RYANN FLETCHER

Rhapsody in Flames

Cover art by indy @strooooble

First edition

This book was professionally typeset on Reedsy.
Find out more at reedsy.com

*To every man who has called a woman abrasive to her face, or a bitch behind
her back.
Fuck you.*

Contents

Chapter One

Verdance was a strange name for a city that spent half its year barren, with nothing more than icy wind to keep its residents company. The dense cloud cover pressed the frigid temperatures down, resting deep in the bones of anyone who was foolish enough to be outside at dusk.

Still, Virginia found her fingers reaching for her cigarette case and a match book, the tiny flame insufficient to heat her frozen hands as she walked, the dying spark withering in the biting wind. The end of the cigarette blazed into life, the bright, saturated orange ember a stark juxtaposition to the dark, grey evening as it drew in around her. The cold was as inescapable as the shame that she'd never managed to quit. She'd gotten close, once, before everything caved in on itself, before she was left on her own to survive the Verdance winters, before she was forty-eight years old and surviving on a diet of smoke and booze, heading home too late in the evening after another disappointing day.

She stopped outside her building, wanting to go inside, weary from the cold and hungry for the relative warmth of her apartment, for the feeling of her fingers defrosting, but she wasn't about to cut a smoke short. Breath curled from her mouth as she leaned against the brick, the roughness chewing through her thick winter coat as if it was delicate silk. In Verdance, nothing was gentle. Not anymore. Not since the Rupture tore everything apart.

Another inhale and she closed her eyes, savoring the taste of ash and tobacco as it gathered at the back of her throat, whispering for more. She was almost out of cigarettes. The paper burned slowly at first, struggling to catch in the biting gusts that swept past her shoes, old and creased, yet polished to an almost mirror shine. She struck another match, but the flame was extinguished before it met the end of her cigarette. She grumbled under her breath, hunting in her pockets for another book of matches, and finding none. Of course. What else could she expect from Verdance other than disappointment and irritation, laced with a side of contempt and a heaping portion of begrudging duty to the city that had taken her in all those years ago?

Going to bed without a smoke was like going to bed hungry: unfulfilled, agitated, and filled with a general sense of injustice. A quiet, gnawing need chewed through her thoughts, interrupting anything that wasn't a meditation on just how much of a disappointment she was to herself.

Virginia pulled her coat close, her breath rising from her lips in frustrated tendrils as she fumbled for the key to her building. Shadows, it was cold. She regretted that she'd waited so long to return home, but there was an unwelcome emptiness that sometimes crept under her door, seeping into her like half frozen molasses.

The key slid easily into the lock, and she shoved the heavy metal door open with her shoulder. The corridor was almost as cold as the outside. Her landlord was cheap as the grave, and it showed in the frosted hand railing that led up the stairs. Her worn brogues slid against the wood, the panels creaking with every weary step.

Fourth floor. Apartment J-22. Virginia froze at the sight of the dark silhouette standing outside her door, already slipping her fingers into the silver knuckles she held in her pocket. "Who are you?" she demanded.

"I live across the hall. I'm your neighbor," the figure responded, the hood of their cloak obscuring their face. Virginia never spoke to any of her neighbors, and as such, didn't know their faces. She didn't know their names, either, and that's how she preferred things to remain.

"What do you want?"

The overhead light in the corridor flickered, the crass yellow glow painting them both in a jaundiced tone, the amber shadows a strange contrast to the deepening darkness outside the window at the end of the hall, the side table beset with dead flowers someone had left there months before. The figure twisted their hands, wringing them anxiously. "Someone on the second floor told me that you're a private investigator."

"If you're looking for your long lost family or whatever, you can come to my office on Phoenix Avenue. Number eleven."

The figure shifted uncomfortably. "It's kind of an emergency."

"Call the cops, then."

"I can't."

Virginia pressed her fingers through the knuckles, balling into a fist, hidden inside the deep pocket of her overcoat. "If it's illegal, I can't help you." Her shoulders tensed, waiting for a fight. It wasn't impossible that one of the runaways she'd returned home had grown up and come looking for revenge, or whatever passed for justice in Verdance those days.

"No, it's not illegal, it's..."

"Spit it out."

"My brother is missing, has been for two weeks. He's..." the figure tugged at their hood. "Different."

"Right." Virginia stepped closer, releasing the grip of her fist, but keeping the knuckles in place over her still-frozen fingers. "What is he, then?"

"Do you promise you won't turn him in?" The figure asked, a tinge of desperation coloring the tone at the edges, betraying their aims more than their nervous fidgeting had.

"Can't promise that until I know what he is. You know the law."

"I know, I know, but they said you could help, you know, in situations like this." The figure chewed their lip and pressed their palms together in a gesture that looked a lot like praying, the way people had every Sunday before the residents of Verdance had largely abandoned the churches after the Rupture.

Virginia sighed, rubbing at her temple. "You aren't going to give up, are you?"

"No, ma'am," the figure replied, shaking their head. "My brother is all I've got left in this world, and I won't abandon him. Please, I'm desperate."

"Come on, inside." Virginia kept the silver knuckles around her fingers, even as the frigid metal bit into her skin. "No sense in talking about this in the hall." She pressed to the door, looking over her shoulder at the figure. "Step back. I've been around the block enough to know that you look like someone with plenty to hide, and I have no desire to bleed out on the floor today."

"I'm sorry." The figure stepped back, leaning against their own door on the other side. "I'm Ursa."

"You already know my name, so I'll refrain from sharing it." Virginia opened the door, flipping the switch on the wall. "Come on."

Ursa entered the dimly-lit apartment, her pale hands almost translucent even under the incandescent bulb. "Your apartment is nicer than mine," they said.

"So what's the problem with this brother of yours?" Virginia asked, flipping the deadbolt. She had little interest in small talk, and even less in the matters of interior design. Besides, if her apartment was that much nicer, she could only imagine the state of Ursa's. The entire building was old, drafty, and poorly maintained, but it was better than the streets, if only by a narrow margin.

Ursa clasped their hands in front of them, pulling back their hood. "He went missing."

"Yes, I gathered that much, but I'm going to need more than that to go on."

"He has the ability to shape shift."

Virginia tossed her keys on the table with a loud clatter, already bored of a case she could predict the outcome of. Missing people were a dime a dozen in Verdance since the Rupture. "He shift in front of the wrong person, maybe? Plenty of crews always looking for someone who can easily slip the net."

"He's a good kid, he—"

"Kid?" Virginia asked. "How old is he?"

"He's twenty."

"Hardly a kid, he's an adult," Virginia replied, bracing a hand against her kitchen counter. "Cops probably wouldn't help you anyway, not for a grown shifter. They might file a report, but that's all you'd get out of them these days." Virginia sighed again, the weight of another hopeless case already settling into her chest. "You know as well as I do that—"

"I do know, and that's why I came to you. Some say... some say that you're the best."

Virginia let loose a derisive scoff. "Depends who you ask."

"The last time I saw him, he was heading off to work that morning." Ursa tugged down their hood, revealing a delicate frame and a fine dusting of scales, barely visible along their collarbone.

"You too, huh?" Virginia said, gesturing.

"It runs in the family."

"What day was that, when you last saw him?"

"Thursday," Ursa answered, picking at the frayed threads poking out of their hood's hem. "Two weeks back."

Virginia pulled a small notepad from her pocket, leaning against the wall as she scribbled barely legible notes on the unlined pages. "Anything unusual?"

"No."

"No new friends he's been hanging around, no new crews hanging around his neighborhood?"

Ursa closed their eyes. "No. Benjamin is a quiet boy, he lives here with me. So unless you know of any crews—"

"There aren't. I make it my business to know who's hanging around this neighborhood." Virginia took out a pencil, worn down to an almost useless nub. "Alright, how about work? He have any problems there?"

"He's always been shy. He used to have bullies in school, but he graduated a few years back."

"Names?"

"I don't know," Ursa replied, shaking their head. "I'm sorry, I... it's hard, you know, trying to work, to keep a roof over our heads, to stay hidden, and—"

"Virginia held up a hand. "Yeah. I get it." She scribbled a few notes at the edges, sucking her teeth as she wrote. "Where does he work?"

"He works as a janitor in the school on Ninth Avenue."

"The preparatory school?"

"He's worked there for about six months. It was hard for him to find a job. You know how it's been."

Virginia nodded. "He's not the only one, that's for sure." She was already calculating how she'd get to the school without hitting rush hour traffic. "Parents?"

Ursa straightened their posture, worried eyes now steely. "As far as Benjamin and I are concerned, we have no parents."

"I know the feeling," Virginia mumbled.

"What?"

She glanced up, blinking away the comment. "Nothing. Alright, no ransom notes, no other clues? He vanished?"

"I know that he didn't turn up for work that day. He walks, I was still on shift." Ursa fussed with their coat, folding and unfolding the hem in their hands. "The school said there was nothing out of the ordinary."

"Hmm. I think I'll be the judge of that." Virginia pursed her lips. It would be an early start, then. She hated schools. Little dens of chaos and trauma, ripe for abuse. "I'm going to need a description."

"Here's a photo." Ursa handed over a wallet-sized picture, almost overexposed. "I know it's not very good, but it's the only one I have of him."

"It's enough. Eye color?"

"Same as mine. Grey."

"Does he..." Virginia gestured to her own collarbone, an eyebrow raised. "Visible?"

"No."

"Well that's something, at least. Not as easy to spot."

"There was a time we were proud of our differences, Ms. Vane."

"That was before all these crews made it their business to snatch up anyone who can be useful to them. Before the government made it *their* business to do the same. It's all part of the same cycle." Virginia snapped the notepad shut. "Without sounding indelicate, I am not a charity." She slid a card across the table. "These are my rates."

Ursa nodded. "I'd pay anything to have Benjamin back, even if it means mortgaging my own kidneys."

"Is there any chance at all that your brother took off?"

"No."

"Are you completely sure? Young shifters have a knack for disappearing into the wind, only to reemerge a year later a few states away."

"I am completely sure that my brother wouldn't do that. He knows that we're all each other has. We have to stick together. He's been doing well at work, and he was about to start some night classes for architecture in the spring."

"You wouldn't believe the number of kids I've pulled out of backstreet drug dens, completely messed up on Nether."

Ursa shook their head again. "No. It won't be Benjamin. He wouldn't touch that stuff."

"You'd be surprised. Not every mythic can cope with how things are these days."

"He *wouldn't,*" Ursa insisted.

"Alright," Virginia said, holding her hands up. "If you say so."

"You have to find him, Ms. Vane. He's all I have left in this world. Without him, I—I don't have much reason to keep on trying to get us out of this place."

"This apartment, or this city?"

"Both."

Virginia nodded, the deep, inexorable need to escape not an unfamiliar one. "Verdance is not the same place it was twenty years ago."

"Is anywhere?"

"No. Not since the Rupture." Virginia studied Ursa's face for a reaction, finding none. "I'll head to the school first thing in the morning, see if I can't track down a lead. Chances are he's just hiding out somewhere. It's rarely anything else."

"Thank you, Ms. Vane."

"I'll keep you updated." Virginia unlocked the door, opening it. "As soon as I know anything, you'll know, so don't be creeping around my door at night. You're lucky I didn't make the assumption that you were trying to jump me."

"Do many people—"

"More than you want to know."

Ursa pulled their hood back up before stepping into the corridor. "I apologize for surprising you at home. With my schedule, I'd never get to your office during opening hours."

"Good night," Virginia said, closing the door. Shadows, the adrenaline was just sitting in her veins now, itching for some kind of release. She locked the door, checking it three times to be sure, still on edge. It wouldn't have been the first time that some grave slug had tried to wait for her at home, though historically, it had never ended well for the other party.

She hung her coat on the hook, unholstering her pistol and laying it on the counter. The silver knuckles rattled against the stained wood, dappled with water rings from years of sticky summers and condensation that dripped down the side of a glass as she pored over another fruitless case.

The radio crackled with static as she honed in on the police frequency, bent over the counter as she adjusted the knobs, the fuzz over the airwaves a constant frustration. Police scanner radios were technically illegal, but always useful. She had a few open cases that had hit a dead end, and any news could jog a new lead. She examined the photo Ursa had left, black and white, one of the edges folded and yellowed from being carried around in an empty wallet. Benjamin was a good-looking kid, with a sharp jaw and wide, soulful eyes. Photos rarely told the full story, but he didn't seem like a troublemaker. More like a sad boy with a broken family and no friends to speak of other than his sibling.

Virginia poured gin into a glass, swirling it around. She'd forgotten to get food on the way back, and there was nothing more than stale crackers in her apartment. The taste was off, as though they'd absorbed the flavor of failure right through the cabinet doors. She pushed them away with a betrayed scowl, sipping at the gin instead. The taste was acrid in a welcoming way, like a half-burned pine forest after a lightning storm, or the smell of rain against ash as it washed down the city's storm drain. Both familiar. Both drawing memories to the surface she'd prefer stayed buried.

Odd, then, that it was her choice of drink, given its effect on her, and there was no explanation for why she continued to indulge in things that only reminded her of pain.

She sank down into the overstuffed chair in the corner, patched with mismatched thread and fabric from years of use. The radio droned on with reports of alley fights, crew sightings, and some slimy fungus of a man being arrested for fraud. The last one would probably be front-page news in the morning. It wasn't as though Virginia Vane was the only one with an illegal police scanner. The damned journalists all had them, too. So did the attorneys.

Gin skidded down her throat, nestling warm in her stomach. It was a comfort on cold nights like those, when the chill crept beneath the windowsills like fingers from the grave, waiting to welcome her into their frigid embrace. The landlord was uninterested in turning the heat on unless the pipes were in danger of freezing, so she'd gotten used to the glacial winters. They beat the humid, cloying summers, at least.

A gentle scratching at the window pulled her attention, even though she already knew it would be that damned cat again. "Alright, alright," she relented, pushing herself out of the chair with a heaving effort to open the window just wide enough to let in the little beast. It sauntered through the gap, long whiskers a stark contrast against its coat, and bright green eyes round as saucers. "Come on, hurry up," Virginia scolded, shivering in the icy draft. "You're late for dinner," she scolded, turning to the kitchen to open a can of tuna. She hated the smell, all metallic and fishy, but it was the only thing the cat would eat, and from its fragile, underweight frame, she knew that wherever it belonged, it wasn't finding enough there.

She dumped the tuna into the cat's bowl and watched it eat, each bite dainty and polite despite the ribs visible through the solid black fur. The cat sat after it finished, licking its chops and showing off an impressive set of fangs.

"You can stay the night," Virginia offered. "It's damned cold out there."

The cat responded by leaping up onto the side table again, staring wistfully out into the frozen night.

"As you wish." Another frigid gust sparked through the window as the cat slunk back into the night, disappearing down the fire escape and into a back alley.

Virginia plunged back into the chair with a quiet exhalation of breath, not so much a sigh as an admission of guilt. She pressed reading glasses onto her face, skimming a book on demonic entities she'd gotten from the library. It was a rare copy, out of print now—the researcher who wrote it had spent the rest of his days as an academic outcast. A pity he had been proved right with the Rupture, but only after he'd spent ten years cold in the grave. She'd spent years trying to track down a copy. The local librarian found one in three hours.

She was so immersed in the chapter about symbiotic possession that she nearly missed the police dispatcher calling for a unit to attend the scene of an unidentified body. Young male, between seventeen and twenty-three, found half-buried in the quarry at the outskirts of the city. Virginia's stomach clenched, knowing what it probably meant.

Tugging her coat around her shoulders, she was halfway down the stairs of her building before the dispatch call even ended.

Chapter Two

Virginia stepped out of the cab, tipping generously. "If anyone asks, you never saw me," she said.

"Hard to forget a face like that," the driver said, gesturing at the scars that dragged down over both cheekbones.

She waited a moment, and they stared each other down in the rear view mirror, despite it being half-clouded with fog. He raised an eyebrow at her, a quiet challenge but one she couldn't ignore. "Fine," she said, stuffing another wad of cash into his waiting hand. He peeled off the moment she slammed her door, leaving a trail of quarry dust in his wake. "Fucking thief," she grumbled.

There were no units on scene yet, and for that, she was grateful. Keeping run-ins with the police to a minimum was for the best, and it was a policy that had kept her out of trouble more than once. If she could just get close enough to confirm or deny that the body was Benjamin's, she'd be on her way.

She stepped closer to the lip of the quarry, peering down into the dark. Virginia squinted, trying to make out what lay at the bottom.

"Are you with the cops?" a woman asked, standing nearby.

"Yes," Virginia lied. "Is this where you saw the body?"

The woman nodded, her hard hat askew on her head. "At the bottom, near where it's flooded."

"You got a flashlight or a lantern or something?"

"Don't police usually have one?"

"Do you have one, or not?" Virginia snapped. "I'm out here, just trying to do my job, and—"

"Alright, *shadows*, here," the woman said, handing her a scuffed metal flashlight, a large dent in the side of the aluminum.

Virginia dragged the beam of light across the floor of the quarry, at least a twenty foot drop from the lip. Enough to kill someone who'd been dumped over the side. The body was along the edge, almost submerged in the frozen lake, formed by the wet winter months and the meters of snow that settled in the crevices, melting, freezing, and melting again.

She huffed out a breath that burst from her mouth in an angry cloud. It wasn't Benjamin. Some other poor kid, and by the looks of him, another shifter. Scales emerged from his hairline, iridescent in the glow of the flashlight. "Not him," she said aloud, forgetting she wasn't alone.

"Not who?"

"Don't worry about it." Red and blue flashed against the cliff side, announcing that the real authorities had arrived. "Thanks." She thrust the flashlight back into the woman's hands, turning to the path that led to the nearest bus stop, a mile and a half away.

"Ginnie?"

The nickname alone dragged a low growl from her throat. No, it couldn't be him. Not there. He was five states away, playing house on the east coast. She didn't turn, choosing instead to lengthen her stride towards the path.

"Ginnie, stop!"

She stopped, but didn't face him. She couldn't, not after that long. "What are you doing here, Arthur?"

The soles of his boots rustled against the gravel, shifting and vaguely unsure. She hated that she knew the look he had on his face, without having to even look him in the eyes. He cleared his throat deftly. "I could ask you the same thing."

"Shouldn't you be far away from Verdance?" she asked acerbically, her chest tight.

He laid a hand on her shoulder, and she flinched away from the contact. "Why are you at a crime scene, Ginnie?"

"You know I always hated that name," she retorted.

He laughed softly, an easy, throaty sound that had once been so familiar and comforting, now like grating metal in her ears. Arthur flapped the edges of his coat in the still night air. "That's not answering the question."

"I have a case." Virginia wished she'd stayed at home. The John Doe wasn't a lead, and the trip had been a waste of time.

"Are you going to look at me, or do I have to discuss this with the back of your head?" Arthur asked, a tinge of bemused humor in his voice. She hated him for that, too.

She turned, glaring. "Fine," she said. "Speak."

"What case?"

"None of your business."

"It is my business, actually." He gave her an almost apologetic smile, but it was tainted with the same smug twinge of his lips that had always driven her into a rage all those years ago. "I'm back in Verdance."

"Great," she deadpanned. "Can I go?"

"Not until you tell me about this case. As far as I was briefed, you're still off the force."

"Yeah, thanks to *you*," she shot back.

Arthur stepped closer. "You can't blame me for that, Ginnie, That was all you."

"You're the one who ratted me out."

"For your own good."

"Please, as if you didn't throw me under the bus to get that nice, fat commendation," she argued, already too tired for the conversation. Their old dynamic hadn't changed much from the last time she'd seen him. "I'm sure it's why you've landed back in this city, what, a captain now?"

"Sheriff, actually," he said.

Something like poison slipped into her stomach, turning the stale crackers and gin to lead. The heaviness pulled at her, and rage rose up in the back of her throat as a threat, or an omen. "Sheriff," she repeated.

"I arrived yesterday," he explained. "I was offered the position a month ago."

"Congratulations. I know it's all you ever wanted." She could hear herself, knew that the snide sarcasm was front and center, but decided to not care.

"It's good to see you," he offered, shoving his hands into his pockets. "It's been a long time."

Virginia narrowed her eyes. "I can't say I share the same sentiment."

"No one ever accused you of being sentimental, Ginnie."

She suppressed a frustrated huff, and her lungs fought against it. "What do you want, Arthur?" she demanded.

"Sheriff Dixon." He corrected with a smirk, and her fist twitched with the urge to punch it off of his face. "I want to know why you are at my crime scene."

"I'm licensed."

"A private investigator?" he mocked. "My, how the mighty have fallen."

Rage burned in her throat, but she swallowed it down, despite the silver knuckles unconsciously slipping over her fingers in her pocket. "It's a living. I solve more than this fucking force does, I'll tell you that for free."

"We both know that's not true."

"Any more information from me will trigger an invoice for consulting," she said, her voice dripping with barely-concealed animosity. "And my rates aren't cheap."

"One more time before I'm forced to arrest you for potential obstruction, Ginnie," Arthur said. "Why are you here?"

She'd hoped she'd never lay eyes on him again, but fortunes were cruel, and she was perennially unlucky. "Missing kid," she said finally.

"Is this one him?"

"No," she answered. "Not mine."

Arthur raised an eyebrow. "That it?"

"Yeah, that's it."

"If this case of yours has a missing person—"

"No."

"I can help, if I know what's going on," he offered.

Virginia glared up at him, his dark skin shining in the glare of the police lights, more units arriving every few minutes. "There's a reason why a significant subsection of this city doesn't trust the cops, Arthur. Maybe if you opened your eyes, you'd know why."

"Listen, all of that conscription stuff is the feds, not us," he said. "We don't have anything to do with that, and I don't like it, either."

"As if you don't happily hand them over whenever the feds ask."

He sucked his teeth, hands shoved into the pockets of his trench coat. "My hands are tied, Ginnie."

The old nickname was enough to boil the blood pulsing in her ears. She shrugged dramatically, her shoulders up high around her ears. "Am I free to go?"

"Sure," he said, waving a hand at her. "Enjoy the walk back. I noticed you didn't drive here, no doubt you didn't want your car to be spotted."

"Among other things." She didn't mention the drink she'd had back at her apartment. No doubt he'd have some choice words for her about that, too, and she wouldn't put it past him to use that against her in order to have her license stripped from her.

Arthur's face softened, tinged with something she couldn't quite identify. Maybe he'd learned a new emotion out there on the coast. "If you could stem the tide of your hostility for an hour, I can give you a lift back to the city. Where are you living, now?"

"What exactly makes you think that we are on terms enough for that?" she asked, barking out a sardonic laugh.

"It's just an offer, Ginnie."

"No thanks."

"Are you seriously going to walk all the way back?" he asked, incredulous. "It's almost two miles, and this is a quarry, and it's pitch black out here."

"I'd rather have my skin slowly peeled off of me by a drunk golem than share a ten minute car trip with you," she spat.

"Sheriff Dixon, the photographers have finished. We need your go-ahead to start excavating the body." The woman who said it was tall and broad, even taller than Arthur, and as a result, Virginia found herself standing on the balls of her feet to look larger than she was. The woman's angular face was sharp in the dense gloom of the night and the flash of the lights, a knife-edged attractiveness that drew Virginia's eye against her will.

He waved his hand. "Yes."

"I'm sure they weren't thorough enough," Virginia challenged. "It's barely been twenty minutes, how could they have gotten enough material to sift through?"

"Ginnie," Arthur said in a warning tone. "Do not undermine me."

"Sheriff?" the woman prompted.

He sighed. "Have them take a full three-sixty, even if they already did. Get the coroner down here, too. Thank you, Captain Lindell."

"Good," Virginia said after the captain walked away. "Really, you should be waiting until morning. The flashbulbs can obscure placement."

"I'm well aware of the limitations," Arthur replied, turning back to her. "Don't do that again."

Virginia shrugged, her mouth set in a line. "It's not my fault you tend to make decisions that ruin cases."

"I'm not having this conversation with you again, Ginnie. It's been what, twelve years?"

"Fifteen." She tilted her chin up, challenging him. Of course, three years could easily slip away, if you were living in the lap of luxury on the coast.

"Even more so, then," he continued. "I can't change the past, and neither can you. You're better off leaving it where it lies, and getting the hell on with your life."

"I *have* gotten on with my life," she hissed.

Arthur threw off a sarcastic chortle, making sure to perform his role as the city's crowned fool. "Oh, I've heard plenty about what you're getting on with," he said.

"What is *that* supposed to mean?" she barked with a derisive laugh, throwing her head back to demonstrate just how ridiculous she found the whole thing.

"Now isn't the time nor the place for us to be rehashing old battles," Arthur said, waving another squad unit past them. "If you come by the precinct—"

"Fat chance," Virginia interrupted.

"Sir?" Captain Lindell called from the lip of the quarry. "Sir, the kid is a shifter."

"Shadows be damned, another one," Arthur said under his breath. "Thank you, Captain. I'll alert the appropriate channels," he called back.

"*Another* one?" Virginia pressed.

"Police business only."

She folded her arms over her chest, doing her best to look as authoritative as she once was. "I have a right to know."

"No, Ginnie, you don't. Licensed as a private investigator or not, you're still just a civilian."

"If there's some kind of war on mythics—"

Arthur rubbed his close-cropped, coiled hair. "There's no war. Just the same crew bullshit as always."

"How would you know, *Sheriff* Dixon?" Virginia asked, sarcasm dripping from her tone. "You already admitted you've only been back in town since yesterday. What in shadows do you even know about how Verdance is now?"

"I've been briefed by some of the top—"

"Please," she said, laughing. "It's a hell of a lot different now than it was when you ran off to the east coast."

He scowled, taking a step backwards away from her, almost losing his footing on the loose rock beneath the soles of his boots. "I didn't *run off*. I was offered a promotion, and I took it."

"Some of us stayed to fix the mistakes we made," she argued.

"Yeah, a bang up job you've done of it too, by the looks of it," he said, the red and blue glow from the units reflecting oddly on his face. "I assume you're holed up in some shitty office downtown, taking on missing person cases? What else, Ginnie? You doing work for the loan sharks, too?"

She narrowed her eyes, arms crossed over her chest. Shadows, she would have killed him right then, given the chance. Or, at the very least, put a permanent dent in that square jaw of his. "My business is none of yours."

"Yet you're here, skulking around for information. I'll even bet you lied to the workers on site, too, didn't you? Because they were explicitly told that no one should get anywhere near that quarry without my say so."

"It isn't my fault they didn't ask for a badge."

"Same old Ginnie, skirting the rules to serve your own ends," he accused.

Virginia scoffed. "Yeah, and same old Arthur, lording around whatever scrap of power you have to the detriment of the city *and* the force."

"And here I'd hoped fifteen years would be enough for you to get over whatever grudge you had—"

"*Fifty* years wouldn't be enough." She stared him down, daring him to chase her off. He'd done it before, and he'd do it again.

"Get off my crime scene."

"Gladly!" she retorted, throwing her hands up as she walked away, her shoes digging mercilessly into the loose ground. She should have worn boots. Fucking Arthur and his smug bullshit. *Sheriff.* As if that sniveling worm had become sheriff.

Virginia's hands were balled into fists at her side. "Of course he came back as sheriff," she grumbled, stalking across the quarry. He'd probably done it just to lord it over her, to rub it in her face how he'd escaped punishment for what they'd done *together.* Now he was sheriff and she was barely scraping together a living chasing after runaway kids and scumbags who had skipped bail.

The more things that changed, the more they stayed the fucking same.

Chapter Three

Virginia awoke to a loud rap on her door. "Shadows," she hissed, throwing off her blankets. "Keep your pants on," she shouted to the invader, buckling her own around her hips.

Pulling on a thick wool sweater, she all but stomped to the door, throwing back the deadbolt. "Listen, I told you already, Ursa, I'll let you know when I have a—"

"Captain Lindell. We met last night, briefly." She spoke with a thick accent, one that had absorbed speech patterns from a dozen different places.

"What do you want?" Virginia snapped.

"You're being called in for questioning," the captain explained, tucking her cap under her arm with one sharp movement.

"Questioning? For *what*?"

"You were at the scene before police units arrived. It's procedure."

"Do you have a warrant?" Virginia asked, still blocking the door.

The captain tilted her head, frowning. "There's no need for all of that, Ms. Vane."

Virginia laughed, holding the door in place. "I disrespectfully disagree."

"The sheriff said—"

Virginia gave a bitter laugh. "I don't give one single rotten ghoul's ass what the sheriff said. We both know that he's an empty suit."

"I am just trying to do my job. If you refuse to cooperate, then I will be forced to go obtain a warrant."

"Good, you do that," Virginia replied, closing the door.

Captain Lindell stopped the door with the toe of her boot. "However, if you force me to obtain a warrant, I will make damn sure that it covers not just your statement, but your home, and your office as well."

"Arthur tell you to say that?"

"He indicated that you may not be the most receptive," Lindell explained. "I improvised the rest."

"Do I get to dress myself, or are you intent on throwing me into the back of your unit in yesterday's clothes?" Virginia asked, the words like acid on her tongue.

"You have five minutes, and I have to wait inside." The captain raised an eyebrow, her short, wavy hair escaping the messy chignon folded low against the nape of her neck. "I don't really feel like chasing you down a fire escape."

"Bold of you to assume this building even *has* a maintained fire escape. I'm surprised that the stray cats don't send it crumbling to the ground." Virginia held the door open. The last thing she wanted was this captain in her apartment, but she was fresh out of leverage, at least until she found out what the hell it was Arthur *really* wanted. "I'll be right out."

"Thank you for your cooperation."

"You didn't really give me a choice, *Captain*."

"This is what happens when you go poking around crime scenes, Ms. Vane. Imagine if we let every half-baked PI wander in and out, destroying evidence, tracking in superfluous evidence that could derail a case."

Virginia slipped into her room, teeth gritted. *Half-baked.* What a bitch. She just had to hope the captain wouldn't spot the illegal radio scanner on the kitchen counter. Those were expensive to replace, and she hadn't been rolling in dough lately. She pulled on a pair of deep, pine green slacks and a white button down, half wrinkled from the day before. She added a jade waistcoat and a tie for good measure, knowing that she'd be heading to do some casework as soon as she freed herself from the grip of the precinct.

"Are you almost done?" the captain called.

"Relax, I'm sure there will be some pastries left for you at headquarters." Virginia pinned her silvery hair back into a neat twist, smoothing the sides.

Good enough. She opened her bedroom door just enough to slip through, closing it behind her. "Let's get this over with."

Captain Lindell was examining the radio. "Interesting contraption. I see now why you weren't keen on a warrant."

"And now that you've seen it without one, it's inadmissible," Virginia said with a wide, mocking smile.

"That's not quite how it works, Ms. Vane."

"I'm overly familiar with how it works, Captain. Or did your sheriff not mention that?"

Lindell frowned, her stance stock-still. "He did not. Were you a consultant?"

"I was a captain," Virginia answered.

"In Verdance?"

Virginia smirked, pleased that she'd caught Lindell off-guard. "Yes. It was before your time." She pulled on her boots, wary of the heavy clouds outside the window. Those were clouds with snow.

"I imagine that we are around the same age, no?" Lindell studied her, even coming close to staring as she searched for something Virginia would never allow her to find.

"Before you transferred here, then."

"Why do you now work as a private investigator, then?" Lindell asked innocently, but the meaning behind her words was painfully obvious.

"You can ask Arthur about that." Virginia gestured to the door, pulling her coat from the hook. "Although, I'm sure the answer he gives you will hardly be the full truth."

"The sheriff has a number of commendations, he—"

"Oh, yes, I'm sure," Virginia interrupted. "He always manages to be in the right place at the right time, ready to accept praise for all the work he had no part in."

The captain clasped her hands behind her back, waiting for Virginia to press her key into the lock. "I'm not sure that you should be sharing this kind of information with me, Ms. Vane."

"If Arthur wanted politeness and decorum, then he should have thought twice before he sent an armed cop to my door first thing in the morning." She locked the door with an angry twist of her wrist. "If he wanted to impress you, he should have sent you to meet his wife, not me."

"We're just trying to get to the bottom of all this."

"*All* this?"

"You know," Captain Lindell said, waving her hand. "The disappearances."

"So there *is* a pattern, then."

"Of sorts."

Virginia led the way down the stairs, hoping none of her neighbors would see her being personally escorted by a VCPD captain. There was already enough gossip about her going around, she didn't need that, too. "I suppose I can assume you're keeping this from the press."

"The sheriff thinks that prudent, at least for the time being."

"People have a right to know what's going on in their city, Captain."

"If you held this position like you say that you did, then you know as well as I do the damage the press can do to an ongoing investigation."

Lindell was right, no matter how much Virginia resented it. She scowled, pushing out onto the street. "Double parked?" she asked, rolling her eyes. "My, it must be nice to have carte blanche to skirt the law."

"Ms. Vane, the less you fight me, the easier this will go. Unless you *want* me to arrest you out here, in full view?"

"Shadows, relax," Virginia said, sliding into the back seat. "Don't worry, Captain, I'm sure Arthur will be thrilled that you're bringing me in."

The captain didn't respond, climbing into the driver's side and throwing the car into gear. Traffic was a nightmare the time of the morning, same as it always was. It had been fifteen years since she'd been in the back of a squad unit, and the reminder made her flinch as though someone had scraped a red-hot blade against her skin. Some things were better off forgotten.

"You get those scars on the force?" Captain Lindell asked, meeting Virginia's eyes in the rear-view mirror.

"No."

"Oh. I guess I just assumed—"

"Drunk pixies."

"Drunk... pixies?" Lindell's lips twitched upwards, unsure if it was a joke or not. Rookie.

Virginia glared. "Have you ever met a drunk pixie?"

"I can't say that I have."

"Alright then."

The captain parked, opening Virginia's door. "The sheriff is—"

"I know my way around, thank you." Virginia strode into the precinct, trying to swallow back the rush of bitter nostalgia that flooded her veins, pulsing insistently at her eyelids. It had been years since she'd set foot in that building, and yet, everything looked the same. The faces were different, but the green tiled floors, the columns, the dingy signs, they were all identical. Her stomach churned, and she was grateful she hadn't eaten anything that morning.

"What do you want, Arthur?" she demanded, standing in the doorway to his office.

"Sit down, Ginnie."

"Not until you tell me what's going on, and why you dragged me out of bed at daybreak."

He sighed, setting his fountain pen down on the leather-topped desk, the nib laying atop a square of scrap paper. "I assume Captain Lindell informed you of—"

"Yes, your lackey gave me a weak reasoning, but that doesn't explain what's really going on here. You could have called, Arthur, or visited my office—how did you figure out where I live, anyway?" She shook her head before answering her own question. "Licensing. Of course."

"Would you like some coffee, Ginnie?" he asked, gesturing towards the insulated bottle on the filing cabinet behind him.

She sat down, her mouth set into a frown. "Why are you being suspiciously nice?"

"I am aware that our... *history*... may make things difficult, working in the same city."

"You think?" she asked with a snort.

"I don't want to constantly be at odds with you. I think you know that we could make each other's lives very difficult, and I am hoping we can avoid that." He stood, closing his office door.

"Ah, of course," she said, leaning back. "You want to be sure I won't rat you out."

"Not quite the phrasing I would use," he muttered. "But yes, in part."

"If I haven't before now, what makes you think I will now that you're back in Verdance?"

He studied her face before sitting back down with a sigh. "Sometimes, when positions change..."

"You think I'm jealous," she answered for him.

"Aren't you?"

Yes, she thought. "No."

"No?"

"It's more complicated than that. I left when I realized I couldn't change things. Not without help, which I obviously didn't get."

"We both know you didn't *leave*, Ginnie."

"Did you really bring me here to rehash things from fifteen years ago?"

Arthur took a breath, leaning his elbows against the desk. "Mona is concerned that—"

"Mona," Virginia said, barking out a laugh. "Of course. I should have known. How is your child bride doing, anyway?"

"I can't change what happened, or how it happened, but my family will always come first." He poured coffee from a thermos, pushing a mug across the table. "She's five years younger than us, Ginnie, hardly a child."

"She was twenty-five when it all happened, Arthur."

"Yes." He drained the thermos into a second cup, adding milk and three sugars to his own. "We have children, now."

Virginia blinked. "Unsurprising."

"Do you want to see photos?"

"Of the children you had with your new wife after you left me? No, Arthur, I don't."

"Ginnie, I—"

"Have you lost whatever semblance of sense you ever possessed?" she said in a low, dangerous voice. "What makes you think that this is a conversation to be had, fifteen years later?" She shook her head, incredulous. "You're a real piece of work, Arthur." Captain Lindell crossed near the window at the side of the office, and Virginia's eyes followed her, unbidden.

Arthur let a long, silent, teeming moment pass without comment, despite the tension so thick it pressed down on both of them, distilling fifteen years of ire into one heavy minute. He blinked at her, swallowing hard. "From what I hear, your... proclivities have changed."

"My *proclivities?*"

He glanced out at the captain, and back to Virginia. "Women, Ginnie."

"And where the hell did you hear that?" she demanded.

"Around."

Seamus. She'd kill him. "What I do in my personal life is none of your business."

"No, but I'm only pointing out that if we hadn't split up, you never would have—"

"I wouldn't have known the shadows-damned *difference* if you hadn't done what you did, Arthur," Virginia spat, bracing her hands against the desk, her knuckles white with the effort.

"I'm just saying, I think it was all for the best."

"Of course you think that, you're the one with the white picket fence and a sheriff's badge on your arm," she shot back.

"I don't want us to be hostile," he explained. "After all, there may come a time when Verdance needs us both."

Virginia narrowed her eyes. "You need me for something." When he averted his eyes, she sat back, taking the hot mug into her hands. "I knew it."

"You weren't wrong last night. There has been a spate of... disappearances. And when many aren't ever reported in the first place, it's hard to keep track."

"I'm not turning over my clients' information, and legally, you aren't allowed to demand that from me."

"That's not what I need."

She searched his face and sighed. "One of your kids is a shifter, aren't they?"

"Yes. She's only eight years old." He took a photo from his wallet, pushing it across the desk. "Her name is Penelope. Penny, for short."

"I trust she's not already missing, or you wouldn't be sitting there all calm at your desk."

"She's fine, she's in school. But Mona is concerned that the move back to Verdance may have been... premature, in light of recent events."

"Go back to the east coast, then. Easy." She sat back in her chair with a nonchalant shrug.

He sighed softly, taking the photo and sliding it back into his wallet. "Ginnie, you know it's not that easy."

"Easy for *me.*"

"My hands are more or less tied here." Arthur ran his hands over the leather, sliding back and forth across the desk. "I'm just asking, if you ever had any affection for me, to keep your eyes out."

"Don't do that."

"Don't do what?" he asked innocently.

Virginia rolled her eyes. "Invoke ancient history to ask for a favor. Just ask me like I'm any other PI, Arthur."

"Fine. Will you please, in your professional capacity, keep your ear to the ground where this is concerned?"

"No promises."

"Ginnie—"

She held a hand up to silence him as she drained the mug. "Is that all, Arthur?"

"Yes, Ginnie, that's all."

"Good." She stood, resting her hand on the doorknob. "Don't send your lackeys to my door with threats. You want to talk to me, you come to my office."

"Understood."

"And tell Mona she makes a good coffee."

His brow furrowed, and he turned to glance at the thermos. "How did you know—"

"Yours always tasted like shit."

* * *

Chapter Four

Virginia stepped off the train platform, grunting at the freezing draft that swirled at the hem of her coat. The cold in Verdance was inescapable and oppressive, at least until the swampy spring humidity arrived—but that was months away, yet. The solstice had only just passed a fortnight ago. Winter was long, dragging its feet across the hemisphere.

The school stood proud, smack in the middle of one of the nicer neighborhoods. Too rich for Virginia's blood, she wouldn't live there even if she had the money. The self-importance cascaded off the wrought-iron gates like a thick fog.

She leaned against the fence, her eyes raking over the empty courtyard. There was nothing to see beyond the freshly-painted front door, crisp and white in its fortitude. It didn't even look like a place where children would play. Maybe they didn't here. Maybe the priorities were different for the offspring of wealthy donors and those sharing tangential genetics with powerful people.

Virginia pressed the intercom. "Hello?"

"No visitors allowed during school hours," the speaker rattled, half-garbled in static.

"I'm here about Benjamin—" Shit, she hadn't thought to ask the kid's last name. "I'm here about Benjamin."

There was a long, empty pause before a reply crunched through the interference. "Are you with the police?"

"Yes," Virginia answered. It was sometimes the easiest way to access information, and as a consultant with the VCPD, it wasn't even a total fabrication.

"We already told them everything we know." The wire mesh protecting the speaker was pristine, not a speck of rust, shining bright in the cold afternoon sun.

Virginia tilted her head. Strange. Ursa had said they hadn't filed a missing person's report, so what in shadows were the cops doing following up on it? "Would you mind filling me in? My partner just left on a sabbatical."

A long, irritated sigh hissed through the speaker. "You're not with the police."

Ah, so they were lying to try and get rid of her. Interesting. "Listen, I'm just trying to help the guy's sibling. I just have a few questions."

"No visitors during school hours," the voice repeated, and cut the line.

Virginia swore under her breath, pulling out her pocket watch. It was at least an hour until school would let out. She'd hoped to be on her way by then—on her way to teach Seamus a lesson, the louse—but kicking in the front gate of a prestigious school was unlikely to earn her the answers she needed to find Benjamin.

Instead, she crept around the side, easing down a narrow alley that ran parallel to the school. It was empty, except for a fire escape at the far end. It was the cleanest alley she'd ever come across, and she'd lived in Verdance her entire adult life. Most places had tiny cyclones of litter and refuse, blown in by the strong winds that never stopped cascading through the city, especially during the harsh winters.

Glancing over her shoulder, she hoisted herself up onto the fire escape, landing deftly on her feet. The window looked in on a broom closet, tidily stacked with mops and various cleaning supplies. The next level looked over the gymnasium, with a gaggle of noisy children screeching as a ball sailed across the court. She winced, climbing another flight.

Whoever was disappearing shifters, they must have a motive. Dragging these kids into a crew, maybe? It wasn't unheard of for established crews to use young ones in their dealings, if they could get their hands on them. Almost always from poverty, like Benjamin, the ones with broken homes, with no one to look out for them.

The roof of the school looked out over the neighborhood, over manicured lawns and polite, landscaped circles of demure, appropriate winter plants, with frost-tipped leaves that defied the weight of the heavy snow resting on them. Every display, every garden looked the same. Virginia grimaced at the visual stench of it. Her gaze dragged over the perfectly cornered blocks, hunting for something that might jog a lead. She watched for a long while, her eyes following figures as they walked along the sidewalks, unaware they were being watched. If there was anything going on in the neighborhood bordering Rickarton, it wasn't on the surface.

By now, children were zooming through the gates, jumping into the backseats of waiting cars, or meeting pretty nannies pushing strollers with babies. It never could have been Virginia. The whole thing felt foreign, somehow. It was like another world, and one she didn't belong in. It was no surprise that Arthur up and left to find someone who did.

The older ones were standing in little cliques, isolating themselves from those they deemed less-than, or too different from themselves, despite the fact that most of them had the exact same start in life, and lived in identical houses, and were sitting on trust funds the size of the federal reserve.

She slipped through the open gate unnoticed. Virginia had learned long ago that if you look like you belong somewhere, the vast majority of people would never question your presence. The white door was heavy, leading into a dark alcove lined with plaques dedicated to donors long dead.

"Excuse me, ma'am? You can't be in here," a woman said, arms folded over her neatly tailored suit, and a harsh, stern expression locked into her gently lined face.

Virginia gestured to the clock on the wall. "It's no longer school hours."

"Even so, you cannot barge in here unannounced. You can make an appointment, if you feel so moved." The woman advanced, trying to intimidate Virginia into backing through the door and giving up her position. Having stood toe-to-toe with more than one brash rookie cop, it was easy to stand her ground.

"I'm just trying to find someone," Virginia explained. "Your janitor, in fact. Anything you can tell me would be helpful."

"We have nothing more to say on the matter." The woman tilted her chin up in defiance, unmoving.

Virginia sucked her teeth, plunging her hands back into her pockets. "From what I understand, you haven't said much of anything on the matter to begin with. At least, that's what his sibling suggested."

"Whatever happens off school property isn't our responsibility," the woman insisted. "I think you'll find that the law backs us up on that front."

"So you won't even tell me if he had issues with staff or faculty?" Virginia asked, reaching for the notepad in the inside breast pocket of her jacket.

The woman narrowed her eyes at Virginia, her hands now clasped behind her back. "You don't strike me as an educator or as an administrator, Ms...?"

"Bale," Virginia lied. "And no, I'm not. I'm just someone trying to track down a missing twenty year old, and you're the one trying to stop me."

"You're free to spend your energies however you see fit, Ms. Bale, however, you must do so off Rickerton property." The woman arched an eyebrow in challenge, a formidable opponent, hardened by decades of students trying to get away with skipping class.

"Do you want me to come back with a warrant?" Virginia bluffed. "Because I will."

The woman smirked at her, a self-satisfied, unworried expression as she adjusted the glasses sitting high on the bridge of her nose, the perfect complement to the tight, unrelenting bun pulled to the top of her head. "Good luck obtaining a warrant, Ms. Bale. I think you'll find that we have friends in the VCPD."

Virginia's eyes slid over the plaques on the wall, catching sight of one with an irritatingly familiar name. "The sheriff of police's daughter goes here."

"I cannot comment on our students," the woman said firmly.

Virginia nodded, not needing the confirmation. Of course Arthur had sent his kid to the richest school in the city. She shouldn't have expected anything else from him. "Can I assume you are the principal here?"

"You may."

"Then I strongly suggest that you reevaluate that relationship, because you're not the only one with ties to the VCPD." Virginia tucked the notepad back into her pocket, already planning to get Arthur to force them to open up their doors and their books.

The principal pressed her lips into a thin line, her face set into a deep scowl. "I've said all I mean to. Good luck with your search."

Virginia raised an eyebrow in challenge. "Can I take a look at the school, at least?"

"No. You may not." The principal nodded at the door. "If you please, Ms. Bale."

"Whoever you're protecting, they—"

"The only people we are protecting are our students," the principal interrupted. "Protecting them from prying eyes like yours, in fact. I'm no fool, I know that you're a reporter. You people like to swarm around Rickarton, looking for scandals which do not exist. We have strict codes of ethics on sharing information with journalists. The families that choose to send their children here rely on us for safety and privacy."

Virginia nodded. "Understood." She'd let her believe the reporter shtick, it was an easy cover. Despite how much most people hated the press, they tended to hate private investigators even more. "Thank you for your time."

She turned, grabbing the doorknob and pushing it open. The frustration of leaving without a lead bit into her, and she waited for a moment, hoping that one would reveal itself.

"Any time now, Ms. Bale."

"I'm leaving," Virginia said, her teeth gritted, turning to offer a smile that was more of a snarl in practice. Three other teachers watched her carefully as she exited the courtyard, and they locked the gate after her, not offering any conversation.

Missing shifter, cagey employer. Could be nothing. *Was* probably nothing, and yet, it sank into her bones, tugging at her mind. She'd been at the investigation game long enough to know not to ignore a gut feeling, even if it didn't always pan out.

For her, though, it usually did.

* * *

She rode the train all the way to its terminal station, turning the corner down a brightly-lit street lined with food stalls, betting shops, and what were most likely fronts for laundering money. Permanently empty shops with windows coated in thick sheets of dust, unattractive displays that hadn't been changed in at least five years. It was obvious to anyone looking with a critical eye that they were nothing more than cash pots for ambitious crews. That much wasn't her business, though. Not anymore.

The door to the gym swung inwards with warm, sweat-thick air wafting out into the street. Virginia shed her coat first, draping it over her arm. She took her clothes from a locker in the ladies' changing room, pulling on the grey, loose-fitting tights and thin navy blue sweater, sliding a padlock through the clasp to secure her belongings. She tucked her hair back into a tight chignon, pinning it securely, and stopping to check her reflection before she left the locker room. She frowned at her pink, half-frozen cheeks as she wrapped her arms, readying herself for a fight.

The humid, stagnant heat of the gym was at least a welcome change to the frigid, frostbitten temperatures outside, and she stretched her arms over her head, relishing the light pops in her shoulders.

"Seamus!" she called, a wide smile spread over her face. Virginia held her arms out as if she was going to hug him, reveling in his confused expression for at least five seconds as she approached. Settling back into a comfortable stance, she punched him squarely in the jaw, her hand throbbing even through the gloves.

Seamus staggered backwards, almost knocked down to the mat from the force, his ungrounded stance easy to unseat. "Shadows, Vee, what the hell?" he demanded, cradling his face.

"You're lucky I didn't keep my silver knuckles on for that," she said evenly.

He straightened, glaring at her with his wide, dark eyes, the tousled mop of hair on his head flopped indelicately over to one side. "Am I supposed to guess why you just cold-cocked me, or are you going to give me a clue?" He tugged at his white sleeveless shirt, sweat patches darkening the middle chest.

Virginia raised an eyebrow, folding her arms over her chest. "You really don't know?"

"No, I don't," he said, rubbing at his jaw. "It's not even your night for sparring, what the hell are you doing here?"

"It felt like the right time to have a chat about keeping the things I tell you to your shadows-damned self." She squared up again, crouched in a fighting stance. "Do you know yet, or do I have to win a few more rounds, first?"

He matched her, sliding a foot back on the mat. He threw a punch, which she easily dodged. "I don't talk to anyone about you, why would I?"

"Too late for lies, Seamus." She ducked, sweeping his legs out from under him. "I thought we had an understanding, but maybe I wasn't clear enough."

Seamus twisted, springing back to his feet and into a combination of jabs. The second one caught Virginia in the shoulder, drawing a repressed grunt as she swung another hit wide, missing him. "Vee, you've been coming here for years, ever since—" He cut himself off, dropping his hands. "Shit."

"I'll say. You didn't think to mention that Arthur was coming back to Verdance?" She landed another hit, square in his gut.

He staggered before coming back into stance, his fists held at his face, his jaw already swelling. "I didn't think you'd want to know."

"It would have been nice to prepare myself." She spun, dancing out of range of his hits. "And to tell him? You told him about—about my personal life?"

Seamus let out a quiet hiss. "I wasn't thinking."

"You got that right," Virginia said, pressing her advantage, connecting with his left shoulder. "What even possessed you to tell him?"

"I was only trying to tell him that you've moved on, alright?"

"Of course I've moved on, it's been fifteen years!" she spat.

"He didn't seem to think so."

Virginia scowled, channeling her rage into the fight. "He's always been a pompous ass."

"He was worried about you," Seamus explained, weaving away from a flurry of punches she directed at his abdomen.

"Yeah, worried I'd kick his ass, maybe."

"You might be right." Seamus popped her lightly in the nose, sending her backwards. "Keep your hands up, Vee."

She grunted, firing off a shower of hits that landed across his jaw and shoulders.

"Alright, alright, I yield," he said, holding his hands up. "I need ice." He stepped off the mat, heading to the insulated cooler against the wall. "I sometimes forget that you're more selective in who you say things to." He turned, grimacing as he laid a bag of ice against his face. "Everyone knows who I am. They know what I'm about." He surveyed her face. "You need ice?"

"No."

"I caught you in the nose," he said, holding up a bag of ice, an offering of peace, but she didn't want it.

"Not hard enough to do any real damage."

Seamus pressed an ice pack to his jaw with a quiet, relieved groan. "Not this time, anyway."

"That was five years ago, and I was fresh off an all-nighter." She sat on the mat, leaning forward to savor the stretch in her muscles. "I'm sorry I hit you."

"No, you're not," he said, leaning against the pack.

She snorted an indelicate, smug laugh. "You're right, I'm not."

"So what's going on that you've already butted heads with Arthur, less than a day since he showed up in town?"

"The usual." She pushed into the stretch, feeling her spine align itself. There was nothing better than a good sparring match to clear her head. "So how did he take it, when you told him?"

"Arthur is a man of few words."

"With you, maybe," Virginia grumbled. "I can barely get him to shut up."

"He seemed... surprised." Seamus raised an eyebrow, but didn't say anything else.

Virginia smirked. "Good."

"Ever the enigma, Vee."

"It's part of the job."

Seamus sat across from her, rocking the ice across his jaw slowly, grimacing from the pain. "My lips are sealed, from this moment forward."

"They'd better be, or I'll seal them for you." She pulled her shoulders, itching for more strain. "Want to go again?"

"Give me a minute, I need to be sure you didn't fracture my jaw."

"Please, I barely touched you," she said, waving him off. "You're fine. I've seen you take worse hits than that."

"How are things, then? With your... personal life, I mean." Seamus shot her a cautious glance, probably afraid she'd pop him again.

Virginia raised an eyebrow at him. "Like a desert."

"Ouch."

"Work has been rough lately. I don't get much time to go out on the prowl."

"Virginia Vane, alley cat of Verdance," Seamus said with a laugh. "Seriously, though, maybe you should come out with me sometime."

"Given the teams we play for, I doubt I'd be a very good wing-woman."

He shrugged, adjusting the ice. "It would be fun."

"You've been asking me to go out for years. Remind me again how many times I've acquiesced?" she prompted.

"None."

She nodded. "None."

"The offer stands, Vee."

"Noted."

He stretched his bare legs out in front of him, the bright red shorts embroidered with his name falling to mid-thigh, showing off toned olive skin. "I bet Arthur fell all over himself trying to talk to you again, after all these years."

Virginia groaned. "Don't remind me how long it's been, I'm already entirely too aware of how old I am." She stood, shaking herself loose. "And yes, he did."

"I knew it," Seamus said, barking out a laugh. "How many times did he put his foot in his mouth?"

"At least a few." She debated sharing the information about Arthur's daughter, but decided against it. "I should have known he wanted my help with something."

"Can you blame him? You're the best in the business."

"Best and broke," she muttered in reply.

Seamus exhaled a light laugh through his nose. "True for many of us. Where else can you find a sparring partner that won't throw you out after being attacked out of nowhere?"

She nudged him with her foot. "Come on, quit bellyaching and let's go another round. I need to work on evasion, I've gotten rusty."

"With a right hook like that, I'm not sure you'll need it." Even so, Seamus dragged himself to his feet, rotating his jaw carefully before tossing the ice to the side. "Square up, Vane, you're not catching me off-guard this time."

Chapter Five

The key fought the lock, metal grating against metal, the door finally swung free after several frustrating minutes of grappling. *Virginia Vane, Private Investigator* was etched into the frosted glass panel, the edges of each letter chipped and worn from fourteen years of waiting there for the one big fish client who could make her a success. Through the window behind her desk, Verdance was blanketed in thick snow, which was why she was already an hour later getting to the office than she had intended. The sparkling white drifts nearly blinded her, and she shielded her eyes against the intrusive light.

She kicked the door shut, the glass rattling angrily. She tossed her charcoal grey wool overcoat onto the green couch against the wall, the large wooden buttons clattering against the armrest. Another day, more cases to solve. If she was lucky, she'd have a few days of reprieve before Arthur tried to worm his way into her business again. No doubt he was sitting at headquarters, seething that she hadn't checked in yet, bouncing his leg up and down as he waited. He was never one for patience, but then, neither was she.

He'd always been terrible at stakeouts, unable to suppress the urge to go rampaging in, guns blazing.

She pored over the case files in front of her: three that had jumped bail, and were probably long gone. Petty criminals, and not worth the expense in dragging them back over state lines. She was an investigator, not a bounty hunter, even if the loan sharks rarely cared about the delineation in profession.

The next case was a man who'd skipped town with his family's entire fortune, down to the grandmother's pearls. A common tale, especially for ones strung out on Nether or harboring a secret gambling addiction. Everyone knew the cards were rigged, but it didn't stop some from trying to play the house at their own game. She examined it again, squinting at the photos his family had given her for reference. Even in the picture, he looked jumpy, unsettled. No doubt the sharks were after him, too. He'd been missing for months, but there hadn't been any leads, not a single one. The casinos were far too tight-lipped to let anything useful slip.

She sighed, assembling a new file for Benjamin. He'd already been gone two weeks, an eternity in investigations. Many times, the trail was long cold by then. The VCPD would shrug him off, shoving the file away in some cadet's desk drawer. "And Arthur wonders why people don't bother," Virginia muttered, tearing the page of notes from her book and clipping it inside the file.

A cagey employer might not mean anything. After all, the rich and privileged loved secrecy, with all their questionably legal enterprises, none of them wanted someone like her poking around in their business. Still, it played on her, and she frowned at the notes. While she wasn't against breaking and entering as a rule, setting a crowbar to the door of the richest school in Verdance was unlikely to be profitable, either financially or in information.

A knock at the door drew her attention, and she lifted her eyes from the desk. "Come in."

It creaked open slowly, cautiously, as though whoever it was wasn't even sure they should be there. "Er—Ms. Vane?" the woman said. She was about five years younger than Virginia, dressed prim and proper, and she likely hadn't ever been that far south in Verdance. She reeked of east coast propriety and mannerisms.

"Mona?" Virginia asked, hoping against the odds that she was wrong.

The woman nodded. "Yes."

Virginia steeled her nerves, her shoulders tensing painfully beneath the cobalt waistcoat she was wearing. She swallowed back her incredulity that Mona would have the bold audacity to show up at her office uninvited, after everything that had happened. "What are you doing in my office? I told Arthur already that if he wants to talk to me, he can make an appointment."

"Arthur doesn't know I'm here." Mona closed the door behind her, unbuttoning her long jacket, the shade of a ripe aubergine. "In fact, I'd ask you to refrain from reporting my visit to him."

"You have my attention, Mrs. Dixon." The name grated at Virginia, even though she'd never chosen to make it her own.

"Mona is fine," she said, tossing her hair. It was black and glossy, pin straight and beautiful like the starlets in the movies.

Virginia gestured to the chair across the desk. "I must say, this is a surprise."

"I was a little worried you would attack me on sight."

"The thought did cross my mind, but I'll admit that my own cockeyed curiosity is winning the battle." Virginia smiled, baring her teeth just enough to set Mona on edge. "For now."

"Should I start by saying that I am sorry for—"

Virginia frowned. "No."

"Okay, then." Mona sat down, crossing one leg over another, her shoes dreadfully impractical for the snow outside, but women who looked like Mona never needed to care much about practicality. "I am concerned about Penny."

"Yes, Arthur indicated as such."

"Did he?"

Virginia raised an eyebrow. "Yes."

"She's a sweet girl, and I... I feel that our return to Verdance may have been ill-conceived," Mona admitted. She folded her hands in her lap, the picture of societal respectability in her matching grey tweed pencil skirt and jacket, perfectly pressed and tailored. "Ms. Vane—"

"I think we know enough about each other to be on a first name basis, don't you?" Virginia interrupted, already desperate for the interaction to be over. "Though I'm sure you know more about me than I do you, which does seem like an imbalance." Virginia leaned against the desk, her forearms braced against the wood. "Get to the point, Mona."

"I want you to convince Arthur to move back to the east coast," Mona said evenly, without even so much as a hint of irony.

Virginia barked out a laugh, tossing a loose grey curl over her shoulder. "He didn't listen to me when we were married, what makes you think he'd listen to me now, fifteen years on?"

"Because in spite of everything, he still trusts your judgment in these matters more than mine." Mona's jaw tightened, her expression pinched. "Much to my personal dismay."

Sunlight cascaded against the desk, reflecting off the chipped varnish into Mona's perfectly unblemished skin. She squinted, and Virginia turned to lower the window's shade, casting them into relative darkness except for the persistent stripe of light that escaped beneath the thick fabric. Virginia folded her hands atop the desk, waiting. "This is not the conversation I thought I would be having this morning, I must admit."

"He thinks he can set Verdance right," Mona said. A shade of irritation colored her tone now, and Virginia was pleased by it. Mona tucked a stray hair back behind her ear before she continued. "Course correct, or whatever it is that he says."

"Things are different here since the Rupture," Virginia replied. "I'm not sure if he has grasped that. He will, before too long."

"I worry he won't, until it is too late."

Virginia rotated her shoulder, still sore from the previous night's sparring session. "Too late?"

"What if something happens to Penny?" Mona asked in a small voice.

"Then Arthur will have the entirety of the VCPD out in force," Virginia assured her, more out of a desperation to get Mona the hell out of her office. "She is safe. Rickarton is staunch in their security protocols."

"How did you know she attends Rickarton? She's only been there two days."

"Mona, I do have a job outside of entertaining you and your husband's anxieties about the safety of Verdance, you know."

"Was it Benjamin?" Mona inquired, and Virginia was irritated that she might have valuable information.

"Hmm." Virginia leaned back, considering. "What do you know about Benjamin?"

"I know he went missing," Mona said. "I know he's the third this year, and the school is hiding something. Benjamin is gone, as are two students from earlier in the autumnal semester. Arthur says I'm just being paranoid, that—"

"You aren't being paranoid."

Mona's eyes widened in surprise. "No?"

"I don't know what it is yet, but something isn't adding up, that's for sure, but it's too soon to say," Virginia answered, scribbling a note in the margin of the file. "Could just be they don't want their shining reputation tarnished." She shrugged. "Could be something more. Could just be crews out looking for trouble again, rounding up mythics."

"Can you find out?" Mona asked.

Virginia laughed. "Are you paying me?"

"You can't tell Arthur." Mona shifted her glance to the side, fiddling with the latch on her bag. "I'm sorry to make this awkward, Virginia."

"Things with Arthur are frequently awkward."

"He's trying to do what's best for the city, but I fear he's losing sight of his family." Mona lay her bag in her lap, the latch abandoned. "It feels like we are losing him."

Virginia nodded. "Not unheard of in law enforcement." She closed the file, sliding it to the side of the desk. "Is your daughter concerned about the disappearances?"

"No. The school told the kids that their classmates moved away."

"And how did you come to find out that wasn't the case?" Virginia asked, tapping a pen against the desk. She'd make notes after Mona left.

"Mothers talk," Mona explained. "I did extensive research on Rickarton before we moved here."

"Fair enough. And your other children?" Virginia had no idea how many children she had with Arthur. For all she knew, it could have been one for each year he was gone.

Mona shook her head. "We just have Penny and her sister, Oren. She's fifteen."

"Shifter?"

"No."

"They run in your family?" Virginia asked, knowing full well that it was almost exclusively a hereditary trait, and Arthur's family had no trace of anything mythic. The man was as boring as she was.

"Yes." She rolled up her sleeve, showing off the iridescent scales that sank into her brown skin. "We manage to fly under the radar, most of the time."

"Arthur never mentioned that."

"I imagine there's plenty he doesn't mention," Mona offered.

Virginia laughed sardonically. "Yeah, you're telling me. I'm intimately familiar with his lies. Or rather, exclusions of truth."

"He never wanted to hurt you, Virginia."

"Let's stick to the business at hand, shall we? I don't think there's much point in dredging up long-buried history. There's too much water under this bridge to unpick everything."

Mona nodded. "Understood."

"Well, then," Virginia said, folding her hands on the desk. "What are you hoping to learn?"

"Why the school is lying to us."

"That it?"

"That's it."

"Then leave me to it. Don't call me, I'll call you when there's information to be had." She slid a slip of paper across the desk. "These are my rates. Under the circumstances, I'm sure you'll understand why I'm not extending my friends and family rates."

"Of course." Mona stood, buttoning her coat back up. "Thank you for being civil, Virginia."

"Why me?" Virginia asked.

Mona paused, tilting her head in confusion. "I'm sorry?"

"Of all the private eyes in Verdance, why ask me? After everything?"

Mona smiled. "Because you're the best."

* * *

Virginia had barely made it through the door before the police scanner announced another corpse had been found, this time at the edge of the park at the center of the city. A young woman this time, an attorney in her mid-twenties, embroiled in a major case targeting the Ruby Thorns, a notorious crew that all but ran the entirety of the west side.

She stood at the counter, waiting to hear the rest of the call. Arthur's voice echoed over the scanner.

"Shifter?" he asked.

"No, sir," came Lindell's voice in reply.

Virginia breathed a sigh of relief. The last thing Verdance needed was some war on mythics. That poor woman just got tied up with the wrong crew, too large and too powerful, with an army of attorneys on standby. She gritted her teeth at the brash injustice.

Two more calls came in, one for a robbery, and one for a street fight just a few blocks down. She sank into the chair, ready to dive back into the chapter on symbiotic possession, when the call came again.

"Sheriff, she wasn't a shifter, but she was a seer," Lindell said.

Shit.

"Copy that," Arthur said. "I'll be down there as soon as I can."

Before Virginia could make it to the door, her phone rang. She dithered, unsure whether to answer it. No one ever called her at home, other than her landlord, and that was a call she preferred to miss. Grumbling, she lifted it from the receiver. "Hello?"

"Ginnie, can I assume you already have your boots on, ready to meet me there?"

"Meet you where, Arthur?" she asked innocently.

He sighed, blowing out the speaker, and Virginia flinched, holding it away from her ear. "Captain Lindell indicated that you're in possession of a scanner."

"So much for privacy," she muttered, rolling her eyes towards the ceiling. She regretted it the moment she spotted the water damage in the corner of the room.

"Are you coming down, or not?" he pressed.

"I'm not a cop, Arthur, you can't just order me around—"

"Come, or don't. I just thought it may prove useful." He hung up, and Virginia huffed. The audacity of that man, calling her at home.

Five minutes later, she was in her car, speeding down the street towards the park. The bastard had always known her too well, even when they were teenagers. She hated it even more at age forty-five than she had at age nineteen. Fifteen years of silence apparently hadn't been enough to untie that particular knot.

She parked behind a squad unit, climbing out and buttoning up her coat, the night's chill already settling heavily beneath her skin. "Arthur," she said casually, announcing her presence.

"I knew you were already on the way out the door," he said, a smug, self-satisfied tone to his voice.

"Why call, then?" Virginia asked, ready to turn tail and go home, if it wasn't for the potential paycheck at the end of the case.

"On the off-chance I was wrong." He smirked. "But I wasn't."

"A seer, then?"

He nodded. "Under the radar. I don't think even her employer knew."

"I don't blame her," Virginia said. "Conscription is a hell of a raw deal just for being born a seer."

"You can't deny that it's a useful skill, especially when national security is concerned." He glanced over his shoulder, eyes flicking across the street. "Could be a million reasons why she's out here."

"And most of them are the Ruby Thorns," Virginia added.

He grimaced. "I wish you weren't right about that."

"You won't have an easy time locking up whoever did it."

"Still, Ginnie, it's not impossible this is related to the boy from the quarry. Mythics sentiment is... evolving."

"Regressing, more like."

"The Rupture—"

"Don't talk to me about the Rupture, Dixon," she hissed. "I was here when it happened. Where the hell were you? Skirting your responsibilities, hiding out on the east coast." Virginia waved her hand casually. "Playing house with Mona."

"I wasn't hiding out," he snapped. "Some of us decided to move on from what happened here."

She snorted a derisive laugh. "An excellent job you've done moving on, too, given you're right back here in Verdance, begging for my help."

"I wasn't begging—"

"Please," she said. "You ran away with your tail between your legs, too afraid of the big bad sheriff to do anything about it. I sucked it up. I stayed."

"Yeah, and look where it got you." He rubbed his forehead. "Ginnie, let's not start this again. I can't have this conversation with you every time we run into each other."

"Fine," she conceded. "I'll keep my opinions to myself."

Captain Lindell exited a squad unit, stepping out onto the snow. "Sheriff." Her gaze slid to Virginia, and she tilted her head almost imperceptibly. "Ms. Vane."

"Captain," Arthur replied with a nod.

"Ruby Thorns?" Lindell asked.

"Could be," Virginia responded. "Or could be connected to the quarry."

"Or both," Arthur added. "We don't want to be premature in ruling anything out."

The irony of it burned in Virginia's stomach, but she swallowed the bile back down. "Photography?"

"They'll be arriving soon," Lindell said in her husky voice, like warm whiskey mixed with honey. "Coroner?" She asked.

Arthur nodded. "Been and gone. Pretty fresh, only a few hours."

"That tracks," Virginia agreed. "Someone would have noticed if there was a corpse in the park all day, this area has pretty high traffic."

"In winter?"

"Yes, *Arthur,* even in winter."

Captain Lindell swallowed back a laugh, covering it with a demure cough. "Ahem. In any case, Sheriff, I think it would be prudent to keep a lid on this where press is concerned, regardless of the findings. You know how they like to spin a narrative."

"Set up a perimeter for now. Let's get all of this done and dusted tonight, so we don't have to deal with onlookers in the morning." Arthur checked his watch and sighed. "Mona is going to kill me."

"What's the matter, she can't handle the life of a sheriff's wife?" Virginia asked. "Seems she should have been informed that came with the—" she cut herself off and rolled her eyes. "Opinions to myself."

"I can take things from here, Sheriff, if you need to get home," Captain Lindell offered.

Arthur shook his head. "No, it's best I stay. It doesn't set a good precedent if I'm running off the scene after only a few days back in the VCPD."

"Very well, sir." Lindell looked back to Virginia. "Are you consulting?"

"Yes," Arthur answered. "Ms. Vane will be consulting on this case."

"News to me," Virginia grumbled, but the VCPD had a much fatter budget than the residents of Verdance City, and she wasn't about to pass up getting double pay on a case. It was most of the reason she was even out there in the first place. "Where is the body?"

"This way," Lindell said, nodding towards the tree line. "She was found by a couple of... well, let's just say that they weren't laying down in the bushes to inspect the local wildlife."

"A bold move in Verdance." They left Arthur behind, greeting the photographers.

Lindell laughed. "A bold move anywhere, I should think."

"How long have you lived here?" Virginia asked.

"Are you asking that out of genuine curiosity, or because of my accent?"

"Oh, I..." Virginia faltered. "I didn't mean to be rude."

"I've lived in Verdance for seven years." She cast a sideways glance at

Virginia. "A pity I'm only meeting you now. You seem like a fascinating woman, Ms. Vane."

"Virginia."

Lindell stopped to look at her, almost an appraisal. "Shirin." She lifted her chin, an eyebrow raised. "But I would appreciate Captain Lindell when I am on duty."

"Noted."

Snow crunched under their boots as they approached, a light dust illuminated by the distant street lamp, blowing across the drifts at the edge of the park. Virginia was no stranger to dead bodies, but it was always jarring. That never faded, not in nearly three decades of doing the work.

"Ligatures?" Virginia asked.

"Doesn't look like it, although we may have to wait for the coroner's report." Lindell crossed her arms over her chest, inspecting from a distance. "The boy in the quarry didn't, either."

"No cause of death?"

"Nothing official, not yet."

"Nether?" Virginia squinted into the darkness. "No," she said, answering her own question. "No purple residue."

"How long have you been off the force?" Lindell asked, brazen in her questioning.

Virginia stiffened, her defenses rising fast and sturdy. "Why?"

"You asked me how long I've lived here, why can't I ask that?"

"It's different."

"Maybe not so different," Lindell said, holding her gaze for a moment before waving over the photographers. "We should get out of their way. We wouldn't want to be the reason that evidence is inadmissible."

"Do you think I could get copies of the quarry?" Virginia asked, keen to change the subject. "I can have a look, see if anything stands out."

Lindell tilted her head, her brow knitted in some sort of unreadable expression. "You don't trust me to see if anything stands out?"

"What would be the point of consulting, exactly, if I'm not given access to the evidence?" Virginia challenged.

"There's a clear chain of—"

"Captain Lindell, I can appreciate your position here. Believe me, I can—some private investigator showing up, stepping on your toes, it can't feel great. But I've got my own cases to solve, and I can promise you that I'm not looking to steal your job." Virginia stepped back, allowing a photographer to take her place. "There isn't enough money in the world for me to work alongside Arthur all day, every day."

The captain lifted an eyebrow. "You assume a lot of things, Virginia."

"Hmm."

"I'll send the photos to your office first thing tomorrow."

Virginia nodded. "Thank you, Captain."

Chapter Six

As promised, the photos of the quarry arrived early, only moments after Virginia had stepped into the office. She nodded a thanks to the courier, slicing open the envelope as the door latched with a quiet click.

The pictures weren't much help. She'd predicted that night photography would be insufficient, and she'd been right. "Damn it, Arthur," she growled, spreading the pictures out. The high contrast, driven by the harsh flash, made it hard to see delicate details of the crime scene.

The victim hadn't been identified, nor had the cause of death. No doubt Arthur had his officers working around the clock to compare the boy with any open missing person reports, but he'd promised he would tell her if anything came up, and her phone remained frustratingly silent.

News of the assumed murder still hadn't hit the papers, thanks to the VCPD throttling information to the press. It was only thanks to quick work that had kept reporters off the scene, carting away all the evidence before they had time to pitch up and snoop around.

Virginia held one photo up to the light, examining it as best she could. No contusions, no defensive marks on his hands. It was like he'd been killed in his sleep. She sighed, laying it gingerly back down on the desk. Verdance had never been what some would call a safe city, but the recent rash of corpses gave her an uneasy feeling much like a brick dropping into her stomach.

Something wasn't adding up.

She scowled, examining another photo. Was it a shadow, or something else? Residue, maybe? The black and white photograph couldn't tell her if it was Nether, gunpowder, or something else. Maybe it was nothing. Maybe it was just mud, or a splash of moisture from the flooded caverns below the quarry.

The phone rang, and she snatched the receiver. "Vane."

"Is this Ms. Virginia Vane?" the voice asked.

"It is."

"The private investigator?"

She stifled a sigh. "Yes."

"Sheriff Dixon is asking whether you've had time to look at the quarry case."

"Tell Arthur he can call me himself, if he wants to talk about work. Besides, I only just got them," she retorted, already tired of the games she was playing with the VCPD.

"He said—"

"I don't give a rat's ass what he said. I'll get back to him when I know something. Otherwise, he can do his own work, for once."

The receiver crackled, and there was a hushed exchange in the background that she couldn't quite make out. Probably Arthur, too high and mighty to call her himself. That badge on his arm was already giving him an inflated sense of self-importance, not that he'd ever needed much encouragement in that department.

"Virginia," came a familiar honey-smooth voice.

"Shirin."

There was a moment of quiet, almost as if the captain was deciding whether or not to correct her. "I'm sorry, I should have called you myself."

"It's Arthur's department, not yours," Virginia said.

"For now," Shirin added, and then laughed. "I tease. In any case, the last thing I would want is for you to feel under-appreciated. It's my understanding that you have been responsible for many cases being closed in Verdance over the years, through one means or another."

Virginia swapped the receiver from one hand to the other, leaning against the peeling wallpaper. "Did you call to flatter me?"

"I called to see if you got the photos," Shirin said.

"A few moments ago, yes." Virginia paused. "Thank you for sending them."

"Any thoughts?"

"Not yet, no. The high contrast makes it a challenge."

"Mm," Shirin agreed. "A pity we couldn't wait until daybreak, but the press..."

"I know," Virginia said. "Always a nuisance."

"Will you drop by if you have any thoughts?" Shirin asked casually.

Virginia leaned back in her chair. "I might."

"You *might?*"

"I do have other cases, Shirin. As it turns out, I am approaching a full caseload."

"My apologies, then. I don't want to waste your time." The captain said something, muffled, as though she had covered the receiver. "I'm lead on this case, so if you wouldn't mind reporting any findings directly to me—"

"I would much rather talk to you than to Arthur," Virginia said, a little too eagerly, and then pressed a hand to her forehead. "I just mean—"

"I know exactly what you mean," Shirin said evenly. "I look forward to hearing from you, Virginia."

The call disconnected, and Virginia replaced the receiver in its cradle, staring at it. There was something about Captain Lindell—Shirin—that made her feel uneasy. Maybe it was her direct way of speaking. It was different to most other people, especially those on the VCPD. The entire department dealt in obfuscation and dancing around the truth, trying to trap people in their own words.

Virginia picked up the photos again, examining them. If she didn't know any better, she'd say it looked like he was killed elsewhere, and transported. Setting the photos on her desk, one by one, lined up in pairs, she pored over them, hunting for any inconsistencies. She gave a quiet hiss, knowing it would have been easier to observe in daylight. She'd only gone to the quarry to make sure it wasn't Benjamin, but *apparently,* she was consulting for the VCPD.

Damn Arthur for that, too.

She sighed, straightening the photos and depositing them back into their envelope, sliding it into a desk drawer. There was a time she would have done nearly anything to be working with the force again, but it felt more like an imposition than an opportunity. She'd seen enough of what happened at the precinct to have a dim view of what went on there.

Going back wasn't an option. Not anymore. It was too far gone, and it didn't matter who was at the helm. Arthur would be subject to the same red tape and politicking as the last sheriff, and the one before that, too. Virginia's jaw clenched involuntarily at the thought of the former sheriff. Coward. Traitor to the city. He had blood on his hands, and did until the day he died.

Virginia stood, sliding her coat over her shoulders and buttoning it against the waiting cold. The only way to get a better reading of the scene was to go there herself. Sure, Arthur would be pissed, but she'd never cared much about that.

* * *

The quarry was covered in snow and even harder to navigate than usual. She parked far off, not wanting to get stuck in a sinkhole, or worse, hauled into headquarters if Arthur had officers out there. She squinted against the bright sun glaring off the untouched snow, drawing a hand to her forehead for shade. She'd be lucky to see anything after the heavy snow, but it was worth a shot. With Rickarton locked down, she was at a dead end with Benjamin's case until she uncovered another lead.

Her boot found the ridges of the squad unit tracks under the snow, following them to the scene. It was clear now, as though nothing had ever happened. The bottom of the quarry pit was covered in wet snow, half-melted and muddy. Virginia frowned at the steep embankment, knowing that if she wasn't careful, she'd wind up trapped at the bottom, clawing uselessly at loose rock. The temperatures were set to drop that night to well below freezing, and dying of hypothermia wasn't exactly how she'd planned to go out.

Sliding and skidding down the slope on her hip, she reached the bottom, looking up to ensure she'd be able to climb out. She dug away snow with her hands, wincing at the sharp pangs of ice stabbing at her skin. Virginia breathed into her hands, rubbing them together and flexing her fingers into fists.

There was almost no sign that there had been a body there at all, nothing more than a slight indentation where the VCPD had dug him out of his shallow, uncovered grave. Poor kid. Whatever it was that he was mixed up in, no one deserved to be unceremoniously dumped in a quarry. Nudging rocks out of the way with the toe of her boot, she examined the impression. There was nothing out of the ordinary, nothing she hadn't already gleaned from the photographs, but something still felt *off*.

She couldn't quite put her finger on it, but she had a strong hunch that they'd missed something. That there was something uncovered, something unseen. Her gut was rarely wrong. It had told her Arthur had been cheating, and she'd been right then, too.

Virginia's jaw tightened. Humiliated, personally and professionally, yet he skated off without consequence to a promotion on the east coast, while she hid in her apartment for almost a year, draining her pitiful pension to make rent.

"Asshole," she muttered. She'd promised to be cordial, even professional, but the man made her blood boil hotter than liquid iron.

She bent, picking through the gravel. No blood. No hair, even, not that it would be easy to find after such a heavy, wet snowfall. No clothing scraps or fragments, although if there had been any, the VCPD would have nabbed them the first night.

They might be incompetent, but they weren't that incompetent. Not usually, anyway. Not anymore.

Her fingers brushed against something soggy and soft, almost turning her stomach with the possibilities of what it might have been before pulling it free from the muck. A matchbook.

She turned it over, examining the faded logo, the cerulean ink bleeding onto her hands. The Sphinx. That kid didn't look old enough to be frequenting jazz bars, but there was no telling if he'd been using a fake identification card, or if he found the matchbook on the street—or if it had been buried there for months, tossed aside by a quarry worker before the whole place closed.

The club was well-known in Verdance, a swanky place with plenty of high-rollers and a basement for illegal bets on the ponies. She'd spent some time there, years back, but adopted a policy of avoidance out of principle. Maybe Astrid didn't work there anymore. Maybe she'd moved on.

Either way, Virginia had to find out.

* * *

The Sphinx was notoriously hard to get into, but Virginia had her ways of bypassing the bouncers. "I'm here to see Astrid," she said, almost expecting him to laugh at her. "I'm her new enforcer. The name's Vee."

The bouncer gave her a strange look, his brow furrowed as he checked something on a clipboard. "She's on in twenty minutes," he said, unclipping the rope.

So she hadn't moved on.

That complicated things, even if it made getting in more convenient.

Virginia sat at the bar, tucking a lock of silver hair behind her ear. She knew how to look the part, and could tell from the curious stares that no one remembered her. Good.

"What'll it be?" the bartender asked, his voice gruff.

"Gin, straight up on the rocks." She glanced at the clock. "Make it a double."

The bartender reached under the counter, producing a cloth to wipe water stains from the marble. "You sure?"

"Of course I'm sure. Do I look like a woman who's not sure what she likes to drink?" Virginia retorted, staring him down with a raised eyebrow. She drummed her fingers against the bar to punctuate her point.

He scowled. "I'm only asking if you want something a little harder, darlin'."

Virginia bristled. "Harder?" She knew what he meant, but wanted to make him squirm.

"You know, a little less..." he leaned over the bar. "Legal."

"If you're asking if I want Nether, the answer is no," she said, her voice firm, and her shoulders tense. Some things at the Sphinx never changed.

He shrugged. "Alright, then." The bartender narrowed his eyes and scrubbed a sticky patch from the corner, tossing the barely soiled rag into a bucket under the counter. "You a cop?"

"No," Virginia answered.

"Cops aren't allowed in here," he insisted. "If you're a cop, you have to say so."

She laid her hands flat on the polished bar. "Are you going to pour me a drink, or do I have to climb over the bar and do it myself?"

"Who let you in here?"

"I'm waiting for Astrid. I'm the new enforcer," Virginia explained, hoping the same lie that had worked at the door would work on the bartender.

He put his hands up in surrender. "Sorry, lady. I didn't know. Haven't seen you around here before."

"Let's keep it that way." She held his stare, glaring until he looked away, turning to make her drink. He'd remember her, of course. Even in the dim light, her faded scars shone, giving her face an eerie glow that reflected back at her from the smoky mirror behind him.

"You a friend of hers or something?" he asked, sliding the glass across the bar.

Virginia shrugged. "Or something."

"Not much of a talker, are you?"

She met his inquisitive glance with a cold, disinterested glower of her own. "No."

"You know what they say, a bartender can be your best—"

"Listen, pal," she interrupted, "I'll tip you well so long as you keep my drink topped up and your lips zipped, are we clear?"

He frowned, leaning against the counter. "Listen, *lady*, Astrid tips better to make sure we aren't letting any creeps hang around waiting for her."

"And I look like a creep?" she asked, the corners of her lips twitching upwards into a derisive smirk.

"You look unfamiliar, which is the same thing where I come from." He set a bottle of whiskey on the bar, sliding it down to a man on the opposite side. "And you wouldn't be the first person to come in here pretending you're one of the new enforcers."

Virginia nodded, taking a long drink of the gin, letting the ice cool her lips. "If you're that worried, you can prance yourself backstage and tell her that Vee is here."

He blinked in surprise. "Oh."

"*Oh?*" she prompted.

"You're *that* Vee?" he asked, his voice almost in awe.

The fact that Astrid had mentioned her to the bouncers and bartender was disconcerting, and probably spelled trouble. Virginia leaned back on the barstool, taking another sip. "Name ring a bell?" she asked.

He nodded. "It's come up, once or twice."

"Are you going to leave me alone, now?"

"Sure thing, Vee," he said, and then corrected himself with, "Ma'am."

Virginia grimaced, rattling the ice against the heavy lead glass. "Vee is fine."

"You want another?" he asked, gesturing at the near-empty glass. "We got a new one in from out of town, real specialty stuff."

"You hold that back for the VIPs or something?" she asked.

He smirked. "Or something."

"The same again is fine, thank you." She drained the glass, setting it down on the bar. The stage was empty, save for a few chairs at the back and a microphone front and center. It was the same staging Astrid had always preferred. She was a holy terror and a harbinger of problems, but Astrid was a creature of habit, despite her profession.

The Sphinx had a reputation for mischief, and was no stranger to intrigue. Plenty of the who's-who of Verdance made it a point to be seen there regularly, the front door frequently plagued with press when the club let out at closing. If everything went to plan, Virginia would be long gone by then. What she didn't need was any reporters getting in her face.

She held the fresh drink between her palms, half savoring the frosty feel of the condensation, and partially resenting its relationship to the frigid draft that continued to waft past the bar every time the bouncer let in someone new. Still, at least the gin was decent. There were plenty of clubs watering it down to make an extra buck.

Virginia watched the club's residents, an old habit that had always served her well. People did all kinds of interesting things when they thought no one was looking, up to and including outright crimes. The Sphinx was no stranger to those, either, and not just because the bartender was apparently handing out Nether like it was candy. An amorous couple in a dark corner of the club, purple tinged at their eyes, leaned into a noisy kiss that nearly turned her stomach. It wasn't as though there weren't enough upscale hotels in the area, and yet, they sounded like zoo animals in a trough.

One by one, the jazz trio wandered onto the stage to a series of murmurs and coughs, the bassist parked next to the baby grand piano, the lid half raised. They were all dressed in black, with matching gold suspenders that matched the chandelier suspended overhead. The pianist settled herself on the bench, adjusting for height, and the percussionist positioned herself over the snare drum, wire brushes in hand.

"Ladies, gentlemen, and folks of all kinds," the announcer crooned into the microphone, his sequined flat cap turned jauntily to the side, "may I proudly present the goddess you've all been waiting for. Please put your paws together for our very own Astrid Frost, returning tonight to the stage."

Virginia didn't clap along with the rest, choosing to swirl the ice smoothly in her glass. Astrid had enough fans, she didn't need to participate in the adoration. Not anymore.

A few in the audience gave loud cheers and whistles as Astrid appeared, a dangerous vision in sparkling silver lace. "Thank you," she said into the microphone, her voice husky and mellow. "It's a pleasure to be here tonight. I hope you'll all come on this journey with me, to the stars and beyond."

Virginia stifled a snort. Shadows, she was laying it on thick. She'd thought someone like Astrid wouldn't need to, but then, with new clubs cropping up all over the city, maybe she did.

The pianist watched for Astrid's nod, settling into a bluesy riff to get the crowd warmed up.

She shouldn't have been surprised when Astrid's voice sent warmth straight to her gut, but she was. After years of freedom, she was right back in it. Instantly, and without hesitation, Virginia leaned towards the stage, her elbows resting on the bar, her drink forgotten.

Astrid was a vision, just like she'd always been. Glittered and sequined, her short hair cropped into a wavy style, adorned with a crystalline comb, she was all but motionless as she performed. Every note she sang drew the crowd further in, enraptured in her voice, watching every shift of her rosy-red lips. Virginia tried to fight it. She lost, even if it had been a valiant effort. Dimly, she wondered why she'd bothered, when Astrid's voice was so beautifully entrancing, like every happy memory bubbling to the surface.

Virginia didn't have many happy memories, but the feeling remained the same. No one moved a muscle during the song, not even the servers or the bartender. The bouncer leaned against the wall to listen, ignoring the waiting crowd outside.

The band paused, shifting around sheet music in preparation for the next piece, and it was only then that the club began to move again. Virginia shook her head, irritated. She knew it was going to happen, and yet, she was frustrated nonetheless.

Astrid gripped the microphone with both hands, looking out to her adoring fans. "Thank you all so much for being here tonight." Her gaze scanned the crowd, landing on Virginia with a surprised flinch. "It's good to see you." She was addressing the whole club, but Virginia couldn't help but smirk. She'd caught Astrid off-guard. Good.

"The next number is one I always like to sing when I'm feeling a little blue. If you've ever felt that way, then I hope you like it."

The bassist shifted a tuning peg before turning to the pianist, counting off a slow pace with nods before lingering on the low notes, reverberating through the club.

Virginia gripped her glass hard, knowing full well what was next. She barely heard the words, despite knowing every lyric by heart. Sadness gripped her, pulling at her chest, encasing her lungs in a vacuum. She pushed away from the bar, fighting it, grimacing against it until she fell into the door to the bathroom. She splashed water on her face, willing herself to break free of it.

Shadows, it had been a long time.

She hadn't missed it.

Or, at least, she'd refused to admit that she had.

Leaning over the sink, she braced herself against the cool porcelain, glancing up at her red-rimmed eyes. She hated the power Astrid held. It's why she'd spent years avoiding the Sphinx, avoiding anywhere she might run into her. Astrid was risky. Treacherous.

She breathed, condensation fogging the mirror's glass. She didn't want to remember any of it, but it came anyway, unbidden, unrequited and unrequested, memories flooding through her like poison, settling into her veins and burning away her insides. Astrid, Astrid. She never should have left. She never should have stayed.

The final bars of the song came to a close, and Virginia's shoulders relaxed. She pushed back through the door, returning to the bar.

"You good?" the bartender asked, an eyebrow raised.

"Fine," she barked.

"Sure you don't want something stronger?" he asked, cocking an eyebrow.

She glared. "I'm sure." Nudging the empty glass over smooth wood, she nodded. "I'll take the good gin this time, though." Maybe it would help numb her for what was coming next.

"This next one is a tribute to my Mama," Astrid said, smiling out to the crowd. "She taught me everything I know, shadows rest her spirit." Her voice etched across the club, equal parts grit and melodic nectar.

Virginia breathed a sigh of relief, taking the fresh glass from the bar. This song held no power over her. That particular collection of notes and words never had, even if half the place was quietly swaying along with the soft, rhythmic beat. She sipped the gin, an eyebrow raised. "Huh. What do you know, it is good."

"Did you think I'd lie?" he asked, holding up the bottle to the light, and it refracted a prism onto the polished black marble.

She took another drink, savoring the taste. "Yes."

The bartender laughed, wiping a glass clean. "Fair enough." He nodded at the glass. "It's nice with a twist."

"Go on then," she said, letting him drop a curl of lemon into the sparkling liquid. She sipped the drink, savoring the citrus notes that danced across her tongue. It was a welcome distraction from Astrid, at least for the moment. No doubt she'd end up back in the bathroom, pouring water down her face again before too long, if the set didn't end soon.

There were two instrumental numbers, a showcase for the other musicians to display their prowess. Difficult walking bass lines, complex piano chords, and no fewer than three drum solos later, Astrid was back on stage for the final number.

"To close out the night," she said, looking straight at Virginia, "one of my old favorites."

Virginia stiffened, ready to bolt.

"An homage to times gone by," Astrid said, the sequins of her dress catching every stray beam of light and reflecting it out into the crowd.

The opening bars were tempting, like the rich scent of coffee from a cafe, or a soft smile from a beautiful woman. Virginia knew the song well, but relaxed into the stool, leaning against the bar. She should have known Astrid would play their song. It was, after all, her signature piece.

Chapter Seven

Gentle light beamed out from the dressing room mirrors, each bulb lit around every frame, the pooling glow falling prettily around Astrid's shoulders. She smiled into the glass as if she already knew that Virginia was her audience of one—a coquettish turn of her lips, with a sharp undercurrent that cut through the tension like razor wire. "Fancy seeing you here, dollface."

"It's been a while," Virginia said, leaning against the door frame with her deep green blazer left unbuttoned, hanging at her waist.

"Three years, at least."

"I wasn't sure you'd still be here."

Astrid met her gaze in the reflection of the mirror. "I own the place now. I would have thought that a woman with your expertise would have figured that out." She sighed quietly, a performance of disappointment. "What brings you back to me, Vee?"

"A case," Virginia replied.

"Always a case with you," Astrid said, irritation coloring her words with an unpleasant, barbed tone.

Virginia nodded, watching her as she toyed with her makeup. "It's a living."

"You still chasing after husbands who ran out on their wives?" Astrid asked.

"You still swindling the general public?" Virginia shot back, not in the mood to play games about how she chose to pay her bills.

"That's not fair," Astrid pouted, turning around in her chair. "I can't help what I am." Her wide, dark eyes shined like tigerseye in the light of the mirror.

Virginia sucked her teeth, doing her best to avoid the obvious traps that Astrid was setting. "Not all sirens find themselves working as jazz singers, either."

"What would you have me do, Vee?" Astrid demanded, sticking out her lower lip. "Starve?"

"We both know it would be a long time before that would ever happen." Virginia crossed the room, her arms folded across her chest. "You've got enough money to rival half the crews in this city."

Astrid shrugged, letting her robe drape a little too far down her shoulder. "A girl likes to be prepared."

"A woman likes to emotionally manipulate the patrons to sell them Nether." Virginia sat next to her, trying her best not to let her eyes wander to where the silvery lace met smooth, dark skin. "Who are you working with, Astrid? Which crew?"

"No crew."

"You're not producing it yourself. Where did you get it from?" Virginia pressed, her elbows braced against the makeup counter, deftly avoiding the scattered piles of blush that were crumbled along the pale wood.

Astrid rolled her eyes, turning back to the mirror. "Did you only come here to play the cop angle with me? And here I thought you missed me, Vee." Astrid gave her a sideways glance, a delicate smirk playing at her lips. "How utterly devastating."

"Please, it's not as if you don't have enough suitors," Virginia offered, knowing it was true. "I'll bet you have your pick of the crowd any night of the week."

"Maybe so." Astrid reached out, tracing circles on Virginia's knee. "They aren't you though."

Virginia shook her head. "Don't."

The singer pulled back, her full lips pressed into a pretty frown. "Not even for old times' sake?"

"We were never going to work, you know that." Virginia tugged Astrid's robe back into place, covering up smooth, untouched skin.

"It worked for a while though, didn't it?" Astrid asked in that whispered, pleading voice that she'd spent years perfecting.

Virginia sat back in the chair, taking her in. "Until you tried to have me framed."

"Water under the bridge, dollface," Astrid said with a delicate laugh. It was practiced, the same as the songs she sang on stage, and just as meant for manipulation.

"I'd say it was a little more complicated than that," Virginia challenged.

"It wasn't personal." She turned back to the mirror, pulling pins from her hair. "I knew you'd beat the rap."

Virginia slid Benjamin's photo across the counter. "Ever see this kid in here?"

"He looks young."

"Twenty."

Astrid tugged at a curl, pulling it apart with her fingers. "Too young to be in here, then. My bouncers know how to do their jobs."

"How about him?" She pulled one of the crime scene snapshots from her inside breast pocket, placing it face down out of politeness. "A body found out at the quarry."

Astrid glanced at the photo and sighed again, but this time it was honest, a frustrated huff of breath let loose because she wasn't getting her way as easily as she once may have. "Why are you getting all mixed up in this? Doesn't seem like your bag anymore. Not for a long while, actually."

"Favor for a friend," Virginia answered. She was finally getting some- where, and she'd get further if she could bring down Astrid's guard.

"Arthur?" Astrid asked, rolling her eyes. "I should have known he'd have you doing his dirty work the second he landed back in Verdance."

Virginia raised an eyebrow, wondering how in shadows Astrid already knew Arthur was back in town. "I'm consulting on a case," she said in a casual, offhand tone, as if it was a normal day for her.

"And you're saving his ass again, just like you always did." Astrid flipped the photo back over, flinching from it. "Sorry, Vee, I don't recognize this one, either."

"Would your bouncers?" Virginia asked.

"I dunno, he looks young, too," Astrid replied. "Got a name?"

Virginia shook her head. "No. Unidentified. He had a matchbook from here, though."

"He could have picked that up anywhere."

"I know. I just thought, if you'd seen him, you might be able to help me put a name to the face. Give his family some closure, you know." Virginia stared at Astrid, unmoving, willing her to give up whatever information she was hiding. "There's been a rash of disappearances lately."

"Shifters."

"Not just shifters. Found a seer in Prosperity Park last night."

Astrid tucked a curl back behind her ear, adjusting the placement of the glittering comb that rested there. "Seers are always getting themselves into trouble," she said. "That's nothing new."

"Might be a crew trying to move into new territory." Virginia put the photograph back into her pocket. "Might be the Ruby Thorns, if you ask me. This seer was an attorney."

"Even more reason it's probably unconnected," Astrid mused, turning back to her own reflection to powder her nose.

Virginia nodded, altogether too familiar with Astrid's nightly routines. "You're probably right."

"Of course I'm right, dollface, I'd argue that I know this city even better than you do." Astrid stood, shrugging off the strap of her dress. "I just wish you'd show up looking for *me*, sometimes."

Virginia averted her eyes, examining the racks of dresses pushed up against the far wall. "Interesting that the bouncer and the bartender knew my name. Why might that be?"

"You're on the list, Vee," Astrid said casually, laying an arm on Virginia's arm. "The skip-the-line list."

"They seemed surprised to see me." Virginia swallowed hard as Astrid shimmied out of her dress, letting the heavy beaded fabric drop to the ground.

"You're the only one who's never showed. No doubt they were curious. You have a memorable—"

"Face, I know," Virginia interrupted.

"I was going to say a memorable *energy*, Vee."

Virginia rolled her eyes. "Sure."

"It's possible that some of them may have heard some rumors through the grapevine."

"And there it is," Virginia said, gesturing with her hand, shaking her head and trying not to catch her own reflection in the mirror.

"There *what* is?" Astrid asked, hanging up the dress, standing in nothing more than her silvery undergarments.

"They know. About us. About our... history."

"Dollface, half these brutes I've got working here barely even read the papers, much less listen to underground gossip. I wouldn't worry." Astrid turned, a hand on her hip. "Why are you so worried, anyway? Embarrassed of me?"

"No," Virginia said carefully. "I'd just rather that half the city didn't know about my personal life."

Astrid turned, the silvery fabric of her garters catching the light and sparkling in a frustratingly tantalizing way, each buckle framing a perfect square of skin. She tossed out a quick giggle, waving away Virginia's concerns. "And I told you, these meatheads aren't the question-asking types. They're the walk me to my car so I don't get pestered by amorous fans types. Or drink pouring types. Occasionally, take one to my bed types."

Virginia grimaced. "I have to say, I don't see the appeal."

"Why did you really come here tonight?" Astrid asked, putting on her sultry, tempting voice. It came so easily to her, that kind of manipulation.

"I told you," Virginia said. "The case."

"Really?" Astrid sat in her lap, draping her arms around Virginia's neck. "No other reason?" she asked, playing with a lock of Virginia's hair. She laid her head on Virginia's shoulder, toying with a silvery curl. "I know what you look like when you're only on a case," she whispered into her ear.

"And this ain't it, dollface."

"Astrid—"

"I know you dressed up for me."

Virginia swallowed hard. "The club has a dress code."

"Mm, a dress code that your usual wardrobe would easily surpass without question. But this," Astrid said, running a finger along the crushed velvet of the blazer, "is extra effort."

"I don't get out much."

"This looks new."

"I've had it for years," Virginia retorted. "Just something I pulled out of the closet." The cuff of the left sleeve was still showing off the fresh mending job, the green thread frayed at the end because Virginia had never been much of a seamstress.

Astrid nodded, her eyes boring into Virginia. "Mmhmm. I'll bet."

"You don't know as much as you think you do," Virginia replied, doing her best to keep her composure in the face of unadulterated adulterous temptation.

"Dollface, when it comes to you, I can read you like a book." Astrid kissed Virginia's neck, pressing her lips against the pulse point she found there and lingering. "And you know how avid a reader I am."

Virginia let out a soft hiss, her resolve melting away. She ran a hand over Astrid's bare thigh, her breath catching in her throat. "Why do I let you do this to me?"

"Oh, says you," Astrid whispered, planting a soft kiss against Virginia's lips. "You show up here looking like that, sitting at the bar all night, watching me, running a finger along the rim of your glass like you wished it was me."

"I was waiting for you to finish, that's all."

"*Please,*" Astrid breathed, waiting a beat. "There is no need for lies. Just admit it. Admit that you wanted the night to end like this."

Virginia swallowed hard. "End like what?"

"With me in your arms."

"You dumped yourself into my lap, Astrid."

"And yet, I can see the hunger in your eyes. I saw it from twenty feet away. I sensed it the moment you walked through the door of my club."

Virginia scoffed, tempted to push her off and leave, yet for some reason, she didn't. "You didn't even know I was here until you spotted me."

"I was looking for you."

"You're a siren, not a seer."

Astrid laughed, soft and musical in her ear, the breath ghosting across skin and drawing goosebumps to the surface. "I don't need to be a seer to notice you. You've always drawn my eye, Vee."

"You're a menace to society," Virginia said, deadpan.

"Then I guess it's a damned good thing you're not a cop, isn't it?"

"Somehow I have the feeling that you've menaced plenty of cops in your time," Virginia replied.

Astrid bit Virginia's earlobe, a sharp, tempting pain that promised so much more. "Only former cops, and only one."

"Should I feel special?" Virginia tensed, suppressing the shiver that danced down her spine, desperate to ignore the trajectory they were on.

"That's up to you," Astrid whispered into her ear.

Virginia fought the urge to shake her off, and then fought the urge to stay. "You probably just don't want to get caught."

"I don't know about that," Astrid said. "Depends who's catching me."

Virginia turned, meeting her gaze. "You're out of my jurisdiction, Astrid."

"The way your hand is traveling up my thigh, I'd wager a guess that you're willing to cross state lines to bust me."

"And what then?" Virginia asked. "We go a few more rounds, a few more months before you try to have me sent off to prison again?"

Astrid rolled her eyes, pulling back. "I already said, I wouldn't have done it if I wasn't sure you'd get out of it. You have connections, you knew how to play your hand, and you did. I don't know why you insist on dwelling on the past."

"Because if it wasn't for a very lucky discovery by my lawyer Sinclair, I'd be sitting in the penitentiary right now, not falling prey to your charms in your dressing room." Virginia wrapped an arm around Astrid's waist, pressing against the soft flesh of her hips. "What's your angle?"

"My angle, dollface," Astrid began, "is that despite everything that went down between us, I did always hold a particular sort of affection for you that no one else has come close to."

Virginia pulled her closer, already regretting what she hadn't yet done. "And why is that?"

"Because no one makes me try as hard as you do." Astrid pressed a hand against Virginia's face, planting a slow kiss against her lips. "And every now and then, it's intoxicating. I've built up a tolerance for everyone except you."

"You have a lot of pretty words," Virginia said, swallowing hard. She was going to lose the battle, and she knew it. "For a siren who's not singing."

"And you have a lot of resistance for someone who's probably had a cold bed for at least six months," Astrid breathed.

"You don't know that," Virginia shot back, despite the truth in the words. It had been much longer than that.

"Oh," Astrid said, loosening Virginia's tie. "Don't I?"

"I have work in the morning," Virginia protested.

"Vee," Astrid whispered, before tracing her tongue up Virginia's neck. "Shut up."

She'd never been good at denying Astrid for very long, even if she did manage to hold out longer than most of the club's patrons did. She was intoxicating in that uncontrolled, wildfire kind of way, sending you careening into the flames without a thought of how you'd manage to keep your skin from singeing right off your bones.

Virginia swallowed back a gasp, feeling the heat of it grip into her like claws, savage and damaging. It was foolish to fall into bed with Astrid, and yet, that's exactly where they were headed, Astrid's legs wrapped around Virginia's waist as she carried her through the back corridor to her private residence above the bar, easily lifting her up the stairs.

The room looked the same, with art-covered walls and a four-poster bed draped with silk sheets. Only the best for Astrid, but when you had that much money, it was a drop in the bucket. Virginia kicked the door shut, dumping her onto the bed.

Astrid reached up, pulling Virginia down by her jade green tie before removing it, tossing it to the floor and starting on her shirt buttons. "I want you to..." she trailed off, biting her lip.

Virginia raised an eyebrow. "Oh?"

"You know."

"Do I?"

"Why do you do this to me, Vee?"

"Because you let me." Virginia removed her jacket and shirt, keeping on her white camisole. She bent, kissing up Astrid's thighs, waiting.

"Dollface, if you make me wait any longer, I might explode," Astrid begged.

"That's the general idea, actually." She smirked into Astrid's skin, pausing again where her thighs met before pressing with her tongue, languidly, tracing circles. It was like touching a hot stove after you'd already been burned, like being once fooled, but not shy enough. Astrid was a landscape of mystery, and Virginia's curiosity might kill her. At least, it might be the reason why she wound up dead.

Even so, she lost herself in Astrid's flesh, giving in, just like she knew she would when she left her apartment hours ago. She never had a chance. Not with her.

It wasn't long before Astrid cried out, pulling Virginia to her with wide, doe-like eyes, the same ones she used on her patrons every night in the club, except now there was a hint of vulnerability that hadn't been there before.

It was that look that always made Virginia come undone.

It was why, despite knowing she had an early start, and knowing she had cases to work, and knowing that Astrid was a shiny lure in the water, she took her again, hook, line, and sinker.

She should have known.

She did know, really, but some things weren't to be resisted.

At least, not for long.

Chapter Eight

Virginia woke with a jolt, startled by the sound of glass bottles rattling somewhere below. She squeezed her eyes shut, willing her surroundings to magically change back to her apartment from the gauzy curtains draped around the bed she shouldn't have wound up in.

Shadows be *damned*.

She slipped out from the sheets, carefully placing a pillow under Astrid's arm. It would be far easier to sneak out before she woke, than to have some big discussion about it. It was wrong, and she was leaving.

"Vee?" Astrid mumbled, rolling over. "Where are you going?"

Virginia didn't want to look her in the eye, didn't want to risk it. "I have work, I told you."

Astrid made a quiet, pleading sound that shot straight to Virginia's gut. "Stay with me."

"I can't," Virginia said, and tugged on her pants, one hasty leg at a time.

"You never stay with me," Astrid pouted.

"I never should have even come here last night. I should have known better."

"What is that supposed to mean?"

Virginia shot her a look as she pulled on her shirt, buttoning it. "You know exactly what I mean. You have power over people, Astrid."

"Yes, but I waited for you to come to me." Astrid propped herself up on an elbow, still naked from the night before. "Which you did."

"I shouldn't have."

"Don't make some big thing of it, Vee. We have chemistry. It just works with us." Astrid tugged at the bed sheets, trying to tempt Virginia to stay, exposing her collar bones and a hint of cleavage.

Virginia turned away, pulling her tie under the collar. It would be easier to leave if she didn't have to look at her. "No, I'm saying that—you know what, it doesn't matter. I'm leaving, anyway."

"You don't have to. We could order breakfast, we could—"

"Listen, Frost," Virginia interrupted. "I'm trying to make myself clear. Last night was a mistake."

Astrid laughed, but it was hollow. "Using last names now, are we? *Vane?*"

"I have to go."

"Come back if you want more answers about that matchbook."

Virginia turned, frowning. She pointed an accusatory finger at Astrid, advancing on her. "You said you didn't recognize either of those boys."

"And I didn't. Doesn't mean I don't know where they might have gotten information from."

"Astrid, I swear on—"

More glass rattled in the alley below, interrupting them both along with the stripes of grey winter light that were peeking through the thick velvet curtains, a deep eggplant purple that matched the club's interior. Astrid shimmied to the edge of the bed, toying the corner of the coverlet. "Listen, dollface, I know how you work. If I give you whatever you want, I'll never see you again." She bit her lip, an eyebrow raised. "And I can promise that I want to see you again."

Virginia laughed. "I'll have you charged with obstruction."

Astrid rolled her eyes, tossing the pillow away. "You're no fun anymore, you know that? Fine. There's a guy who goes by the name Franky Fiske. Sometimes people call him Sweet Cakes."

"What does he have to do with any of this?" Virginia asked.

"I don't know, Vee, I've just seen him around, alright?" Astrid replied with a huff. "He supplies for us sometimes, and he's got mythics helping him. Shifters usually. That's all I know."

"You could have told me that last night."

"I could have," Astrid agreed. "But you would have left."

Virginia pulled her blazer on, sliding her feet into her boots. "Maybe not. Next time you should try giving me a straight answer before I wind up late for work."

Astrid sat up, holding the sheet around her, no longer interested in games. She glanced at her reflection in the mirror of her vanity, adjusting her hair and wiping the remnants of the previous night's eyeliner from the corners of her eyes. "Come back and see me, dollface."

"Yeah," Virginia replied. Maybe she could manage another four years without seeing her, without falling back into that trap of soft skin and brown eyes and—she shook her head, heading down the back stairs. This was exactly why she never went out.

The bartender from the previous night was already there, scrubbing down the bar. He caught her eye with a smirk and a nod. "Take care, Vee."

"Piss off," she shot back, grabbing her coat from the rack. "I was never here."

At least he didn't know her real name, not that it would be hard to find out if he wanted to. There weren't many people who looked like her running around Verdance, getting mixed up with whatever Astrid was up to now. She should have known the club would be dealing in Nether. Astrid was never one to miss a trick, especially the kind that lined her silk pockets with plenty of cash. Beauty and brains, not to mention the ability to make you feel the lowest you've ever felt, just to pull you to the highest highs.

It was what had first attracted Virginia to her in the first place, and it was also what she hated most about her. Astrid was always hiding something, stowing away information for later, for extortion, or worse. Virginia had never trusted her, and still wound up ensnared in her social-climbing bullshit.

The streets were cold, and bitterly so. A storm front was blowing in across the lake, and the piles of slush at the edges of the road would soon be rock hard ice, just waiting for a car to spin out. Virginia snatched the parking ticket off her windshield, swearing under her breath. There had been a last-ditch attempt to make sure she was out of the club before five in the morning, but even the threat of a ticket hadn't been enough to drag her out of Astrid's bed.

She groaned at the traffic along the lakefront, gripping the steering wheel, hoping the effort would warm her hands. It didn't, and the cold settled into her knuckles with a dull ache.

Her stomach rumbled, but she ignored it. Breakfast always felt like an imposition. When she woke, she wanted to dive headfirst into the day, scouring case files and evidence, not standing over a stove to cook, what, porridge? Horrible, bland porridge. It was like eating horse feed.

The car shuddered to a stop when she parked, surprised to see Captain Lindell already waiting outside her office door. "Captain," she said, climbing out and slamming the door. "You're here early."

Lindell frowned, dragging her eyes over Virginia, lingering on the jacket and tie. "Late night?"

"No, I went for a run," Virginia replied sarcastically. "Can't you tell?"

"Funny, I didn't think you were much of a morning runner."

The door swung open. "Now who's making assumptions, Captain?" Virginia gestured for her to step inside, and knocked the snow free of her boots against the shallow concrete step, sending a spray of clumpy, muddy slush splattering across the pavement.

"There's been a break in the case," Lindell said casually, her posture still ramrod straight.

The hinges creaked in protest as Virginia closed the door, the glass panel rattling quietly as the latch caught. "Which one?"

"The quarry," Lindell answered. "They got a positive identification."

Virginia shrugged off her coat, tossing it onto the couch. "Rickarton?"

Lindell shook her head. "No, much to Arthur's relief. You know his daughter—"

"Yes, I'm aware."

"His wife asked me to pay close attention to this case in particular," Lindell added.

It seemed like Mona had been making the rounds to ask for extra surveillance. Virginia sat in her chair, pulling close to the desk, the wheels scraping against the wood flooring. "I'm sure she has concerns."

"In any case, he's a kid from three states over," Lindell said. "A runaway."

Virginia nodded. "Not uncommon, unfortunately."

"His parents were... how can I put this delicately." Lindell sat, her elbows resting on the arm rests, one hand holding her jaw. "Somewhat less than pitiable. Sounded to me as though they were trying to press him into working for some crew out there, running Nether."

Virginia sat back, chewing the inside of her lip, unsure of how much to share with the captain before she followed up on Astrid's tip. "Where are they now?"

"Already on their way back home."

"Peachy."

Lindell scowled. "The peachiest."

"Poor kid."

"An unjust end, no matter how it played out." The captain leaned forward, scanning the file names on the desk. "A fascinating assortment, Virginia."

"Do you mind? *Shirin?*" She stacked the files, pulling them into a drawer with a sharp snap. "I don't waltz into the precinct and stick my nose in your business, do I?"

Lindell tilted her head, the sparkle of challenge in her eye. "I'm not a consultant for the VCPD."

"Cases I work on aren't your concern, I think you'll agree." Virginia held her stare, challenging her. "These are people who couldn't get help from the VCPD, so they come to me instead. Not even Arthur would be brave enough to barge in here and comment on my work."

Lindell laughed, and it was husky, almost friendly. "That's because the sheriff is afraid of you." She smirked. "I'm not."

"Maybe you should be," Virginia replied.

Lindell shrugged. "Perhaps."

"Was there anything else, Captain? Or did you just want an excuse to snoop through my office?" Virginia sniped, staring across the desk, willing Lindell to excuse herself and leave. An argument, a parking ticket, and an interrogation. What an inauspicious start to the day.

"If my sole goal was to pry, I would have broken in while you were away." Lindell's eyes fell on Virginia's attire again, an eyebrow raised. "Seems I would have had ample opportunity."

Virginia sucked her teeth. "Jealous, Captain?"

"There's no one here, Virginia. You can use my name."

"*Shirin.*"

"I rarely get to taste Verdance nightlife. Despite my snide remark the other night, I made my own assumptions about you." Shirin shrugged lightly, and the delicate motion caused a lock of thick, wavy salt and pepper hair to fall into her face. She tucked it back behind her ear, eyes trained on Virginia with interest.

"And what were those?" Virginia asked, flipping through her files.

Lindell rubbed a hand against her jaw. "I did not think you would be one for spending all night at the Sphinx."

"How did you—" Virginia rolled her eyes. "The parking ticket."

"It was logged this morning," Lindell explained.

"Keeping tabs on me now?" Virginia asked, scanning her desk for anything else Shirin might be able to use against her, and sweeping papers into the top drawer.

Shirin shook her head, hands folded in her lap. "No. A coincidence borne of protocol. It is my week to log traffic infractions for that district."

"I would respectfully ask that you try not to notice things about me, alright?"

"That will be difficult," Lindell replied. "You are very noticeable."

Virginia rolled her eyes, resisting the strange urge to cover her scars. Their ugly encroachment across her face didn't bother her so much anymore, but they made it so much more difficult to move through the world unnoticed. "I hardly think that a night out precludes me from consulting work, unless things have drastically changed since I left the force. Or maybe captains *aren't* having boozy lunches anymore?"

Shirin shifted uncomfortably, the chair's wood creaking with the motion. "For whatever it's worth, not all of the captains do that."

"A marked improvement, then, to be sure." The words were barbed, and

Virginia knew it, and she didn't care.

"I wasn't trying to be judgmental, Virginia."

"Weren't you?"

"No. Many enjoy winding down," Lindell offered. "I prefer to do so off-duty, but I will admit that not all my peers share the same opinion."

"You'd be fighting a losing battle on that front," Virginia replied, letting the snide tone worm its way into her speech.

"This didn't quite go how I had hoped," Shirin said, smoothing back her short, wavy hair.

"And how had you hoped for it to go?" Virginia asked.

"I'm not sure anymore," Lindell answered. "I feel I have made several errors."

Virginia raised an eyebrow. "Was there something else you needed?"

"No." The captain didn't move for a moment, and then stood, straightening her uniform. "If you hear of anything else, you know where to find me."

Virginia chewed her lip before responding with a curt nod. "Will do, Captain." She leaned back in her chair, considering. "Shirin."

* * *

Nights were long in Verdance. The winter chill snaked through the gaps between the buttons on Virginia's coat, and she gritted her teeth against it. Without the glow of the sun, even behind heavy clouds, the city was plunged into frigid temperatures that made it easy to see why so much of the local wildlife migrated south for the season.

She'd migrate, too, if she could.

Virginia parked a long way away from the back entrance of the Sphinx, off the road. She didn't need Captain Shirin Lindell poking through her business again. *Protocol,* sure. More like monitoring her. Most cops didn't like private eyes, and it looked like Lindell was no different, despite her initial attempts at warmth.

She waited, watching for deliveries to the club. There was only one, but when she leaned forward, balancing her weight against the steering wheel, it was clear that it was only food, with no Franky Fiske or mythics in sight. Virginia even recognized the man making the delivery, he'd made them even years before when she was spending far too much time hanging around the club. Too much time in Astrid's bed, more like.

Grimacing, she tapped her fingers against the dashboard. She should have been smarter than to wind up along with Astrid, but at least she'd gotten a lead. That was something. No doubt Arthur would have demanded to wire the whole place up with bugs, and no doubt Astrid would have fought the whole thing tooth and nail, involving press and lawyers from the jump. No, it was best to check this out quietly. Privately.

An hour passed, and then another. Midnight came and went, and Virginia sighed, about to turn the key in the ignition and head for home. Deliveries that late would interrupt the show, surely. Just as the engine started, a wide van turned into the alley, the lights off. She waited, hoping she hadn't been spotted.

The van stopped at the back entrance, and a boy jumped out, knocking on the back door. Virginia squinted. Was it Benjamin? At a distance, it looked like it could be him, but it was dark, and the deep shadows obscured his face. She released the key, letting the car's engine die, climbing out but leaving the door ajar. She needed a closer look.

"Hey! Open up!" the young man yelled through the door. "Come on, man, we can't be waiting around all night. We have other deliveries to make."

Light spilled out as the door opened, the bartender leaning against the frame. "Alright, keep your pants on. Not my fault you're three hours late."

"We got held up," the young man retorted. "Not our fault, either."

"Yeah, yeah, be that as it may, I've got customers to serve, so hurry it the hell up." The bartender glanced over his shoulder, a worried crease in his brow. "You're going to interrupt the set."

"Fiske says it's a double shipment today."

The bartender ran a hand through his hair. "Didn't ask for a double."

"Well a double is what you're getting, alright?" He looked strong, lean with muscle visible even under his winter outerwear.

"You'll have to talk to Astrid about that," the bartender replied.

"I don't have time for bullshit negotiations, pal," the young man said, his voice a pleasant tenor but ridged with put-on grit. He dropped a large crate at the door. "She can take it up with Franky."

The bartender shook his head. "No, no, you don't get to just drop extra product at my door, and—"

"Wait." The young man turned towards the dark, staring.

Virginia froze, hand poised over the holster of her revolver.

"Someone's out there," he said, stepping into the light pooled at the door.

Benjamin. It *was* him. Even at a distance, she saw his eyes rimmed with bright purple. The kid was blown out on Nether, that much was obvious. Ursa had a long road ahead of getting him out of that racket, and it wouldn't be easy. She straightened, shoving her hands in her pockets. "Benjamin?" she called.

"What's it to ya?" the young man shouted back.

"Your sibling is looking for you," she explained. "Ursa hired me to track you down."

He wavered for a moment, rocking back and forth on the balls of his feet. "Tell them to piss off."

Virginia raised an eyebrow. "They're paying a pretty penny to make sure you're safe."

"I'm fine," he shot back.

"You don't look fine, in fact, even from here I can see that you're on Nether," Virginia said, wondering how fast she could get that kid into the car. Maybe she'd even be able to finish that damned book if she got home early enough.

"So?" he asked.

"So that stuff has long-term effects, Kiddo," she explained.

The bartender squinted. "Vee?"

"I told you to forget my face," Virginia shouted. "Close the door and don't tell Astrid I was here."

Benjamin's shoulders tensed. "Mind your own business, bitch."

"You are my business, at least until I complete the contract." Virginia nodded towards the car. "Hop in, and let's talk."

"Piss off," he yelled.

"I don't think I will. In fact, now that I know where you are, I'm going to make it my life's mission to tail you at every opportunity, turning any and all information over to your sibling." She smirked, putting a hand on her hip. "Maybe the cops too, we'll see how things play out." She had no intention of so much as breathing a word of it to Arthur, but it was a useful threat.

"You have no idea who you're messing with," Benjamin growled. His eyes glowed white, the first sign of a shift.

"Shit," Virginia mumbled, settling into a fighting stance, her silver knuckles at the ready. She left her gun in the holster where it belonged. No one hired her to bring their loved ones back dead or riddled with bullets.

Shifts were unsettling to watch, the first few times. Fur or scales bursting from smooth skin, the crack and crunch of bones breaking, only to reform as something else. The soft, guttural wheeze as they tried to scream, but no longer could.

He sprang at her, an almost fully-grown panther, his sleek black fur almost invisible in the night air except for the glint against the club's neon light.

Virginia braced for the impact, but it wasn't enough. He slammed into her, knocking the wind from her lungs. She landed a few hits to his side, rolling out from under him as he swiped.

"Oh, shit," the bartender yelled, disappearing back into the club. It wouldn't be the cops he called, not with a shipment of Nether on the doorstep.

She rolled to her feet, the sole of her boot sliding against the black ice, sending her knee slamming into the concrete. Virginia groaned, feeling the inevitable pop, reeling back to punch at the panther once more, the silver knuckles biting against velvet muzzle.

The cat growled, its fangs bared as it lunged. Virgina staggered against the ice, and teeth sank into her shoulder.

She growled back, hitting it in the eye with a wild flail. This time, the silver broke skin, and the cat reeled backwards, pawing at its face.

Two Sphinx bouncers burst from the back door of the club, holding bats aloft, the wood encircled with barbed wire.

"Wait!" Virginia wheezed, clutching her shoulder. "Wait. He's just a kid, he's hopped up on Nether—"

"All the more reason," one of them said, advancing.

She unholstered her gun, aiming it. "Not one more step towards that cat," she hissed.

"That shifter just tried to put you down, who's he to you?" the other called out.

"No one." She staggered to her feet, bracing her weight against the car. "Don't hurt him."

The cat leaped over the low fence at the back of the lot, slinking back into the thin woods behind the club.

"You know he's just going to go hurt someone else," the bouncer said. "And you let him get away!"

"I'll keep an eye on him." Her vision swam, and her knees buckled.

"Lady, you're about to keel over." The bouncer lowered the bat. "Shit and shadows. Bryce!" he called through the door. "Call Anya. Tell her it's an emergency."

Virginia barely had time to holster her gun before she blacked out.

Chapter Nine

Virginia stirred, wincing away from the pain and pressure at her shoulder. "Stop that," she mumbled, her limbs strangely unresponsive when she tried to sit up.

"I can guarantee that you don't want me to stop," a voice chastised. "What do you think will hurt more, a poultice, or losing your arm to infection? Lie still, for shadows' sakes, you're worse than the men."

"Not worse than a man," Virginia grumbled, prying open an eye. "Who are you?"

The woman's bronzed skin glowed in the candlelight, her thick, silvery hair tied back in a low bun. "I'm the person saving your arm, so you could stand to be a little more polite."

"What are you doing to me?" Virginia asked.

The woman pressed her down onto the steel table, holding her in place. "I just told you. Lie still."

The room was dark, except for a ring of candles that surrounded them, black and white, interspersed. Their strange, ethereal glare echoed against the pristine, sterile white wall. "You're a witch," Virginia said.

"Of sorts," the woman replied casually, dousing a bloody rag in a horrible smelling poultice once more. It had the scent of something dead in the summer, and didn't at all seem like something that should be pushed into a wound.

"What's in that stuff?" Virginia asked with suspicion, willing her vision to stop swimming in front of her.

The witch flicked her gaze away from Virginia's shoulder. "You're lucky, you know. Even a few moments later, and you'd have had some real problems." Her eyes fell on Virginia's scars. "Although something tells me you're no stranger to those."

"Oh, these?" Virginia said, gesturing at her face with her good arm. "Nah. Just some unlucky ghouls."

"Strange, you don't hear about them attacking humans." The witch continued to work, tossing aside one rag and reaching for a clean one. She poured more poultice onto Virginia's shoulder, and immediately the white cotton began to bloom deep red, beset on the edges by the sticky brown substance that was threatening to bring up whatever she had eaten last.

"Not usually, but it does happen," Virginia explained, flinching away from the witch's fingers pressing deeply into the wound.

The witch raised an eyebrow before returning to her work. "Whatever you say."

Virginia breathed out of her mouth, trying not to smell the poultice, but decided that tasting the air laced with it was worse. "How long is this going to take?"

"It will take as long as it takes. It will take less time if you stop interrupting me." The witch drained the bottle of poultice, setting it aside. The dark green glass almost sparkled in the candle light, throwing odd little reflections to rest on the blue fabric of her skirts.

Pain shot through Virginia like she was being attacked all over again. She moaned, reaching for the wound herself, desperate to dull the sharp ache.

"Don't touch it," the witch said, slapping her hand away. "You'll get yourself infected, and then I'd have to have you here even longer." She resumed pressure, adding more poultice to the wound from a different bottle, this one a light fuchsia purple with a squeaky cork stopper. "But now that you know how I am helping, maybe you can keep your mouth shut."

"Fine." Virginia turned her head, not wanting to be confronted with the grisly wound. She was no stranger to gore, but seeing your *own* meat laid bare was another story entirely.

The witch changed the poultice several times, and each time, the pain was lessened, until Virginia's shoulders relaxed, and she breathed deep for the first time since she'd left the office hours before.

"So, where did you find a shifter that could do this much damage?" the witch asked, sensing that Virginia was waking from her pain-induced stupor.

"Just a kid. Well, a young man, I suppose. He was on Nether," Virginia replied.

The witch nodded knowingly, keeping her focus on the wound, one hand holding pressure as the other reached for another bottle, yellow with a black screw top and smelling strangely of daffodils. "Not the first attack I've seen lately. Verdance is changing."

Virginia nodded, still staring at the wall. At least it wasn't the hospital. Emergency rooms and clinics would have had far more questions for her, none of which she'd be interested in shedding light on. "It's been changing for a long time."

"Hey, Anya, you almost done? We have to get back to the club," the bartender—Bryce, apparently—called through the thick velvet curtain over the doorway.

Anya glanced at the door with a vaguely irritated expression, her brow furrowed in concentration. "It will be a while yet."

"I can get myself home," Virginia said. "No one has to wait for me."

"They are waiting to make the payment," Anya said, dropping more dried herbs into a wide mortar and pestle. "I hope you didn't think I work for free." The grinding of marble against itself was oddly soothing, even as it crunched and crackled with the pulverizing of whatever strange ingredients were in there.

"I'll pay for myself, thanks," Virginia said, her tone clipped.

"Astrid's orders," Bryce said.

Virginia squeezed her eyes shut. Of course Astrid found out. Virginia nearly died in her back lot. "Tell Astrid I don't need her charity."

"Tell her yourself," Bryce said. "But it's not on me, I have my own job to do."

"Get out," Virginia snapped, propping herself up on an elbow. "Tell

Astrid to stay out of my business."

"Leave the usual fee on the desk," Anya said, pressing Virginia back down onto the table again. "I'll settle any excess with her later."

The front door slammed, followed by the angry tinkle of wind chimes. "I'm sorry if they woke you up," Virginia grumbled. "I would have been fine."

"I don't know why you're tangled up with Astrid, but frankly, I don't want to know." The healer turned away, rummaging through a squeaky drawer with the light jingle of small vials and the telltale rustle of envelopes. "The less I know, the better." Anya added the ground up herbs to a flask, shaking it vigorously. "I prefer to have nothing to tell the cops, if and when they show up."

"I won't report it," Virginia promised. "I know most shifter attacks do, but I'd rather this stayed quiet."

"Drink this," the witch said, thrusting a small bottle into her good hand.

Virginia held the flask to her lips, nearly spitting out the foul concoction. "What's in this? It tastes like sewer water."

"It's sewer water," Anya said casually, offering a smile. "Verdance's best." She tilted her head and smirked before she continued. "It's just herbs and some potent extractions, Vee, or whatever your name is. Might not be pleasant, but it's effective."

"Fine." Virginia choked it down, swallowing back the gag itching at the back of her throat. Whatever in shadows was in that stuff, she'd prefer to never find out. Witches were sometimes fond of illegal or disgusting ingredients. "Can I go now?" Virginia asked. "I have a lot of work to do."

Anya raised an eyebrow, heavy with skepticism. "At three in the morning?"

"Yes, *actually*," Virginia insisted. "I have to go back to the club and find where the hell that kid went."

"The shifter?" Anya asked, her long, elegant fingers poised over several jars as she chose which she needed, pulling the one from the center off the shelf and pouring the slightly pink liquid onto a wad of fresh gauze.

Virginia winced as Anya pressed against her shoulder once more. "Yeah."

"Probably long gone by now, and a good thing, too," Anya replied. "Conscription, fighting rings, you name it. Too much danger."

"How does a witch like yourself stay out of trouble, then?" Virginia asked. "Plenty of people in need of good healers, these days."

"I stay out of trouble," Anya answered. "I make sure I don't know anything about anyone. They bring me someone, I heal them, they leave money on the counter, that's it. No questions, no answers."

"They?" Virginia prompted.

Anya met her eyes for a moment. "Astrid's people. I don't work for her, she's just a loyal customer. Seems she keeps enough of her people in peril that it keeps me busy enough, along with the other jokers in this town." Anya chewed her lip for a moment, taking another roll of gauze from a stack against the tiled wall, and dropping it into the jar.

Virginia watched her, curious who she might know. "You ever hear of a Franky Fiske? I think he's who's nabbing these young ones, maybe. At least, the one who attacked me. Maybe others, hard to say."

Anya pulled her hands away. "Are you a cop?"

"No," Virginia answered.

"You work with the cops?" Anya pressed. "Do *they* know you're working with the cops?"

Virginia tried for a shrug, but the pain almost sent her unconscious again. "Astrid knows."

"That's a shock, given what she's dealing in," Anya said, returning pressure to the wound. "I'm surprised she didn't shoot you on sight."

"Her aim was never very good," Virginia said acerbically, remembering a particularly nasty tempest she'd found herself in with Astrid, just before the framing.

"I'd be careful, if I was you," Anya warned. "You could have died. You could have lost the arm, or—"

"Listen, lady, I know what I'm about, alright?" Virginia interrupted. "Relax."

"It's your funeral," Anya said easily. "I've seen worse things here on my table than you have. Take my word for it, this is a nasty wound."

Virginia tried to sit up again, but Anya was already pinning her shoulder to the table. "I don't have anything to do with Nether, thank you very much," she growled.

"If you're hanging around Astrid, then you have everything to do with Nether," Anya said, straightening the roll of wet gauze, the liquid dripping fat droplets onto the steel tray. "I'm tired of treating overdoses. The dealers are loading them up too fast, too soon, and it's messing everybody up. Not even mythics can handle those dosages." Anya brought her to a sitting position, bending to wrap the soaked bandage around the wound. "Recreation is one thing, but this stuff is stronger. More potent, and it doesn't leave residue."

"Where is it coming from?" Virginia asked.

"How the hell should I know?" Anya snapped, tucking the edge of the bandage in. "I told you, I do my best to *not* know things. I'm not sure how much clearer I can make myself."

Virginia risked a glance at her wound, cringing at the sight and regretting that she'd allowed herself that impulse. "How bad is it, really?"

"Another half an inch and you'd have been dead before they dragged your unconscious ass in here," Anya replied in a cold, deadpan voice. She worked in silence for long moments, allowing the room to fill with thick tension as she ground herbs down with methodical, rhythmic circular motions. She scraped the mortar and pestle clean and paused to light incense, the ember burning bright as she placed it into a small wooden holder. She dragged the incense around the bowl, the smoke heavy. "And did you know that most cats, be they domestic or feral, have specific attributes in their saliva that can cause rapid blood poisoning if left untreated?"

"No."

"No," Anya repeated, tossing her a smug, self-satisfied expression. "Once again, I ask that you trust me long enough to treat you."

Virginia pressed her palm against the metal, warm from her own body heat. "I'm just hesitant about witches. Plenty of frauds these days, you know. I've had more than one try to poison me."

Anya re-lit the incense, her lips turned into a deep frown. "I am not a huckster, nor am I selling serpent tongues to heal impotence, nor do I prey on the weak and vulnerable with the goal to separate them from their money. I am a witch, yes, but also, I am a healer, and a damned good one. So if you don't want to wind up back here tomorrow, doubled over with fever and hallucinations, you will shut up and let me finish."

Virginia swallowed back the snide remark she had prepared, her jaw clamped firm. She knew all too well what it was like to have people doubt her abilities, and she'd long grown tired of it. Still, her wariness remained, and every time Anya turned her back, she eyed the ingredients on the wall, trying to make out the names.

"It's nothing you haven't heard of," Anya said. "I can hear you shift your weight every time I turn around."

"Sorry," Virginia grumbled.

"I will send you home with enough poultice that you won't have to recreate it," Anya said, decanting a mixture into a small tin. "Some of the ingredients are rather rare, and would be hard for you to obtain. Onyx blossom, for one." Anya turned back to her, adding more fluid to the bowl. "And frost sweat."

"Expensive," Virginia commented. Those reagents went for premium prices on the black market.

Anya shrugged, lifting the bowl to swirl the concoction together gently, the odd glow of candlelight on fluid reflected in her aquamarine eyes. "Astrid pays a premium for the best care. Who are you to her, anyway?"

Virginia sighed. "No one."

"Lover?" Anya asked.

"A long time ago, maybe," Virginia mumbled.

"Ah." Anya poured the remaining mixture into a flask, setting it inside a cloth bag with a stack of clean wrap bandages. "I should have guessed. You aren't the first, and I suspect, won't be the last, either."

"Encouraging." Virginia sat up, poking gently at the bandage. "Pain isn't as bad now."

Anya handed her the bag. "Change your bandages once a day, soak in the poultice. If anything looks inflamed, come back, I may need to alter your dosages." She scanned Virginia's figure, chewing her lip. "I think you'll find that it's fine, though."

"Right. So that's it?" Virginia asked, anxious to be let loose. "Are you going to take Astrid's money?"

Anya floated into the front room, sweeping the curtain aside. She thumbed through the bills before setting them inside a locked box. "Yes. Emergency fee, rush fee."

"And you won't let me pay for it?" Virginia asked, reaching for the money clip she had shoved in her bra. It was safer than a pocket. "Money isn't a problem." It was, but Anya didn't need to know that.

"I try not to make a habit of crossing Astrid." She snapped the box closed, setting it inside a drawer. "I recommend you get a cab home. It's too far to walk back to the Sphinx in your condition."

"I'll be fine," Virginia assured her, despite her legs nearly buckling under her weight.

Anya rolled her eyes. "Do whatever you want. I'm sure as hell not your keeper."

"Great."

"Arrogant," Anya muttered under her breath, the wind chimes not enough to obscure her remark. Virginia pretended that she hadn't heard it, only because she was too tired and broken for a fight.

Chapter Ten

Virginia pulled up outside the precinct, wincing at the lingering, pulsing pain in her shoulder. If she was going to get Benjamin back to his sibling, she was going to need Arthur's help.

Unfortunately.

She walked through the front doors, heading straight to his office, finding the door shut. "Arthur, it's me. Open the damn door."

"Ginnie," he said, easing it open with the quiet groan of the tarnished brass hinge that probably hadn't been oiled since before Virginia had set foot in the precinct at twenty. "I wasn't expecting you."

"Virginia," Captain Lindell said, already getting up from her chair. Her broad frame seemed to take up half the room, nothing but visible muscles and badge and the gun holster slung under an arm, the leather strap visibly worn and dull. "What happened to your shoulder?"

"Long story," Virginia said dismissively. "Arthur, do you have a minute?"

He closed the door behind her, pulling the blinds to shroud them all in a strange, muted morning light. Arthur tugged at the lapels of his jacket, immaculately pressed, almost certainly by Mona, because Virginia had never seen the man lift a finger to do his own shadows-damned laundry. "Is this about a case?"

"It sure as hell isn't a social call," Virginia shot back, irritable from a lack of sleep and the persistent ache that still shot down her arm, despite the pounds of poultice that witch had packed into the deep wound. She hadn't been able to bring herself to look at the dressings quite yet, knowing they'd be oozing with mashed up herbs and her own half-clotted blood.

Captain Lindell tilted her head. "Your shoulder, Virginia, have you had it seen to?"

"Yeah, some witch on the north side," Virginia answered, waving her uninjured arm casually. "I'm fine. That's not why I'm here. Well, it is, but it's not." She sat in the seat next to the captain, and immediately felt the heavy pull of exhaustion. It had been too long since she'd slept. "I found someone."

"Who?" Arthur asked, sitting back down. "Who did you find?"

"Benjamin. A private case," she explained. "And not reported to the VCPD."

Arthur's tell had always been the way his eye twitched when he was irritated, and she couldn't help but notice it in that moment. He sighed, adjusting the pin that sat above his badge, glowing dimly. "I assume there's a reason you're here, then, and not just to brag that you've solved a case?"

"He's a shifter, and he's also on Nether," Virginia offered after a long moment.

"Is that what happened to your shoulder?" Lindell asked. "A swipe?"

"Bite, but yes."

"But the toxins—"

Virginia waved her away for a second time, punctuated with a dramatic roll of her eyes. "Yes, yes, I'm aware. I'm fine. The thing is—" she halted mid-sentence, unsure whether she should give up Astrid for selling Nether or not. If she did, they might never find this Fiske person to track down other mythics. "The thing is," she continued, "according to this kid's sibling, he's never touched the stuff."

"People lie all the time," Arthur said. "Especially to their families." He shot her a pointed glance, but Virginia chose to ignore it.

"Obviously, but I've just got this strong feeling they're not wrong about that. This kid, he had a decent gig working as a janitor at Rickarton. His sibling says he was about to start some night classes, really try to make something of himself. You think he'd give all that up for a few hours of a high?" Virginia shook her head. "It doesn't add up."

"I hardly think that a hunch is grounds for evidence," Lindell said, her hands perched on her knees, fingernails scratching lightly at the wool of her pants.

"If you've got anything better to bring to the table, then let's hear it," Virginia snapped. "But last I heard, you two were fresh out of leads."

"Any ideas where the kid wound up?" Arthur asked.

"Jumped the fence back behind the Sphinx," Virginia answered. "I'd guess he was wandering around back in those woods for a while."

Arthur nodded. "We'll send a team to take a look."

Lindell shook her head, incredulous. "Sheriff, you can't seriously be allocating officers based on a *feeling.*"

Virginia stared at her, wondering where in the hell Shirin found all that audacity that made her so irritatingly confident. She sucked her teeth, deciding just how far she was willing to go to prove a point. "Shirin is right," Virginia said. "I'll go."

"You can't go, Ginnie, look at you. You're beat to hell and back, and you look like one good hit would take you out for good." Arthur gestured at her shoulder before topping up Shirin's mug with coffee from his thermos, rusted at the edges from years of daily use. He held it out to Virginia, but she shook her head. "And what if this kid takes a punch at you again?" he asked. "Do you really think you can take that in your current state?" Arthur shook his head again, rubbing at his hair, the wedding ring on his hand looking the exact same as his old one had. "We should be sending a specialized team." He paused, his hands laying flat on the desk, and the gold ring glinted. "Hold on there, Ginnie. The Sphinx?"

"So?" she asked casually, not wanting to divulge any more details than she had to. He'd already heard more about her personal life than he should have from Seamus.

"What were you doing there?" Arthur asked, in a resigned tone that suggested he already knew the answer, and didn't particularly want the truth.

"Trailing the kid, obviously," Virginia replied.

He pressed his fingers into a steeple, boring into her with that look that meant he was about to figure something out. "How did you know to look there, though?"

She shrugged. "Got a tip."

"From who?" he pressed, leaning across the desk.

Virginia rolled her eyes, a dramatic show that she knew would irritate him. "Why does it matter from who? The tip was good, the kid was there. I just hadn't anticipated he would be on so much of that stuff. He could be in trouble, Arthur, and if I don't find him I'll have to tell his sibling he's gone forever, and you're in here giving me an interrogation about where my information came from." She stood, reaching for the door. "Forget it."

"Sit down, Ginnie," Arthur warned.

"I have work to do." Virginia yanked the door open before she felt a hand on her arm.

"I'll go, Sheriff," the captain offered. "Just give the woods a cursory look, and call in dispatch if we find him."

Arthur drummed his fingers against the oak desk. "There's something you're not telling me, Ginnie," he accused. "I know you well enough to be too aware when you're hiding something. What is it?"

"I'm under no obligation to share my information," Virginia spat. "This department spent almost two decades all but pretending I didn't exist, and now you want me to spill my guts just because you can't figure shit out for yourselves?" She shook her head, allowing a disenchanted, sarcastic laugh to bubble up in her throat, cascading over her lips like high tide. "Fat chance."

"You're a consultant!" Arthur shouted, pointing an accusatory finger at her. "You *are* under an obligation to share information you uncover about open cases!"

Captain Lindell glanced between them and the bullpen with a wary look. "Sheriff, maybe we should—"

"Come or don't, but I'm not waiting," Virginia said, storming out of the office. "That's one thing this place always did wrong, waiting until all the pieces are together before you make a move, and then people wind up hurt." She threw another look at Arthur, twisting her face towards the overhead fluorescent lights. "Or dead."

"Ginnie—"

"I've always told you not to call me that." She crossed the bullpen in four wide strides and slammed through the stairwell door, stomping down the stairs despite the sharp throb of pain with every step. "Shadows-damned pretentious little *fuck*," she hissed under her breath.

"Virginia, wait." Captain Lindell stood at the top, arms crossed over her chest. "You shouldn't be driving with that shoulder." The captain descended a few steps, wary, as though she was afraid she would spook Virginia like an untrained, nervous horse. "You can't deny we'll get there faster if we use my squad unit."

Virginia faltered, her hand on the railing. "Fine. But hurry up, I don't want to be in this building any longer than I have to be."

"I'm parked at the back," Lindell said, gesturing towards the bottom of the stairwell. She jogged down now, easily catching up with Virginia. "Are you going to tell me what that was all about, or are you keeping those cards close to your chest, too?"

"You were there, Shirin, you heard what happened."

The captain raised an eyebrow before putting her hands up in surrender, a curious smile playing at her lips. "Whatever you say, Virginia."

"Good."

"Why does the sheriff call you Ginnie? A woman gets curious," Lindell said with an easy shrug and an irritating glint in her eye, the same kind seen in card sharks at Verdance card tables.

Virginia huffed out an aggravated breath, still heading for the door. "A captain gets nosy and thinks she's entitled to know everything about everything."

"Not everything," Lindell said. "Just that."

"I'm surprised half the bullpen isn't talking about it. There's at least a few who know who I am." Virginia shoved open the door to the parking lot, wincing at the pain it sent echoing across the muscles in her arm. "Bastards."

"Third unit on the left," Lindell answered after a long, thoughtful pause.

Virginia climbed into the passenger side, wincing at the dull throb in her shoulder. She could only imagine how much worse it would be if she hadn't seen that witch—healer—and felt a begrudging gratefulness to Bryce the bartender for dragging her there. "Do you know how to—"

"Yes, I know how to get there," Lindell interrupted. "Lived here seven years, remember?"

"There's the service entrance off Highlake, that's all."

Captain Lindell glanced at her sideways. "Service entrance?"

"Yeah, for the park rangers." Virginia bit back a groan at the stab of pain in her arm, resisting the urge to press against the dressing. "It used to be more densely wooded in there, before the city grew up around it. Not much need for rangers now, but the entrance is there."

"I didn't know that Verdance once had a reserve within city limits," Lindell said. She started the car, the engine roaring into life despite the temperatures. Even so, freezing air slipped around the gaps of the windows, making itself at home under their thick coats. Not even goose down could keep Verdance out.

Virginia nodded. "The city council voted to have it thinned. Too much crime in there, after the Rupture."

"So, the attack," Captain Lindell said, pulling onto the road with a cursory left and right glance, shifting into gear with a confident thrust of her wrist. "Care to explain? Or is that a big secret, too?"

"I don't know what there is to explain," Virginia replied. "I saw the kid, tried to get him to come with me, he shifted and attacked me. An almost fully grown panther."

Lindell gave a low whistle, slowing the car as they hit the inevitable traffic downtown, too many cars and not enough lanes to hold them. The captain turned down a side road to avoid the congestion. "Shadows, Vane, you're lucky to be alive. A panther on Nether?"

"Yeah, that's what the healer said, too."

"What was this kid doing at the Sphinx?" the captain asked. "Seems an odd place for someone so broke to hang out. It's my understanding that Astrid charges a premium."

"While I can appreciate that it's your job to weasel information out of me, especially when Arthur can't, I'm going to ask you to remember that I had your job, once, and am keenly aware of what it is you're trying to do," Virginia said casually.

Lindell nodded, her brow furrowed as she drove. "I apologize. Old habits."

"If the kid overdosed on Nether, he's going to need help, and I won't be able to drag him back myself." Virginia grimaced, rubbing her arm where the spikes of pain were clustered. "Not with my shoulder in this condition. When I know more, you'll know more." She sighed, leaning her head against the frosty glass of the window. "Arthur has a habit of going in, guns blazing, and then before you know it, the whole thing is blown. You give these creeps the opportunity and they'll be burning the evidence faster than you can break down the door." Virginia fiddled with a button on her coat, hanging on by one shredded thread that matched the thick wool. "Burning, shredding, there won't be a single thing left to log into evidence."

"What happened with you two?" Lindell asked, blunt and obvious.

Virginia tensed, and then winced away from the pain it caused. So much for Anya's magical poultice, she was still in agony. "Nothing."

"I'll just ask one of the other captains when I get back to the station if you don't tell me," Captain Lindell said, her forearm resting on the steering wheel as she waited for pedestrians to cross the road. A woman with a stroller and a toddler, a shabby looking priest, his fraying collar a visible display of the church's financial struggles, and a man that almost certainly had a large revolver hidden beneath his coat. Lindell gestured lazily at the woman, waving her across the road. "I can either hear about it from you, or from them."

"Find out from someone else, then," Virginia sniped. "I don't feel like dredging up ancient history."

The captain glanced at her before setting the car into gear again, nodding. "Ah. I'm sorry, I hadn't realized."

"Hadn't realized *what*?" Virginia demanded.

"That you and Arthur were... well. I can put the pieces together well enough." Captain Lindell turned onto a side street, looking to Virginia for confirmation. "Down here, yes?"

"Yes." Virginia pointed towards the fence gate. "There." She scanned the line of trees, hunting for movement and finding none other than the gentle sway of empty, leafless branches. A sick feeling oozed into the pit of her stomach, sliding into her gut like raw eggs. "I don't see anything."

"Let's take a look," the captain said, removing the keys from the ignition. "He might still be around here, or maybe a trail. Did you hit him?"

"Of course I hit him," Virginia snarled. "He didn't take me down without *some* damage. I use silver," she added, slipping the knuckles around her fingers to show the captain. "Caught him in the muzzle at least twice. He won't heal fast from that."

"Most people would have shot him." Captain Lindell glanced at her and her gaze lingered for just a moment. "I'm sure the boy's family will be grateful for your restraint."

"I can't imagine they'd want to pay me if I returned him in a body bag," Virginia retorted.

The captain raised an appreciative eyebrow, her stare falling on the mound of gauze hidden beneath Virginia's shirt. "Still, a panther on Nether... it's surprising you even survived. Most wouldn't. Haven't."

"Stop digging, Shirin, I've already said I'll tell you when I know more." Virginia eased the gate open, the hinge squealing in protest. She grimaced at the sound, a headache already creeping at the edges of her vision, borne of a sleepless night and a tragic lack of strong coffee. She should have taken Arthur's offer at the precinct, but she didn't want things with him to start feeling too familiar. "So much for a quiet entrance," she muttered as the gate shrieked once again. "Snapped twigs on either side of this path. He probably came through here, looks like in a hurry."

"Any blood trails?" Lindell asked.

Virginia shook her head. "None that I can see."

The captain followed, nudging the moldy, wet leaves with the toe of her boot. "Fur. Black. What do you think?"

"Yeah," Virginia said, nodding. "Looks like his, I'd imagine."

"Where does this park dump out on the other end?" Lindell asked.

"Where's the other service entrance?"

"Fifth and Haven," Virginia answered, examining the clumps of fur, some of them crusted over with brown, dried blood. "He may have shifted back by the time he made it over there," Virginia offered, straightening once again and swallowing back the groan that was growing in her throat.

Captain Lindell sucked her teeth. "Or someone circled back around after you passed out."

"You think they tried to nab a panther?" Virginia asked.

"I think we shouldn't rule it out. Sedatives, if they had a gun, or..." Lindell trailed off, thinking. "Or force."

"It would have taken at least ten to wrestle a panther down, and not without injury. Shirin, he was strong. Stronger than a twenty-year-old should have been, even a shifter."

"Maybe we can check the local hospital logs, or—"

"The kinds of people trying to subdue a shifter to cart them away aren't the kinds of people who will visit a public hospital with a shifter wound." Virginia cocked her head, not wanting to give too much away. "They tend to visit private healers."

Lindell scoffed. "So what you're saying is that we have no idea whether they circled back for this kid or not." She grumbled something in another language, a curse maybe. "Fantastic."

"Unfortunately. Keep looking, we might find something. A half melted footprint, even," Virginia offered, scanning the unremarkable landscape for something else that would give them a clue as to where he'd gone.

"Do you think the Sphinx has connections to the producer of this Nether??" She leaned in, examining a large branch. "I'm just trying to get a clearer picture of who we're dealing with."

"And I already told you to stop prying. If you continue to ask ridiculous questions, I'm going to assume you know as much as a cadet, and I'll respond in kind." Virginia pointed back at the gate. "We won't be able to get prints off that gate, Cadet, not from a shifter who's shifted."

Shirin laughed quietly, resting a hand on her hip and running the other through her hair, cap grasped between two fingers. "You're a fascinating woman, Virginia."

"And why is that?"

"You don't pander," Lindell replied evenly, with a hint of admiration.

"I'm not interested in ass-kissing," Virginia said. "I'm interested in results."

"A rare quality." The captain gave her that strange, appraising look again. "A pity that the VCPD lost you. You're a force to be reckoned with."

Virginia bit her tongue to keep back the words gathering in her mouth away from her vocal cords. "Blame Arthur for that," she said finally, and left it at that.

"Tire tracks there," Lindell said, pointing.

Virginia nodded. "I see them, too. They don't look too fresh, though."

"Seems unlikely they'd use this place to hide shifters, no?" Lindell asked, shielding her eyes against the harsh sunlight to scan the thinning park. It was more windswept garbage than trees, a candy bar wrapper blowing against the chain-link fence for a moment until it scraped itself away from the steel and escaped into the parking lot of the Sphinx. "Too barren, too easily seen from the street."

"I don't want to say for sure, but..." Virginia trailed off. "Let's just say I think I would have noticed."

"Spending lots of time at the Sphinx lately?" Lindell asked, always questioning. "Were you staked out?"

Virginia blinked, her mind a reel of what had happened with Astrid. "You could say that."

"And you didn't see anyone?" Lindell pressed.

"Not then, no. And not last night—at least, not before I was knocked out, anyway."

The captain bent, examining the tracks. "Iced over. Definitely wasn't last night. If he's still out here, he's freezing."

"Yeah, and that's my worry," Virginia said. "He'll have had a hell of a come down after that shift. He'd have needed food and sleep somewhere warm. If he's hitting withdrawals, even more so."

Captain Lindell eased around the back of a small thicket of bushes, picking her way past winterized, bare thorned vines that snaked out from their stem, brittle yet still damaging. "Shadows," she swore. "Vane! Over here!"

Virginia vaulted back over the tree, regretting it as soon as she hit the ground, the impact reverberating around the pulsing wound in her shoulder. "Ah—fuck—hang on," she said, clutching her arm as she staggered towards the thicket.

"He doesn't look good," Lindell shouted. "Help me get him into the car."

"Here," Virginia said, stripping off her coat, "Put this over him. Poor kid doesn't need humiliation on top of everything else."

"There are blankets in the unit for him, too." The captain spread the coat out over him before jostling his shoulder, her gloved hand rubbing against the dark grey of the wool. "Hey, kid." She gave Virginia a questioning look.

"Benjamin," Virginia supplied.

"Benjamin, wake up," Lindell urged. "We're going to get you somewhere warm, alright?"

He stirred, coming to. "Shit," he spat, scrambling to his feet, pulling the coat around him. He shoved his arms through the sleeves, stumbling over the hedge as he tried to run, his breaths quick and desperate. He skirted Virginia's grasp, but landed squarely in the captain's grip.

"Stop!" Lindell barked, but it had an air of kindness. "Stop. You're not in trouble."

Benjamin fought her grip, trying to wriggle out of it. "Leave me alone!"

"Hang on, kid," Virginia said, already chilled from the cold and missing her coat. The kid was damned lucky to have survived the night. "Ursa sent me to bring you home."

"Ursa?" he said, shaking his head. "No, no... they can't know. They can't. You can't tell them. They won't understand, not after everything—"

Virginia faced him, watching for the telltale glow of the eyes in case he decided to shift again. She wasn't sure she could take another fang to the shoulder without missing a few weeks of work. "Whatever it is, I'm sure they'll understand."

"No!" he wrenched from the captain's grasp and took off running down the overgrown path with ragged, uneven strides that suggested he was unbalanced and close to passing out.

"I've got it," the captain said, suppressing a laugh as she followed in pursuit. She was fast, and lithe, and Virginia couldn't help but be a little impressed when Lindell plucked the kid off the fence he was climbing, holding him by the shoulders. "Relax," she said, commanding now. "You need to get inside before you're hypothermic, if you aren't already."

"That's the least of my problems," he spat, struggling with the buttons on his borrowed coat.

"Care to elaborate?" Virginia asked, approaching. "Someone tie you up in all of this?"

"No, it was me, only me," Benjamin said. His stare fixed on Virginia's shoulder, the bandages lumpy and obvious beneath her shirt. "You're the lady from last night."

"*Lady,*" Virginia repeated, cringing. "Shadows. When did *that* happen?"

Captain Lindell snorted a laugh at that, keeping a firm hold of him.

"Yes, I am the *lady* from last night," Virginia confirmed. "What of it?"

"I thought—I thought—" Benjamin stammered.

"You thought you killed her," the captain filled in.

"Nah, takes more than a kid to take me out," Virginia said, an eyebrow raised. "As you can see, I am fine, except for the gaping hole in my shoulder and my very dangerous lack of both caffeine and tobacco."

Benjamin slumped, covering his face with his hands. "I'm sorry, I couldn't—"

"I know. Come on, in the unit." Virginia gave Captain Lindell a sideways glance. "We'll take you home."

"Food first," the captain said. "What do you like?"

Benjamin glanced from one of them to the other, considering his options. "I'd kill for some chicken."

Virginia barked a sarcastic laugh. "No need for homicide, we already tried that once, haven't we?" She gestured towards her shoulder again. "Sorry that you didn't quite manage to punch my ticket."

Benjamin's face burned crimson as he pulled her coat tight around himself. "I'm sorry, I—"

"Donny's?" the captain asked, heading for the squad unit.

"Yeah, probably easiest," Virginia said. "It's on the way to his place."

"Where do you live, Benjamin?" Lindell asked.

Virginia climbed back into the car, struggling to withhold the wince that yearned to burst free from the swollen wound. "The apartment across from mine."

"He lives in your building?" The captain arched an eyebrow, but turned the key, checking the mirrors first, and then the police scanner before she turned it down again. "Interesting."

"It's not that interesting, Shirin, it's where his sibling hired me."

"You're *her?*" Benjamin asked, closing the door behind him. "The lady across from us? Ursa always said to stay away from you." He shrank against the seat.

Lindell laughed again, and Virginia gave her a scowl. "I'm a private investigator, not a member of the fae."

"They didn't think that, it's just—"

"Can it, kid," Virginia said with a beleaguered sigh. "It doesn't matter."

Benjamin pulled the coat tighter around himself. "They thought you were a federal agent."

"I could see it," Captain Lindell said, pulling the car back onto the road. "You have that aura of cloistered rule-abiding about you, Ms. Vane."

"You can zip it too, *Captain,*" Virginia spat back. "I'm not a federal agent." She scowled. "I would *never.*"

Chapter Eleven

Ursa wasn't home when they got back to the building. "I don't suppose you have your key anywhere," Virginia said to Benjamin, rubbing her temple. The lack of sleep was starting to eat at her, and her shoulder throbbed in protest.

"No."

"Should have checked for his clothes behind the club," Lindell said. "Maybe I can go back—"

"Do not," Virginia said emphatically. "You show up there, everyone is going to scatter, and we won't find out another damned thing."

"I'll take a cab, leave the squad unit here." The captain glanced down at her navy blue uniform, the piped silver trim shining in the mid-morning light. "And I'll change."

"You'd still look like a cop, Shirin," Virginia argued. "I'll go."

Lindell's face scrunched in comic disbelief. "Absolutely not," she said. "You look half-dead already."

"Wow, the first real compliment I've heard all year, thank you." Virginia rolled her eyes and unlocked her door, shoving the door open with her good shoulder with a loud, protesting creak. "Come on, Benjamin. I'll get you something to wear. You can shower and eat, and we'll wait for Ursa."

"I could take him to the station," Lindell offered.

"Like this? No. Poor guy would never recover from that. Twenty is hard enough as it is." Virginia ushered them both inside, throwing the deadbolt behind them. She plucked a clean pair of pants she wore for sparring from the top of the laundry pile, along with a shirt, tossing them to the kid. "Bathroom is the first door on the right. Turn the knob all the way to the left, you'll get more hot water that way, and you need to warm up."

"Thanks," Benjamin mumbled, disappearing into the bathroom, the door latching with a soft click.

"You sure you're alright?" the captain asked when the pipes groaned with the effort of redirecting the hot water from the radiators. "You took fangs to the shoulder."

"And lived to tell the tale," Virginia mused.

Lindell cast a skeptical glance in her direction, straightening the cuffs of her uniform. "You should rest."

"I will, when the kid is back safe with his sibling." Virginia sighed, too afraid to test her shoulder's movement. "I worry that whoever got him into all this will be back for more."

"The sheriff is going to want you to press charges," Lindell said. "He almost killed you."

"But he didn't," Virginia argued." It was an accident. Come on, you saw his face. He was horrified. That wasn't him, it was the Nether."

Lindell leaned against the counter, the silver thread of her uniform catching the light. "Sheriff isn't going to like it."

"I don't give a shit what the sheriff likes," Virginia said with a caustic tone, opening one of the steaming takeout boxes and thrusting a fork into a golden mound of buttery mashed potatoes. "It wasn't him with the puncture, so it's not his call to make."

"He could try to get the kid on public endangerment," Lindell said. "I could be subpoenaed as a witness."

Virginia glared, gesturing with her fork. "All you know is we found a kid freezing to death in an old, blown-out reserve. You didn't see shit, Shirin."

Shirin offered up a half-hearted shrug, taking off her cap to tousle her hair. "I don't think we should be letting him free to run the streets unsupervised."

"Fine," Virginia said. "I'll keep an eye on him."

"What, you're a babysitter now?" Lindell asked.

Virginia stabbed the fork into some chicken. "Shirin, you don't know what it's like, being a kid that age with no parents and a shaky support system. His sibling does their best, but you know, it's Verdance. Your best isn't enough. Not here."

"And you *do* know what it's like?" Shirin asked, probing, always probing for more information, trying to peel back Virginia's layers, to delve where she shouldn't.

"I barely know you," Virginia deflected. "Pardon me for not baring my soul on the table over some lukewarm fried chicken."

"Can I use your phone to call the sheriff?" Shirin asked after a beat, tilting her head. There was a silence in the apartment outside the wheezing of the outdated pipes that was oppressive.

Virginia swallowed. "Be my guest."

"Thank you." The captain's voice was guarded, stilted. "VCPD headquarters," she said into the receiver, waiting to be transferred. "Sheriff, it's Lindell. Yes, we got him." A pause. "No." Another long pause. "No, she said she won't, I already asked."

"Give me the phone," Virginia said, standing.

Lindell handed it over, her face stony. "Here."

"Arthur, I'm not pressing charges," Virginia announced into the phone. "End of discussion."

The line crackled through the silence, and she could hear that he was drumming his fingers against his desk. "Ginnie, you don't know what this kid is capable of."

"I'd argue that I'm the only one of us that *does* know what he's capable of. I have evidence, if you're so desperate to see." Virginia smirked, even though he couldn't see it. "Or perhaps not. You've always been squeamish, haven't you?"

"I'm not *squeamish*," he protested, sighing. "I would appreciate if you'd consider pressing charges."

"Fine."

"Thank you, Ginnie, I—"

"I've considered it, and the answer is no," Virginia interrupted.

He breathed a sigh down the line so loud, she had to hold the receiver away from her ear. "I never understood why you're like this. He needs to be brought in for questioning, and that's final," he ordered. "And you need to press charges. It's the only way we can start to untangle this mess, and you know it."

"Get a fucking warrant, a subpoena, whatever it is you need then, Arthur," Virginia said evenly. "I'm not bringing him in."

"I will, then!"

"Fine!" She slammed down the receiver, turning back to the captain. "What?" she snapped.

"He's going to post officers around the building, you do realize that, right?" Shirin asked, leaning against the counter with one hip.

"Arthur can do whatever he wants."

"It would be easier if you cooperated. The sheriff is committed to—"

"The VCPD does an excellent job of getting people killed," Virginia spat. "Maybe instead of running your mouth, trying to pry into my private life with parking tickets and stakeouts, you could do your fucking job."

The captain's face hardened even further, her brow knitted into a tight expression somewhere between rage and violence, her eyes glittering with the temptation of it. "I can't pretend to know what you work so hard to keep secret. I also can't help you if you aren't willing to work with me on this, Virginia. He's going to come down like a ton of bricks after that call."

"Good," Virginia replied evenly. "Let him try."

"You only make things harder for yourself by acting like this," Lindell replied.

"And as always, the VCPD is blameless, is it?" Virginia asked, resting one hand on her hip and another on the dated telephone hanging on the wall, the black paint chipped at the edges and the rotary tarnished from years of abandonment. She'd gotten more calls in three days from the damned thing than she had in years.

"Whatever your baggage is, you need to get over it. We can't have consultants on cases running around getting impaled by shifters, and then refusing to bring them in." Lindell straightened, pointing out at the bathroom door. "I could drag him out here right now and arrest him for public indecency."

"Oh, please, give me an excuse," Virginia said, squaring her shoulders. Even the subtle action made pain pulse through her, and her eye twitched with the effort of holding back the pained groan that was rising in her throat.

"You really think you'd win that in your state?" Lindell asked, not even trying to stifle a laugh.

"Sure," Virginia said. "I'll take that chance."

Captain Lindell scoffed, her hands balled into fists at her side. "Virginia!" the captain shouted, pressing fingers to her forehead. "Please, I am begging you to listen to me. I know you have some shit with Arthur, and I get that, but you need to think about what's best for Benjamin. If we don't find out where he was getting Nether from—"

"I know where he's getting it from," Virginia admitted.

Lindell took a step backwards, steadying herself against the counter once again. "And you just, what, decided not to share that information? We have an entire taskforce dedicated to the Nether rings, this is one hundred percent within VCPD's scope, and you know it."

Virginia shrugged, an eyebrow raised in challenge. "I can't force you to trust me, but I can ask. Trust me."

"Why should I?" Lindell snapped.

"Because," Virginia explained, "I took a fucking fang to the shoulder in the middle of the night trying to unravel this, and if you clowns bust in there, you'll never find a scrap of evidence."

"Why, because you'll tip them off?" Lindell accused, pointing at her. "That's obstruction, and the sheriff will have you arrested for it."

"No, not because I'd tip them off, because they'll know that kid got picked up. You think they weren't looking for him? You think they didn't see your squad unit poking around in the woods behind the club? I can guarantee they were, but it was three in the morning and the kid was well-hidden. They'll be hiding whatever they've got and burning the receipts."

"Who is they?" Lindell interrogated.

"*They* are the ones shipping this crap all over the city, using mythics to do their dirty work," Virginia supplied. "You go in and bust the Sphinx for

Nether, you'll never find the fucking source."

Captain Lindell folded her arms tightly over her chest, constricting herself more effectively than a python would have. "That excuse isn't going to fly far at headquarters."

"Then it's a good shadows-damned thing I don't work there," Virginia replied lightly, still watching the captain for any sign that she would run for the bathroom door.

"You're making it very difficult for those of us who do," Lindell snapped.

"Honestly, Shirin, that's not my problem."

Benjamin cleared his throat, standing in the narrow, short hallway. "Sorry," he mumbled, sliding a box towards himself as he sat at the counter, grabbing the water-stained fork Virginia had left for him.

"How are you feeling?" Virginia asked.

He shrugged, loading up the fork with frigid mashed potatoes. "I'm fine. Cold doesn't bother me much after a shift."

She nodded, pressing a hand to her hip once more, edging the captain towards the door. "Captain Lindell was just leaving, weren't you?"

"This isn't over, Virginia," the captain said coolly. "The sheriff isn't going to let this go so easily."

"Fine. He can take it up with me later," Virginia answered.

"As for the club—"

"I said, Arthur can take it up with me later. I'm in no mood to keep scratching at the surface of this, not when the only shut-eye I've had in over twenty-four hours has been me passed out on a table." She leaned against the counter next to the kid, advancing on Lindell. "Okay?"

"Fine." Captain Lindell yanked her jacket sash tight, opening the door. "I'll be back later."

"Bring a warrant," Virginia shouted after her.

The door slammed, and Virginia moved to lock it behind her. "Shadows," she hissed, pressing against her shoulder. Whatever pain management Anya had put into the poultice was rubbing off, leaving her with enough pain to blur her vision and buckle her knees.

"Are you okay?" Benjamin asked, fork poised halfway to his mouth.

"Uh huh, yep, I'm fine," Virginia replied.

"I'm... sorry. For attacking you."

"Not the worst I've had." His eyes landed the scars that laid across her face, and she tilted her head to meet his gaze. "Neither was that," she offered casually, despite the pain wracking through her shoulder, shooting down her arm into her fingertips.

"What was... that, then?" he asked, shoveling more food into his mouth.

She braced herself against the counter, trying to look casual and knowing she looked like a lukewarm mess. "Werewolf."

"You sure it was a were, and not a shifter?" he asked.

"I'm sure."

Benjamin swallowed, reaching for another box of chicken. "How, though?"

"The bright shiny thing in the night sky made everything rather obvious," she said sardonically, sitting across from him. "Eat your food, kid. You'll need it to regain your strength."

He nodded, chewing another bite. "Thank you for not pressing charges." When Virginia raised an eyebrow, he continued, "I heard through the bathroom door. I only started shifting last year. Ursa thought maybe... maybe I wasn't, after all."

"A baby shifter, too," Virginia said with a sigh, rubbing her temples. Shadows, she was tired.

"I'm not a baby," he said, sitting up straight.

Virginia laughed. "Relax, kid. I just meant you're new to all this." She took a bite, savoring the creamy potatoes despite their temperature, and swallowed. "So how'd you get mixed up with this Franky Fisk character?"

Benjamin tensed, empty fork held aloft, offering a dull shine in the mid-morning Verdance glow. "Who?"

"Cut the act, Benjamin, I know more than you think. If you don't tell me, then I guarantee the sheriff of police is going to roll in here with some bullshit charges to drag you into the station. Given your job at Rickarton, I can only assume that you don't want that."

"Ursa works hard," he said quietly.

"So it was for money." Virginia sighed. She should have known. It wasn't a difficult puzzle to piece together, not in Verdance.

"I never meant for any of this to happen," Benjamin said. "He said the Nether would make me invincible. Said we might be dealing with some shady people on the delivery routes, and it was a safety precaution, that it was some new strain that wasn't dangerous."

"He lied," Virginia said. "Let me guess, you didn't go home because—" she gestured at the way his hands shook, the fork bouncing in midair, "you didn't want Ursa to see?"

"They would have known." He set the fork down, as if it would hide the truth. "I was ashamed. I thought maybe, if I could just make enough to get us out of the hole, we could start over again somewhere else."

Virginia finished her food, pushing the box aside. "Split the leftovers?"

"Yeah."

She emptied out the contents, putting slightly more into his box. "Here."

Benjamin returned to his food, but held the box in his lap to hide the tremors, as if she hadn't already seen it. "If Ursa knew what I'd done, they wouldn't blame you for hitting me."

"If we play this right, they don't have to know about the Nether," Virginia offered.

He poked at the food, stabbing through a chunk of meat with the tines of his fork. "Alright."

"Can I trust you not to leave if I sleep for a bit?" She asked, her knees beginning to buckle.

"Yeah," he replied.

She eyed him suspiciously, wavering on the spot. "You sure about that?"

"I won't go anywhere," he assured her.

Virginia nodded, adjusting the stool at the counter, its metal legs scraping against the bare wood floor. "Good," she said, "because if I don't get some shut-eye I'll either die or turn feral myself." She gestured towards the icebox. "Not much in there, but have at it. Knock if you need me. Yell if there's danger. If the cops show up, don't let them in, even if it's Captain Lindell." Virginia sighed. "*Especially* if it's Captain Lindell."

* * *

Virginia woke with a start, the darkness in her room weighty and oppressive. She'd slept too long. Grabbing her pocket watch, she squinted at the time and groaned. Nine in the evening. No wonder she felt groggy. No wonder her shoulder was pulsing with the stabbing pain of at least three hundred razor blades.

She'd slept in the same clothes she'd been wearing the night before too, now wrinkled and smelling of sweat, dried blood, and whatever was in that awful poultice.

"Benjamin?" she called, opening the door. Her stomach lurched at the silence. "Benjamin." There was no reply, and the knowing sank into her as her spine prickled with the fear that was crawling through her veins. "Shit," Virginia hissed.

She yanked open the bathroom door, finding it empty. The living room and kitchen were empty, too. Virginia smacked herself on the forehead. How could she have been so stupid? Maybe he'd heard Ursa arrive home from work, maybe they'd gotten home earlier than usual.

Virginia unlocked the door, padding across the hallway. "Ursa?" she said, knocking, and then pounding at the door.

"Ms. Vane!" Ursa said, throwing open the door. "Do you have a lead? What happened to you? Are you okay?" Ursa gestured at her shirt, stained with blood.

Virginia pulled the shirt away from her skin, brown and splattered in the yellow corridor light. "It was, uh, your brother."

"*Benjamin* did that to you?" Ursa asked, horrified.

Guilt settled deep into Virginia's wound, sending roots straight through to her spine. "He's not... here?"

"Why would he be?" Ursa replied.

"Shadows be damned," Virginia hissed, the corridor spinning around her. Her vision swam, and her head was pounding with a punishing rhythm. She couldn't admit to Ursa that Benjamin had been so close, but slipped through her fingers. "We overturned a hornet's nest," she said. "I hoped it would have sent him home where he belonged."

"You saw him?" Ursa demanded, their voice rife with worry and panic. "Where was he?"

"Working for some club," Virginia replied. "On Nether."

Ursa took a step backwards, their brow furrowed, the heavy wool of their robe almost black and trailing along the cracked tiles behind them. "No, no. That can't be right. Benjamin knows how dangerous that stuff is. He wouldn't dare."

"Some distributor lied to him, said it was a different strain," Virginia explained. "He wanted to help with money."

"No!" Ursa shouted, covering their face with their hands. "Where is he now?"

"I don't... know." Virginia braced herself against the door frame, her head spinning to such an extent she wasn't sure she'd make it back to bed without passing out. "I'm sorry, I have to go. I'll let you know when I know more."

"You can't just leave him out there!" Ursa argued. "What if he gets into more trouble, what if the cops pick him up—"

"The cops are the least of our worries right now," Virginia replied, wincing. "I'll find him. The cops don't have anything on him, not really. If they picked him up, we'll just have to bail him out," Virginia lied, knowing Arthur would throw the book at that kid just to get a hint of a lead. "Let me handle it."

"I can't believe you let him slip through your fingers," Ursa said softly.

Virginia looked up at them, defeated. She had let him slip through her fingers. She'd been weak, undisciplined. Foolish. She should have known better, should have stayed awake, should have known the kid would take off the second she slipped from consciousness. Another failure in her files, another black mark against her name, another opportunity to prove to everyone that she was exactly what they all said she was—a fraud. "I'm sorry."

Back in her apartment, she reached for the phone. "Arthur Dixon's residence," she said into the receiver. "Tell them it's Virginia Vane, they'll accept."

The line rang twice before someone picked up. "A Virginia Vane is on the line."

"I'll accept," Mona said.

The operator disconnected, and Virginia waited a moment before speaking. "Mona, I need to speak with Arthur."

Mona heaved an uneasy sigh into the receiver. "I don't think that's a good idea. He's practically spitting tacks."

"Great," Virginia said. "Well, he's about to be in a worse mood, so, sorry for that." Virginia bit back a groan, sinking into the chair. "Damned kid sneaked out while I was out cold. He was blown out on Nether."

"Shadows," Mona whispered.

"Yeah, you're telling me." Virginia moved the receiver to her other ear. "I need to talk to him, Mona."

"Are you sure about that?" Mona asked.

"I'm sure." She waited on the line until she heard Arthur's telltale grumble. "Arthur."

"What do you want, Ginnie? What's so important that you called me at home? How did you even get through?" he demanded, and the sound of his voice over the line was so damned *familiar* that she resented him for it.

"Mona accepted the call," she said evenly.

He growled, holding his hand over the phone. "Well, out with it."

"The kid took off," Virginia said.

He breathed into the receiver with an angry, whistled exhalation. "Please tell me that you're kidding."

"Unfortunately, I am not," she replied. "He left when I was asleep. Lindell left earlier." Virginia glanced at the door, checking that the deadbolt was engaged, noting the empty takeout boxes still on the counter. "He's just a kid, Arthur, I'm asking you to wait."

Arthur made a strange sound in his throat. "He's twenty, a grown man, and capable of nearly taking out one of the most skilled fighters I've ever worked with."

"Shadows, Arthur, that was almost a compliment."

He sighed again, and she knew that he was pacing in a tight circle from the sound of his shoes against the wood flooring in his house. "Don't get used to it, Ginnie, I'm about to tear into you for not letting me take the kid in earlier. At least then we'd know where in the hell he was."

"Yeah, and so would the feds," she replied.

"I can't help that."

Virginia leaned against the desk, allowing herself a private grimace at the growing ache in her shoulder. "You really should grow a spine. What are they going to do, storm the precinct?"

"Ginnie, I begged you to let us look for the kid. Captain Lindell wanted you to let us question him, it would have at least kept him in one place. At least we would know where he is!"

"I'll find the kid myself." She huffed, and flinched away from the pain once more. He was quiet on the line for a long moment, as static crackled in the background.

"Ginnie," he said, a dark tone weighing down his voice.

"What, Arthur?" she snapped, yearning for a little gin to take the edge off the stabbing throb beneath her skin.

"Turn on your radio."

Her stomach clenched, sending bile into her throat. "Why?" she asked, and her voice was hoarse from the lump already lodged in her throat.

"I think someone beat you to it," he said. "They found him."

"Are they bringing him in?" she asked, her eyes squeezed shut.

"Ginnie, he's dead." The line fuzzed with static for a moment as she twirled the cord around her fingers, cutting off the blood supply. Arthur waited for her to reply, and when she didn't, he cleared his throat lightly. "I'll pick you up. Don't tell the sibling just yet. We don't need press getting hold of this."

"Fine," she relented. "I'll wait at the back entrance."

Chapter Twelve

By the time they arrived, the scene was already heaving with squad units, photographers, and the coroner. The house was inoffensive from the front yard, lights warming the window frames, the mailbox dusted with snow, and a trail of blood that led from the side fence out to the street, where it disappeared. Virginia squeezed her eyes shut, willing it to be an infection-induced hallucination. The coroner. The coroner, because the kid was dead. Benjamin was dead, and it was her own fault, and she'd been a fool.

A hapless, stubborn fool.

"This is *your* fault, Virginia," Captain Lindell accused, pointing a finger at her the moment she stepped out of the car. "I told you we needed to bring him in, and you flat out refused."

Arthur held up a hand. "Captain, let's not let emotions cloud our judgment, this is a challenging—"

"You're supposed to be sheriff, and you just let her do whatever the hell she wants. What hold does this woman have over you?"

"Watch yourself, Lindell," Arthur said carefully, his dark eyes steely. Despite his calm demeanor, Virginia saw the fiery rage flash in his eyes. Lindell did, too, and held her hands up in surrender.

"Fine," she snarled, turning back to the crime scene.

"I know it's my fault," Virginia said finally, closing her door behind her.

"You couldn't have known the kid would take off," Arthur replied with a tired sigh, rubbing his close-cropped hair. "He made his own decisions."

"It's not good enough." Her fingers curled into a fist, unable to release the tension from her hands. She bit the inside of her lip, trying to remain emotionless. There was no room for overly dramatic displays at a crime scene, especially not hers. Not when she was the reason there was a crime scene at all. "I should have been better." She followed Arthur through the front door, pushing past a sea of detectives all crowded in the living room, the side of the wall torn to shreds.

"This is why mythics need to be reporting missing people to the VCPD," Arthur said, picking his way through the now-dilapidated building. "They need to file reports or we don't know which end is up."

"Not now with that, Arthur," Virginia snapped. "It's not always the answer."

"It would have been in this case," he argued.

She turned her head to hide the roll of her eyes, the ruined room drawing her attention. "Looks like a hell of a fight."

"Would you believe that this place looked normal this afternoon?" he asked. "Neighbors say nothing unusual at this address for years, not until today. Now it looks like it's been empty and rotting for twenty years. Water damage, half the ceiling torn down, three walls hanging on by threads."

Virginia took in the scene, her stomach churning with guilt. "Any witnesses?"

He shook his head as he picked through some of the rubble, tossing aside a broken chunk of brick. It clattered against the others in the corner, a hollow, dull sound. "None that have come forward, but we should be ready to accept that we won't find any. Seeing a fight like this would scare most reasonable folks into convincing themselves they'd never seen anything to begin with."

"Other casualties?" she asked.

"Not as far as we can tell, although there is a blood trail that exits through the front door. Disappears over the grass, and doesn't pick back up."

Virginia chewed her lip and grabbed the arm of the passing coroner. "Time of death?"

The coroner stopped, her black hair braided tightly at either side into wide loops. "Around five this evening, give or take."

"Thank you," Virginia said.

"Which means he probably left not long after you crashed out," Arthur said, waving the coroner away. "Kid probably went straight back to whoever he was working for. "

"Why, though?" Virginia asked, sifting through the piles of wood and brick. "He even admitted he never should have started up with all of that in the first place."

"Could be he felt the itch for Nether," Arthur suggested, examining the deep claw marks in the wallpaper that exposed the layers of outdated decor beneath it. "Could be that he just lied to you, Virginia."

"Yeah. Could be." Her gut twisted in on itself, and she resisted the urge to retch. "I don't think so, though."

"Don't beat yourself up, Ginnie," he said. "We see this every day."

"Twenty year olds? Every day?" She scoffed, shaking her head. "You've been back less than a week, and you're trying to tell me how this city runs."

"Nether is the same coast to coast," he said. "Doesn't matter which city we're talking about, the results are the same regardless."

Virginia pressed a hand to her forehead, as if the pressure there could erase what had happened. "What in shadows am I supposed to tell the kid's sibling?"

"I can handle that, if you want," he offered. "Some people take it better when it comes from someone official."

"Not with mythics, and not with you," she said, shooting him a look. "Absolutely not. It's going to be me. My mess, my cleanup. It's only right." Virginia rubbed a smudge of soot from the wall, examining it between two fingers. "Do we even really know what happened? Other than a fight between two seriously overpowered mythics?"

Captain Lindell stepped over a pile of rubble, her eyes steely with angry determination. "No. We don't, and that's thanks to you."

"Yes, I got that much," Virginia retorted. "If I'd turned him over to you, he'd be halfway to the capital by now."

"Better than dead," Lindell shot back.

"Is it?" Virginia demanded. "Are you sure about that?"

The captain leaned down until she was nose-to-nose with Virginia, glaring. "Positive."

"Lindell," Arthur said, his tone warning now. "I've already said enough. Don't make me take you off this case."

"Me? You want to take *me* off this case?" Lindell asked in disbelief, shaking her head with a derisive laugh. "The whole reason we're out here in the cold, scraping frozen blood off the floor, is standing right there. You're not taking *her* off the case?" The captain threw her hands up in frustration. "I should have left this shadows-damned city when I had the chance."

Arthur's jaw set firm, his hands shoved deep into his pockets, the way he always did when he was angry. "Get back to the precinct, Lindell. You're done here."

"Fine," Lindell hissed. "It's not like I wanted to be here anyway."

Virginia watched her go, stomping through the building, throwing open the door just to disappear into the night, a soft mist of powdery snow swirling under the flickering street lamp. "She's not going to make this easy for you. For either of us. She knows something happened back then."

Arthur blew out a sigh, the breath a frosted cloud in the night air that had poured into the building through the collapsed outer wall. "What did you tell her?"

"Nothing. But she's going to keep digging, and sooner or later, someone is going to say enough for her to put the pieces together."

"I'll keep an eye on it."

"You'd better. I don't want to live through that again, especially not now. You know how much the press loves a salacious story." Virginia turned, examining blood splatter on the wall, a spray of tiny droplets in one corner, and fat, thick blobs in another that had dripped down into the rug below, staining the golden fringe. "Don't underestimate it, Arthur," she said in a low voice, conscious of all the other people within earshot. "There are plenty in Verdance who would use anything to have either of us knocked down a few pegs." She smirked. "More you than me, but still."

"Thanks for looking out for me," he replied. "Ginnie—"

"Don't," she said. "Let's just get this over with."

"It's through the next room." Arthur led, brushing past three photographers who were busy setting flags next to blood spatter, thick and arterial, pooled on the unpolished wood floor.

Virginia nearly chewed through her own tongue, trying to remain stoic at the sight that awaited her. Benjamin lay crumpled in the corner, half-dressed, still wearing the pants she'd lent him. The shirt was torn, flung over a hanging lamp. The wall behind him was concave where his panther form had connected with the harsh studs, bent but not broken.

He looked so small in comparison.

She drew a breath, and then another. "I need some air," she said, backing out of the room. All the mistakes of her past came flooding back, every misstep, every time she fucked up and someone else got hurt. The memory of it shot through her like a red hot knife through waiting meat.

"Are you alright?" Arthur asked, but she was already pushing past the coroner, shoving her way out the door where she plunged her hands into the fresh snow, collecting atop the mailbox. She let the sharp stings of ice prickle up her knuckles and past her wrists, her eyes squeezed shut.

"Ginnie?" Arthur prompted, now at her elbow.

"I'm fine," she said through gritted teeth. "It's just the fever. I'll be alright."

"If this is too much for you, then—"

"I said I'm fine!" Virginia snapped, rounding on him. "Stay out of the way and let me do my shadows-damned job."

He searched her face, looking for something she'd never let him find. "The photographers are almost done. The coroner will be loading up the body for the morgue in just a few minutes. I imagine they will need next of kin to be the positive identification."

Virginia nodded. "I'll prepare a statement for Ursa. My mistake, my penance," she said, heading back inside. "I shouldn't have fallen asleep."

"You have a hole in your shoulder the size of a half-dollar that could have easily killed you. Anyone would have fallen asleep after all that." He waited for a response, but she wouldn't give him one. "Any ideas about the other mythic?"

"Not yet." She examined the room, bending to search the rubble for anything telltale, like a missing tooth, a ring, even a scrap of hair, but found nothing that clearly pointed to the identity of his attacker, not even a clump of fur that didn't match Benjamin's.

The coroner nodded as she passed, Benjamin's body now atop a cot, being wheeled out. "I'll have the full autopsy tomorrow, Sheriff," she said, looking at Arthur. "Though we're all pretty confident of what we'll find."

"Nether?" Arthur asked.

She nodded. "And plenty of blunt force trauma."

"Thank you, Mayumi."

Virginia trailed a finger along an overturned desk, squatting down to see the room from another angle as she rubbed the dust from her fingertips. "I think they knew each other."

"What makes you say that?" he asked.

She gestured at the door that was still on its hinges, the lock intact. "No forced entry. Whoever it was, they were let in."

"Could be whoever it was had a key," he suggested.

"Not impossible," Virginia said, crouching in front of the lock. "But these old locks are noisy. Would have alerted whichever of them was inside." She stepped over a broken picture frame, and pulled the photo free. "Recognize any of them?" she asked, passing it to Arthur.

"No, but I'll send it up to records."

"Why here," she wondered aloud, her brow furrowed in concentration. "Why some random house in a residential neighborhood? Was it business, or personal?"

"Business," Arthur said, gesturing to a bag of cash on the ground, the bills at the top splattered with blood. "No Nether though, not that my officers found."

Virginia turned, chewing her lip. "Unless someone lied."

His frown deepened, the creases in his forehead sharp. "I doubt that."

"Stranger things have happened in this town, Arthur," she said. "The VCPD is no stranger to corruption."

"Why do you think they offered me sheriff?" he said. "To come back from the east coast and clean this place up."

"Hm." She pried up a corner of the carpet, having spotted purple residue on the wall, faded, but still visible, if only just. "Looks like you have a lot of cleaning up to do, then." She pulled at the busy patterned wool, revealing a trap door left gently ajar.

"That doesn't mean it was an officer," he said defensively.

"No, but if it wasn't, then they need some remedial investigation classes." Virginia tugged on the brass ring and the door came loose, descending down a precarious ladder into a cold, dank basement, the chill wafting up towards them. It almost sucked the breath right from her lungs. "A safe house for Nether."

"That can't be," he said, almost laughing. "This is a respectable neighborhood."

"What, Arthur, and you think *respectable* people aren't doing Nether? Please pull your head out of your ass." She rolled her eyes again, climbing down into the floor, her boots slipping on the icy rung. "Don't let anyone lock me in here."

"I might, if you don't stop harassing me," he argued.

"If you didn't need me, I wouldn't be here." She grasped the ladder, grimacing at the cold, rusted metal. She'd be lucky if she didn't pick up at least a dozen different diseases down there. "Empty," she called up the ladder. "Whoever found it, they cleared it out, and fast. Spilled vials down here," she explained, nudging the inert residue with the toe of her boot. "Definitely Nether, though."

"Nothing else?" he asked.

"No." She shifted, feeling the unfinished grit under her feet. "Get one of the photographers to toss me a camera. That ladder barely held me, it's not going to last much longer."

He left the room, and she listened to his footsteps rumble against the floorboards above her. How many normal looking homes were hiding Nether drops? Probably more than she even wanted to know.

"Here," he said, waiting at the trap door. "Don't break it."

"I'm not going to break it." She caught it, heavier than she'd thought, and set it on an old table, holding the flashbulb to make sure the vials were visible before taking the photo. She got pictures of the ladder too, and the worn out desk that wobbled with any pressure or weight.

"Done," she said, passing it up to him.

"Let's get out of here then," he said. "It's freezing, and Mona might kill me if I pull another all-nighter."

Virginia's breath was oddly luminous in that crawl space, the clouds of vapor rising from her lips and dissipating, "What's the matter, sheriff, the family life you so craved not quite lining up with your job expectations?"

"Hurry up. I still have to go catch Lindell," he said, ignoring her barbed comment. He'd always been good at ignoring her. "I can't leave you unsupervised at an active crime scene, especially if you're only a consultant for the department."

"Then you can wait, I only need a moment." She bent, running her fingers under the table, half expecting to find vials taped underneath. There was nothing. Virginia frowned, sitting back on her haunches. Something about the room felt strange, like there was something hidden that she hadn't quite uncovered yet.

"Ginnie—"

"I said, hold on," she growled, her voice more barbed than she'd meant it, but nevertheless, he backed off, busying himself with returning the camera. She climbed under the table looking for a hidden seam in the woodwork, maybe, or another secret door beyond the concrete.

She ran her hand along the wall, pulling it away as though she'd been burned, as though the cold concrete was still hot. "Arthur," she called. "I think someone else was in here." It was a gut feeling, one without much basis yet, but she couldn't ignore it.

His footsteps thudded back, pausing at the entrance. "A third party?" He stroked his beard, peering down at her. "A third party who killed the kid?"

"No. Well, maybe," she relented. "Or they're less connected to Fiske than we think."

"Whoever it was, they must have been involved," he said. "A lackey, or a transport."

"Or," she suggested, "someone was tailing the kid, found the stash—"

"And whoever the distributor is, showed up with the cash and killed the kid for losing the Nether?" he finished.

Virginia nodded. "It's the best working theory we've got for now."

"I'd agree, but we don't have any evidence to support a third party."

Something glinted in the dim light, filtering down through the uncovered floorboards. "Get your evidence team," she ordered. "I just found proof that Benjamin wasn't the only one down here. Red hairs, caught in the brick."

"There are none of those up here, or in the other room." He peered down, shining a flashlight into the darkness. "How many?"

"Multiples," she said, counting at least three caught on a rusted, protruding nail. "Long, curly. Almost frizzy."

"Frizzy?" he asked.

"Yeah, you know," Virginia said, motioning with her hands. "Frizzy. Verdance is murder for curly hair."

"How do you know that?" he asked.

"Arthur, really? We lived together for ten years. You've known me since we were kids. I have curly hair, I just, you know."

"What?" he prompted.

"Style it!" She rolled her eyes, irritated by the conversation. "Shadows, it's a wonder you even know how many children you have with your pitiful observation skills."

"How am I supposed to keep track of—" he turned, taking gloves and a bag from the evidence team. "Whatever, Ginnie, it's not important. Here, do the collection. You remember how, right?"

She shot him a withering look as he passed down the evidence bag. "I still collect evidence, you know, even if the chain of custody starts and ends with me." The hairs came away from the nail easily, deposited into the bag and sealed before she passed it back up. "Toss me that flashlight, I want to see something."

"What are you trying to see?" he asked.

"Can it, Arthur." She examined the protruding nail with a frown. "Damn. Was hoping we'd have something else here, but it's clean."

"What are you thinking? Distributor gone rogue?" Arthur asked, penciling notes into a small pad from his pocket. "Crew turf wars?"

Virginia turned around again, taking one last look at the strange room. "Hard to know. Would need some more information, a witness, or maybe someone knows who the family in that photo is. Hell, even some chatter from the usual suspects might help put some pieces together." She climbed the ladder gingerly, lifting herself out of the hole. If she hadn't been proving a point, she would have keeled over from the pain. "We don't even know how much was down there to begin with." She nudged the trap door. "We'll assume the boxes would have to be smaller than this to fit. Cube-shaped for easy stacking and a relatively indiscriminate parcel size." She stepped around it, considering. "Usual vial size, stacked eight deep..."

"Ginnie—" he started

"Maybe fifty vials per box," she interrupted. "You could easily fit at least a thousand down there."

Arthur sucked in a breath. "A thousand. Not the biggest ever, but at least in the past a few years," he said. "Not to mention, some of the Nether we've been confiscating lately, is far more potent."

Virginia nodded, the pieces coming together. "Benjamin said his distributor, or whoever was making him do the drop-offs, said that this new batch wasn't addictive."

"We haven't found that. Rather, the opposite is true." He held the clear evidence bag to the light, examining it. "What do you think?"

"Can't tell much from a hair," Virginia said, her mouth set in a frown. "I'd have thought at least the sheriff of Verdance City police would know that." The fiery hairs glistened in the yellow glow of the flashlight. "Hard to say, but if I was guessing, I would guess it's a girl, young."

"Young like Penny?" he asked.

Virginia shook her head. "No, young like nineteen, maybe twenty. Too young to afford the more expensive hair treatments, or..." she paused, tilting her head. "Could be older, if unhoused."

"That's a lot to guess from a few hairs," he grumbled.

Virginia shrugged. "You're the one who asked."

"I didn't think you'd claim to know her entire life story," he said, taking the evidence bag back from her. "What's next, Virginia, are you going to hire yourself out as a medium?"

"I've never been very good at talking to the dead," she snapped. "If I was, our jobs would be a hell of a lot easier." She stepped over the shards of glass again, catching one under the heel of her boot with a grinding snap. "I only say that from personal experience. You might do well to remember where in shadows I came from."

He swallowed, searching her face. "I remember. I'm sorry, I forgot."

"Lucky for you, being able to forget," she sniped.

"Sheriff, I—" Captain Lindell stopped short, her eyes fixed on Virginia. "Apologies, I didn't realize she would still be here."

"Just cleaning up your mess," Virginia shot back with an insulting smile. "You folks missed the glaringly obvious trap door, leading down to a likely stash drop."

"How much Nether?" the captain asked, ignoring her, speaking only to Arthur.

"None, it was cleared out," Arthur replied.

"Oh, so what you're saying is that you didn't really find anything, did you?" she asked, smirking at Virginia now, tucking a wavy lock of hair back into her regulation cap. "An empty room, fantastic. I bet that will solve every case in the backlog."

"Captain," Arthur interjected, casting an irritated glare at Lindell, "I thought I made myself clear. You're off the case."

"I came back to apologize for my behavior," Lindell said evenly, brushing powdery snow from her shoulder with a swift flick of her wrist. "I know that I can be a strong asset for this case. I will—" Lindell glared at Virginia, seething, leaning towards her with shoulders squared up and ready to fight. "I will defer to your judgment on consultants and positions alike. I was out of line. I just find it a challenge when cases are impeded by *civilians*."

"I find it challenging when the captains assigned to a crime scene miss the glaringly obvious," Virginia retorted. "So how about we both keep our opinions to ourselves?"

"Ladies—" Arthur started.

"What?" both Virginia and Lindell snapped, then turning their glare on each other.

"Let's take a breather, shall we? Ginnie, with me, we'll get this evidence dropped off. Captain, please follow up with the records office, see if that crawl space was a sanctioned addition, if it was dug out without a permit, or if it was built that way."

"Sure thing, Sheriff," Lindell grunted, all but hissing the words through her gritted teeth.

"I have another case to follow up on before…" Virginia trailed off, taking a breath to fill the suffocating silence. "Before I deliver the news to Ursa. I'll find my own way back."

"Ginnie, it hasn't even been twenty-four hours since you were attacked," Arthur said. "You really should let me drive you."

"The way you drive, Arthur, I'll take my chances with going septic."

Chapter Thirteen

Virginia peered through the tinted glass of the apothecary, hunting for any sign that Anya was in there. "Hey," she called, knocking on the door. "It's Vee." No sense giving her a full name when she didn't have it yet. "I, uh... had some questions."

The shop was dark and deserted at that time of night. Astrid's lackeys probably had a private number.

Or, Virginia thought, edging down the alleyway, *a secret entrance.* She vaguely remembered a different door, more like a barn than a shop, wide, with a metal shutter that rolled up. It was possible she'd hallucinated it, given her condition at the time. Her shoulder throbbed with the memory of it, and with the stabbing reminder of her exhaustion and probable infection.

Trash littered the alley, torn up posters for the Sphinx lying in snow-melted puddles, Astrid's face looking up at her from the concrete with that infuriating, devilish smile. Virginia climbed over some old crates, marked with purple splodges of paint along the sides. Her brow furrowed. A Nether drop?

She bent, examining the half-rotted wood for signs of it, finding none. Perhaps it was for something else. Purple was just a color, after all.

"Is there a reason you're skulking around behind my shop?" Anya asked, looking down on the alley from the window above.

"Oh, uh—I had a few questions," Virginia said.

Anya raised an eyebrow. "About aftercare for that bite?"

She shook her head. "No, I got all that."

"That's all I have to discuss with you, Vee, or whoever you are."

"I wanted to ask if you saw anyone come through here earlier this evening, maybe around five?" Virginia asked. "A shifter, would have been pretty messed up."

"Shop was open all day, closed at seven." Anya gestured to the street. "Any of the shops across can verify that. For someone who's not a cop, you sure as hell act and sound like one."

"Former," Virginia admitted.

"That explains the attitude," Anya chirped.

Virginia snorted. "Attitude?"

"Entitled." Anya waved her hand and shrugged. "Arrogant."

"Arrogant!" Virginia protested.

"Officer Former Cop, I didn't see anyone today. No clients. I sat in the shop, I sold a few poultices, helped a teenage girl with some bad menstrual cramps, and read a book on the transient nature of bioluminescent fungi."

"Are there other healers like you in Verdance?" Virginia pressed.

"Yes," Anya said, offering nothing else.

"Can you give me a list?"

Anya laughed. "No. You run close enough to police and federal circles that I'm already considering skipping town myself. I'm not handing you a golden list on a silver platter of all the witches you can go round up." Anya waved her hand again, shooing her away. "Good night."

Virginia pressed a hand to her hip with an exasperated sigh, the pavement slippery under the treads of her boots. "I'm trying to find a shifter that killed another shifter."

Anya's face faltered. "The same one as..." she trailed off, but pointed at Virginia's shoulder.

"Yes," Virginia replied. "Found him in the park this morning, pretty messed up. Got him warm and fed, he skipped out while I was sleeping. And now he's dead." She huffed, her breath a wide cloud of vapor. "Anyway, I don't have to explain myself to *you*."

"I've got nothing for you, sorry," Anya replied, more softness in her tone. "Haven't seen anyone. A quiet day, for which I am grateful, given the state of you. Have you even changed your clothes since last night?"

"No," Virginia answered. "Haven't had the opportunity. I will, when I get back home."

"On a scale of one to *I'm literally being burned alive by a fire demon*, where is your pain right now?" Anya asked, staring down at her with a strange sort of concerned suspicion.

Virginia winced. "Somewhere near the *I now have a worrying amount of blackened flesh crisping over my skin* level," she answered.

Anya sighed, rolling her eyes once more. "You're probably well on your way to blood poisoning. I'm surprised you haven't passed out in a gutter yet." She waved towards the street. "Meet me at the shop door."

"I'm fine."

"I'm going to wager a guess you don't know how quickly *fine* becomes *dead* in these matters."

Virginia hesitated. "Okay, alright." She dragged herself back through the alley, dusting off her trousers when she reached the street. She needn't have bothered, given she already looked like a mess.

"Look what the panther dragged in," Anya said, unlocking the door. "You cops never listen to medical advice."

"Former," Virginia insisted.

"Whatever. I call them like I see them, and leopards don't change their spots," Anya said dismissively. "You've got that weird hero complex all tied up in there with a total lack of self-preservation and from what I can tell, about thirty-seven brick walls to keep everyone else out. I know your type, alright."

Virginia scoffed, stepping over the threshold and grateful for the warmth inside. "My *type?*"

"Yeah. You take pride in having no one around, like it's a badge of honor that people find you completely insufferable," Anya explained.

"I have... people," Virginia countered. "My sparring partner—"

"People that you don't pay to interact with you." Anya raised an eyebrow at silence, giving Virginia a self-satisfied smirk. "That's what I thought. What did you even talk about, the last time you saw him? Work?"

"No, actually," Virginia retorted. "I punched him in the jaw for outing me to someone."

Anya threw the deadbolt with a loud click. "Do you punch all your friends, Vee? Should I invest in padded gloves and a mouth guard if you're going to keep showing up here in the middle of the night?"

"Why, you planning on outing me to an ex?" Virginia asked, surprised at her own honesty.

"An ex!" Anya pushed aside a bookshelf, revealing the hidden clinic door. "Okay, I admit that may be deserving of being punched in the jaw."

"It's not *not* public knowledge, I just didn't want to get into it with my ex who's suddenly back in town." Virginia unbuttoned her coat, and then her shirt, laying back on the table. She could only assume that she was septic, and that's why she was being so loose-lipped about her personal life. "So," she said, eager to shift the conversation, "how long have you been here?"

"I was born and raised in Verdance. Inherited the shop from my aunt. She was a witch, and a healer, too." Anya pulled several jars from the shelf, pouring bits of herbs into the mortar and pestle. "Left me the shop, everything I know, and a hell of a lot of debt."

"I know the feeling." Virginia flinched when Anya peeled back the bandage, the dried blood crunching against fragile scabs. She hissed a pained sigh through her teeth, turning her face away.

"It's already infected, just like I said it would be if you didn't follow my instructions," Anya chastised, sucking her teeth. "And you're still running around in the same clothes, climbing through parks and down alleyways, and I'm guessing you've barely slept."

"I slept long enough for that kid to hightail it out of my apartment," Virginia growled, the guilt still fresh in her gut.

"I'm sorry." Anya pressed a hot compress against the puncture, drawing out the infection. "The streets are tough, these days."

"These streets have always been tough." Virginia tried not to think about her raw, exposed meat, oozing out over scraped skin. "How long before this bastard wound heals?"

"A week, maybe less," Anya answered. "But only if you listen to me this time."

"I swear on my mother's grave." Virginia neglected to mention that as far as she knew, her mother was still alive. Probably.

"Brace yourself." Anya leaned into the cloth, pressing her palms firm around it, laying flat against Virginia's skin.

"Shadows burn!" Virginia swore, almost catapulting off the table, pushing Anya backwards.

"I told you to brace yourself!" Anya shouted, catching herself against the shelf of bottles, creating an unholy racket.

"It would have helped to know what I was bracing myself *for*!" Virginia protested, her vision still weak from the pain.

"I have to lessen some of the infection, or you'll be halfway to joining your mother in that grave by sunrise." Anya glared, her hands raised as she approached. "*Brace* yourself."

Virginia turned her head, her eyes watering at the pain. She swallowed back the plaintive cry that lodged itself in her throat, begging for relief. Instead, she muttered a stream of curses under her breath, her eyes squeezed shut.

"Ten more seconds," Anya said, and her voice was gentler now. "Done."

"That was terrible," Virginia said, gasping for air. "I'll bet you did that just to prove a point."

Anya laughed. "Not just to prove a point, no. But I'm sure you won't forget that lesson any time soon, will you? You'll have to drink this again," she said, handing over a flask of the same foul beverage. "Helps the healing process."

Virginia choked it down, stifling the gag that originated deep in her gut. "So you learned all this from your aunt?"

"I did," Anya replied, tossing the soiled rags into a tall, lined bin.

"What else did she do? Love potions?" Virginia asked, setting the flask on the table next to the cot.

Anya glared at her for a long moment before she returned to her mortar and pestle, crunching up an assortment of dried herbs and reagents. "No."

"Did I say something wrong?" Virginia asked, her eyes following Anya as she moved around the room, collecting bits of this and that, tossing them into the mortar after a quick examination, her dress a pretty blue that matched her eyes.

"Love potions are deeply unethical," Anya explained. "It removes the basis of consent." She pounded the herbs into a fine powder, adding liquid. "Lucrative, yes. Ethical, no. My aunt never took part in it, and it's why she died with unpaid debts. I don't take part in it, either."

"I'm sorry I asked," Virginia apologized.

"People want who they want. That much is fine. It's when they decide that their want should supersede the other person's that it's trouble," Anya explained. "Always, always trouble. You can't build real love on that kind of foundation. It's like sand, always running through your fingers, always running out of time to make it work."

"When emotions run hot, things get messy," Virginia agreed.

Anya glanced down at the wound with disapproval. "I don't think you're one to talk about messy. Personally, I never would have gone by myself to collect a shifter bulked out on Nether in the first place." She pressed the poultice down into the wound, roughly this time, packing it full with the dense mixture.

"Ouch!" Virginia complained, trying to pull away from the pain. It was like fire, flooding into her muscles all at once. "What are you trying to do, heal me, or punch that hole down deeper?"

Anya paused to offer her a dangerous smile before scooping more poultice out of the mortar. "You should think more about what you say to people."

Virginia would have laughed at the absurdity of the conversation, but the ripples of pain were too sharp to overcome with wit. "You're picking a fight with a stranger you're knuckle deep in."

"You'd think that someone on the receiving end of that would be more pliable." Anya dug in further with a disgusting squelch. "But apparently not."

"Do you mind?" Virginia hissed, her vision fuzzy from the overwhelming pain.

"I'm trying to make sure you don't wind up back here again," Anya said, adding another scoop of poultice into the wound. "I'm tired of you waking me up in the middle of the night for this."

"I didn't ask you to do this, I only asked for information," Virginia argued.

"And yet, this is far more achievable for me." Anya spread the remaining poultice against the wound, snipping a fresh bandage from the roll. "Besides, if you die in my back alley, that's a lot of frustrating paperwork for me. I'd have cops swarming this place for weeks."

"Hiding something?" Virginia accused, only half joking. "Nether?"

Anya tucked the edge of the bandage in, turning to wash her hands. "No."

"Never tried it?" Virginia pressed, hoping for another clue that would lead her to Franky Fiske.

"Have *you*?" Anya shot back.

Virginia shook her head. "No. There's not much I'm scared of, but I'm scared of that."

"You're not a shifter, what are you worried about?" Anya asked derisively.

Virginia waited a moment before she replied. "Death," she replied.

"Fair answer," Anya replied, the hint of a smile playing at her lips. "Most people are too timid to admit that they fear death."

"The one thing you can never come back from," Virginia mused. "Besides, necromancy is illegal," she offered, unsure if she was making a joke or being frighteningly serious. Bringing people back was powerful magic, but dark.

"With good reason. It's never what people hope for." Anya dried her hands, looking down at Virginia. "Are you planning on leaving, or are you sleeping there tonight?"

Virginia steeled herself, standing up out of the bed. Her legs nearly collapsed out from under her, and she was left to scramble back onto the table, knowing she looked completely ridiculous. "You could have helped, you know."

"Yes, but then I would have missed the evening's entertainment." Anya smirked, offering her hand to steady Virginia. "Now, can I leave you to your own devices, or do I have to babysit you?"

"You don't have to—shadows," Virginia groaned, doubled over. "No. I'll let myself out."

"I'll wait until you're ready." Anya flipped a page, cracking the spine of her book casually and without regret or concern.

Virginia grumbled, climbing to her feet again, steadier this time. "I'm leaving."

"Excellent. I will enjoy the rest of my evening." Anya set the book aside. "A friendly reminder, Officer Not A Cop—whatever happens to you after you leave my establishment, it's not my doing."

"Trying to absolve yourself of culpability?" Virginia asked sarcastically.

Anya nodded. "One has to cover one's ass."

"Alright, shadows, I'm going." Virginia's vision swam, and she gripped the door frame with such force, her nails created crescent moon indentations in the soft wood.

"I already called you a cab," Anya said, flipping another page. "They'll be out front by now, I expect."

Virginia couldn't see a phone in the room, and so worried the infection was already impacting her cognition. "When did you do that?"

"I'm a witch, Vee. I am incredible at multi-tasking," Anya said airily. "How are you feeling?"

"Like shit," Virginia grumbled.

"Sounds right to me." Anya picked up her book again, waving Virginia towards the door. "I'd say I hope I don't see you again, but I think that would be far too optimistic."

Chapter Fourteen

The cab home was mercifully silent, the driver keeping her mouth shut until Virginia shoved several bills into her hand. "Keep the change."

"Have a good night, ma'am," the driver said with a polite nod, her stare on the dried blood on Virginia's coat for a second, and made the wise choice to remain quiet on the matter. She'd probably seen worse.

Virginia gripped the hand railing, silently cursing herself for living on the fourth floor. Under normal circumstances, she preferred the quiet and the privacy it afforded. When every step was like a long sparring session with Seamus, she resented every single creak of the wood, every subtle ding in the brass rail, and every scuff against the once-white walls, long in desperate need of repainting.

She almost expected someone to open their door and see her nearly bent double, holding one hand to her shoulder, and the other clutching the railing. Maybe Anya had poisoned her, instead. Maybe she was just dying of some slow-acting herb that was sapping her energy, clouding her mind and making her inefficient at defending herself. Maybe there would be a pack of shifters waiting outside her door to finish the job. Maybe the poison was so strong that there wouldn't need to be any shifters to finish the job, because her elevated heart rate as she climbed those *fucking innumerable steps* would do the job for them.

Every step felt like an hour. Maybe it was, except the light outside didn't change. It was still pitch black, except for the waning moon and the distant, flickering street lamps that called them all home. She shook her head, reaching for clarity that never came. It must have been poison. She'd been a fool to trust that witch, no matter how well-regarded she was, no matter how much Astrid had paid her.

When Virginia finally reached her door, she sighed with relief, until remembering for the fourteenth time that Benjamin was gone. He was dead, and she had to tell Ursa, and it wasn't going to be easy. She should have been practiced at delivering bad news by then, after dozens of missing people turned up dead, addicted, or disappeared. After nothing could be proved. After the crews and loan sharks had all gotten away with it, *again*.

Her stomach burned with the memories, stripping away the inside of her, one ulcer at a time. Eventually, there'd be nothing left of Virginia Vane other than a worn overcoat, a well-oiled revolver, and a set of slightly dented but highly polished silver knuckles.

Pushing into her apartment, she left the door ajar and leaned against the counter. She reached for the bottle of gin, pouring two shots into a glass and throwing it back, grateful for the burn in her throat that reminded her what had to be done. She poured another as she waited for the first to take effect, hoping it would dull the pain in her shoulder. When it didn't, she had the second swig, too.

The glass slid against the wood as she pushed it away. Virginia turned, facing the door across the corridor, knowing. A deep and dreadful knowing, the same kind that always grabbed her by the throat and shook her soul loose, leaving it to rattle somewhere inside her where she could never quite reach.

There would have been silence, if not for the persistent ringing in her ears, a result of a concussion she didn't know she had, or the gin, or exhaustion, or fear, or poison. Ursa's door was open. The door was open, and something like tar slipped into her lungs, and she knew.

She should have known.

The ones running the Nether racket were never ones to go quietly, or be ignored, or resisted. Virginia's slush-covered boots dragged across her floor, and then the corridor, her hand poised above the door knob. Filled with a desperate, foolish hope, she called through the crack. "Ursa? Are you in there?"

There was no answer, of course. Virginia had known there would be no answer. Still, she continued, "I need to talk to you about Benjamin."

She eased the door open, the hinge protesting with a loud whine. "Ursa?" The apartment was dark. Virginia reached for where she knew the light switch would be, pressing it against the wall. She closed her eyes to keep out what she knew she'd see, but she couldn't ignore it forever.

The tattered couch was overturned, plates smashed on the ground. Picture frames shattered, the glass crunching under her boots. "Ursa? Are you in here?"

At that point, Virginia knew that they weren't in there, but it would have felt somehow worse to not pretend. At least that way, she could pretend she wasn't imposing on the family's second tragedy of the day. "Ursa," she whispered, bracing herself against the wall.

She'd failed twice.

Twice in the same day, even.

Her jaw firmly clamped to keep the tears at bay, she swallowed back the lump at the back of her throat, pressing against her, daring her to give into the hopelessness, that tempting void of impossibility.

The bedroom was empty, too. The wardrobe had been looted, clothes strewn all over the floor, drawers overturned. Whoever had taken Ursa, they must have been looking for something. The Nether taken from the secret cache, maybe.

Virginia picked up the phone in the kitchen, dialing the station. The dispatcher answered with a bored voice. "Department?"

"I need to speak to Captain Lindell, if she's in."

"Please hold."

Static echoed across the line as she waited. Arthur would be home, probably asleep by then. Lindell might still be there. If not, she'd have to call in someone else, and given the nature of the case, she'd rather not. Just when she was about to hang up, the line crunched.

"Lindell," she said, all business and no nuance.

Virginia cleared her throat. "It's me. Ursa is gone. The—Benjamin's sibling."

"They are probably just out for the evening," Lindell said evenly. "Surely someone like you would recognize that as a possibility."

Virginia covered the mouthpiece and took in a deep breath before continuing. "The apartment was tossed. Door was standing wide open, no one is here."

"Shadows burn," Lindell hissed through the receiver. "Did you call the sheriff?"

"No, I figured he'd be at home, and I didn't want to piss him off twice in a row." She leaned against the ice box, her head swimming. "I'm surprised you're still there."

"Someone has to be." Lindell sighed. "So much for getting some sleep tonight. I'll be right over with a full team."

"A full team?" Virginia asked. "There's no body."

"No, but given your unreasonable standards, I might as well come prepared," Lindell retorted. I hope you didn't touch anything."

"Just the phone." Virginia bit back the cutting remark she had locked and loaded about how she *understood evidentiary protocols, thank you very much, Captain*, and said, "I'll see you when you get here."

The line went dead, and she waited in the corridor, half slumped against the peeling green wallpaper. Shadows, all she wanted was some rest. Her head was pounding a punishing rhythm, blood pulsing its drumbeat in her ears. It had probably been poison. Maybe, if she was lucky, she'd be dead in the morning. Good riddance, Virginia Vane, the world is far better off without you.

"You look like hell," Lindell said, the first to arrive, her boots scuffing softly against the worn wood flooring. "Have you even slept?"

"Have *you*?" Virginia shot back.

Lindell gestured to her shoulder. "I'm not the one walking around with a panther puncture."

Virginia stood upright, grimacing with the effort. "Worried about me, Captain? A few hours ago you were ready to separate my head from my shoulders."

"I'm on the clock, Vane. Too much paperwork to kill you right now." Lindell smirked from the corner of her mouth, making sure Virginia saw it.

"Never thought *paperwork* would be what saved me from an early grave," Virginia mused.

Lindell turned her head to hide a quiet laugh. "It's always the things we don't expect."

"I've left it as it was," Virginia said, nodding towards Ursa's apartment. "I didn't see any blood. It seems unlikely that this is unrelated to the missing Nether drop from that secret cache."

The captain nodded. "Too coincidental for both in one night. It has to be connected."

Virginia leaned against the wall again, trying to hide just how rough she was feeling from the poultice or poison coursing through her veins. "I imagine having cops swarm the place where the money was dropped may have spurred some scum-sucking leech to try and extract it elsewhere."

"Wouldn't be the first time," Lindell said with a heavy sigh.

"No, far from it," Virginia agreed. "Won't be the last, either."

The photographer arrived, bleary-eyed, tipping his hat to the captain with a wordless wave.

"Sorry," Virginia offered, knowing her call had dragged at least a few officers out of their beds. She'd always hated those emergencies in the middle of the night, stumbling to the door half asleep with mismatched shoes, Arthur at her heels.

"Don't be sorry, they're getting overtime," Lindell said, her eyes following him as he pushed into the apartment. "It's more than some of them deserve."

"Harsh words, Captain."

"True words, Vane, and you know it."

Virginia's shoulder pulsed, and she pressed against it, feeling the bandage grow soggy beneath her hands, beneath the thick cotton of her shirt. "Yeah. I know it."

"Go sit down before you pass out," Lindell ordered.

Virginia shook her head, insistent. "I'm fine."

"Suit yourself." The captain disappeared into Ursa's apartment, barking orders. It wasn't long before the officers and the photographers filtered out, leaving Virginia alone with Lindell in the corridor once again.

"Anything interesting?"

Lindell pulled her cap down over her eyes. "Hard to say without a prior comparison. Did you ever see the inside before today?"

"No," Virginia answered. "I didn't really know them. I do know they work at least two jobs, maybe three. One of them is as a cleaner in the financial district, but that's all I know."

"Any previous domestic disputes with their brother?" Lindell asked, scribbling in the margins of her notepad.

Virginia blinked, her brow furrowed. "No."

Lindell glanced at her, pen poised over the paper. "You can say that with certainty?"

"Do you think I would have mentioned that, Shirin?" Virginia asked, letting the snide tone slip into her words, comfortable like old training clothes.

"Captain," Lindell corrected.

"Shadows' sakes," Virginia hissed, turning away. "As far as I am aware, *Captain*, there were no disputes between Ursa and their brother. They were very distraught at his disappearance."

Lindell tapped the end of the pen against the paper, chewing her lip. "Yet they waited two weeks to hire you?"

"I imagine money was a concern on that front," Virginia replied. "Not everyone in Verdance gets a cushy pension, you know."

"Why not report it to the police?" Lindell asked.

"Are you really asking that?" Virginia said with a derisive snort. "Seriously? With the feds creeping around every case that involves a mythic?"

"Surely it would be better to be alive and conscripted into a salaried job, than to be dead after running a Nether racket," Lindell retorted.

"It would be better to be alive and free from both of those nets," Virginia shot back. "But in this country, especially in Verdance, that's too shadows-damned much to ask for."

The captain narrowed her eyes, her head tilted with suspicion as she slid a pad of paper back into her breast pocket, threading the silver button through the buttonhole with one hand. "All I'm saying, Vane, is that something isn't adding up here."

"So what do you suggest?" Virginia asked in a mocking tone. The pain and the potential poison was grinding her tolerance to a nub, and she wanted nothing more than to be left alone for the night.

"That you stay out of police business from here on out," Lindell answered. "This is now a homicide and a Nether drop issue. The person you were hired to look for is dead. The person who hired you is missing or dead. As far as I can see, your case is officially closed."

"I guess we'll see what Arthur has to say about that," Virginia said lightly.

Lindell leaned in, her dark amber eyes flashing. "I guess we will."

Chapter Fifteen

Virginia stretched her arms over her head before she remembered the puncture. Feeling little pain, she pressed at the bandage with curiosity, feeling skin spring back beneath her fingertips. She raised an eyebrow. Anya hadn't poisoned her, after all. A shame, really. She'd been looking forward to the deep rest of a shallow grave.

She picked up the pocket watch from her bedside table, squinting at the face through the bright glare of the sun that still managed to cascade through the dark curtains hung on the window. Midday. She'd slept, finally.

Virginia stripped off her clothes as the shower heated, and she was grateful that she'd missed the morning rush for hot water. Most days, even on the bleakest winter day, she had to make do with a brisk shower. Most days, she didn't mind, but after the past few days, she craved the comfort of steam.

The phone rang, and she shot a glance at it down the corridor, willing it to stop. When it didn't, she cinched a robe around her waist and stomped towards it, wrenching it off the wall.

"What?" she demanded.

Arthur cleared his throat nervously, crunching over the static on the line. "Ginnie?" he asked. "I was about to send over a unit, I've been calling all morning. You're not at the office?"

"No, I'm not." She rolled her eyes, despite the fact he couldn't see her. "Clearly."

"I need you to come into the station," he said firmly.

"Why?" she demanded. "Captain Lindell made it very clear last night that my involvement in this case—these *cases*, in fact—is at an end."

"Lindell isn't the sheriff, in case you haven't noticed," he retorted, taking a noisy slurp of what was probably lukewarm coffee. "I just need you to come into the station to make a formal statement about last night."

"What, me trading barbs with Lindell in the corridor wasn't official enough?" Virginia sniped, regretting that she wasn't already enjoying a hot shower.

Arthur sighed again. "I just need the formal statement. Any more involvement is up to you. I'll take your consultancy, if you want to give it, but if you prefer not to, then I understand." He waited a beat, and through the phone she could hear him running his hands over the leather pad on his desk. He cleared his throat again, loudly, an uncomfortable, aggressive sound. "You can't tell me you don't love being back at this."

"We both know that if you dangle that carrot, I'm going to bite." Virginia pressed her palm flat against the wall, biting the inside of her cheek until it bled. "That's it though, Arthur, and I mean it." It was a lie, and she knew it. There was no rejecting the allure of a case, but then, having to be in a room with him was like picking at a scab. "I'll be in soon," she said. "I have to finish up some things here first." She hung up without waiting for a response.

The bathroom was filled with delicious steam, and she hung her robe on the back of the door, reveling in the sheets of hot water that cascaded over her skin. The building was run-down and in desperate need of serious renovation, but the water pressure was impeccable.

She peeled off the bandage carefully, almost afraid of what she'd find. A big black hole, maybe, a festering wound so far gone that she didn't even feel the pain of it anymore. Or a purple-tinged glow, the damning sight of someone who'd fallen too far to get back up again.

There was still a wound, red and angry at the edges, but scabbed over despite the size of it. The swelling had all but vanished, and Virginia rotated her shoulder with curiosity, pleased that she'd regained almost all motion. She'd even be able to make her sparring match in a few days, so long as

Seamus didn't sink a punch right into it.

Rinsing off the remains of the poultice, she groaned under the water, feeling it wash away days of dirt, but no matter how hard she scrubbed, she couldn't get rid of the guilt. It stayed under her skin, permeating into her muscles, untouchable. Another indelible stain that sank into her, becoming a part of her, fusing with her bones.

She scraped mud from her hair, her face twisted into a scowl when she thought about how awful she must have looked the previous night. No wonder Shirin said she looked half-dead. No wonder Anya felt compelled to drag her into the shop and fix her, she'd probably looked like a feral cat that someone had kicked into the gutter.

Virginia wasn't a vain woman, but she had some sort of propriety, or at least, not wanting to draw attention to herself by looking unkempt. Her mother's words were in her ears again, and she shook her head, sending droplets flying against the cracked tiles.

Wrapping herself in a towel, she wiped the condensation from the mirror, the edges ugly and de-silvered. She frowned at her reflection, tracing the six scars that draped over her face, one by one. She'd had plenty of time over the past fifteen years to get used to her reflection, and she had, but it didn't change the fact that they were a permanent, visible reminder of the thing she regretted most.

She squeezed the water from her hair before pulling it back into a braid, pinned against her head. It was good enough. Clean clothes slipped over her body like silk, despite their cotton and wool fibers. The sky outside looked like snow, overcast with heavy, water-laden clouds. She added a jacket for good measure, and topped with a thick, insulated coat.

The drive to the station was overly-familiar. Sinister, in a way, to slip back into a routine so long abandoned, fifteen years gone. She was supposed to be older and wiser, but the only sign of either was the gray hair and the slight wrinkles at the corners of her eyes. Wisdom, it turned out, was not automatically granted with age, and she'd blown right past it.

There was something about the way the lights flickered in the lobby of the station, about the slick feel of the marble tiles under her boots, and about the vaguely stale air, smelling of abandoned paperwork and day-old coffee that made her stomach lurch. In another, fairer life, she'd be sitting at Arthur's desk, and not him.

Instead, she was a two-bit private investigator with a mean streak and just enough money in the bank for rent and cheap gin.

"I'm here, Arthur, now what do you want?" she asked, leaning against the door frame.

"Close the door behind you, and I'll get a formal statement," he said.

She latched the door, sitting at the edge of the chair across from him. "I arrived back at my building late, probably around midnight, maybe a little later."

"Where were you before you discovered the scene?" he asked, a little too innocently.

Virginia raised an eyebrow. "If you're asking me for an alibi, Arthur, we're about to have a very different kind of conversation. If you're trying to pin this on me—"

He gave her a strange look. "Why would I be trying to pin anything on you?"

"Because it wouldn't be the first time," she spat. "Or have you forgotten?"

"I don't think that's quite how I remember what happened, Ginnie," he replied evenly.

"Of course it isn't," she growled. "I went to a healer on the north side, alright? My shoulder was bothering me, and I wanted to make sure I wasn't going to end up septic in the middle of the night."

"Which healer?" he asked, and when she opened her mouth to shoot back a snide answer, he interrupted her. "Ginnie, I'm just trying to make sure you're alright. Some of these healers have been using Nether in their treatments."

"This one wasn't," she retorted. "I'm old enough to know better," she growled, "and I watched her the entire time. Now, is this some strangled attempt to get an alibi, or not?"

He sighed. "It's not."

"Excellent. I saw a healer, I was there for around ninety minutes if I had to guess. I returned home to my apartment, and noticed that the door across was standing open. I investigated, the place was tossed, no one was home, I called the station." She leaned back in the chair. "That's it."

"Captain Lindell had some frustrations with how things went at the scene." He arranged a cluster of pens up on the side of his desk in size order, choosing the tallest one to continue his notes with. "Ginnie, you're a brilliant investigative mind, but you have to try harder to not piss off my captains."

"All I did was exist in the same space as her, she's the one with the problem," Virginia replied.

Arthur rubbed his head in frustration, tossing the pen down onto the desk. "My concerns right now revolve around finding the other participant in that fight at the earlier scene."

"You saw the hairs I pulled from the basement, I'd start there," she suggested. "Any ex-con shifters with long, curly red hair that just got out? Anyone on the list of usuals?"

"No," he said. "We tried that already."

"Then I don't know what you expect me to do, short of trying to question every person in Verdance with hair like that. Assuming they haven't already cut it all off, either," she added. "I would, if I thought I'd left evidence behind."

"You have a knack for these things in a way I never did," he said calmly.

"And yet, there you sit." She let the words hang in the air, heavy and leaden, and something poisonous inside her rose up into her throat. "Mona has been after me and Lindell both to look out for this Rickarton shit."

"What?" he asked, leaning forward in his chair, the wheels squeaking against the wooden floor.

"She came to my office, said she was worried about your kid," Virginia explained. "Three disappearances at Rickarton since the school year started, and they're naming you as the reason they can't divulge anything."

"Mona shouldn't have gone behind my back like that." He sighed, rubbing his temple. "Especially to you."

"According to her, I'm the best. No telling why she asked Lindell, then," Virginia sniped.

He picked up the pen again, grasping it between two fingers. "I'll have a word with her."

"Don't bother," Virginia said. "It's fine, Arthur, why wouldn't I want to be deeply involved in your marital strife? I was for ten years, why not just pick up right where we left off?"

"Ginnie—"

She put a hand up to silence him. "I'm already looking into the Rickarton stuff. Consider it a favor. I just thought you should know." Guilt again seeded itself in her stomach. She shouldn't have said anything about Mona, but she felt the need to fire back, to have ammunition of her own. After fifteen years without a word from him, it was all she had.

A long, heavy moment passed, and she was about to get up out of her seat when he spoke again. "I need you to give me everything you know on the Sphinx."

She drummed her fingertips against the arm of the chair, the wood's varnish chipped. "No."

"We all know you were there that night, and that their people took you to a healer," he said. "Why would they do that for a stranger?"

She shrugged, staring him down. "I imagine they didn't want to risk the press hearing about it. Hushing up Nether is easier than dealing with an investigation, even if it means dragging an old lady to the north side as she threatens to bleed out all over the backseat of your car."

Arthur's mouth shifted from a grimace into a frown. "You saw the same healer? That night, and last night?"

"Yes, it made sense to me to visit the same practitioner," she answered.

"You should have questioned her about other injuries from last night, if—"

Virginia interrupted him with a heavy sigh. "Yes, Arthur. That's why I went there."

"But you said you went there for your arm," he argued."

"I lied." She rotated her shoulder again. "I didn't get any information about other shifters. She said she had no one all day.

He eyed her suspiciously. "Are you sure this healer wasn't using Nether? Your shoulder is looking much better today."

"Do you want me to strip for you in your office to prove it, Arthur? So you can see there's no purple tinge at the edge of the wound? Despite the improvement, it's still pretty disgusting, and we all know how squeamish you are."

"No—no, Ginnie." He rested his forehead in his palm. "That won't be necessary." Arthur straightened a stack of papers on his desk. "And I'm not squeamish."

"Was there anything else, or are you done interrogating me?" she demanded.

He tapped the pen against the arm of his chair. "It's not an interrogation, I just needed a formal statement."

"Lots of questions in there for just a statement, don't you think?" She tilted her head in challenge. "You must think I'm a fool, Arthur. I know Lindell has her own ideas about what happened last night."

Arthur glanced at her over the rim of his coffee mug, the steam long since dissipated from the liquid inside. "She's just being thorough. You know it's not beyond the pale to investigate whoever called it in."

"So I *am* under consideration." Virginia gripped the edge of the chair, her fingernails digging into the underside. "I'm a suspect."

"I wouldn't call it that, it's a formality!" he argued.

"Formality," Virginia repeated with a scoff. "Fine, you need an alibi? I was seeing a healer on the north side. Runs an apothecary, it's called Moonshadow Botanicals. Her name is Anya. Owns the place too, so I'm told."

"She do much healing for these Nether rings?" he interrogated.

Virginia released the chair, smacking her hand against his desk. "Don't you think I would have fucking led with that, Arthur?" she hissed. "You drag my ass in here for a statement, when what you really want is an alibi, because your holier-than-thou captain has it in her head I have motive. Which I didn't, by the way, but I suppose that's neither here nor there. You seriously can't understand why I might be a little *fucking* angry?"

"Keep your voice down, Ginnie," he warned.

She leaned into the desk, willing herself not to pick him up by the collar and toss him out the nearest window. It was only the third floor. He *probably* wouldn't die. "As if you'd do this to me *again*," she spat. "I took the fucking fall for you, and you *let* me." She could hear her breath, fierce and measured, barely contained in her lungs. Every exhalation felt like fire, burning her throat with each syllable she spoke. "And you have the audacity to show up here and act like we can pick up where we left off before any of that shit happened." She inhaled. "No."

He sucked his teeth. "I can see that you're upset."

"Oh, well done, Detective *Fucking Obvious*." She barked a laugh, shaking her head. "With investigative skills like those, it's a wonder you need me here at all."

"I did expect this on my return, I will be honest," he admitted. "Although, I expected it back at the quarry. I was almost surprised you didn't hit me."

Virginia sat back in her chair, arms folded over her chest. "You'd have deserved it." If she didn't get out of there soon, she was going to lose whatever cool she had left. "Am I free to go?" she demanded.

"Yes, Ginnie, you're free to go."

"Excellent." She stood, trying her best to ignore her legs shaking beneath her. "I'll call if I learn anything about Rickarton."

"Ginnie," he pleaded. "Come on, can't we start over?"

"No." Virginia opened the door, her hand wrapped around the knob. "Absolutely not."

"Ginnie, Captain Lindell had some—"

"I don't give a shit what Captain Lindell has or doesn't have. If you want me consulting on these cases, then you'd better tell her to stay the hell out of my way." She turned, coming face to face with the captain. "Shit."

"You have a loud voice, Virginia."

Arthur stood, coming between them. "Okay, Ginnie, how about you get back to your office, and I will let you know if anything jumps?"

The captain shook her head in disbelief. "Sheriff, you can't just let her—"

"She has an alibi, Lindell!"

"What, did she go spend the night at the Sphinx again?" Lindell asked, loud enough for half the bullpen to hear her.

Virginia reeled, her fists twitching at her side with the impulse to sink a punch right into Lindell's smug square jaw. "My personal life is none of your—"

"Please, Vane, it's obvious that you're hiding something. You go to that club, spend all night there, and then the next night you're back getting torn apart by a shifter?" Lindell asked, laughing. "Come on, you can't think I'm that stupid, can you? You're involved in this somehow, I can feel it."

"I'm not involved in a shadows-damned thing," Virginia snapped. "You're just a paranoid cop who's mad that the sheriff doesn't trust her as much as his disgraced ex-wife."

The captain raised an eyebrow and blinked. "So that's the big secret, is it? That's why he lets you do whatever the hell you want?"

"Honestly, Shirin, the fact that no one else told you should be a clue about your personality."

"Ginnie," Arthur said in a warning tone. "Now is neither the time nor the place for this conversation."

"Don't worry, Captain Lindell, I'm going." Virginia released the door knob, pulling at her lapels to straighten her coat. "This whole shadows-damned place can go to hell."

Chapter Sixteen

Seamus weaved around her, throwing another punch. "Are you gonna say anything, Vee, or just remain moody and silent all night?"

"I'm not moody and silent," she retorted, dancing around him to land a hit to his side, lightly jabbing him in the ribs. "I'm hardly a woman of many words, even when I'm not in the middle of kicking your ass."

"I can tell something is up." He dodged her swing, ducking under her arm. "The last time you were this quiet, it was when Astrid—"

"Shut up, Seamus," Virginia growled, not willing to dredge all that garbage up in the middle of a sparring match.

He threw two punches and aimed for a sweep. "All I'm saying is that I can tell you're frosty about something. You've been weird since you got here."

"Shadows, Seamus, let it go." She flinched, taking a hit to her shoulder. She let out a breath as a tight hiss as she recovered, setting up for another jab. "I'm fine."

"Alright, alright." He bounced away from her hits, setting up to come at her again. "If nothing is wrong, then you're just off-form for no good reason tonight."

Virginia blocked his attempt, irritated that she'd spent most of their time sparring on the back foot. "I was half dead three days ago, give me a break."

"What?" he asked, still coming for her.

"Shifter. Panther." She dodged, but took another hit in her ribs, wheezing lightly from the force.

He stopped, holding up his gloved hands. "Vee, what the hell?" he asked, stepping backwards off the mat.

"What now?" she demanded, not following him but throwing up her own gloves in frustration. "Get back on the mat, Seamus, we still have thirty minutes in this slot."

"You didn't tell me you got attacked this week," he accused.

She offered up a dramatic shrug, a performative gesture she knew would fall short. "I'm fine now."

"Yeah but—you've been letting me wail on you for twenty minutes," Seamus argued.

Virginia pressed a glove to her hip, the other resting at her side, the wound in her shoulder still pulsing with every heartbeat. "I didn't want you to go easy on me."

He smirked and stepped back onto the mat, jabbing in with a punch. "Left shoulder?" he asked, and she nodded. "That explains why you've been favoring your right side all night." Seamus hit her twice now, exposing her weakness.

"Fuck," she said with a grunt, taking a step back. "Okay, it's still a little sore, but it's nothing to get wild about, alright?" Virginia recovered, hooking a foot behind his ankle. "We both know I've fought through worse."

"Anything else happen this week?" he asked innocently, but it was all too easy to see through the ruse.

Virginia sent him to the mat, pinning him. "You talked to Arthur, didn't you?"

"No, but now that you've said that, I can make a pretty good assumption on what it was." He tapped the mat, signaling his surrender.

"It was nothing." She released him, sitting back on her haunches. "You know how he gets."

"It was never going to be smooth, you know," Seamus said from the mat. "Him coming back to Verdance."

"He should have stayed out at the coast," Virginia grumbled. "Leave this festering shit hole to people like you and me, and he's more than welcome to return to his boring neighborhood and his enormous house."

Seamus nodded. "Probably would have been best for everyone, given what's going on in the city lately. At that school, too."

"Has Mona been talking to you, too?" Virginia asked, an eyebrow raised.

"No," Seamus replied with a laugh, before he realized she was being serious. "Why, is she talking to *you*?"

"Asked me to keep an eye on things. She's worried about her kids. Told me she wants me to get him to move back east." Virginia rotated her good shoulder, leaning into the stretch, knowing the other side wouldn't be as pleasurable.

Seamus lifted an unkempt eyebrow, reaching behind himself for a bag of ice. "I'm surprised you didn't kill her on sight."

"I considered it," Virginia admitted.

The gym door opened and closed, sending a frigid draft towards both of them. Seamus waved at another client, giving him a winning smile before he returned to their conversation. "A rare display of restraint on your part," he said. "Did you tell him that Mona was in your ear about all this?"

"No," Virginia said. "Not the last part."

"Why?" Seamus asked, stretching out his arms. "Thinking you might be able to?"

"No," she replied. "I don't know. He wants forgiveness, I guess. Penance." She tightened her braid, tucking two stray locks back into the folds. "He's looking for the wrong thing."

"You had to have known he'd come back someday. This place is in his blood, there's no denying it." Seamus tossed a weighted ball over his head, and it landed neatly in its wire cage, along with all the rest of them.

Virginia bit back a sigh and several choice words about Arthur's inability to let things lie. "I'd hoped he would have resisted that particular urge." She rolled her eyes to the ceiling. "Though I suppose his track record on that front is pretty abysmal."

"Just don't skip town on me, alright?" he said, his face knitted into a stern expression. "I barely kept you here the last time."

"I'm going to be honest with you, Seamus, it's very tempting right now." She stretched her legs out in front of her, still avoiding her busted up shoulder. She'd thought she'd be fine to spar, but he'd spotted her weakness right away.

"You don't have it in you to disappear, Vee. You love this damned city even more than he does." Seamus tossed her a bag of ice, nodding towards her shoulder. "So what now?"

"I continue to avoid VCPD headquarters as long as I can," Virginia said with a casual shrug. "Not much else to do about it."

He nodded, but in that way she knew he thought she was full of shit. "Because you're trying to convince yourself that you don't miss it?"

"No, because he's getting on my nerves," Virginia said, doing her best to ignore the pulse in her shoulder. "Lindell too, shadows damn her. Nosy fuck."

"Are you just mad she's investigating?" Seamus asked.

Virginia gave him a playful shove from her seated position, knocking him backwards onto the mat. "Yes."

"It's her job, Vee," he said, neutrality permeating his voice in an obnoxious way. "Of course she's going to get cagey if you're not sharing all the information."

"Regardless, I don't appreciate accusations," Virginia argued. "Not after... well, you know."

Seamus nodded. "I know." He sat up again, crossing his legs. "Other people would have run for the hills the moment all of that started to break down. Not you, though."

"No." Virginia tilted her head back, dust particles dancing across the high beams of the ceiling, far above them. "Not me. Because I'm nothing else if not a fool."

"You're not a fool, Vee."

"Feels like it."

"We're all just stumbling through life, ass over tits," Seamus said, tossing another ball into the wire crate. "Mistakes happen, feelings happen. It's just mess, all of it."

"Some messes are messier than others," she grumbled, pressing the ice to her shoulder and swallowing back the relieved gasp in her throat at the frozen pressure. "Some messes tend to follow you around."

Seamus waited a moment, watching her, and then resumed his stretches, despite the fact he'd have another sparring appointment in less than an hour. "What happened wasn't your fault."

"Sure it was. I'm the one who made the call. I was captain, I made the call, and people got hurt." She sighed, already itching for a cigarette and a large glass of gin. "People died."

"Arthur should have backed you up," Seamus said. "He should have fought for it."

"Yeah," Virginia agreed. "He should have, but he didn't."

"I know he and I still talk but..." Seamus trailed off, tying another bandage around his knee. "I never really forgave him for what he did to you. Leaving like that, and so soon after you were pushed out."

"You and me both," Virginia growled.

"He's never been as strong as you," Seamus said quietly. "Arthur wants, above all, a quiet life. Chose the wrong profession for it, though."

Virginia chewed the inside of her cheek. "He couldn't handle the proximity to downfall. I was an embarrassment for him. I was an embarrassment, and I wouldn't give him what he wanted anyway, and Mona appeared like a figure out of the mists, and that was that."

"Still, at least your sex life is better now, right?" Seamus asked, poking her lightly in the ribs. "That has to count for something."

"Seamus," Virginia chided, laughing. "Stop."

"Tell me I'm wrong!" he teased.

She threw a roll of bandages at him, clocking him in the shoulder. "You're not wrong."

"You spent the night with Astrid, didn't you?" Seamus asked, wiggling his eyebrows. "A return to the siren of Verdance?"

"No," Virginia lied.

He squinted at her with suspicion. "Vee."

"Fine," she relented. "Yes."

He gave her a stern look, wrapping the roll of bandages back into a misshapen lump before he tucked them into his gym bag. "I can't say I'm highly enthusiastic about that development."

"You're one to talk, I bet you're still bouncing around with that guy who never gives you the time of day when other people are around." Virginia tilted her head, challenging him. "Aren't you?"

Seamus raised an eyebrow, and then blew out a sigh. "I know. I still think you should be careful around Astrid."

"It won't happen again. I just... I lost my head. You know how she is," Virginia said, her defensive walls starting to reclaim the real estate in her mind because the sparring match was over, and was no longer effective at distracting her from thoughts of Astrid.

"I know how *you* are," Seamus taunted.

Virginia waved him off, wishing she had something else to throw at him. "Zip it," she warned.

"I can't blame you," he said with a deferential gesture. "Astrid Frost sure is beautiful."

"Yeah, like one of those flowers with the poisoned thorns." Virginia stood, resting a hand on her hip. "Are we done talking about my personal life, now?"

"I'm surprised you even gave me that much," he grumbled, keeping his place on the mat.

"It's been a hell of a week." She bent into a fighting stance, sliding a foot back, and for the first time that night, she felt grounded and prepared. "Ready to go again?"

He shook his head, pointing at the abandoned bag of ice that was already beginning to melt in the gym's humid heat. "I think you should cool it until that shoulder heals."

Virginia rolled her eyes. "Fine. But I'm going to expect a double session next week."

"I'll bring extra padding."

"Good, you'll need it."

Chapter Seventeen

Virginia pulled at the shutters in the office, blocking the bright morning light that aggressively reflected off the freshly fallen snow. She squinted, looking out over Phoenix Avenue. It was the same as it had always been. Snow gathered at the sides of the street, crushed into a dirty slush by the cars that passed.

There was still no sign of Ursa. It was as though they'd vanished, no trace. No word from Arthur or Lindell, either, though it might just mean that her outburst had formally ended their arrangement. They'd deserved what they got. No regrets.

She sifted through the files again, running her tongue over her teeth. Her coffee was cold by now, bitter and undrunk in the mug. Virginia slid it across the desk, annoyed by its presence. One more reminder of things yet to do.

Rickarton was still playing on her mind. A few kids missing, Benjamin hooked into a crew, probably the Ruby Thorns. The seer at the park. The kid at the quarry. Maybe they weren't connected, but it nagged at her, pulling at her gut like a secret she was never supposed to know. The new Nether wasn't leaving signs of use, which meant the coroner might not catch it. And the hairs from the scene where Ursa's brother was found—who the hell was that? Certainly wasn't Ursa, nor anyone else in the usual ranks. She'd left it for days, unsure of the situation with the VCPD.

The door burst open, the glass pane rattling angrily. Virginia jerked away from it, half expecting to see Lindell or some goon wanting her to stop poking around, but instead found herself surprised. "Anya."

"What in shadows are you playing at?" Anya demanded, slamming the door behind her. Once again the glass rattled, but this time there was an almost crunching sound, like the spiderwebbing of a crack.

"I'm sorry?" Virginia asked, sitting back in her chair with her hands folded across the desk.

"Cops, Vee." Anya gestured at the door, where the blocky letters emblazoned the name of the office. "Or should I say, Virginia? Cops swarming my shop last night, overturning everything. They said you mentioned me as a person of interest!"

Virginia shifted in the chair, the wood creaking softly under her weight. "So you found me."

"It wasn't hard."

"No, I suppose not if you met Captain Lindell."

"How did you know it was her?"

"We had words." Virginia leaned forward, gesturing at the chair. "I will explain."

"I don't really give a damn about your explanations," Anya snapped.

Virginia licked her lips, preparing an attempt to defuse the situation. "If that was true, you wouldn't have come here."

Anya sat, throwing herself into the chair. "Alright then, talk. I'd love to know why you decided to sell me out after I went out of my way to keep you out of the cemetery. Twice."

"Yes, uh... thanks for that." Virginia nodded at her shoulder. "Basically good as new."

"Fantastic," Anya deadpanned.

"I didn't mean to pull you into this, and I..." she sighed. "I should have realized they would toss the place, but I wasn't thinking. My last interaction at the precinct was somewhat less than positive."

"And?"

"They were trying to pull me in over something I had nothing to do with."

Anya's jaw ground down on itself, the sound more than a little grating, and oddly louder than the noise of the street outside the office window. "So

I was your alibi."

"Yes."

"You do realize that some of my reagents are less than legal, right?" Anya snapped.

Virginia drummed her fingertips against the desk to dampen the enraged noises coming from the other side of it. "Please tell me it's not Nether."

"Of course it's not Nether," Anya hissed, her long, silvery braids still dusted with snow, despite the sun. "If I was using Nether, you'd have known, with that enormous fucking hole in your shoulder," she seethed. "They confiscated four rare ingredients!"

Virginia prepared a notepad, poised above the page with a fresh pencil. "Tell me what they are. I'll replace them."

"Easier said than done, Vee." Anya sighed again, straightening the deep navy wool of her belted coat. "Tell me exactly what you said. I have to give a formal statement later."

"And you came here, in broad daylight?" Virginia demanded. "Great, that won't look like conspiracy at all!"

"My phone is tapped, I couldn't exactly give you a call."

Virginia set the pencil down, a deep, familiar rage and worry bubbling up inside her, eating away at her gut. "Then we're in more trouble than you realize."

"I didn't do anything wrong," Anya insisted. "All I do is patch up whoever gets dumped at my door, you included. And for that matter, you got me into this mess, and I'd prefer if you got me out of it."

"Lindell is just overzealous. She's convinced I know more than I'm letting on."

"And do you?"

Virginia sighed. "Yes, but if I tell the VCPD, they're going to fuck it all up. The only way to get hands on whoever this Fiske guy is, it has to be done quietly. Dragging north side healers into the station, tossing shops, it's only going to drive it all further underground."

"You're protecting Astrid," Anya accused, gripping the sides of the chair with enough force that Virginia thought she might snap the wood in half.

"No, I'm not," Virginia explained. "I knew that kid would likely wind up at the club, so I waited. All I wanted was to drag him back to his sibling and be done with it. I didn't anticipate that he'd be boosted with Nether, and I damn well didn't anticipate getting my ass kicked."

"Is getting your ass kicked a rare occurrence, then?"

Virginia bit back a smirk. "Yes, actually."

"You could have shot him."

"It doesn't matter, because he wound up dead anyway." The shame of it boiled inside Virginia, threatening to expel what little of the coffee she'd swallowed. "I'll do what I can, alright? Tell them the truth about when I was there, and what for. They already know about the attack, and my subsequent visit."

Anya raised an eyebrow, her pink lips still set in a deep frown. "And if they ask why I was here today?"

"That's not an if, that's a guarantee. Lindell is like the damned panopticon of Verdance." Virginia ran her fingertips over one of the files. "Tell her the truth, you came here to read me to rights about mentioning your shop. You can even tell her that you flipped my desk, if it helps."

"Is that an invitation to commit vandalism?" Anya asked evenly. "Can I get that in writing?"

"Listen, Anya. I've known a lot of cops like Lindell. She's going to try to get on your good side. She'll try to get underneath your skin, she'll try to trap you with your own words. She doesn't like my involvement at the precinct, and she wants me out. She'll do whatever it takes to make that happen, even if it means taking you with me."

Anya blew out a huff, brushing a hair out of her face and tucking it behind her ear, glinting with silver hoops all lined up in a near little row. "Great."

"I'm sorry, I never would have gone back there if I'd known she was going to pull this." Virginia sifted a pen from her desk drawer and closed it.

"This isn't what I need in my life," Anya said. "This kind of bullshit threatens to upend everything I've been trying to build since my aunt died. Do you even know how much commercial rent is on the north side?"

Virginia nodded, glancing through the blinds out the window, almost expecting to find Lindell standing on the sidewalk, staring in with a triumphant smirk. Instead, there was an empty sidewalk and the blinding flash of sun against snow. "I have an idea, yes."

"It's taken years to clear her debts. A lifetime of bad investments, of getting tied up with the wrong sorts of people left her penniless at the end. She had nothing and no one, other than me." Anya released the chair, following Virginia's stare between the worn-out window coverings. "I spent a decade gathering supplies for what I'd need, traipsing through bogs and backwaters digging up roots and reagents, just to have some upjumped cop bust in and start moving around all the furniture."

"I'll deal with Lindell," Virginia promised.

"And my reagents?" Anya asked. "What about them?"

"I'll do my best to have them returned to you, but I can't guarantee that."

"Get me a job with the VCPD and we'll call it even," Anya said evenly, without a hint of irony.

Virginia snorted. "What?"

"If I'm keeping busy healing their broken bones, then I don't have to worry about Astrid's enforcers showing up in the middle of the night with all kinds of injuries." Anya shrugged. "Money is what I'm after, I don't care who it's from."

"You have to give them more than that if you want Arthur—Sheriff Dixon—to hire you," Virginia replied. "Information. Anything."

Anya chewed her lip. "Fine. This Fiske guy... I've never seen him. Couldn't tell you what he looks like, or where he is, and that's the shadow's honest truth. However, I do know he's been picking up a lot of mythics lately, mostly shifters, having them run Nether for him. Sometimes they end up in my back room, and it's messy." She exhaled quietly, running her fingers over the sleeve of her coat. "I think they're looking for someone specific."

"I was hoping that wasn't the case," Virginia muttered. "Any deaths?"

"No, I'm good at my job."

"You ever see this one?" Virginia slid a photo of Benjamin across the desk.

"No."

"What about that seer in the park, the attorney? Was she one of his?"

Anya shook her head. "I don't know, it's not like they gave me a roster. All I know is that she was asking too many questions, at least from what I heard. A couple of enforcers were talking in front while I was working on someone." Anya tugged at one of the silver hoops in her ear, and when she released it, there was a quiet, polite jangle as it rejoined the others. "Rumor has it she was digging too far into the Ruby Thorns."

"That tracks," Virginia agreed. "It's what I had assumed when I realized she was a lawyer."

"I don't know anything else."

"Don't tell Lindell the part about the deceased seer," Virginia said after a long beat of silence in which the only sounds were the cars driving on the street outside, the oddly calming whoosh of tires against wet tarmac.

Anya's brow furrowed. "Why?"

"It will make her watch you more, not less. If she thinks you're the designated healer, she's going to have cops posted up outside your door twenty-four seven." Virginia made a note on her page. "Any healers on the south side?"

Anya inhaled slowly, breathing out a hiss. "There is one, but from what I hear, he's not the favorite anymore. He's cagey about healing mythics."

"Why?" Virginia asked.

"Not sure, never met the guy. In fact, I couldn't even tell you where he's located." Anya paused, making a strange noise in the back of her throat that might have been affirmation and might have been rage. "I can tell you that it's why I've been busier the past few months."

"So Fiske is upping the game, then, and it's recent."

Anya nodded, leaning back in the chair, finally releasing some of the rage she'd entered with. Too late for the glass pane, however. "In my estimation, yes."

"And if that's where most clubs and distributors are getting their Nether from—"

"Then it stands to reason he's the top of the pyramid, so to speak," Anya finished. "The head of the snake."

Virginia nodded. "We need to redirect suspicions. If Lindell knows the Sphinx has Nether, she'll run a raid, and we won't hear from Fiske for at least eighteen months, and that's if we're lucky. But she won't want to hear it from me."

"You really pissed her off, huh?" Anya asked.

"I'm surprised she didn't take a swing at me."

"What did you say?"

Virginia searched Anya's face, and then laid her elbows against the worn wood. "I'd rather not get into it. It wasn't pretty." Virginia jammed her hands into her pockets, desperately seeking warmth in the frozen office, frost edging in at the corners of the window, its fractal pattern spreading more with every frigid midnight. "I'm sorry for the trouble."

Anya stood, straightening her skirt. "Sort it out, Vane. I can't have this be the thing that pulls me under. Not after everything I've done to keep my head above the water."

"Understood."

Chapter Eighteen

She shouldn't have been surprised when the news hit the papers, but a small part of her was anyway, in spite of everything. *MYTHICS TARGETED BY MYSTERIOUS KILLERS*, the headline of the nightly news read. No doubt someone at headquarters had leaked it. Arthur was probably spitting tacks.

Virginia slid the coins across the newspaper stand, tucking it under her arm. No doubt it was full of suppositions and thinly connected accounts, with a healthy dose of hysteria for good measure. Journalists would be all over this whole thing, now. There'd be no getting away from it. "Thanks," she said, nodding to the man who took her change.

"As always, Ms. Vane," he said, tipping his hat.

Fifteen years of nightly news editions.

Fifteen years of meaningless pleasantries, and she didn't even know his name.

"Have a good one," she replied, turning towards the alley that led to her street. She'd walked home, not wanting to drive in the snow. It was about to be a blizzard, no matter what false hope the forecast was peddling. The clouds hanging low, obscuring half the skyline with their grey heaviness, were waiting for their moment of opportunity to dump snow over the city. It was too bad that seers couldn't predict the weather, nor the future at all, they could only see snippets of what had already come to pass.

An icy draft snaked up her thick wool coat, flipping the hem to and fro in its own private storm. It was dark already, despite the relatively early hour, and the sun had set while she was still sitting at her desk, poring over the files one more time, but finding no leads. She gave in to a shiver, letting it vibrate through her limbs and down into her core. Verdance residents learned to live in the dark, to accept the frigid fate that the lake cast over them.

The alley was barely lit, the only scattered beams of light coming from the street lamps at either end, yellow and dim in their own disappointing estimation of daylight. Her boots skidded along the ice, and she reached up to catch herself on the chipped red brick of the building. Something felt off.

Hairs on the back of her neck prickled, and she spun around, expecting to see someone standing behind her. But there was no one, and she was alone. Unsettled, she hurried through the alley, one hand slipping into the silver knuckles, and the other reaching inside her coat to rest on the revolver, holstered under her arm. She hesitated at the other end, looking back over her shoulder once more, and finding nothing.

Virginia shook her head, chewing her bottom lip. It had been a long day, and she was feeling paranoid. Lindell hadn't showed up at her office, which was unexpected. She'd been preparing to go another round with the woman, arguing about sins past and present, locking horns about her cases, about information, about Astrid and the Sphinx and missing Nether. No leads for Benjamin or the others who'd gone missing from Rickarton.

She looked over her shoulder once more, seeing nothing. It was probably just her imagination, the obvious result of a tiring few days. It hadn't even been a week since she'd been attacked, and despite her shoulder healing well, the memory of it was fresh. She almost expected to see glowing white eyes staring out at her from behind a dumpster, ready to pounce, ready to exact revenge for Benjamin.

A discarded newspaper leaf blew down the alley, catching on an overturned crate, the splintered wood reaching up towards the sky. The sound of it tearing in the wind made her jump.

"Get a hold of yourself, Vane," she grumbled, turning down the street. She'd been jumped by mythics at least a dozen different times, maybe more, but this was the only time she felt haunted by it. He'd been just a kid. All she'd wanted was to send him back to Ursa, to collect payment, and close the case. She'd failed, just like she'd failed before, and it was scraping at her like sandpaper against bone, chipping away at whatever was left after so many empty years.

Once more up the steps to her apartment, once more catching the sleeve of her coat on the unfinished wood on the second floor banister, once more sliding key into lock and sighing as she barred the door behind her, flipping the deadbolt. Once more, pouring cheap gin into a glass, kicking off her snow-covered boots. Routine and comfortable, even if strangely reminiscent of another life she'd never had the chance to live. One where she wasn't being tracked down by cops, witches, and shifters. One where she worked as a researcher in some dark basement across the city, unbothered by the politics of the city council, or the governor, or the press.

The gin was cold because her apartment was cold. Heat was expensive, and cases she could solve were thin on the ground. She slid off her coat and into a thick, wool sweater, a deep forest green, textured and rough. It was almost enough to keep out the chill. Virginia savored the burn of the gin, swirling it in the glass.

She was missing something.

It was obvious as daylight that she was missing something, but it was just out of reach, dangling right at her peripheral vision. She pinned Benjamin's case file contents to the wall and stepped back, examining them, studying the photographs from the quarry, and from the park. One more unsolved case to shame her from the cork board, and his photo sat right next to Juliette's, her first unsolved case that had remained open for decades.

No doubt Lindell would never let her get her hands on the photos from Ursa's apartment now, but that was her own shadows-damned fault for losing her cool. She sighed, her knuckles balled into a fist. Mona. Lindell. *Sheriff* Arthur Dixon. They obscured the truth, somehow, keeping her from clarity.

Virginia paced with her glass, sipping from it now and then. She needed to figure out how the school was involved, or not involved, maybe. It could be a coincidence but the broken latch was the only disrepair that place had seen in years, and why? She set the glass on the coffee table, sinking down into the couch, her elbows on her knees.

From outside, the sound of breaking glass, and a scream. Another. She bolted to the window, peering out into the darkness, searching, but finding nothing at first, until the dance of strange shadows pulled her stare.

The alley.

It was lit with the glow of orange flames, irregular and cascading feverishly over the bricks. Arson, maybe, or a torch. She threw open the window. "Hey!" she shouted.

There was no reply. Virginia hesitated, waiting. It could just be kids getting into some trouble, trouble she had no business interfering in.

But if it wasn't, it would be one more guilt to lay on her conscience, which was already too heavy to bear.

She went to the phone, her hand hovering over the receiver. To call VCPD would have the whole place swarming. It would mean Lindell breathing down her neck again, and Arthur doing whatever it was that he did best, and having to explain how it was that she kept finding herself in the middle of all this shit.

Virginia drew her hand away, still staring at the window.

Another scream, this time, "Get away from me!"

Without even thinking this time, she flew out the door like it was her own apartment on fire, jumping down the stairs three at a time. She nearly broke the glass on the building's door when she threw it open, already running breakneck towards the alley.

"Hey!" she shouted again, nearing the entrance. Her eyes were slow to adjust to the darkness, and she blinked rapidly, trying to see into the inky black of the alley. "I called the cops already," she lied, shifting one leg forward for balance.

"Piss off, lady, this isn't any of your business," a man said, his face masked by the darkness.

"I'm not going anywhere," Virginia shot back, slipping a hand into her coat.

"I strongly suggest you leave."

Virginia smirked, pulling her fist from her pocket, the silver knuckles in place. "I could say the same to you."

"What are you, neighborhood watch?" he asked, laughing. "I could blow you away in two seconds flat."

"Try me." Before he could even reach for his weapon, her revolver was unholstered and ready. "I don't think you know who you're dealing with," she said coolly, tugging back the hammer with a satisfying metallic snap.

"Come on, man, let's just go," a second voice said. A shadow moved at the far end of the alley. "This one isn't worth it."

"The hell she isn't," the first said. "She's better than any shifter. Could be the one he's looking for."

Virginia stepped into the alley, her shoulders squared. "I don't know what you're doing in this neighborhood, but whatever it is, you're done, now."

"I'm not letting some old lady scare us off, what's she going to do?"

Virginia laughed, and it echoed down the alley. "Try me."

A shadow surged towards her, coat flapping in the wind. She evaded, turning on the toe of her boot to land a knuckled punch against cheek. He went down hard, holding the side of his face. She landed a kick to his ribs, keeping the revolver pointed at the other. "Care to try again?" she asked.

A shot fired off, glancing against brick. She laughed again. "That was a terrible shot." She fired her own gun in response, rewarded with a loud squelch and a strained hiss of pain as he bent double, clutching his leg. Virginia's eyes finally began to adjust, and she spotted the girl, edging backwards at the other end of the alley. "Hey," Virginia said, "wait a minute."

"Sorry," the girl said, her voice wavering. "And thanks." She slipped around the corner and out of sight, her bright ginger hair blowing in the draft.

"Shit," Virginia muttered, stepping over one of the goons to give chase. She holstered her weapon and ran, eyes on the sidewalk, looking for ice, while still trying to keep tabs on the girl that was much younger and faster than she was. "Wait!" she shouted again. "I'm not trying to hurt you."

The girl bent into her run, gaining speed and weaving around the parked cars.

"I'm not a cop!" Virginia offered. "Or a fed."

The girl wavered for just a moment. "You could be lying," she shot back, panting.

"I'm not."

The girl picked up speed again, vaulting over an iron fence that enclosed the local library. She vanished into the shadows given by the tall oak trees, planted hundreds of years ago when Verdance was new.

"There's nowhere to go from in there," Virginia called from the street, trying to catch her breath with icy cold air that burned at her lungs. "Come on out." She stood waiting on the street, scanning the small property for movement and finding none. Her hands in her pockets, she sighed. "Come on, kid, don't make this any harder. Why don't you come on out and tell me why those two enforcers were after you? Are you a mythic?"

No response. No movement.

Virginia squinted into the darkness. "I saw fire. Are you a witch?" She'd have to be very powerful to have flames that large as a witch, but it wasn't unheard of in some family lines. It would make sense that Fiske was trying to round her up if she had power like that.

She sighed. That kid wasn't going to come out, and if she went in, there was a chance she'd miss the kid escaping. The same was true if she left to find a phone to call the station. Virginia groaned. She'd have to call the shadows-damned station to report it. An inferno witch would definitely get hauled in by the feds, probably before morning. "Listen, kid, if those guys are after you, it won't be long before they send more."

The library stood tall, its edifice dark and imposing regardless of the time of day. Wrought iron accents across the windows and the door gave a dull shine in the limited glow from the distant street lamp behind Virginia. She jammed her hands into her pockets, the cold starting to numb her fingers. If those fools came back for more, she'd need to be ready. "I don't want to be out in the cold any more than you do," she called. "Let's get out of there and we can talk."

Still, there was nothing.

"I'm not interested in playing games," Virginia snapped, losing her patience. "Either come out now, or you can freeze to death hiding behind the library. I'm sure Ms. Zin will be thrilled to deal with your corpse come morning. It wouldn't be the first time she's had to do it."

When there was still no sign of movement, she flapped her coat angrily. "Fine. Be it on your own head, then." She turned, walking back up the street, but listening for the sound of steps, or the creak of a gate, or the soft whisper of boots on snow-covered grass. There was nothing.

There wasn't anyone in the alley when she returned, either. No evidence at all of what had occurred beyond the faint smear of blood against the concrete. It wasn't enough to indicate death, so she'd probably nailed the sucker in the leg or the shoulder. Good, it served him right. Was that really what things had come to in Verdance? Kidnapping teenagers to run drugs? She shook her head, pushing back into her building.

She checked her apartment before locking the door, wary. Those goons hadn't seen where she had come from, but it was impossible to know who was already watching her. Could Fiske already be aware that she was poking and prodding into matters she shouldn't be? Benjamin was dead, she was off the case and she should just leave it alone.

Still, it pulled at her. Benjamin was dead. Benjamin was dead, and it was because she didn't involve the VCPD when she'd grabbed him. Now there was another kid out there, and despite what she was, she was in danger, and not just from Franky Fiske.

Her hand hovered over the phone as she stared out at the alley through the rain-stained window. With a heavy, defeated sigh, she dialed the precinct. "Sheriff Dixon, please."

"The sheriff has left for the day. Would you like to leave a message?"

"No. Is…" Virginia turned her head, hissing out a sigh. "Is Captain Lindell in?"

"She is. May I ask who is calling?"

"Virginia Vane."

"Please hold." The line was quiet for several minutes, long enough that Virginia wasn't surprised when the dispatcher returned with, "I'm sorry, ma'am, she's not taking calls right now."

"Right. Thanks." She hung up, rolling her eyes to the empty apartment. "Not taking calls from *me*, she means," Virginia muttered. Lindell was becoming a real thorn in her side, a bonafide pain in the ass. To the station, or leave it until morning? No, if she left it until morning that kid could be halfway to another state, and Fiske would be even harder to track down.

She growled, throwing on her coat again. Goddamn kids.

Chapter Nineteen

"Captain," Virginia said, standing outside the scuffed, chipped door to Lindell's small office. "I know you'd rather throw me into the fiery pits of my own personal hell right now, but I need to talk to you."

A chair squeaked from within, a muted consideration of her words until the captain cleared her throat. "I'm not interested in your pathetic apologies, Vane."

"Oh, I'm not here to apologize," Virginia said coolly. "I meant every word."

"Get out."

"Shirin, don't make me kick this door in. We both know that I'd do it," Virginia threatened, eyeing up the old, worn out hinges and the rattling knob. It wouldn't last much more than a few hits. She leaned against the door frame, her hand on the knob. "There was an inferno witch outside my apartment tonight, and I thought you might want to know."

There was a moment of quiet shuffling, paired with a sigh of resignation. "Come in," Lindell grumbled, her chair squeaking as she shifted her position.

"Thank you for being reasonable," Virginia said, opening the door to the tiny office that had once been hers. The cracks in the wall behind the desk were the same, peeking out from behind Lindell's framed certification, hung there to hide Virginia's sins.

Lindell toyed with her cap, flicking the silver chain that laid across the brim. "Tread lightly, Virginia. I mean it. I will not hesitate."

"Yeah, I got that much," Virginia replied, sitting down in the threadbare, understuffed chair. "Shadows, I think you might even be more annoying than I was when I was a captain."

"I'm older than you were then."

"Been checking my records, have you?"

"It felt prudent after our last interaction." Captain Lindell folded her hands on the desk, leaning forward. "Get to the point."

Virginia stifled the urge to roll her eyes. The familiar water stain in the corner had grown considerably over the previous fifteen years, spreading to the adjacent tiles. "I was home, saw some flames, heard some screams, kicked the shit out of a couple goons in the alley."

"Where's the witch now?"

"Lost her. She jumped the fence at the library."

"You didn't pursue?" Lindell asked, a harshness to her tone that grated in the same way as nails against a chalkboard.

Virginia swallowed hard, struggling to remain civil in the face of an infinite inquisition. "Somehow, given your confidence that I'm a Nether running mastermind, I felt like trespassing might not do anything to disabuse you of that notion."

"And these other two?"

"Rough shape, but able to walk. They scrambled when I was chasing the kid."

Lindell paused from taking notes to flick her gaze up at Virginia. "So you didn't bring any of them in, then?" she asked.

Virginia rankled once more, taking a deep breath to stem the tide of irritation growing stronger and more insistent in her gut. "What would you have had me do? I didn't have to come all the way down here, you know. I could have just said nothing."

"I'd have thought you would be trying to harbor an inferno witch for yourself."

"For myself?"

"You were adamant you didn't want us to take in Benjamin," Lindell said, tapping a pencil against the margins of the empty page in front of her.

Virginia tensed, drawing in another pointless, cleansing breath. "Yes, and he slipped through my fingers, as did his sibling. I wanted to make sure this one didn't wind up dead in a warehouse."

"Warehouse?"

"The two trying to pick her up were almost certainly Fiske's. Said she was better than any shifter. I can only imagine they'd want someone that powerful to be guarding the bulk of their wares."

Lindell raised an eyebrow, finally noting something down. "Did you tell the sheriff?"

"Dispatch said he'd gone home."

"I'm surprised you didn't use his personal number."

An aggrieved sigh escaped Virginia's lips at last, coming to rest at the tail end of a derisive laugh. "Is there something you want to get off your chest, Shirin? Because I'm sure I'd love to hear it."

Lindell laid down the pencil, sitting back in her chair. "Alright, I'll bite. I don't think you should be consulting for the VCPD. I think it's a conflict of interest."

"No shit," Virginia replied, rolling her eyes. "You think I don't know that? It was hardly my intention to wind up back in this precinct, but you know Arthur, he gets what he wants."

"Please, as though you didn't jump at the chance to get your fingers back into these kinds of cases. Look at you, it's almost midnight now, and you're standing here at my door telling me about some inferno witch." Lindell shook her head, pushing away the notepad. "You've been desperate to get back into the precinct ever since you were dismissed. It's embarrassing, Virginia."

"What's embarrassing is you taking orders from the sheriff's wife to keep tabs on me."

"Excuse me?"

"Please, I'm not a rookie fresh on the force, Shirin. You were tailing me that night, it was you who put the parking ticket on my windshield. Clever, actually, to use that to cover your tracks. It's just too bad they weren't quite covered enough." The wood of the chair's armrests was fractured and split under her fingers, promising a splinter.

Lindell glared, and then sighed, turning to stare out the window at Verdance's nightscape, barely visible beyond the glass. "I wasn't taking orders from Mona. I was just doing my *job*, Virginia. You're some ex-cop who got thrown off the force for corruption charges and a failure in the line of duty and I'm *not* supposed to follow up on that?"

"Are you interested in finding this inferno witch, or not?" Virginia demanded.

"I'll send a squad unit to check things out," Lindell offered. "That's the best I can do."

"That's it?"

"What would you have me do? Mobilize the entire force to look for a kid you think *might* be a witch? Is that really a good use of our time?"

"I don't know what to tell you, Shirin. If you want to find Fiske, you need to be proactive, not sit here on your ass, in your office, hoping I deliver him to you on a silver platter."

"A silver platter?" Lindell repeated, her graveled whiskey voice drawing out the second word. "Is that what you think I'm hoping for?"

"Sure as hell seems like it," Virginia shot back. The entire interaction had her craving another cigarette, and it had only been about twenty minutes since she'd finished the last one on the drive over.

Lindell drummed her fingertips against the wood of the desk, a pulsating, driving rhythm. "I need you to tell me exactly what happened fifteen years ago. Convince me you're not playing both sides on this, and maybe I won't toss you out on your ass the first chance I get."

Virginia shrugged, despite the tension growing between her shoulder blades. Lindell had no right to pry, and yet, she was the one holding all the cards. "You read the file," Virginia said evenly. "You know what happened."

"We both know there's plenty that doesn't show up in the official reports," Lindell replied.

"Ask Arthur, if you're so curious. I'd love to see how that goes for you." There was a growing, insistent apprehension that Virginia never should have gone to the precinct in the first place, and no amount of trying to swallow it back down was working.

"I was surprised to hear you'd been married," Lindell said. "You don't seem like the marrying kind."

Virginia blew a breath out of her nose, almost a laugh. "I guess I wasn't. If you want to know the real story..." She sighed. "You'll have to ask Arthur." The reality of it was that she had no desire to recount the whole messy thing, and if Lindell wanted to excavate the past, Virginia wanted no part of it.

"I can't say this assuages all my concerns."

"No, I wouldn't expect it to. I wouldn't let it go either, if I was sitting where you are."

Lindell nodded, at least somewhat satisfied with the explanation. She slid the notepad back to the center of her desk, poised above the page with the dull end of a used pencil. "So, this Fiske guy. Any thoughts?"

"Listen, Lindell, I am trusting you to not fuck this up."

"How nice of you to say that. Twenty years on the force, and you're trusting me to do my job."

"I'm serious, Shirin, if you bust in there with a full squad, you're going to drive this all further underground," Virginia warned.

"So what would you have me do? Ignore a tip like this? Let the Sphinx keep doling out Nether to whoever asks for a hit?" The captain pointed across the desk. "That's corruption. That's not going to happen. Just because you want to protect your girlfriend—"

Virginia barked out a laugh. "My *girlfriend?*"

"Was there *another* reason you spent all night at the club?"

"If you'd bothered to do even a single shred of prep work for this, Shirin, you'd know that prior to that night, I hadn't seen Astrid in over four years." Virginia shoved her hands into her pockets, eager to clench her fingernails into her palm, anything to distract her from the slow, precise extraction of secrets she would have preferred remained hidden. "This isn't about Astrid. Once we get Fiske, you can do whatever you want with the Sphinx."

"Is that so?"

"Yes, that's so."

The captain tilted her chin before opening a drawer, laying a file flat on the desk. "You've protected her before, Virginia."

"Not intentionally."

"You seem to have a habit of throwing yourself to the wolves," Lindell said.

"She tried to frame me, it wasn't altruistic," Virginia replied. "Listen, I am telling you that if you want Fiske, if you want to really disrupt this shit in a meaningful way, you have to aim for the big fish. To get him, you're going to need cooperation, which you won't get if you charge in there." Virginia flexed her fingers, still stiff from the cold walk to the station. "Astrid has a lot of contacts, and more money than you or I will ever see in this lifetime. Set her in your sights if you want, but she has an army of lawyers and battalions of flunkies ready to take the fall for her even if you do manage to pin something on her."

"Flunkies like you?" Lindell asked again, setting the scalpel to Virginia's past once more. "Why were you at the Sphinx?"

"Because I needed information."

"Information you neglected to share with us, despite being a consultant for the VCPD."

"The cases at the time were unrelated," Virginia explained.

Lindell leaned across the desk. "And now?"

"I'm telling you everything I know. This kid, this witch? She might match the hairs we found at the scene of Benjamin's death."

"If we bring her in—"

"If we bring her in, the feds are going to be on top of this department like flies on shit," Virginia said. "Inferno witches are rare, and they're going to want her. I know that you don't want them crawling up your ass and getting involved in your cases, so that's why I am telling you, this has to be done quietly."

"That's not protocol."

"It's your decision, Lindell. You can go along with protocol, let the feds stampede all over you and everyone else here, probably messing up cases left, right and center, or..." Virginia shrugged, an eyebrow raised. "Or, you can say *fuck* protocol, and try to get this case solved."

"You are a dangerously persuasive woman, Virginia."

Virginia shrugged. "I'm just trying to save you some trouble."

"Bullshit. You're trying to save *yourself* some trouble," Lindell corrected.

Virginia shoved her hands back into her coat pockets again, the flickering light overhead sending strange shadows to jump across the desk in an odd dance. "More corruption with the feds than you'll ever see here at headquarters, and that part isn't in the file."

The captain rolled her sleeves back down, buttoning the cuff links at her wrist, the silver shining. "I'll give you a lift to the library, we can take a look around." Lindell stood, smoothing her uniform. "Virginia," she began, looking down at her, "if you ever speak to me like that again, especially in front of other members of this force, there will be no coming back from that."

Virginia didn't respond, she couldn't, not with all the rage bubbling up in her throat. She gave her a curt nod and rose from the chair, following her out the door.

"Detective Moer, I'm leaving the station. Call my unit if anything goes wrong."

"Yes, Captain," the officer said, nodding. He looked young, but then, half the force was looking young to Virginia lately, an unfortunate side effect of the inescapable passage of time. "Will you be returning to the station tonight?"

"It depends."

"On what, ma'am?"

"On whether Ms. Vane can follow instructions."

Virginia bit down on her tongue until a thick, stomach-turning coating of iron laden blood flooded into her mouth. She was already regretting involving Lindell. The captain had the high ground there, and she knew it, and she was going to use it to her full advantage to get back at Virginia for embarrassing her in front of half the force.

She couldn't blame her, really.

Still, the anger bubbled just beneath the surface, hissing between Virginia's teeth with every beleaguered exhalation.

In the stairwell, Lindell turned to face her. "Relax, Vane. I can feel the tension from all the way over here."

Virginia huffed, gripping the banister. "I'll relax when we find that inferno witch." The stairs were an irritating familiarity beneath her boots, every creak expected. "The sooner this is over with, the better."

"So, Astrid," Lindell began again. "She's a siren?"

"Yes." Virginia followed her through the emergency exit door to the rear of the building. "How did you find out?"

"I had my suspicions for a while. Reports of people losing everything they had just to go to the Sphinx every night. It's not illegal, outside the Nether, so there's not much we can do," Lindell replied. "I'm sure plenty of them can figure out what she is."

"Have you ever seen her perform?"

"No."

Virginia smirked. "You should, she's damn good."

The captain thrust the key into the ignition, shooting Virginia a smirk. "Some of us have the good sense to not get tangled up with sirens."

"I didn't know she was a siren until later," Virginia lied. In truth, she'd known what Astrid was the moment she'd opened her mouth to sing. Sirens were rare, but not extinct by any means. "And, for the record, her band is decent. Probably one of the best in the city."

"Money can buy many things, including a crew of skilled musicians."

"She's buying their loyalty most of all, not their ability to sink a clean arpeggio."

Lindell flipped the switch on the radio, which began to utter dispatch calls for the city. "Quiet night."

"Nah. The real juicy calls are the ones that never make it to dispatch," Virginia replied.

Captain Lindell stopped at a light, glancing over at her. "None of them have a bad word to say about you, in case you were wondering." The captain eased the car into gear again, the late night streets clear and quiet. "You still command a respect there."

Virginia shifted uncomfortably in her seat. "And yet I get paired with you, the one captain who thinks I'm trying to run a Nether ring by myself."

"I don't think that," Lindell said evenly. "I find your reluctance to share information deeply irritating, Virginia, but I don't think that you're a criminal mastermind."

Virginia gave her a dry laugh. "You were ready to toss me into interrogation a few days ago."

"I was frustrated."

"Oh, good. Every time you have a bad day at work, I can expect you to show up at my house with cuffs."

Captain Lindell coughed loudly, watching the sparse traffic. "I would at least take you to dinner before that, Virginia."

"On the left," Virginia replied, turning her face to the window to hide the flush crawling across her face. "This kid might be long gone by now."

"Alright, we'll have to force entry," Lindell said. "Since neither of us has a key."

"Zin isn't going to like that either, but I'll smooth it over."

Lindell shot her a look. "You have history with her, too, I take it?"

"Yes, one peppered with several hundred books and a shared enthusiasm for rare copies. Get your head out of the gutter, Shirin." Virginia stepped out of the car, moving to the gate with a lock pick.

"What, you're a cat burglar now, too?"

"No, but it's one less thing to replace than if you cut the padlock off, Captain." The chain fell free, and Virginia turned back to her with a smug smile. "See?"

"Get on with it then," Captain Lindell said, nodding towards the front door, imposing, intricately carved with hundreds of delicate vines and their reaching leaves, grasping for sun they would never feel.

Virginia popped the deadbolt, pushing the door open to reveal the dark library. "If that kid is in here, she'll be on the second floor. There's a tree with several strong limbs that lead to the windows, and those locks aren't very sturdy." She flicked her hand with a casual gesture towards the tall oak. "Sometimes you just really need a book in the middle of the night." Virginia shot her a smirk before ascending the grand staircase, the wide, polished ebony shining in the moonlight that cascaded through the second floor windows that extended up to the ceiling. "The windows I mentioned are on the east side of the building."

"The reference section?"

"That's the one."

Lindell nodded. "You take left, I'll take right."

"No, I'll take right. There's an extra shelf on that side towards the back you might miss." Virginia crossed in front of her, crouching behind a shelf. "Kid, I know you'll have heard us break in here. Just come on out and let's talk."

She moved from one shelf to the next, hunting for any movement that wasn't Lindell on the other side of the room. Virginia frowned. "She's not in here."

"Well where the hell did she go, then?"

As Virginia turned back towards the door, there was a crash on the first floor, followed by the sound of a roaring fire. "Shit," she muttered, already heading for the stairs.

"You didn't check the back entrance first?" the captain accused, following close behind. "That's rookie crap!"

"There isn't a back entrance," Virginia shot back, vaulting over the banister as she neared the bottom. There was a steaming, smoking hole in the back of the building. "Shadows," she swore. "Zin is going to fucking kill me."

Chapter Twenty

Virginia leaned against the imposing oak tree, waiting for Zin to be done chewing her out. She deserved it, so she waited, the red and blue lights of the squad units casting an eerie glow across the library's entrance.

"And do you have any idea what that smoke damage could have done?" Zin demanded, pushing a stray blond hair out of her face, her eyes still filled with accusation, and, to Virginia's horror, disappointment.

"I didn't know she was going to blast a hole in the wall."

"You were chasing an inferno witch through my library!"

"I'm sorry, Zin."

"Sorry," Zin repeated with a loud scoff. "*Sorry* doesn't cut it, Vane. What in shadows did you think was going to happen?" Zin's arms were folded over her chest, her lips pressed into a thin line. It almost made her look younger than she already was. "Why didn't you call me?"

"It was the middle of the night."

"And?" Zin demanded. "You've dragged my ass out of bed for reference materials at three in the morning, you think I wouldn't want to know there was an inferno witch running rampant?"

"How much was damaged?"

"You mean, other than the huge hole in the side of the building?" The librarian sighed, her resolve finally softening after fifteen minutes of scolding. "The damage to books is minimal."

"Are you two done, or can we get a move on?" Captain Lindell asked, propped against the hood of her squad unit, illuminated in the oscillating lights, the flickering highlighting the sharpness of her cheekbones.

"Is the VCPD going to pay for these damages?" Zin asked, an eyebrow raised.

"I don't know, do I look like the budgetary committee?" Lindell asked with a laugh, waving her away. "File the paperwork."

"And do what, have an enormous hole in the library in the meantime?"

"You'll have to pin her down with that paperwork," Virginia said, enjoying the shift in power. She'd grown tired of Lindell's lectures. "Captain Lindell doesn't have much affinity for reading."

"I can still hear you, you know," the captain said.

Virginia threw her an overly enthusiastic smile. "I'm aware." She rubbed her hands together before shoving them deep in her pockets. "If you need anything, Zin, you know where to find me."

"Thanks, Vane." Zin gave her a suspicious glare. "That book you have is almost overdue."

"I know, don't worry."

"I know how you are, you conveniently forget, and then I'm left cleaning up the mess that is the holds list."

"Oh, yeah? How many people are on the list for this one?"

"One."

Virginia tilted her head. "Really?"

"Yes, really."

"I didn't think many even knew it existed, much less that you managed to unearth a copy of it."

Zin sighed heavily. "It doesn't matter who they are or why they want it, Vane, just make sure it's back on time. Tick-tock, alright?"

"Yeah. Tick-tock."

"Vane, we have work to do. Let's go," Lindell said, checking her watch.

"Duty calls," Virginia said, giving Zin a nod as she pushed off the oak tree and trudged through the iced-over snow, the cold seeping through her thick boots and settling deep in her bones.

"We need to find that kid, or we're going to start having problems, and fast," Lindell said under her breath.

"Yeah, no shit, Shirin. I did mention that last night, if you recall."

"I'll admit I didn't quite believe you, at first."

"What changed your mind? The giant, smoldering hole in the back of the library? The plumes of smoke that were all but blocking out the moon? What?"

"Yes," Lindell said carefully, climbing into the car. "That did settle my mind, on some scores."

"Did you call Arthur?"

"He's aware."

"And?"

"And what?" Lindell asked, setting her cap on the dashboard.

Virginia sighed, slamming the passenger door as she slid into the seat. "And what did he *say*, Shirin?"

"He wants us to find this inferno witch and bring her in as soon as possible," Lindell replied. "He's concerned that if there is another incident, the press will grab hold of it. And if the press gets hold of it, that kid is as good as dead. No doubt she's who they've been looking for."

Virginia nodded. "True. Zin will keep her mouth shut, assuming she gets the funding she needs to get repairs done quickly, but there's no telling what someone else might say to a reporter."

"Does Zin usually cover things up for you?"

"For *me*? Try for *us*, Shirin, you were there too."

"I meant previously."

"Nothing Arthur doesn't already know about," Virginia answered.

Captain Lindell's jaw flexed.

Virginia sighed. "It had nothing to do with that. Small things. Reference materials. Checkout logs, that sort of thing."

"You seemed pretty cozy with her."

"What is your problem?" Virginia demanded, ready to throw herself out of the moving vehicle in order to save herself from the imposition of the captain's questions. "You've been nothing but hostile to me about my personal life since we met, and to be frank with you, it's grating on my nerves."

"Personal relationships can obscure investigations."

"My only relationship with Zin is that of a librarian and a shitty investigator who sometimes needs a little extra help tracking down information."

"I disagree," Shirin said with a shrug.

Virginia scoffed, choking on the noise in her throat. "You *disagree?*"

"That you're a shitty investigator. You're quite good, actually."

"Great."

"She's cute, Virginia."

"Yeah, and nearly twenty years younger than me."

The captain shrugged. "So?"

"So she's too nice. Too fragile. This damned city hasn't completely decimated her hope quite yet." Virginia sighed, bracing her head against the cold glass of the window. "Not my type. Not interested."

"Who *is* your type?"

"I'm not having this conversation with you."

"Why not? We're trying to be friendly, aren't we?"

"Okay, who's your type then, Shirin? Let's start with you," Virginia shot back, desperate for the conversation to end.

Captain Lindell drummed her fingers against the steering wheel. "I don't have a type."

"Cheap answer."

The dispatch radio crackled noisily. "Squad unit twelve, what is your location?"

"Downtown, leaving the library," Lindell answered.

"Sheriff needs to see you—both of you—as soon as possible," the radio replied with a static crunch.

"Headquarters?"

"No, he's at the lakefront. Be... advised."

The captain placed the radio back in its clip, looking over at Virginia. "I assume I don't need to explain what that means."

"No. For one, it means we're in trouble, and for another, they've found another body and they don't want the garbage-starved rat press who hunt for stories on this frequency to know."

"Aren't you also a garbage-starved rat who hunts for stories on this frequency?" Lindell asked, pulling a u-turn in the middle of the road to head back towards the lake.

"For cases, not for articles," Virginia shot back. "You wouldn't catch me dead writing for the papers."

* * *

Arthur sighed, pressing two fingers to his temple. "And here I thought I was going to have to throw you both in a cell for a day to work things out. Instead, you were up the entire night chasing after inferno witches and setting fire to the public library."

"It wasn't us who set the fire," Virginia explained, a hand resting casually on her hip. "That was the inferno witch."

"Regardless, in light of the recent press attention, I think it would be best to avoid garnering further inquiry, don't you?"

She shrugged. "Didn't you already say you want us to track the kid down?"

"How do you know it's a kid?"

"I saw her. Slight little thing."

"Regardless," Arthur pivoted, wilting at Virginia's glare. "We've uncovered another body down at the shoreline."

"Identifiable?" Lindell asked, taking off her cap and holding it under her arm.

"Perhaps, if we can find next of kin. It hasn't been too long," Arthur said. "Coroner says two days, maybe, and the water's temperature slowed decomposition."

"Mythic?" Virginia asked. "Shifter?"

"Unfortunately." Arthur cast a skeptical eye at the police boundary and sighed. "We won't be able to keep this from the press for long. No doubt some of them are already on their way here."

Virginia frowned, pulling her coat tight around her, trying to block out the incessant chill from the lake's wind. "Age?"

"Mid-thirties, maybe. He had a wallet on him, but it was mostly empty except for an old photograph and a matchbook."

"From where?" Lindell asked, leaning forward.

"You don't know it was from the Sphinx," Virginia countered, knowing where she was going with that line of thinking. "It could be from anywhere. Verdance is a big place. Lots of clubs."

"Impossible to tell," Arthur said. "Too much water damage."

"I'm sure we could tell where it's from, Sheriff, maybe a fleck of ink, or—"

"He said it's impossible," Virginia interrupted. "So how about we focus our energies elsewhere?"

"Trying to protect your girlfriend again?" Lindell challenged, squaring her shoulders with an infuriatingly well-sculpted eyebrow raised in defiance.

Arthur shook his head, blinking rapidly. "Girlfriend? Ginnie? You have a girlfriend at the Sphinx?"

"Ex," Virginia supplied.

"You didn't mention that."

"Why would I? It was years ago."

"She's still creeping around there, though," Lindell said. "Or did you leave that part out, too?"

"That depends, did you leave the part out where you've been tailing me because Arthur's wife asked you to?"

"That's not fair, Virginia, you know that—"

"Enough!" Arthur shouted, loud enough to draw the attention of the photographers at the shore line. "I'm starting to rethink my position on locking you two in a cell together. Although, given my apparent misfortune, I fear one of you would kill the other." He glanced at Virginia, and she smirked in response, knowing it would irritate him. He frowned, holding her stare for a long moment, long enough for another lake wind to curl around their ankles. "Lindell, we're going to discuss this later. Ginnie..." he trailed off with a heavy sigh. "I know you'll hate me for it, but we will need to debrief on your... er... more intimate encounters."

Virginia threw her head back with a single, sharp burst of laughter. "Absolutely the fuck not."

"I don't mean details, I just need to know where any conflicts of interest may lie," he explained.

"No," Virginia repeated. "Anyway, you know now. I used to hang around Astrid Frost, owner of the Sphinx. It was for about nine months, four years back. She tried to frame me, it didn't work."

"I am going to regret this," Arthur grumbled. "I'm *already* regretting this."

"I'm going down to the shore line," Virginia announced, walking off before either of them could argue with her. Both of them were far out of line, demanding details about her personal life. It's not as though Astrid was the one ordering hits on shifters. She was a jazz singer and a hell of a business woman—maybe too good—but she wasn't a murderer.

"Move," she said to the man standing in her way as she approached the corpse.

The photographer leaped out of her way, standing a foot further to take the picture. The morning was cloudy and grey, the haze of the night's fog still lingering above the water with no unimpeded sun to burn it off. "Did you get everything you need?" she asked, looking up at him from her crouched position.

"Yes," he said, taking another snap of the man's hand. "Hell of a week, eh?"

"Hell of a week," she repeated. "Anything off about this one?"

"We'll have to wait for the coroner's report, but looks pretty obvious to me. No defensive wounds, no gunshots, no stab marks."

"Nether?"

"Probably. Won't know for sure until they open him up."

Virginia nodded. "Overdose?"

"If I had to guess." The photographer pulled out a cloth, cleaning the lens of the camera and squinting out over the water. "Too many, these days."

"You've got that right." She tilted her head, examining the position. "Did anyone move the body?"

"Not that I know of."

"He's face down."

"Yeah, that's how he was when we showed up."

A sick feeling in the pit of her stomach was starting to grow, shooting tendrils of unease to root in her veins and choke her lungs. "Was anything else found with him? Other than this empty wallet with the photo and the matchbook?"

"Waterlogged revolver. No identifiers, mass produced." He squinted at her. "You new on the force?"

Virginia flinched. He was young, probably in his mid-twenties. He wouldn't know who she was, or what had happened. "No."

"I don't know why anyone touches that stuff," he scoffed, putting his camera back in its bag. "Nether. All it ever does is ruin lives."

"Yeah, get back to me when your life is already ruined, and let me know how that goes for you."

"You've tried it?"

She blinked, taken aback by the earnestness of his tone. "No," she lied. "Never."

"Oh." He buckled the latch on his bag, standing upright. "Well, I'm sure I'll see you around."

"Likewise."

"Ginnie," Arthur said, his gait unsteady on the rocky sand. "Find anything?"

"Nothing anyone else hadn't already," she replied. "When are they coming to pick up the body?"

"Now. We want to get clear as soon as we can."

She nodded. "Good."

"What's the deal with you and Captain Lindell?" Arthur sucked his teeth, watching the road for signs that the press had descended on the scene. "I'd hoped you two would work well together."

"Hope doesn't do any of us any good, Arthur. Not in Verdance."

He crouched to match her stance, his coat dragging in the damp sand. "We need to get this figured out. I just got back, haven't even moved into my office yet, much less my house, and already we've got shifters piling up in the morgue."

"It's good to see some things never change," she said, bitterly.

He blinked. "What's that supposed to mean?"

"You're more concerned with optics," she said coolly, waving her hand. "It's just how you are. It's why you're the sheriff, and I got tossed out on my ass." She stood, grimacing at the scrape of sand inside her sock. "I hate the beach."

"Some things about you never change, either."

"It's cold, I'm freezing my ass off, and there's enough sand inside my boot to backfill several lots. No, I haven't grown to like beaches."

Two medics came down the embankment with a stretcher, preparing to load the body up into an ambulance to take to the morgue. Arthur waved them through, stepping out of the way. "Anything else before we let them move the body?"

Virginia shook her head. "No."

They turned him over, and she squeezed her eyes shut. "Shadows," she swore.

"Friend of yours?" Lindell asked, already behind her.

"No. An open case. Gambling. Loan sharks were looking for him."

"Sounds pretty open and shut to me," Lindell said, watching as the medics carted him away. "Sharks aren't known for their patience and generosity."

"He was still a shifter," Virginia said. "I'm betting he got in over his head, went to Fiske for some extra cash."

"Why would Fiske be killing off enforcers?" Arthur asked. "That doesn't make much sense."

"Nether," Virginia answered. "It's making them too powerful, too much of a challenge to control."

Captain Lindell glanced up at the gathering reporters with a frown, turning to block their view of the body. "Or it's about that money we scraped up at the last scene. If Nether and money went missing, there's no telling what they'd do."

"I want you two on this until there's a break," Arthur said.

Virginia snorted back a laugh. "Yeah, okay, *Sheriff,* I'm pretty sure we already had a conversation about how the VCPD wouldn't be monopolizing my time and energy, consultancy or no."

"If Ms. Vane isn't up to the challenge, I'm sure Detective Moer will be," the captain said, shooting her a smirk. "He's far more versed in the intricacies of these kinds of cases."

"Piss off, Lindell, you're just trying to get under my skin."

"Is it working?"

Arthur pulled at the hems of his coat cuffs, his eyes squeezed shut. "Ginnie, for once in your life, can you please try to tone down the overt hostility?"

"*Me?* I'm not the one—"

"Ginnie."

She huffed out a breath, the angry cloud dissipating into the air. "Fine."

"We need to find the connection between these bodies," he said firmly. "That is the priority for Verdance City right now."

"What about the inferno witch?" Lindell asked.

"Back burner," he said. "Important, yes, but... we need to get a lid on whatever this is, and fast. There's no telling how long before someone calls the press before they call us. Especially when the press are handing out bribes and finder's fees like candy."

"With respect, Sheriff, I think tracking down this inferno witch should take precedence. If what Virginia says is true, then—"

"*If?*" Virginia spat.

Lindell ignored her. "If what Vane says is true, then it could be an opportunity to see what's happening at the beginning of this funnel of exploitation, and in my experience that's the best way to stop this from happening again."

"Captain Lindell, if I want your opinion, I'll ask for it." Arthur's tone was harsh now, with an edge Virginia hadn't heard in fifteen years. "Find Fiske, or whoever the hell it is doing this. Don't enter my office until you have some real answers."

Chapter Twenty-One

Virginia leaned her shoulder into the door of the cafe, letting loose a relieved sigh at the burst of warm air that fell from within. It was her usual haunt, quiet that time of day, private enough, and usually, no one bothered her. The only interlopers were the cases of pinned butterflies, splashes of bright blues and oranges against the backdrop of the charcoal-colored walls. "Morning," she mumbled, sliding into the booth.

Shirin glanced up from the menu she was perusing, her tousled hair falling into her eyes. Her uniform was pristine and freshly pressed, the blouse under her jacket peeking out only with the flash of a bleached collar. "Good morning. You're early."

"I didn't want to provide you with any more ammunition to shoot me with."

The captain nodded thoughtfully, as if she hadn't really heard what Virginia had said. "It seems we have some business to discuss," she said, taking a sip of the room temperature tap water that filled a water-stained glass on the table.

Virginia unbuttoned her coat, grateful for the cafe's warmth compared to the icy wind outside, blowing a small whirlwind of garbage down the street as several cars passed. "Another riveting interrogation about what I do in my free time, I'm guessing?"

"No. I think we need to find that inferno witch before someone else does," Shirin said. "How is the coffee here?"

"The coffee is excellent," Virginia answered. "Going behind Arthur's back is a bold move, especially for you."

"It's not going behind his back, it's... delegating."

Virginia gave her a bemused smirk. "Delegating."

"If you find her when you're not working on VCPD consulting cases..." Lindell shrugged, flashing a smile. "What can he really say, then?"

"He's going to know."

Shirin shrugged easily, as though they weren't discussing things that would get them both fired. "Of course he will but at that point, who will care?"

"Arthur will."

"You underestimate yourself, Virginia. I bet you could burn that precinct to the ground, and he wouldn't say a word." Shirin waved at the owner, a tall, lanky woman with delicate tattoos that sat on either side of her throat. "He feels guilty."

Virginia laughed. "Good. He should."

"Use it. Find this girl, bring her in. We'll keep her protected, shielded from this Fiske person."

"And then dump her into the Feds' lap?"

"I will do my level best to... lose some paperwork." Lindell opened her hands, a questioning gesture. "Is that good enough?"

"I guess it will have to be." Virginia leaned back against the cracked vinyl upholstery, loosening her jade green tie. "Hey, Eden. Fresh pot?"

"For you? Always," Eden answered, taking a short, stubby pencil from her unkempt updo, tendrils of hair spilling out over the top of a brightly patterned scarf. "And you? What can I get you?"

"Whatever Ms. Vane's usual is," Shirin answered, flashing Eden a winning smile. "This place comes highly recommended."

"It better, she's in here at least three times a week." Eden leaned against the edge of the booth, scribbling notes onto an order pad. "Vee, we've got the regular and the almond today. What's your poison?"

"Almond," Virginia answered. "Two, I suppose."

"Coming right up," Eden replied with a casual wave, and disappeared into the back.

"We've got no leads there, Shirin," Virginia continued. "Unless the kid shows up in that alley again, or burns another hole in the library—"

Lindell slid a report across the desk. "The fire marshal sent this over about an hour ago. Magical supplies shop, burned to shadows and back."

"Could be her," Virginia said, scanning the page. "If it's not her, then it's an accomplished arsonist. Did you go out there yet?"

"No, I can't," Shirin answered, shaking her head. "Not with the sheriff watching me like a hawk to make sure I'm focusing on this other shit."

Virginia nodded. "I can head over there, scope things out. Is this fire marshal going to give me any push back?"

"He might. Ignore him. He's..." Lindell waved her hand in the air, searching for a word. "He's a slimy bastard."

"Understood," Virginia confirmed. There were all too many of those in Verdance, and it seemed like most of them were in positions of power. Of all the things in the city that had changed, that aspect had only gotten worse since she left the force.

Shirin tugged at her cuffs nervously, picking at the silver links as she stared out the broad window into the mid-morning grey sunlight of winter. "Virginia—Ms. Vane, I—"

The cafe's door jingled, and of course, there was Arthur, looking as pissed off as he did cold. "I thought I'd made myself clear that you two were to work on the case at hand," he accused, just as Eden set down two steaming mugs of fresh coffee on the table. He sighed, rubbing his head. "I'm almost surprised to see you haven't killed each other yet."

"Give it time, Arthur, the day is still young," Virginia said, her hands braced on her knees as she inhaled the rich scent emanating from the mug.

"If we could tone down the outright violence today, Ginnie, that would be appreciated." He rubbed his hands together, breathing into them for warmth. "It's a cold one out there today."

"Was there something you needed, Sheriff?" Lindell asked.

"I was just making sure you two were following orders." He glanced at Virginia as he slid into the booth next to Captain Lindell, his coat still pulled tightly around him, and belted at the waist. "I'm not surprised that I found you here."

"Old habits die hard," Virginia replied, waving at Eden for another coffee. "You never liked this place."

"I prefer to work at my desk, not at a table covered in sticky residue." He ran his fingers over the wood, frowning at the deep scratches in the surface. "I came to make sure you weren't going behind my back, Ginnie."

"I only just got here, Arthur, you'll need to give me at least ten minutes to get up to speed on things," she replied, holding her hands eagerly around the mug, absorbing the heat through the worn black ceramic, glazed to match the dark decor.

He raised an eyebrow. "Has there been a new development?"

"Not as such," Lindell answered, sliding the report into her briefcase. "I just thought that Ms. Vane and I should discuss an appropriate plan of attack where all this is concerned."

"I think the best place to start would be the coroner's reports," he said, pulling several envelopes from his inside pocket and dropping them onto the desk. "They are illuminating, even if they are what we had all suspected from the beginning."

"Were you waiting for the right moment to theatrically produce those?" Virginia asked. "Or did you forget that they were already in your pocket?"

He ignored her, nodding at the envelopes. "Nether, all of them."

"Unsurprising," Lindell said, unfolding the reports one at a time. "It was clear when Virginia was attacked." She looked over the top of a page. "How are you feeling, anyway?"

"Fine," Virginia answered.

"Seems awfully soon to—"

"I said, I'm fine. What else is in those reports? Was the seer from the park on Nether, too?"

Lindell nodded. "Autopsy showed her heart couldn't handle it."

Virginia shook her head, frowning at the report. "We need to get this stuff off the street." She flipped through the pages one at a time, looking for anything that could be an inconsistency. "What about Benjamin?" Virginia asked. "We know from the way that place was smashed up that he didn't die from an overdose."

Lindell handed her the report. "Blunt trauma."

"I guess that much makes sense. What about the other one, from the lakefront?"

"Nether."

"And the quarry?"

"Nether again."

Virginia huffed. "Something isn't adding up here Arthur, and you know it."

He accepted a mug of coffee from Eden, sniffing at it suspiciously before taking a noisy sip. "If you can find Fiske, we can disrupt the distribution long enough to get a handle on things," he said. "All of us know how bad things have gotten in recent years—"

Virginia snorted. "Lindell and I have been here in Verdance, where the hell were you?"

"Doing my job, which is all I'm asking the two of you to do," he shot back. "I know you have your issues with me, but I am asking, *professionally*, for you to cut the shit, Ginnie. I've had about enough, and I've barely been back a week. The sooner we can get this under control, the better things will be."

"For you," Virginia finished. "The better things will be for *you*."

"Two specials," Eden announced, returning for the third time, carrying two small black plates, each with a perfectly shaped crescent pastry, dusted with powdered sugar and slivered almonds. "Did you need another?"

"I'm not staying," Arthur replied.

Eden glanced at Virginia before topping up her coffee from the pot and vanishing behind the counter once more.

"And what is your suggestion?" Arthur continued, not willing to let it rest because he'd never let anything be, not for a single moment, and not throughout his entire career. "Allow Nether to fill the streets? For clubs like the Sphinx to be allowed to throw this stuff at anyone who stumbles through the door? For teenagers to be scooped up off the streets and pushed into running this stuff?"

"You'll never really get rid of it, Arthur," Virginia replied, blowing on the mug as the steam caressed her wind-chewed face.

"I can try."

"Your problems are with Fiske, fine. Lindell and I will find Fiske."

"Thank you," Arthur said, nodding. "Captain Lindell, you're on deck for the late shift tonight, remember. I have plans with Mona."

"Anything fun?" Lindell asked casually, taking a polite bite of the pastry.

Virginia inhaled, holding the air in her lungs until they burned. "Maybe I should just—"

"It's our anniversary. I've made reservations at the Saffron Rose."

"Saffron Rose?" Virginia asked, reeling but trying very hard not to care. "Really?"

"What?" Arthur asked, pushing his half-full mug across the table.

Virginia stared, wondering if he could feel the same heat that was singeing her cheeks. "The same place we had our—you know what, never mind."

"It's a nice restaurant!"

"Arthur, you swan back into Verdance with no notice, you ask me to consult, your wife asks Lindell to tail me, you're what, I don't know, trying to rub my face in this, or something?"

"No," he said carefully. "That is not my intention."

"I am happy for you," she said. She'd intended it to sound genuine, but it left her lips hostile and dripping with disdain. She tried again. "I am happy for you, Arthur. That you found someone who fits. We didn't, and that was clear from the start. I... well, I've found my own way now, and that's in the past, and that is where I would like it to stay."

"Okay."

"I mean it. If you want me consulting, no more of this." She turned her ire towards Lindell, who was halfway through her pastry. "And *you* need to stay the hell out of my personal life."

"I'm just being thorough, Virginia," Lindell replied through a mouthful of sweet dough and sugar.

"Great, you are more than welcome to be thorough in any other direction than mine. You want respect? Fine. But I'm due some as well, I think you will agree."

"Okay, Ginnie," Arthur relented.

Virginia bit into her pastry angrily, tearing off a wide piece and sending a fine dusting of sugar to whisper across the table. "Excellent. Good talk."

"I should get home, get some sleep before tonight," Lindell announced, draining her mug. "Virginia, I'll meet you at your apartment for consultations over the next week as discussed. Those two from the alley might be tailing you, so don't come to the precinct unless you have to."

"Get some sleep," Virginia replied as Shirin buttoned her coat. "You look like you need it.

The cafe filled with a gust of frigid wind as the door opened and then closed again, leaving Virginia and Arthur in the midst of an uncomfortable, pressing silence that she'd do almost anything to escape.

"Do you..." he trailed off, searching her face. "Do you have someone?"

"Arthur, for shadows' sakes—"

"I just... I worry. And Mona worries, and—"

Virginia pressed a hand to her forehead, the headache already pulsing behind her eye. The same ache that Arthur's bullshit had always wrought, ever since they were young. She took a long drink of her coffee, trying to keep from losing her patience with his incessant bullshit. "I can handle a lot of things, but Mona feeling sorry for me isn't one of them."

"You shouldn't let what happened keep you from being happy," Arthur said quietly. "I feel bad about what happened between us, and I don't want to see you miserable."

"Who says I am? Just because you were out on the east coast dancing on the grave of my career doesn't mean that I'm... I don't know, some kind of... actually you know what, there isn't anything wrong with being alone."

"No, perhaps not." He shrugged off his coat, laying it over the back of the booth, the deep navy of the wool almost black in the dim light. "I've known you nearly my entire life, Ginnie."

Obviously, he was preparing for an extended conversation, much to her dismay. She finished her pastry, savoring the final bite. It would probably be the only half-decent thing she ate all day. "Except the past fifteen years," she countered.

"It would be nice to make up for that. We were friends, once."

"Yeah, what a mess we made of that." Virginia trailed a fingertip through the leftover powdered sugar, letting it collect on her skin before she touched it to her tongue. "What a mess *you* made of that, I should say."

"You'd have left eventually, if I hadn't."

"Maybe."

He chuckled, leaning into the table, taking a stray slivered almond from the plate. "I could already see it in your eyes when you'd look at me. *Contempt.*"

"Contempt?"

"After it all happened," he explained. "I'd get up in the morning and you'd be sitting at the table like you wanted to ram a butter knife through my eye."

Virginia rattled the utensils on the table, still wrapped tightly in a napkin."I *did* want to ram a butter knife through your eye." She met his eyes for the first time since he got back to the city and sighed. "What's done is done, Arthur."

"Yes," he agreed. "What's done is done."

"I'll work with Lindell to find Fiske," Virginia said after a long, impossible moment. "After that, I'm done."

Chapter Twenty-Two

Virginia knew better than to walk in the front door of the burned out magical supplies shop, having taken Captain Lindell's advice. The fire marshal was still out there, shouting about only shadows knew what. He seemed like a real piece of work, and his face, red with rage, was supporting evidence.

Scraping her fingers through the loose ash pooled on the floor, she frowned. If it had been arson, an accelerant would have been obvious, but the scorch marks lining the walls were random, devoid of any kind of pattern, and lacking any trail between them. No wonder the marshal was pissed. To him, it wouldn't make any sense.

The inferno witch was powerful, that much was clear. Holes seared clean through layers of wallpaper and paint, through drywall, through support studs and through to the other side of the wall. Virginia stepped around the corner, peering in. A bathroom. So the fire had burned through thick plaster, too. Impressive. She caught her reflection in the singed mirror, almost surprising herself with how tired she looked. It was no wonder she looked beat down, not with Arthur back in town. There was a quiet, ignored part of her that still hated him for what he'd done.

Virginia ran her hands over the unburnt wallpaper in the living room, crouched to stay out of sight of the marshal. There had been a fight between the witch and someone else. Not a shifter, there was no evidence of claws, teeth, or fur. No evidence of other magic either. In fact, the shop felt strangely inert, devoid of magic entirely. She wasn't a witch, but magical areas had always felt charged to Virginia, like static electricity if it permeated through the air and solid objects alike.

She picked through the remains of several melted spell candles, the wax pooled on the singed carpet. A smashed scrying mirror, an overturned display of crystals, and several books burnt past recognition, their spines nothing more than crunchy charcoal. If Zin saw them, she'd be outraged.

The fight hadn't involved the shopkeeper. He'd been the one to report the fire that morning, early, when the ruins still smoldered even after the heavy dawn snowfall. What had a young inferno witch been doing in a supplies shop in the middle of the night?

Looking for something.

Virginia sat back on her haunches, scanning the path of the room. The witch had broken the window and unlocked the door. Aside from the shards glittering in the sky's grey light of day, there was no other damage at the front entrance. She hadn't come for a fight.

The bookshelf had been the first hit, judging by that. It was on its side, leaning against the stairs that led to the second floor of the shop. Virginia leaned in close, examining each title on the shelf, and finding nothing that made any sense. She glanced up the stairs, seeing no further damage. The fight hadn't lasted long, then. It made sense, given that no disturbances were reported in the area, according to Lindell.

She shifted the bookshelf gently, peering behind it, her fingers finding a wide bullet hole. An inferno witch versus, what, a non-mythic? Virginia frowned. Who in shadows would be foolish enough to take on an inferno witch, if not one of Fiske's enforcers? Even so, a revolver against some far more serious firepower was never going to end well. No body, though. No one had died, and if someone was injured, they'd left no trace of it.

Virginia had only met one other inferno witch before, and it had been decades ago, when she was fresh on the force. She was a serial arsonist, dangerous, setting fire to anything she could, and even her destruction was nothing compared to the damage in the shop. This witch might be young, might be small, but she was wielding some incredible power.

It would be almost impossible to hide her from the Feds, even if Lindell kept her word, which Virginia doubted that she would.

She backed out of the shop, stepping around the delicate dusting of snow, blown in from the outside, being careful to not leave anything that even looked like a footprint. Her truce with Arthur was shaky at best, and going behind his back to do exactly the thing he'd said not to was a great way to shoot it dead in the water.

Her sights fell on the overturned bookshelf once more. The witch was looking for a book. First the library, now the shop. It was the only logical explanation.

* * *

Virginia eased the library door open, the gust of icy air swirling around her face. The hole at the rear hadn't even been taped over yet.

"I was wondering when you were going to show up."

"Hey, Zin," Virginia offered, already sensing overt hostility from the librarian.

"Did that captain sign off on my petition yet?" Zin gestured towards the gaping fissure in the wall, her pin-straight, platinum hair swaying with the exaggerated motion. "Shockingly, the wall hasn't fixed itself."

"I don't know, I'd have to ask."

"What do you need?"

Virginia toyed with the book of matches in her pocket, even as she examined the passing scorch marks in the light of day. "I came by to ask if anything was stolen."

"Not to my knowledge. We've been thorough with inventory, but everything seems to be accounted for." Zin nodded towards a study room. "Let's talk in there. I don't want to disturb anyone."

"Are there many patrons here, when half the building is missing?"

"The need for a public library never stops, Vane." Zin closed the door behind them, sliding into the worn wooden chair with a soft creak. "Tell me what you're really looking for."

"There was an incident at one of the shops downtown."

Zin frowned at a book left behind, a page folded in the corner. "Oh?" she prompted, trying her best to flatten out the paper.

"I'm thinking this witch is looking for a book. First here, then the shop?"

"Could be coincidence."

"It's not." Virginia sat across from her, drumming her fingertips against the desk. "Can you think of anything an inferno witch might be looking for?"

Zin frowned, eyes closed in concentration. "We have a few books about inferno witches, but none of them were touched, not even close. They were on the other side of the library."

The dull white paint reflected the yellow light of the overhead lamp back at them, giving both an eerie, sickly pallor. Virginia sat across from her, still frozen from the short walk from the car. "I'm missing something, I can feel it."

"That's not like you."

Virginia blew out an exasperated sigh, tilting back onto the chair's back legs for just a moment. "It's more like me than you'd think."

"No, it's not. You'll figure it out. Shadows, I'll bet the useless drips up at VCPD haven't even figured the book part out yet."

"It's just me on this one."

Zin raised an eyebrow. "And why is that, when I have a hole the size of a small elephant in my library?"

"Priorities will always lie with murders." Virginia's gaze fell on the black paint of the wall, the corner chipped. "And I'm not exactly supposed to be working on this one."

"Now that sounds more like the Vane I know," Zin said, closing the book, finally satisfied with the work she'd done to uncrease it.

"The sheriff is... frustrating. We'll never get to the bottom of whatever this is if we don't figure out who was trying to snatch her in the first place and why."

"Any ideas?"

"Nether, probably." Virginia slid the book across the table before stacking it atop several others. "It's always Nether, these days."

"You'll find her," Zin replied. "You always get your person in the end."

"I don't know about that." Virginia picked at a chip in the desk, right next to some rather unsavory graffiti carved into the wood. "I lost two just a few days ago. One dead, one vanished and probably dead. Another one yesterday morning, found on the lakefront."

"Sounds like a busy week."

"It's been a while since I've worked a case like this," Virginia admitted. "I feel rusty."

"Virginia Vane is anything but rusty." Zin straightened the pins at her collars, matching silver ravens, both facing inward. "Here I am wandering through the stacks every day, and you're facing down killers and what, taking panther fang to the shoulder?"

"And where did you hear that?"

"Captain Lindell has a big mouth."

"Something I am learning," Virginia muttered. "I'm unclear how that came up in a conversation about the library, though."

Zin gave a delicate shrug. "I might have overheard her talking to the police sheriff."

"Overheard."

"I'm a librarian, Vane, part of my job is to overhear things."

"I'm not quite sure that's true, but alright, Zin." Virginia gestured to her shoulder. "Fought a shifter, got my ass kicked, saw a healer."

"There's a lot more story in there somewhere."

"Another time." Virginia stood, unnerved by Zin's curiosity. "I should get out of your hair."

"If you find out what book this witch is after, give me a call. Or stop by, whichever, and I'll see what I can do. Maybe we plan a sting operation."

"I'm not so sure she'd return to the scene of this crime, given what happened last time."

"What I can't figure out is why this witch wouldn't just come during the day. Why break in at night?"

Virginia leaned against the back of the chair, pressing her weight down into the wood and letting it creak under her weight. "She's being tailed, that's why. Night provides more cover, more safety. Easier to slip the net of whoever is trying to bag her.”

“What if I stayed late?”

“I’m not so sure that would help. She knows she’s in trouble if she’s breaking into shops now, too.”

“You’ll find her.”

“Yeah, let’s just hope I find her before someone else does.”

* * *

The newsstand was busy that time of the evening, and so Virginia waited as others crowded the counter, desperate to get home to their spouses, their lovers, their children. She waited because she didn’t have any of that. She’d grown used to the quiet, even reveled in it, the sweet silence after a day of nothing but Verdance’s unending, unrelenting cacophony. She craved the familiarity of the gentle sound of ice in a glass, of a struck match and a lit cigarette, of more takeout noodles and hours of deliberating old, abandoned cases.

“Ms. Vane,” said the newsstand owner, once the rush had cleared. “Always a pleasure.”

“Evening paper and three packs of my usual.”

“Three?” he asked, an unsettling note of concern to his voice that irritated her.

“It’s been a stressful week.”

“Stress is no good for you, Ms. Vane. Bad for the heart and bad for the brain.” He slid paper across the counter first, folded in half. “You seem like a woman who needs a vacation.”

“If I ever get to take one, you’ll be the first to know.”

“I’ll know if I don’t see you, eh?” He smiled, setting three packs of Charmed cigarettes atop the paper, the mint green band at the top indicating the menthol. “Don’t smoke too many at once, alright? I don’t restock until next week.”

"I'll try. No promises." She flipped him a few bills, taking her purchases. "And if you ever notice I haven't been around for a few days, you should probably just assume I'm dead. That's more likely than a vacation at this point."

He laughed, waving her off. "Good night, Ms. Vane." His glasses caught the glare of the street lamp, shining a flash of light.

She shoved the cigarettes into her coat pocket, unfolding the newspaper as she walked the now-deserted streets. No front-page article about the body found at the lakefront, at least. Arthur would be happy about that, even if he was the one who leaned hard on the press to keep it that way. No news about mythics at all, in fact, to such an extent that it was almost suspicious.

The newsprint was soft and smooth in her hands, bleeding ink on her fingers as she scanned the headlines, pressing the door open with her hip. "No news is good news," she muttered as she rounded the second floor. "What horseshit."

Tucking the paper under her arm, she unlocked the door. Something crashed inside, and in an instant, her hand was on her revolver, the newspaper dropped to the floor with a quiet flutter of pages filled with nonsense. She threw the door open, already leveling her gun, her hand braced against her wrist for more control.

"Come out, or I start shooting," she growled, pulling back the hammer. The crash was too loud to be that damned cat, and she was certain she'd locked the window before she'd left earlier.

The drapes tacked above the window waved gently with a deadly breeze. She took three silent steps towards them, keeping her eyes moving, roving over every spot in the apartment. Keeping her back to a wall at all times, she yanked at the drapes, pulling them down with a loud, distracting crash, but there was no one.

"I will not hesitate," she said, glancing beneath the sofa. "I will not hesitate, and in twenty minutes you'll be on the way to the morgue."

She turned, glancing over her shoulder to check the hallway, but as she did a sphere of flames flew right over her shoulder, close enough to singe a lock of hair at her shoulder. Virginia pivoted, firing in the direction it had come from, lodging a large forty-five caliber round in the wall. She squinted at the corner, bracing herself for the recoil of another shot.

"It's you," said a girl, still not visible to Virginia. "From the alley."

Virginia wavered, still holding the gun in position. "Come out."

"You're going to shoot me."

"I'm not going to shoot you." She holstered the revolver and held her hands up, the silver knuckles glinting in the light from the corridor. "What are you doing in my apartment?"

A young woman emerged from beneath the coffee table where she'd wedged herself. "I didn't know it was your apartment." Her stare flicked up over Virginia's shoulder. "Your wall is on fire. You might want to deal with that."

"Thanks very much for that," Virginia replied, patting it out with her coat, keeping her stare fixed on the young woman. "Do you make this sort of thing a habit?"

"No, I was—" she glanced around, nervous. "I was looking for something."

"Nether? You won't find any in here."

She wrinkled her nose. "No. That stuff makes me feel terrible."

"Money, then? That's similarly unavailable. If you're looking to rob places, I strongly suggest you try the north side. You won't find much down here."

"You said you weren't a cop." The young woman's arms hung at her sides, her fingers flexing and releasing in a rhythmic manner that suggested she might still be convinced to shoot more fire. "The other night, in the alley."

"I'm not."

"You shoot like a cop."

Virginia frowned. "No I don't. I'm a much better shot than a cop."

"You stand like one, then."

The wall still smoldered, the burnt plaster crunching with the dying embers. "What kind of trouble are you in that you're such an expert then?"

"Not hard to have run-ins with cops when you're from this side of the tracks."

"True enough," Virginia agreed. "But you still haven't told me why you're in my apartment."

"I told you, I was looking for something," the young woman repeated, her hair frizzy and unkempt, a fiery halo around her head.

"But you haven't said what for."

The young woman clasped her hands in front of her, fidgeting. "A book."

"A book?" Virginia glanced at the round table next to the sofa, which still featured the remains of the previous evening's cocktail, and the book Zin had already been harassing her about returning. "You're not an inferno witch, are you?"

"I don't know what I am," the young woman replied softly. "I was trying to find that out for myself."

"You think you're a fire demon?"

"I guess."

"How long?"

She chewed her lip. "How long?"

"How long have you had your powers?" Virginia asked. "Since birth?"

"I'm not sure. There were some strange occurrences when I was younger, but I didn't notice anything major until about six months ago." She looked at her hands, ashamed. "It's hard to control."

Virginia nodded slowly. "And those brutes in the alley, who are they to you?"

"I don't know who they are."

"Then why are they after you? Did you use your abilities somewhere they could see?"

"Not exactly." She looked up at the ceiling now, deliberately avoiding eye contact. She could be lying, or she could just be scared. "Are you going to call the cops?"

"Should I?" Virginia pressed, hand resting on the holster once again.

"I would rather you didn't."

"And I'd rather you hadn't just burned a hole in my kitchen wall, but we can't always get what we want, now can we?"

"What do we do now?"

Virginia looked from the phone to the young woman again. "This is new territory. I imagine if I move for that phone, you're going to try and crisp me like a roasted chicken again."

"If I run, you'll shoot me," the young woman replied.

"Probably."

"What do the cops want with me?"

"I think you were at a crime scene. Someone was killed, a shifter. Young, powerful, jumped on Nether." Virginia eased closer, shifting her weight against the creaking floorboards beneath her feet. "Know anything about that?"

"No."

"I'm willing to bet that the hairs we found there will match the ones growing out of your head."

"I didn't know him," the young woman protested. "I don't know any of them, I was just looking for an easy score."

"So you *are* casing places looking for Nether."

She balled her hands into fists. "No! I went there to destroy it."

Virginia nodded, watching the young woman closely. "A common story when someone gets picked up for distribution."

"I don't have it anymore. Those guys in the alley came looking for it, but I already dumped it all."

"Seems silly to dump something that could have paid rent for a year." Virginia raised an eyebrow at her. "Seems even more foolish to be messing with guys like Fiske."

"I don't know who that is."

"He's the one whose Nether you dumped," Virginia informed her. "Assuming that isn't a lie, anyway. You wouldn't be the first one to try for that kind of defense."

"I don't have it! I watched that drop location for weeks. I knew when it was getting delivered, I knew how long it would be in there more or less unguarded, I made my move, I left."

"Why not take the money?" Virginia asked, taking another step towards her. The kid had clearly been squatting somewhere, maybe an old ware-house by the looks of her. Cold, dirty, and desperate, all of it picking at the scab of an old wound.

The woman pulled at the ends of her bright ginger hair. "I got surprised."

"By?"

"Some shifter."

"So you killed him," Virginia finished.

"No! I didn't, I—I wouldn't. I ran. I don't know what happened once I left."

Virginia searched her face for a trace of a lie. "A likely story." She sighed, already hating where the evening was headed. "How old are you, anyway? Sixteen?"

"Eighteen."

"Eighteen," Virginia repeated. "Shadows." She rubbed the smooth silver of the knuckles against her temple, grateful for the frigid metal. The kid was barely done being a kid, being chased down in alleys and pulling off some damned heist out of what, misjudged altruism? "Old enough for a drink, then."

"You're offering me a drink?"

Virginia shrugged, keeping her stare fixed on the young woman. "Neither of us know how to proceed at this juncture, so in my estimation, it can't hurt."

"Are you going to poison it?"

"Do I look like a woman who keeps poison in the cupboard next to the porridge?"

She tilted her head. "Yes."

"Well, I don't. I prefer my methods to be a bit more direct than that." Keeping the young woman in her line of sight, Virginia poured two glasses of gin, sliding one across the counter. "It's there if you want it."

"I'm sorry that I broke in."

"You got my name and address from the library records," Virginia supplied. "That's how you wound up here."

She nodded. "It was the only copy I could track down."

"Next time, just ask Zin. If it can be found, she'll find it."

"I was afraid she would know what I am. What I might be, I guess." A cold gust blew through the open window, and the girl flinched. "Night is easier for me."

"Zin doesn't go around reporting mythics." Virginia took a sip, bracing her palm against the wood.

"Are you a mythic?" the girl asked.

"No."

Her brow furrowed, head tilted in confusion. "Oh."

"Did I give the impression that I am?"

"No, I guess not. You're definitely not a shifter, anyway."

"What gave it away? The gun?" Virginia asked, sipping at the gin. The coarse intimacy of the drink was enough to ground her, at least.

"Mostly the gun, yeah."

Virginia swirled the glass in her hand, creating a tiny storm inside it, the clear liquid surging to and fro, lapping at the rim. "This Fiske guy is responsible for a lot of bad shit lately. We're trying to track him down."

"We?"

"Me and my…" Virginia waved her hand in the air. "Me and my colleagues."

"Why?"

"Like I said, he's been up to no good, picking mythics up off the streets, pressing them into being distributors, enforcers, that kind of thing. Young ones mostly, but he'll take the odd desperate adult up to his eyeballs in loan shark debt."

"I saw the headlines in the papers the other day, about mythics turning up dead. Is that him?"

Virginia nodded. "I think so." She swirled the gin in her glass. "Maybe you can help me out, and maybe I don't have you tossed in a cell for breaking and entering."

"Okay," the girl said carefully, still standing on the balls of her feet like she'd run the moment she had the opportunity.

"I need to make a call."

The young woman flinched, already stepping back towards the window. "You're going to call the cops."

"Listen, kid, if we're both going to make it out of this without burns and bullet holes, you need to calm down. You're not going to get arrested, alright? I guarantee it." The young woman nodded, and Virginia reached for the phone, dialing the precinct.

"Lindell's desk," Virginia said.

The line paused. "She went home for the day."

"Reroute to her home, then. Tell her it's Vane."

"Just a moment, ma'am."

After a moment, two rings, three, and a fourth before she picked up, her voice even huskier than usual. "This is Shirin."

"It's me. I need you to come over."

"What? Why?"

Virginia watched the girl in the hallway, shivering and far too lean. She'd need blankets and some hot food. "For that thing we were talking about earlier."

"What did you find at the supplies shop?" Lindell asked, her voice husky like she'd been sleeping.

Virginia watched the young woman sink into the couch. "It's complicated. Just come to my apartment the way we discussed."

The line crackled with quiet static. "Is everything alright?" Shirin asked.

"Oh yeah, peachy. Come on, Shirin, quit fucking around. I need you."

"Alright, shadows, Virginia. I'll be right over."

"Bring food."

"What?"

"You'll understand when you get here." Virginia hung up, keeping her hand on the phone. "So."

"So," the young woman repeated.

"You know my name, but I don't know yours."

"Jolie Laar."

Virginia nodded. "And I'm going to guess you don't know much about me other than my name and my taste in reading material, or you wouldn't have broken into my apartment."

"No, I don't."

"Some free advice, kid, never wander into somewhere you don't know the full story. Things might have ended very differently tonight."

"What are you, some kind of mercenary?"

Virginia laughed. "Sure." She finished her gin, setting the glass back on the counter. "I guess you could say that."

"Why were you reading that book?"

"Research."

"For what?"

"I have some—" Virginia almost started to explain her cold cases, but stopped herself. "I have some interest in the area, that's all. Rare books fascinate me, especially ones like that."

"Have you ever met a fire demon?"

"No." Virginia leaned against the counter. "Not before tonight."

Chapter Twenty-Three

Captain Lindell arrived as promised, with a stack of takeout boxes, and mysteriously, a bottle of wine. "Alright, Vane, I'm here, but next time you could ask me to come over in a slightly less dramatic way."

"What's the wine for, Shirin?" Virginia asked, arching an eyebrow.

"You called me late, and asked me to come over," Shirin replied, twisting the bottle in her hands to show off the emerald green and gold label, a relatively rare vintage. "I thought a little lubrication might make strategizing easier."

Virginia pushed the door open further, revealing the girl on the couch. "I found our inferno witch. Except she's not an inferno witch at all, she's a fire demon."

"How did you catch her?"

"She broke into my apartment. Apparently I had the book she was looking for." Virginia glanced at the bottle of wine. "I'm more of a gin woman, by the way."

Captain Lindell looked different out of uniform, her thick wool coat brushing just past the curve of her hips, the slate grey mottled with tweed. She unbuttoned it, revealing a sharp button down shirt, a deep aubergine, tucked into black trousers.

Virginia took her coat and bolted the door. She leaned in, whispering. "I told her I wouldn't call the cops, so let me handle this." Her eyes roved across the captain. "You clean up good."

"I told you I'd come without uniform," Shirin replied, her voice low.

"How did you think I'd show up?"

"I hadn't thought about it."

"She's staring."

Virginia cleared her throat, hanging the coat on the hook. "This is Shirin, she's my... colleague," she announced. "Shirin, this is Jolie Laar."

"She looks like a cop," Jolie said, her eyes wary as she pushed herself back into the lumpy couch cushions, the mossy green upholstery crinkled at the edges.

"What's wrong with cops?" Shirin asked, before Virginia could silence her with a glare.

"To be frank, I'd rather go inhale several lungs full of river water before I open my mouth to someone who could have me locked up or carted off by the Feds." Jolie showed off a petulant shrug, her young age on full display.

Virginia grimaced. "I'd happily accept jail over even getting near that river. You're braver than me, I'll tell you that much." She poured out another measure of gin, this time pushing it across to the captain. "Here."

"Thanks," Lindell replied, bringing it to her lips and swallowing it down. "So," she said, setting the glass back on the counter, "what's the deal with this book, then?"

"I wanted to know what I was," Jolie said. "There aren't many... resources. Most people think it would be impossible for me to even exist."

"Which side?"

"Side?"

"Which parent did you get it from?" Lindell asked, hooking a thumb through a belt loop. "It's usually hereditary."

Virginia pressed the cork back into the bottle of gin with a soft squeak of resistance. "I didn't think you would be an expert on rare mythics."

"I'm not," Shirin said simply, not elaborating any further.

"It's not always hereditary, in any case." Virginia gestured towards the book, still sitting on the side table. "Occasionally, there can be a symbiotic possession. Jolie, have you had any near death experiences? Anything that might trigger something like that?"

"No," the young woman said, her fingers running over the fabric cover.

"Nothing out of the ordinary."

"Could be hereditary then."

"I wouldn't know. I, uh…" Jolie trailed off, staring out the window. "I didn't grow up with my birth parents."

Captain Lindell glanced at Virginia before looking back down into her half-empty glass. "This Fiske guy, how does he know what you are?"

"She stole the Nether from that scene," Virginia answered. "They chased, she fought back. Although I'm willing to bet they have no idea what she actually is. They probably think she's an inferno witch, just like we did until tonight."

"You've gotten yourself into some deep shit," Lindell said, gesturing at Jolie. "Guys like Fiske don't give up easy. It's probably better off if you leave the city."

"Shirin—" Virginia protested, setting down her glass with a heavy thud. "We can't take her in, Arthur will demote me faster than you can say—"

"She can't stay *here*, not after what happened last time."

"What happened last time?" Jolie asked. She was clutching the book to her chest now, perched at the edge of the sofa. "What does that mean?"

Virginia hesitated, laying her palm flat over the top of her glass, almost bracing against it, almost willing it to shatter under her weight and break the inescapable tension. "There was a missing shifter kid. He attacked me. I brought him here the next morning, once he'd calmed down, and he left."

"Left."

"He died." Virginia sighed, quiet and coated with regret. "He died in the house you stole that Nether from."

"Oh."

"I didn't mean for it to happen." At that, Shirin looked at her with something that was akin to pity, and Virginia flinched away from it, dragging the glass closer to the edge before refilling it. "But it did, and now here we are."

"I'll tell you whatever you want to know about those distributors—enforcers—whatever they are," Jolie offered. "Just let me stay the night."

"No," Virginia said.

"I won't steal anything. I won't even—"

"No. Listen, kid, you broke into my apartment and introduced yourself by shooting flames at my face." Virginia nodded at the scorched wall, already dreading the awkward conversation she'd have to have with the landlord about it. No doubt he'd add it to her growing tab. "It's hardly the way to start things off, wouldn't you agree?"

"You shot at me."

"Yes, after you tried to kill me," Virginia replied. "A common response, I think you will find."

"I didn't know you were the same person that saved me from the alley at first. It wasn't until—" Jolie interrupted herself, her eyes following Virginia's scars.

"Right."

"It was dark, but—"

"I've got the picture, thank you," Virginia said, the icy words hanging in the air like troubled mist, a ghost from fifteen years ago that had never quite crossed over. "Thank you for not continuing to try to kill me, but you can't stay here."

Shirin leaned into the counter, thoughtfully rotating the glass against the wood. "Just one night, Virginia, and we could solve this thing. With the right intel, you know we can."

"*No*," Virginia insisted.

"Come on, I thought we were on the same team with this."

"You take her home, then. Deal with it yourself."

"I can't," Shirin said shortly. "It has to be you."

"Can't? Or won't?" Virginia pressed, already trying to remember where in shadows she'd left the spare linens.

Lindell laced her fingers together, elbows propped on the counter. "Sometimes that difference is rather more nuanced than you might want to think."

"I don't know about that."

"And I don't want to get into this right now, Virginia."

"You have a wife at home, or something?"

"Or something," Lindell answered icily. "Let's just say I can't be dragging any fire demons home, alright?"

"Ever the enigma, aren't you?" Virginia asked dryly, rolling her eyes. "Fine," she said, looking to Jolie. "One night, and that's it." She glanced back at Lindell. "And I'm staying awake the entire time."

"I can ask a unit to—"

Virginia shot her a look. "And Shirin here will keep her ears to the ground about Fiske, won't she?"

"How did they find you at that supplies shop?" Lindell asked, turning away from Virginia.

Jolie pulled at the frayed cuffs of her coat. "Tailed me, I guess."

"No other reason? You're sure they didn't know you were looking for something specific?"

"I don't think so."

"Fiske's goons are too empty-headed to figure it out," Virginia said. "She was tailed, that's the end of it. I'd be surprised if any of them could tell their asses from their elbows, much less spot that she's a young fire demon, and not an inferno witch."

"Are there any other copies of this book around?" Shirin asked.

"Not that I know of."

Shirin stood, crossing the room to take the book from Jolie. She turned it over in her hands, examining the pages, running her thumb over the fabric cover. "Virginia, I think we should check out that apothecary on the north side again. Moonshadow Botanicals."

"What? Why?" Virginia asked, already dreading the inevitable interaction with Anya on the topic. So much for finding her a job with the VCPD.

"In case she's heard anything since," Lindell said. "And because when I was there the other day, I thought I noticed some rare books."

"Not that one."

"How do you know?" Lindell pressed, a lock of wavy hair falling into her eyes that she brushed away with a suave, casual gesture.

"Because I already checked," Virginia answered. "Besides, I don't think she's going to be very receptive to helping, going forward."

"She already wasn't receptive."

"Yeah, and can you blame her? You show up with a dozen—you bust in there, demanding information, confiscating reagents, and expect her to be *receptive?*"

Shirin gave the book back to Jolie, turning to face Virginia again. "Lean on her harder, then."

"This is why I didn't want you involved with this," Virginia hissed. "You're like a werewolf at a moon spa, all hammer and no finesse."

"I have *finesse*," Shirin argued.

"Please, you have about as much of that as Arthur does."

"Are you two going to start shooting at each other?" Jolie asked, crushing herself into the corner of the couch. "Because if so, I can just leave."

"No one is shooting anyone," Virginia growled, locking eyes with Shirin before flicking her gaze back to the delicate swirl of the clear liquid in her glass. "Fine. Jolie, you can stay one night, but that's it." She waved her hand at the closet in the narrow hallway. "There are fresh linens and towels in there, I think."

"Thank you, Virginia," Lindell said, her voice low. "I know we can solve this one."

"I guess we'll see about that, won't we?"

Shirin offered her a mischievous grin. "We could say that I owe you one?"

"Oh, you're already racking up quite the debt. Don't worry, I'm keeping your tab open."

Shirin raised an eyebrow at that, picking at the label on the bottle of wine, bending the corners and exposing the sticky underside. "I should get to the office. I can try to start going through some of the usuals."

Virginia shook her head. "Arthur's already had people on that, it didn't turn up much. Not without more information."

"The ones from the alleyway, anything distinguishing?" Lindell asked, looking from Jolie back to Virginia, running her thumb over the lip of the glass. "Tattoos, accents, hair." She glanced up at Virginia. "Scars."

"I would have mentioned it already," Virginia shot back. "I'm not a total rookie, you know."

"I know, Virginia."

Jolie shifted on the sofa. "One of them had a tattoo."

"See?" Shirin said, throwing Virginia a smirk. "Sometimes it's worth asking the obvious questions."

"It was… I don't know, it was dark, but I think it was a squid, or something. Tentacles over the elbow." Jolie pointed to her own arm, drawing a circle and dragging down towards her hand, ending at the delicate, bird-like joint of her wrist.

Virginia sighed. "Shit."

"Is that bad?" Jolie asked, her arm dropping back to her side.

"It's not good, I'll tell you that much." She locked eyes with Lindell, who was already moving for the door. "I take it you know the same thing that I know, then."

"Unfortunately."

"Wait," Jolie protested. "What do you know? Why is that important?"

"He's part of an underground ring. Well, *is*, or *was*. Hard to say. We thought they'd been eradicated, but maybe not."

"He could be a holdout," Shirin said, plucking her coat from the hook. "A holdout, or it could be they're rebuilding, or it could be they've been there the entire time and we were too stupid to see the signs right under our noses."

Virginia stacked the empty glasses in the sink, the white porcelain staring back up at her. "Could be Fiske, could be nothing. Could just be some fool who ran with the Krakens back in the day, made parole."

"Bold to be running around with that tattoo, if so," Lindell said. "All of them knew that the cops would be on them in an instant if they saw it."

"The boldness is what's concerning," Virginia agreed. "Jolie, was there anything else?"

"No. Nothing that I can remember. Nothing else that stood out."

"I'm going to go pull files," Lindell said, her hand on the door. "Call you in the morning?"

"Yeah," Virginia agreed. "Call me in the morning."

"I'll let you know what I find."

"Lindell, be careful. If Arthur finds you down in records, pulling files from decades' old cases, he's going to know something is up."

"Don't worry, Virginia, I know how to cover my ass." She gestured at the boxes of food. "She looks like she could use a good meal. You probably could, too, if my own observations are correct."

"Stop observing me, Shirin."

"Impossible." Lindell's face faltered for a moment, and then she was gone, closing the door behind her with the soft click of the latch. Virginia pulled the chain across the door, checking three times that it was settled in the lock. Jolie was just a kid, but her intrusion had set the evening on an edge.

"Here," Virginia said, sliding a box across the counter. "Looks like noodles."

"Thanks." Jolie sat at the counter, plunging a fork into the still-steaming food, sauce dripping back into the box. "I can't actually remember the last time I had a hot meal."

"I know the feeling."

"You do?"

"It's been a while, but..." Virginia trailed off, turning to face the cabinets. "Yeah."

"I wouldn't have thought someone like you would have come from the streets."

"Didn't come from them, not really. Not like that. I don't know, kid, it's complicated, alright? I don't want to get into it." Virginia poked at a box of noodles, resenting the smell making her mouth water greedily. "Just eat your food."

"Thank you. For letting me stay."

"Just the night."

"I know." Jolie glanced out the window, giving an involuntary shiver. "Beats trying to find a space out there tonight. Verdance is..."

"Verdance is hostile. Even at the best of times." Following the girl's stare, Virginia spied two green eyes in the darkness. The cat. She opened the window to let it in, reaching for the can opener.

Jolie's face broke into a wide smile as she stood and scooped up the cat with surprising ease, snuggling it under her chin. "Hello, angel," she cooed. "What's your name?"

"Doesn't have a name," Virginia grumbled. "It comes here for a free lunch. No such thing, unless you're a cat." She dumped the tuna into a small bowl, and the cat wriggled free of Jolie's clutches to eat its fill, not even leaving a crumb behind. It returned to Jolie for another scratch behind the ears, leaning into her hands.

"It's not yours?" Jolie asked, nose to nose with the cat.

"No." Virginia filled the kettle, the heavy cast iron a pleasant, grounding weight in her hands. "Coffee?"

"It's almost midnight."

Virginia set the kettle on the stove and opened the window again for the cat to escape into the night. "I'm not planning on sleeping."

Chapter Twenty-Four

Virginia downed her fifth cup of coffee, her eyes dry and begging for sleep. But it was barely dawn, and the kid was still asleep on the sofa, curled up tight beneath almost every blanket in the apartment. Virginia couldn't let her slip through her fingers, not when they could take Fiske out once and for all if they played their cards right.

She held her hands around the green ceramic mug, grateful for the heat that radiated through it, staving off the midwinter chill that crept beneath the windowsills like an invisible, suffocating fog. She pulled her sweater tighter around herself, and huddled over the coffee. The combination of the unexpected late night and the smell of the bitter grounds pulled her back to her VCPD days, when sleep was infrequent and rarely restful.

Her relationship with sleep had changed much in the intervening fifteen years. A notoriously early riser who stayed up far too late, she rarely got more than half a night's sleep, even when her caseload was thin.

Her fingers traced over each page of Ursa's file once again, desperate for a clue to jump out at her. None did. Ursa had disappeared without a trace, and it was driving Virginia senseless. There was always a thread, some crumbs to follow, but there were no bank accounts drained, no signs of a struggle, no witnesses reporting they'd been seen somewhere downstate starting a new life with a new name.

She envied people who could do that. She'd wanted to, after being removed from the force. After Arthur left, there was nothing and no one. Still, she'd stayed, despite the fact that no one would have blamed her if she had left. Maybe a fresh start would have changed things. Maybe it would have spelled out a better future somewhere else, where she wasn't just a disgraced private eye, where she was respected, where she was unknown and free from obligation and expectation alike.

Or maybe that fresh start would have landed her in an early grave. There was no way to tell which way the paths would have turned, which life would have led her to the purest conclusion. All she had was all she had done, and lingering on what-ifs never did any good for anyone, least of all her.

Virginia let out an exasperated sigh loud enough that Jolie stirred, turning over on the sofa. The young woman shivered once, and then twice. Delicately, but with irritation, Virginia pulled a blanket from her own bed, laying it over Jolie to keep her warm.

It was months away, but Virginia was already looking forward to the gentle, almost imperceptible shift towards spring, when the mornings were still cold and crisp, frost laid itself delicately against the windows in its ostentatious fractal patterns, and geese flew overhead, returning from their sabbatical, but before the stickiness of summer let itself be known. Heat pressed like death. Cold pulled like the temptation of sleep to the drowning.

It was six-thirty in the morning when Jolie sat up, her chest heaving.

"You alright?" Virginia asked.

"Yeah. Just... a bad dream."

"Go back to sleep."

Jolie swung her legs over the side of the couch, hands smoothing the extra blanket. "Thank you."

"Bathroom is down the hall, if you need it."

"Thanks." Jolie stood, stretching her arms over her head, gaze fixed on the scorch marks from the night before. "Sorry again about that."

"Could have been worse. Could have been me." Virginia smirked. "Or the gin."

"When is Shirin coming back?" Jolie asked, wiping sleep from her eyes.

It was strange, hearing Lindell's first name from someone who probably should have known her as Captain first and foremost. "I'm not sure. It's still early, yet."

"Do you think she'll find some answers?"

"Yes." Virginia nodded towards the kettle. "Coffee?"

"Have you been up all night?"

"Yes. Had to make sure you didn't sneak out, didn't I?" Virginia turned the brass tap, filling the kettle once again. "Shirin would never let me live it down, I can tell you that much."

"I told you I wouldn't leave."

"So did the last kid, and look where he ended up. Parked in the morgue." Guilt twisted in Virginia's gut, and so she knocked back the rest of her barely-warm coffee to drown it. "I'm fine."

Jolie hesitated, tugging at the hem of her thin sweater, the edges frayed with split threads, and a hole at the side seam that was already pulling apart. "I won't leave."

"Okay." Virginia fussed with the coffee grounds, pouring the old ones into the trash, and replacing them with fresh. "I'm still not going to go anywhere, regardless." She waved a hand towards the hallway. "Towels are in there somewhere. I imagine you'll want to shower, so you'd better be quick. The hot water goes quick around here."

"Thank you again, for all this."

"It's not a big deal, kid. I'd do it for any of my informants." She cringed, hearing her own voice speak the words. "Well, you know. Colleagues. Clients. That sort of thing."

"Informants?"

"Slip of the tongue."

Jolie frowned, turning to open the linen closet. "I hope you aren't a bounty hunter or anything like that."

"I'm not."

"Because if you were, I wouldn't feel bad anymore about almost burning your apartment down with you in it." Jolie untied her hair, letting it loose it from the band that had secured it overnight. "I'm going to shower."

Virginia nodded, both at the observation and the announcement. She set the kettle on the stove, lighting it with a long match once again, stretching out her hands to absorb the ambient warmth before the steam became too hot to touch. The phone rang, and she moved to answer it when it stopped. She frowned, looking back at the kettle.

She called the precinct again, vaguely annoyed that her fingers remembered the dial pattern so easily and without prompting. "Lindell," she said, waiting to be redirected.

"This is Lindell."

"Did you just call here?" Virginia asked.

"Yes."

"Why did you hang up?"

Lindell cleared her throat lightly. "I'm in a meeting."

"It's not even seven," Virginia said, glancing at the clock above the stove. "Oh. Is Arthur standing right there?"

"Mhmm."

"Are we busted?"

The line crackled. "Not yet."

"Call me when he leaves."

"Yup."

The kettle whistled, piercing in its comfort. She'd watched it each time through the night, taking it off the heat before it raised the alarm and woke up the kid. Poor thing looked like she'd been on the streets a while, and Virginia knew all too well what that was like, especially in the windy cold of Verdance. Maybe it wasn't so bad for a fire demon. At least she could commit some casual arson to keep herself warm.

Another cup of coffee, another stare at the clock, more desperate blinks as she convinced herself that she wasn't tired at all, actually. It hadn't been that long since she'd pulled an all-nighter, but that time the activities were somewhat more strenuous than standing at her counter, drinking endless cups of coffee, trying to make sure one of the rarest mythics in the world didn't run out her door and into the hands of Franky Fiske and the Ruby Thorns or one of the Krakens.

Virginia folded the blankets from the sofa, stacking them neatly on the back. She picked up the book, leafing through it once again. It was a hell of a coincidence, having the kid she was chasing break into her apartment, but if there was one thing she'd learned in her forty-eight years, it was that fate, or whatever it was, had a strange way of dealing with people, leading everyone down winding, twisting paths until they were all so tangled up that there was no finding your way home again.

She scoffed. Home. Where even was home, anyway? Verdance, she supposed. Her apartment, organized just how she liked it. Her office, an extension of that. But she'd never felt that deep, inexorable pull back to where everything had started for her like so many others had. They'd all but sprint home at the solstices to see family. She remained firmly rooted in Verdance City.

A knock at the door pulled her from her thoughts. "Just a minute," she said, pulling her knuckles from her coat pocket. She opened the door, half expecting to see Fiske himself on the other side.

"Expecting a fight, Virginia?" Lindell asked, raising an eyebrow at the glint of the metal.

"I thought you were still at the station," Virginia replied, slipping the silver off her fingers.

"I came as soon as I could."

"Break in the case?"

Lindell closed the door behind her, shaking the powdery snow from her scarf. "The sheriff is onto us."

"What?" Virginia demanded. "How?"

"He came in early! I wasn't expecting him until later. He wanted to know why I had pulled an all-nighter."

"You didn't sign out?" Virginia asked with a scoff. "Rookie move."

"You can't just sign out if you're still in the building," Lindell replied dismissively. "What if there was a fire, or some other kind of emergency?"

"Yeah, what if you were trying to hide the identity of one of the only known fire demons in the entire world? It would be a shame to make damned sure no one was poking around through your business, wouldn't it?" Virginia huffed out an angry breath, pacing back to the kitchen counter, her socks sliding against the chipped wooden floor, the heel catching on an exposed nail. "Why didn't you just lie?"

"Of course I lied, but I'm not a very good liar." Lindell shrugged. "Besides, he's less likely to take a pound of flesh from me for this if you're the one who's spearheading it."

"So I'm the scapegoat."

"I wouldn't call it that."

Virginia returned to the kettle, pouring hot water into the press. "You want me to take the fall for you?"

"No, I just want you to get him to ease off this for a few days," Lindell explained. "Just until we can unravel it. Once we've got Fiske behind bars, he's not going to care how we got there."

"A few days? I thought you said *one* day."

"You know how these things are," Shirin said, tilting her head towards a beam of light that illuminated the amber sparks of her irises.

Virginia bent over the counter, keeping an eye on the bathroom door. "She can't stay here, Shirin."

"Did you sleep?"

"No, of course I didn't."

"You should sleep. Go, I'll watch her."

"You haven't slept either, by the looks of you." Virginia smirked. "I'll bet Arthur was very curious about why you weren't in your uniform."

"He made some assumptions that I did not disabuse him of," Shirin said casually, leaning against the counter with one palm planted on the imitation marble.

"Maybe it won't be the last time you have an early morning jaunt to the office after a hot date." Virginia fumbled. "Not that you were—not that we uh—"

"Relax, Vane, don't strain yourself."

"Coffee?" Virginia offered, trying her best to shake the fog from her mind.

"Sure. Already had seven, what's one more?"

Virginia exhaled a soft laugh, pulling two more mismatched mugs from the cabinet, one a plain white ceramic, and the other a dark blue with an angular, irritating handle, emblazoned with a bold floral print. "And here I thought I was throwing caution to the wind with five.”

“Amateur,” Lindell replied, taking the blue mug once it was filled with coffee. “Did the kid sleep?”

“Yeah.”

“She give you any trouble?”

Virginia shook her head. “No. She barely moved all night.”

“Probably the first time she’s had a soft place to land in a while.”

“Maybe next time you can take her.”

“I told you, I can’t.” Shirin shifted, holding the mug even as she blew across the rim, sending the steam in erratic, coiled directions.

“So you *do* have a wife at home?” Virginia asked. “That’s... interesting.”

“She’s not my wife.”

“Partner, girlfriend, whatever,” Virginia offered. “Whatever we’re calling it these days.”

“She’s my sister,” Shirin answered. “She’s not been well.”

Virginia looked down at her mug, watching the swirls of milk blend seamlessly into a creamy brown. “I’m sorry to hear that.”

“She doesn’t really have anyone else, so...”

“Yeah.” Virginia pulled a pack of cigarettes from her coat pocket. “Do you mind if I smoke?”

“No.”

“I’m in desperate need, I didn’t want to open the window while she was sleeping and let all the cold air in.”

“That’s surprisingly thoughtful of you.”

“Surprisingly?” Virginia asked, shooting the captain a wry smile over her shoulder. “I’m not a complete monster, Shirin.”

“I know you’re not a monster. I never thought that.”

The match struck, sizzling its acrid flame as she lit the end of the cigarette, holding it out the cracked window and trying to ignore the cold that immediately set itself deep into her hands. Virginia bit back a comment about the wine, choosing instead to take a long, relaxed drag. “We run the risk of them finding her here, you know. I’m hardly an unknown entity in those circles.”

"Because of Astrid?"

"No," Virginia replied acerbically. "Because I probably broke the jaw of one of them, and shot the other in the leg. And I tend to have an obvious face."

"I can move some patrols around, get more beat cops down this way."

"No, that's not necessary. It would only complicate things, anyway." Virginia closed her eyes, savoring the sweet burn of the tobacco in her throat. "She's jumpy."

"Understandable." Shirin leaned against the counter, thumbs resting through her belt loops. "The sooner we nab these guys, the better."

"Any word on Ursa?"

"No. Not a single thing. Even the sheriff thinks it's odd."

"Not that odd, if you ask me. They either took off, or..." Virginia took another drag, blowing the smoke through the window. "Or Fiske got to them, too."

"Bold to go after a fully grown shifter."

"The stiff at the lakefront yesterday, too. They're getting more confident. I don't like it."

Shirin reached for the coffee press, refilling her mug. "This makes eight." When the phone rang, she flinched, nodding towards it. "And that will be the sheriff."

"Great," Virginia said, stubbing out the cigarette into a green glass ashtray. "I can't wait to be interrogated again."

Chapter Twenty-Five

Arthur glared at Virginia and Shirin, shifting his eyes from one to the other. "Took you both long enough."

"There was traffic," Virginia lied. They'd had to wait for Jolie, bundle her in the car, and make sure she'd stay there, handcuffing her to the back seat. She still felt guilty about that. "I don't have a lot of time, Arthur, so spit it out."

"I need you to start sniffing around all the clubs in the city, see if Fiske is supplying them all."

"Of course he is," Virginia deadpanned. "That much is obvious."

Arthur sighed heavily, the effects of the case weighing heavily on his shoulders. She'd seen that pressure before, but it had been a long time. He straightened pages against the desk with several sharp snaps, tidying the files before sliding them back into his desk drawer. "We need evidence of that."

"I'm sure it won't be a problem. I mean, hell, I almost got taken out by a shifter last time, what's one more near-death experience?" she mused.

"I don't want you to get involved, Ginnie, I just want observations. Patterns, delivery times, something we can latch onto."

Virginia rolled her eyes, hands pressing into her hips instead of clenched at her sides because she'd promised that she would at least try to relieve some of the tension from their interactions. "That will take weeks to get anything worth using."

"These things take time, you know that."

"And in the meantime, shifters are showing up dead because you aren't willing to do what it takes to shut this down once and for all."

"My predecessor left me with a mess, Ginnie," Arthur said, exasperated, exhausted, probably harangued at work and at home. "I can't help that."

"Clearly."

Captain Lindell cleared her throat, leaning against the door frame. "Sheriff, I think we could potentially find some more useful information if we focus our attentions on these underground healers."

"We didn't find anything of use at the apothecary on the north side, what makes you think anywhere else will be different?" Arthur asked, flicking through the stack of papers still present on his desk.

"Different people, different priorities. Some may be more... easily motivated."

Virginia shook her head. "You don't know what you're talking about, Shirin. *Captain,*" she corrected, catching the warning glance. "They're not going to sell out someone like Fiske, hell, Anya wouldn't even drop any information on Astrid, and comparatively speaking, she's a small fish."

"On a first name basis with this healer, are you?" Arthur asked.

"Only because I wasn't there long enough to catch her last name, Arthur."

He nodded thoughtfully, watching Virginia the same way she'd seen him watch suspects. "She may still be the key to getting the Sphinx shut down."

"I doubt that." Virginia cocked an eyebrow. "Unless you can give her a job."

"What?" Lindell barked, tacking on a laugh at the end. "That's absurd."

"Put her on the special unit squad," Virginia suggested. "She's a good healer, knows what she's doing. Quick, efficient, and—"

Arthur leaned forward against the desk. "You want me to put someone on payroll who has been involved with a crime syndicate as recently as last week?"

"I don't think healing people is crime syndicate behavior, do you?"

"It is when the people you're healing are at the center of it."

"Are you including me in that?" Virginia asked.

"No," Arthur said, but it was unconvincing. "No, of course not. I'm only suggesting that it may not reflect well on me that I would be adding a healer to the roster who we just confiscated several illegal reagents from."

"You have to give her something to work with, or she's never going to help you," Virginia said, staring out the window at the cold day outside. Jolie would be cold out there in the car, even despite the extra blankets.

He straightened a stack of papers. "Maybe we don't have to give her anything at all. Maybe we just... watch. We wait, and see, and sooner or later, one of those enforcers will lead us right back to wherever Fiske is keeping these hired guns. Wherever he's keeping the Nether."

"Yeah, or they lead us directly into an obvious trap," Virginia argued. "Fiske isn't oblivious, he'll know we're onto him now after Benjamin. And Ursa."

"There's no murder without a body, Ginnie, and Ursa hasn't been found anywhere."

"Not *yet*."

The captain unbuttoned her coat, sitting down across from Arthur with an ankle resting on her opposite knee, pulling the twill fabric of her trousers taut over her thighs. "I think we can workshop this, Sheriff. Find a method that works for everyone. Right now, Virginia has to get going, don't you?"

"I do," Virginia answered with a nod. She didn't want to leave the kid out in the cold, even if she was a fire demon. "I have other obligations that need attending to."

Arthur glanced between them with a sigh. "Something tells me I'm going to regret pairing you two up on this, one way or another." He rubbed his shining forehead, a broad glare against it from the window. "Just... tell me if anything jumps."

"Will do." She exchanged a glance with Shirin, and Arthur sighed.

"Whatever is going on, just... stop it," he said, pleading.

Virginia flashed him a smile that she knew he would know was bullshit. "Nothing is going on." She closed the door behind her, knowing that Shirin was about to get at least a dozen questions about what was going on. Served her right for tailing Virginia in the first place, especially on the request of Arthur's wife. Something about it all still smoldered in her chest, as dangerous as it was inevitable. Wounds like that never really healed. They just scabbed over, scarred, leaving a fresh canvas for the next betrayal.

"Good to see you back around here, Vane."

"Detective Kang. It's been a while," Virginia said. He was older than when she'd last seen him, salt and pepper hair peeking out from beneath his regulation cap, but his blue eyes as piercing as ever, and his smile warm.

"Lieutenant, now."

She nodded. "Lieutenant." The same rank she'd been, once.

"Are you coming back to the force?" he asked.

"No," she answered, twisting her keys in her hands, letting the metal bite into her flesh. "I think the time for that has passed."

"Consulting?"

She nodded. "On a case or two. Don't worry, I'll be out of everyone's hair soon enough."

"Ah," he said, hands clasped behind his back, white collared shirt starched and ironed to perfection, no doubt by his wife. "Is it the shifter thing?"

"It is."

"Pain in the ass, that is," he said, blowing out an exasperated breath. "We've got newshounds showing up at every scene now, regardless of what it is. It's becoming a damned nightmare just to keep them out of the way."

Virginia exhaled a laugh through her nose. "Good luck with that, Kang."

Kang's glance flicked between her and Arthur's office. "None of us expected him to take the job, you know. None of us that were around then."

"It was a surprise to me, too." She sighed. "Blindsided, actually."

"Take care, Vane. Don't let it get to you. You're still the best damned investigator this piece of shit town has ever seen."

"Thanks." She tapped on his desk, fingertips against wood. "Don't let him work you too hard."

The back stairs echoed with every step she took, her boots heavy against the creaking, worn wood, split from years of salt-encrusted soles pounding grit into the grain every winter. Something about the Verdance City precinct settled in her chest, weighty and wanting, like the shadow of a long-forgotten dream, or the piercing sharpness of memories she'd spent fifteen years trying to forget. The sooner this case was closed, the better, and she could go back to pretending none of them even existed anymore.

She opened the driver's side door, glancing into the back. "You can sit up, now."

"Took you long enough. It's freezing out here."

Virginia handed her a paper cup, filled with coffee she'd taken from the bullpen. "Here."

"Thanks." Jolie met her eyes in the rear view mirror. "Why did you lie?"

"Lie?" Virginia asked, inserting the key into the ignition, firing up the car's engine with a resounding growl that echoed against the concrete pillars. "You're going to have to be more specific."

"You said you weren't a cop."

"I'm *not* a cop."

"No, but Shirin is." Jolie gestured. "I know this is the precinct, I'm not ignorant."

Virginia sighed. "I should have made you wait until we were back on the road to let you uncover your eyes."

"I did when you were gone, anyway."

"It's great that you're so good at following instructions," Virginia grumbled, grateful that Kang hadn't followed her out to the car. "I think there's more to this than you're telling me, Jolie." She caught her glance again in the mirror. "I'm a private investigator."

"I just wanted to know why I am the way that I am. I wanted to get revenge for—" Jolie stopped short, staring out the window as Virginia pulled onto the road. "For nothing."

"Revenge for nothing isn't very convincing."

"It's a long story."

"Good, we've got a lot of traffic to sit through to get to the north side," Virginia encouraged. "I'm more than willing to listen."

"Why are we going to the north side?" Jolie asked, holding the paper cup to her mouth and nose, inhaling the twists of steam that were already fast depleting.

"Because someone there might have more information than she's telling me."

"Is she a cop?"

That same, familiar headache began to pound its rhythm once more, thudding weakly against Virginia's temples. The day's moderate winter sun was enough to exacerbate it, the glare from the snow drifts at the side of the road painfully blinding. "No," she answered.

A moment passed, with only the sounds of the engine rumbling, and the noise of traffic as Verdance residents went about their days, tires against asphalt and demanding horns orchestrated into a dire cacophony. "Are they going to report me to the Feds?" Jolie asked in a quiet voice.

"Shirin—Captain Lindell—has promised that the paperwork will conveniently get lost," Virginia assured her. She wasn't even sure just how much of that she believed, but she was out of options that didn't involve the VCPD.

"Do you believe her?" Jolie asked.

"I don't know," Virginia replied, her own honesty surprising her. "I haven't known her for very long. She's very dedicated to her job." She glanced at the traffic light, turning onto a busier road, lined with parked cars. "But she also seems like a fair person, and one who understands the gravity of the situation."

Jolie exhaled a quiet sigh, more of resignation than frustration. "I never wanted this, you know."

"What, breaking and entering? Getting caught?"

"Being what I am." Jolie drained the cup, crunching it up in her hands. "Life was complicated enough before I started shooting fire out of my hands. I wanted to at least try to use it for good, but it looks like I wound up making the same kinds of mistakes I always made before, bandied around as some sort of trade, being chased after by a bunch of assholes."

"You have run-ins with the law before in Verdance?" Virginia asked, already planning how much extra trouble that would cause if the feds did get involved.

"Not here, no. Other places."

"Record?"

Jolie nodded. "Probably. I got into a few scuffles when I was younger."

"I bet you'd lay them out now," Virginia said with a smirk. "Not many people can fight against fire. It's why Fiske wants you so much. You'd be unstoppable."

"Fuck Fiske."

Virginia laughed. "A relatable sentiment, to be sure."

"Aren't you tired?" Jolie asked, stretching her arms over her head as she yawned.

"Not my first all-nighter, kid. I'll be fine."

"I'm not a kid."

"Close enough."

Jolie shifted in the back seat, pulling the blanket they'd used to hide her tight around her shoulders. "Why aren't you a cop anymore?"

"Where'd you hear that?"

"I heard you and Shirin—Captain Lindell, I guess—when I was in the bathroom."

"You haven't even divulged half of what I've asked yet, so, no, I won't be answering that question," Virginia said, tapping her fingers against the steering wheel. "Besides, what I did was a million years ago. What you did was last night."

"I said I was sorry," Jolie grumbled.

"I need more about Fiske."

"He's been—well, his enforcers—have been after me for weeks," Jolie explained, grimacing as the car hit a pothole in the road that nearly splashed the remains of the coffee against the threadbare seats. "Seems I can't go anywhere without one of them showing up."

"How many have you killed?"

"What? None of them."

At a stop sign, Virginia turned to look at her, searching Jolie's face for hints of the truth. "Are you sure about that?"

"Yes, I'm sure. Why, how many people have you killed?"

"Enough."

"Shadows," Jolie whispered. "No, I just... I just wanted them to leave me alone. It's been the same van a few times, though."

"You could have mentioned that before, that's something we can work with."

"No, it's too generic. Black, no distinguishing marks."

"Plates?" Virginia asked.

"Different every time. Probably stolen."

"How do you know it's the same van, then?"

"The enforcers are always the same," Jolie said, wincing as the car sailed over another bump in the road. "The two men you saw in the alley—well, saved me from, really—and a woman."

Virginia nodded, assembling a suspect list in her head of known ex-cons who ran in those circles. "What's the woman like?"

"Worse than the men," Jolie grumbled. "She's tall, broad, and has a mean right hook."

"We'll see about that," Virginia said, tapping on the steering wheel. "Anything else about her?"

"Blond hair, usually in a braid, and I think she might be a mythic."

"Shifter?"

Jolie nodded. "Probably. I've never seen it, though. She's bad enough as a human."

"What's your plan once we catch Fiske?" Virginia asked. "Are you going to keep breaking into libraries and apartments, or what?"

"I don't know. It's been—I've just been trying to survive."

"Mm," Virginia agreed, being all too familiar with the pressures of baseline existence, and how sharp Verdance could be. "I guess we're all just trying to survive," she offered.

Chapter Twenty-Six

The front of Moonshadow Apothecary was dark, and a closed sign hung on the door. Virginia ignored it and knocked anyway.

"It says it's closed," Jolie said, standing behind her.

"She's here, just trust me."

"But what if—"

"We're closed," Anya shouted from the alley. "Come back tomorrow."

Virginia released the door handle, moving to the side of the building. "It's just me."

"I'm busy, Vee," Anya growled. "Go away."

"Clients?"

"None of your business," Anya answered, but her voice wavered just enough to pique Virginia's curiosity.

"Are you okay?"

"I'm fine, thank you. Get lost." She glanced at Jolie, an eyebrow raised. "What are you doing, babysitting?"

"Something like that."

"I'm not a baby," Jolie grumbled under her breath.

"Anya, I wanted to talk about... well, you know, I'm guessing, judging by the tinge of blood on your apron," Virginia said, doing her best to be deferential, but knowing it wouldn't be enough. "Please."

"I don't know, *actually*, and whatever I'm doing in my shop is none of your business," Anya shot back, wiping her hands against the stained white fabric. "You want in? Get a warrant."

Virginia shrugged, making sure her shoulder holster was visible. "And here I thought you'd be a little more cordial to someone who was working on getting you what you wanted."

"Liar."

"It's not a lie, I had a conversation with the sheriff just this morning." Virginia said the last part louder, almost a shout. "And if you want me to keep my voice down on the matter, then I suggest you stop stonewalling me."

"You're all the same, you know that?" Anya spat. "You know exactly what you're doing." She gave an exasperated huff, waving them both off. "Come back in an hour. I'll be done by then."

Virginia shrugged, grateful that her shoulder didn't pulse in response. "We can wait."

Anya pointed at her, the threat clearly made even from the side alley. "Vee, come back in an hour, or there won't be any discussions to be had about any of it. Are we clear on that matter?"

"Who's in there, Anya?" Virginia stepped closer, her fingers instinctively lacing through the silver knuckles in her pocket. "Is it him?"

"No."

"Are you lying?"

Anya stood against the door, her bright aquamarine eyes flashing. "You're not going to force your way in here. This is my place of work, and you have no authority here."

"Technically, I don't have authority anywhere, but that's never really stopped me before," Virginia replied casually. It was true, but not something she wanted to be bragging about.

"I will report this."

Virginia yawned, stepping closer again and bracing an arm against the door as she leaned closer to Anya. "Oh? And who are you going to report me to? I doubt VCPD would care. Even if they did, I'm just a consultant. To be honest, getting me fired from that gig would be doing me a favor."

"I am warning you, Vee," Anya said. "Leave. One hour."

"Are you going to hex me?"

Anya tilted her chin down at her, leaning hard against the door in order to keep her out. "I'll do worse than that, if you don't listen to me right now." She all but hissed the final two words, their remnants coasting on the wind like noxious fumes. "If you want my help, and we both know that you do, because you wouldn't be here otherwise, then leave. Come back when I am finished with what I am doing."

"Or, I could just..." Virginia reached for the knob, turning it. The door fell inward, sending Anya sprawling onto the sun-faded tile of the shop, and revealing Ursa on the healing cot. Virginia jerked back in surprise. "Ursa?"

"Ms. Vane, I—" Ursa struggled to get up, holding their side. They were covered in deep, mottled bruises interlaced with thick lacerations. "I didn't expect to see you here." They looked around, their breathing labored.

"What the hell, Anya?" Virginia demanded. "You didn't think this might be important?"

"I didn't know who they were until this morning," Anya retorted, getting up from the floor. She dusted off her skirts, so deep blue they were almost black. "And given what they've been through, I thought they deserved some privacy."

"We were about to start a murder investigation!" Virginia argued. "Have you completely lost your mind?"

"You have no right to come barging in here, harassing my patients, you are trespassing, Vee." Anya pointed at her, shoulders tight with rage. "Get out."

"No, I don't think I will." Virginia nodded to Jolie, who stepped inside and closed the door. "Ursa, what happened? Did you even know that your apartment had been tossed?"

"I knew," Ursa admitted. "I came home, saw what had been done, and I left."

"And you've been hiding out here ever since?"

"Not here, no." Ursa glanced at Anya, who shook her head. "Around. Nowhere important."

"And these injuries?" Virginia demanded. "Where did they come from?"

Ursa looked away, their long, chestnut hair tied back into a long braid, usually hidden by their hood. "Fiske's enforcers found me," they explained. "I barely got away. They wanted me to be a distributor, because…"

"Because you're a shifter," Jolie finished. "Yeah."

"Vee, you need to leave," Anya said again, hands on her hips. "You can't just do things like this, not if you want my help."

Virginia shrugged at her, keeping a blank face. "Seems to me you weren't actually wanting to help me, if you were keeping all of this silent and under wraps. Seems to me you were actively interfering with an investigation."

"You're not even a real cop," Anya spat. "You're just an upjumped nobody."

"That is not news to me." Virginia folded her arms over her chest, looking back to Ursa. "When did Fiske catch up to you?"

"Few nights ago," Ursa answered, staring down at the floor, anywhere other than at Virginia.

"Before or after your brother…" Virginia trailed off, letting her arms fall to her sides. "I'm sorry about Benjamin."

"He made his own choices," Ursa said, and their pain was palpable in the way their voice cracked when they said the words.

"I know, but I should have been more careful."

Ursa grimaced against invisible pain. "I don't blame you, Ms. Vane. We both tried our best to keep him safe. It's not your fault that he slipped out. He did the same to me before."

"You said he wasn't known for antics like those."

"He wasn't. Not until Fiske got involved, and then…" Ursa waved a hand in the air, defeated. "And then it all went downhill. I could barely keep tabs on him, and then when he went missing…"

"Anything you can tell me about Fiske or his enforcers might get us closer to finding justice for your brother," Virginia said. "Anything at all."

Anya made a choked sound that was somewhere between a scoff and a snort.

"Do you have something to add, Anya?" Virginia asked, raising an eyebrow in challenge.

"*Justice*," Anya spat. "As if people like us ever really get justice."

"It's better than the alternative of just letting Fiske run rampant all over Verdance, wouldn't you agree?" Virginia challenged, already regretting the decisions to visit the shop. She had a lead, but at what cost? She'd have to deal with Arthur again, and sooner than she'd intended.

"Get rid of Fiske, another will fill that void," Anya said, lining up tiny bottles with a series of angry, tiny clanks. "It's just how things are in this shadows-damned city, and you know it. Going after this guy isn't going to get justice for Ursa's brother, or for any of us."

"Things are worse now than they have been, Anya, I don't know if you've noticed," Virginia retorted. "How many dead mythics have to show up before you start taking any of this seriously?"

"I've seen more grit and blood in this city than you ever will," Anya hissed, moving closer. "I've seen things you cannot even begin to imagine, Vee. Horrible, soul-destroying things, and it all lives up here." She tapped against her temple, now leaning over Virginia, using her considerable height as an advantage. "I know better than you or anyone else in the whole of the VCPD that these streets don't change, at least, not for the better. Every year is another step down into irrevocable depravity and chaos."

"Are you done with your little speech?" Virginia asked, glaring up at her. "Because I have work to do."

"You don't get it, Vane. You don't get it, and you won't, not until you realize what happens when the cops aren't looking."

"Oh? And what is it that happens when the cops aren't looking?"

"You're worried about a few mythics being found in public places as though there aren't at least five a month being quietly dumped into landfills, used up, cashed out, hidden from public view. You're so busy thinking about how many, and you haven't even stopped to think where the rest end up when no one wants them to be found," Anya said evenly, a cold calm to her voice despite the content of her words.

Virginia took a step back, instinctively, as though she'd been thrown off balance. "You're saying that Fiske *wants* them to be found."

"Obviously," Anya replied.

"He wants them to be found, because he wants to send a message."

Virginia shook her head, angry that she'd missed it. "He wants other mythics to know they'd better not step out of line, or risk the consequences."

"Now that you've figured that little gem of information out, do you mind getting the hell out of my shop? I have work to do, and I can't very well do it with you two standing around." Anya fixed her attention on Jolie. "What's your story, anyway?"

"I'm an intern," Jolie replied easily.

Anya glared at Virginia. "An intern?"

"Tax breaks," Virginia said with a shrug. "She can handle herself."

"She could get hurt!" Anya protested. "She looks like she's sixteen years old!"

"Jolie, you know what you signed on for, right?" Virginia asked, knowing that the girl would confirm their story, despite their abbreviated history together. "You're aware that shadowing me may incur risks?"

"I'm aware," Jolie answered, inspecting her cuticles. "Not all of us are afraid of the dark, you know." She flashed an uncompromising grin at Anya, and Virginia had to bite back a laugh.

"Don't leave town," Virginia said, looking at Ursa. "We might need you to make a formal statement about Fiske's enforcers."

"I won't, I promise," Ursa replied. "But I won't be going home. They know to look for me there."

"Where are you staying?"

Ursa shook their head. "I can't say, I'm sorry, Ms. Vane. What I can do is offer to meet you in Independence Park the day after tomorrow, at noon. We can talk more then."

Virginia searched their face, and then gave a slow nod. "Alright. At noon." She turned back for the door, nodding again at Jolie, when Anya blocked her exit. "What do you want, Anya? I thought you wanted me to leave, now you're keeping me from doing so."

"If you ever storm into my shop again, you *will* live to regret it," Anya warned."

Virginia looked her up and down, sizing her up, doing her best to look intimidating. "I'm not afraid of curses or hexes."

"Oh, you should be," Anya whispered. "I will make every last day on this mortal plane a living hell for you, are we clear?"

"Yeah, whatever," Virginia said, rolling her eyes in full view. "Crystal."

"You think I am weak, Vee, because I am a healer. Let me reveal something—I *choose* to heal. I am more than capable and experienced in a range of other magic that most wouldn't even dare dream of using." Anya leaned down, almost nose to nose with Virginia, before she shifted her glance to Jolie. "It's not me who needs to be afraid of the dark." She moved, opening the door, her steely glare boring into Virginia. "Don't come here again without calling ahead."

"Fine," Virginia shot back, trying not to look as rattled as she felt. "Shadows, Anya, you don't have to be like that." The door slammed in her face, punctuating the sentiment for her.

"So, she's a little intense," Jolie said, leading the way back to the street. "What's the deal with you two, anyway?"

"The deal?"

"Yeah, you got history or something?"

Virginia laughed, trudging through thick, wet, snowy sludge. "No. We don't have history."

"Well, there's something there." Jolie looked back over her shoulder with a shrug and a smirk. "I thought she was going to kiss you."

"There's nothing there," Virginia insisted. "I barely even know her. She's probably got a husband on the east side or something."

Jolie shrugged. "If you say so."

"I do say so." Virginia climbed back into the car, nodding at the passenger seat. "You can sit in front."

"Oh, you trust me now?"

"No, if I leave you in the back, you might strangle me."

"I wouldn't strangle you, that's not my style." Jolie climbed into the front, slamming the door. "I would just crisp you up with fire. Where next?"

"Ursa was lying," Virginia said.

"What?"

Virginia rested her hands on the cold leather of the steering wheel, running her hands over the stitches. "They're lying. I never told them that I had Benjamin in my apartment. They couldn't have known that unless they saw him before he died. Even Anya didn't know that I had him."

"That's big, right?"

"It might be." Virginia glanced at Jolie. "It might be nothing, maybe, but... no, something is telling me that I'm missing something."

"Missing what?"

"I don't know, but I mean to find out." She started the car, checking the roads. "And we need to get you a warmer coat. I don't want you freezing to death on my watch. Arthur would never let me hear the end of it."

Chapter Twenty-Seven

Virginia kicked the radiator and it let out a long, recalcitrant hiss. "Damned thing," she muttered under her breath. "I'm sorry it's so cold in here."

"It's better than outside," Jolie replied, an old, frayed blanket draped around her narrow shoulders.

"Is that where you've been sleeping?"

There was a pause as Jolie sat at the counter, considering her answer. "Sometimes."

"How long?"

"Few weeks. I was sleeping on couches for a while, but you can only do that so long before you burn out your welcome." She snorted. "Get it? Burn?" She hovered her palm over the mug, savoring the steam. "Because I'm a fire demon?"

"I know what you mean." Virginia turned away to hide the upturned shape of her lips, almost a laugh that escaped over something so juvenile. "It's easy for people to get bored of you."

"You were on the streets for a while, weren't you?" Jolie asked, shooting an ember at the kettle, heating it almost instantly.

Virginia tugged on a second sweater, this one a faded grey and even more worn than the first one, though she'd always liked the patched elbows. The kettle whistled loudly, and with a towel, she removed it from the stove. "Nice party trick." She prepared the coffee, grinding beans into powder, scooping powder into the press, all in silence. "I was for a while, yes. I was young, my mother threw me out. I came to Verdance without anything."

She waited for the coffee to steep before depressing the plunger, focusing on the silent, gradual deepening of the liquid. "It was a long time ago, but you never forget it."

"Why did she throw you out?"

"She didn't like who I had become." Virginia laid her hands on the counter. "Milk? Sugar?"

"Neither."

"You might change your mind, this stuff is pretty intense." She added both to her own, sliding Jolie's black coffee across the wood. "There's milk in the icebox if you change your mind. Sugar in the cabinet."

"Do you still talk to her?"

"Not for almost thirty years." Virginia stirred her coffee, allowing the milk to bloom through the coffee, dragging the creamy spirals from one side of the mug to the other. "She could be dead now, for all I know." She chewed the inside of her cheek, feasting on the reliable, tolerable pain. "But I don't think I'm that lucky."

Jolie sparked an ember between her fingertips, letting it dance from one to the other before snuffing it out. "What are you going to do about Ursa?"

"It depends on whether you can keep your mouth shut or not."

Jolie took a sip, looking at her over the rim of the mug. The tendrils of steam ebbed and flowed with her every breath, curling to the ceiling and framing her bright amber eyes. "Who are we lying to?"

"It's not a lie, it's just an... omission. I want to figure part of this out before we tell Shirin and Arthur." Virginia waved a hand, still clutching her coffee with the other. "Captain Lindell and Sheriff Dixon."

"Why?"

"Do you always ask this many questions?"

"Do you always avoid answering them?" Jolie countered.

"They haven't started a murder investigation on Ursa yet, because there was no body. Clearly, now we know why we never found a body, but..." Virginia trailed off, leaning over to balance her forearms against the counter. "I know Ursa was lying, I just don't know why."

"Do you think they're working for Fiske?"

Virginia took a sip of her coffee, perfectly brewed. "It's not impossible, but I really don't think so. If they were making money with Fiske, they wouldn't have been trying to hold down two different jobs. But Ms. Anya Quinn didn't want me asking more questions."

"No, I think if you had, she might have murdered you on the spot."

"Probably," Virginia agreed.

"Murdered you or *married* you."

"Stop."

Jolie shrugged, a smirk playing at the corners of her lips. "I'm just saying, there's clearly something there. I think she was just drawing a line in the sand."

"That's enough, thank you," Virginia sniped, an edge to her tone. "How would you know if there was something between us, anyway? You saw ten minutes of interaction."

Jolie snapped her fingers, a small flame sparking where she did. "I'm a fire demon. I can sense heat."

Virginia set her mug on the counter with a little too much force, so much that she was afraid she'd cracked the ceramic, or fractured the handle of the mug. "I'm going to check Ursa's apartment. Don't go anywhere." She shoved her feet back into her boots, flinging the door open to stomp across the hall, ducking under the police tape blocking the entrance. They'd left the door unlocked. A failure on Lindell's part, and so Virginia would save that piece of leverage for when she needed it.

Ursa's apartment looked the same as the last time she'd seen it, over-turned, trampled through, broken glass shards still spread across the floor. They sparkled in the late morning light, shooting lazy glares against the poorly painted off-white walls. The clothes in the bedroom were still strewn over the bed, and the bathroom wore the marks of use, the tub etched in lime scale, the sink water-stained along with the small round mirror that hung above it on the wall.

Virginia crept around the debris, careful to not disturb anything. Photos, coats, two pairs of shoes. None of it was out of the ordinary, none of it added up to finish the open ended equation that was still playing in her mind. Why would Ursa lie? What had their plan been?

"How is it warmer in here than in your apartment?" Jolie asked from the doorway, still clutching the mug.

"Because the building is made of cardboard and empty promises," Virginia answered, bending to examine the back side of a shattered photo frame. "I told you to stay there."

"I'm sorry if I overstepped."

Virginia glanced at her. "It's fine. I'm not angry."

"Are you sure? Because you look angry."

"Listen, kid, this is just how I look, alright?" Virginia snapped. "Leave me alone and let me do my job."

Jolie nodded, but didn't leave the doorway. She stayed, watching, observing, but silent. It was more than Virginia had expected to get, so she didn't fight it.

The photo frame laying smashed against the floor was wood, intricately carved at the corners by someone with a practiced hand and a quiet mind. Deep swirls graced the oak, smooth and never rough. The photo was a landscape, looking off a small peak over a wide valley filled with trees, the crisp black and white drawing you into the scene. Virginia opened the back of the frame, looking for an inscription and finding none.

She frowned. Why put this photo in such a prideful frame? What was its meaning? Turning it over in her hands, a slight impression against the frame's backing caught her eyes. "There was something else in this frame," she said, more to herself than to Jolie. "Money, maybe."

"Maybe the enforcers found it."

"And carefully replaced the back of the frame?" Virginia shook her head, frowning. "That's unlikely. That's not their style, they're more of a smash and grab and leave everything a disaster."

"Maybe whatever was in there got taken long before Ursa went missing?" Jolie offered. "Or, you know, before everyone thought they went missing."

"Normally I'd agree with you, but look." She held out the frame, waiting for Jolie to set down the mug and take it. "You can see the indentations across the back aren't deep. Whatever was in there wasn't meant to be accessed regularly, and also," Virginia said, crouching down, gesturing at the shards. "There are no shards under where the frame was. Someone smashed it before putting it on the ground."

"Do you think Captain Lindell caught that?" Jolie asked.

"I don't know, I haven't seen the reports, and if I ask for them, she'll want to know why."

"Can I assume you aren't supposed to be in here?"

"Correct." Virginia shot her a glance over her shoulder. "And you're not going to utter a word of this to either of them."

"You know my opinion on the VCPD. I'll keep it to myself." Jolie huddled with the mug, the blanket a strange cape that swept behind her.

Virginia ran her fingers over the exposed photograph. "I wonder where this is."

"Hmm." Jolie examined it, tilting her head with concentration. "Maybe north? I can do some digging if you want."

"No, that's a waste of time. Chances are it was just a decoy to hide whatever was in the back of the frame."

"Anything else seem out of place?" Jolie asked, handing the frame back.

"Other than everything?" Virginia cast another glance around the apartment, willing something to jump out at her, to announce the secrets it had been hiding all along. She stood and ran a finger along a shelf, picking up a layer of thick dust. "I'm going to look at the bedroom again. Keep an eye out."

"What do I do if I see someone?"

"If you see someone, we're already sunk. I don't know, yell, or something. Unless it's Shirin, in which case she'll probably throw both of our asses in a cell before we can even try to explain why we're in here."

"Okay." Jolie closed the door with a shrug. "Harder for anyone to know we're in here."

Virginia nodded, picking her way around the remaining shards. Ursa's bedroom, or what she assumed was Ursa's bedroom, was difficult to parse. The dark curtains were drawn, leaving it in a damp darkness where shadows crept around every corner. It was unsettling, but then, crime scenes always were. A strange liminal space of violence or flight, tossed, left for someone to investigate, waiting to be solved by people who were never meant to stay.

The closet was empty, the clothes tossed to the floor, some still on their hangers. Long, flowing garments, most of them black, some of them peeking out from under the bed.

Virginia threw open the drapes. The electricity for the apartment had already been cut off, no doubt by the landlord trying to save a few pennies, not wanting the VCPD to run up the meter. She turned, willing herself to see the room afresh, without stagnant memories clouding her judgment and her mind. Everything looked the same, but the grey light from outside almost gave it a more haunting pallor, telling a story that wasn't meant to be told.

"If Ursa knew the enforcers were coming, why wouldn't they get out sooner?" Virginia wondered aloud.

"Maybe they thought they'd be safe."

"They're a shifter, too, you'd think that..." she trailed off, squeezing her eyes shut. "No, I'm missing something. The pieces don't fit."

Jolie followed her into the bedroom, the blanket sweeping behind her, stirring up tiny cyclones of dust and dirt tracked in by Shirin's team. "Maybe Fiske threatened them."

"Maybe, but that doesn't seem like his style. He's more murder now, ask questions never."

"Doesn't seem very efficient."

"Mythics are a dime a dozen since the Rupture," Virginia said. "He's got a steady stream of people desperate enough to try anything to stay alive." She leaned into the closet, straining her eyes against the relative darkness. "Come here, I need light. Do that thing with your fingers, you know, the snapping thing."

"It's not a very good light, but okay." Jolie leaned over her shoulder, snapping, a flickering glow dancing across the bare wood panels. "See anything?"

"Yeah. Look, there's a loose board here." Virginia pried it off, and it came easier than she'd expected. "I'm betting someone opened this recently.

The nails are all bent."

"What's in there?"

Virginia bent, examining the empty space. "Nothing."

"So someone took something from the picture frame, and something from the closet?"

"Looks like it."

"Money?"

"If I had to guess," Virginia agreed, and ran her fingers along the inside of the hole. A protruding nail caught the side of her hand, drawing a thin line of blood. She brought her palm to her mouth, sucking at it. "Shadows," she swore. "Damned thing." Her head exploded with pain, as though someone had swung a bat, the wood connecting with her exposed brain. She leaned back on her haunches, almost toppling over, head in her hands. "Fuck," she hissed.

"Virginia?" Jolie asked, her eyes darting with panic. "Are you alright?"

"It's nothing. I just need a minute." Virginia rocked back and forth on the balls of her feet, blinking, trying to clear the static and fog from her mind.

"Should I call Shirin?"

"No! Do not call anyone."

"But—"

"There was something here, something..." Bile leached into her throat and she coughed, trying to swallow it back. "What the fuck," she muttered under her breath, vision still swimming. "I don't think it was money in here."

"Nether?"

"Maybe." Virginia squeezed her eyes shut. "No." Pain radiated across her forehead and down her neck, setting uncomfortably at the top of her spine. "Valuables, maybe. An heirloom. Something to pawn." She reached for the closet again, brushing against the panel, careful to avoid the nail that time. "There's a hook in there," she said. "A necklace. Look, you can see where a pendant blocked the dust."

"Someone is coming," Jolie hissed, closing the bedroom door. "Come on, we have to go."

"Alright, yeah." Virginia took Jolie's offered arm, staggering to her feet. "The window," she whispered, still off balance, still unsure. The lock popped easily, and she hoisted herself out onto the fire escape. "Close the window behind you," she uttered, climbing up to the roof.

Verdance was a beautiful city at a distance. The skyline rose into the sky, almost midday, the glow of the pallid sun illuminating so many windows, a ghostly pallor that hung over them like a fog. It was one reason why Virginia had never been able to bring herself to leave, even after everything that had happened with Arthur.

"Wow," Jolie breathed. "It's beautiful up here." She looked over the side with a grimace. "It's the cops. Squad units on the street, parked up on the sidewalk."

"Shit. Go on, get to the other side." Virginia rubbed her eyes, still woozy. "If it's Lindell, she's going to know something is up if my car is down there but we're not in my kitchen."

"Oh no."

"Please don't tell me you left that mug in Ursa's apartment," Virginia said with a quiet hiss. "That will be a dead giveaway."

"Of course I didn't, I'm not a total brainless ghoul." Jolie waved the empty mug in the air. "The oh no was because there is no fire escape on your side of the building."

"Amateur," Virginia said, lowering herself to hang from the gutters.

"You've got to be kidding me."

"I've done this a million times, kid." She levered the window open with the toe of her boot, silently thanking herself for leaving it open after her morning smoke. She'd need another one as soon as this was all over. With a swing, she landed heavily on the floor of her apartment. "Come on, hurry up," she said tightly, holding an arm out. "I'll catch you."

Jolie uttered a string of curses before clattering off the gutters and grasping for Virginia's hand. "Pull me in," she whispered. "Hurry!"

"Alright, shadows," Virginia replied, dragging her inside just as someone knocked on the door. She moved to open it, arms crossed over her chest.

"Vane," Lindell said, looking past her into the apartment. "I have some bad news. We found a body." Lindell looked back at her, brow furrowed. "Are you alright?"

"Of course I'm alright, why wouldn't I be?"

"Your window is open."

"I was about to smoke."

"And your eyes are bloodshot."

Virginia turned. "Are they?" She caught Jolie's eye, who grimaced and nodded. "Oh. Maybe I just didn't get enough sleep or something."

"I already saw you this morning, Virginia. What happened?"

"Nothing!"

"We're never going to get through this investigation if you don't start sharing any and all information, and that includes whatever scrap you obviously got involved in after I left."

"I wasn't in a scrap." Virginia looked across the hall to the detectives flooding Ursa's apartment again. "What does this body have to do with Ursa's missing person case?"

"Because," Lindell said slowly. "It's Ursa's body we found."

Virginia almost laughed before she realized that Lindell was being serious. "When?"

"An hour ago. It's an active murder case now, Vane, and the sheriff wants you on this one, too. He thinks they're all interconnected, and to be quite honest, I am inclined to agree."

"Where?" she prompted. It had only been two hours since she'd seen Ursa alive and mostly well in Anya's shop.

"North side river branch. Coroner hasn't pinned a time of death yet."

Virginia stared. "No, that's..." She shook her head. "That's not possible."

"Yesterday you were climbing up my ass for not preemptively turning their case into a homicide investigation, and now you're staring at me with your mouth hanging open? What's the deal, Virginia? It doesn't take a genius to know that there's something you're not telling me."

"We were looking at the apartment again," Jolie offered, setting the empty mug on the table. "She didn't want you to get angry about it."

Virginia shot her a look, despite being grateful for the cover. "Thanks a lot, kid."

Jolie shrugged. "She would have figured it out sooner or later, just look at her."

"What does that mean?" Lindell asked, shaking her head. "Never mind. Virginia, what in shadows' hells were you doing? I could have you arrested for half a dozen different things with that admission. I could have your investigator's license pulled, I could—"

"But you're not going to," Virginia finished, smoothing her hair back, noting the dust clinging to the strands at the back. "You're not going to, because you need me, and Arthur needs me, and because I caught something your brilliantly brainless detectives missed."

Lindell crossed her arms, leaning back. "And what is that?"

Virginia licked her lips, almost flinching at the cracks stinging, an inevitable result of Verdance wind in the winter. "The photo frame in the living room. There was something behind the picture, I think removed recently. The glass is smashed, but there are zero shards beneath the frame. It was broken after the fact and placed there."

"That will be hard to prove, if you're thinking the whole thing is a setup."

"We don't need to prove it, Captain Lindell, we just need to use that to get us to the next piece of information." She chewed on her lip, savoring the pain and the gentle taste of blood on her tongue. "Ursa is really dead?"

"They really are. I'm sorry, I know you probably had hopes you'd find them alive. Was there anything else?" Lindell looked at Jolie, an eyebrow arched. "Anything else you'd like to share?"

"Don't ask *her*, Shirin, ask me," Virginia scolded. "I'm the consultant here, not the feral fire demon. There is a false panel in the closet," she said simply. "It is empty, but I think there was something valuable in there. A necklace, by the looks of it."

"How do you know it was a necklace?" Lindell demanded.

Virginia rolled her eyes. "If someone knew Ursa had it in there, or even if they knew to look for a false back in the wardrobe, it would have been easy pickings. Plus the arrangement of the dust in there suggests a heavy pendant.”

“We can’t prove that. It still might have been Nether.” Lindell glanced at Jolie again, watching her, searching for a weakness in her story, or a fracture in the case to pry at.

“I don’t think so.” Virginia shrugged, turning back to Jolie. “You can have them take swabs, I guess,” she said over her shoulder. “Then you’d know for sure.”

“I’m perfectly capable of running my squad and this investigation, thank you,” Lindell snapped. “I think sometimes you forget that you’re only on this case as a consultant.”

“Your own detectives missed two crucial things,” Virginia retorted, offering up a sardonic laugh. “I have no interest in wearing that ugly uniform, and as far as I’m concerned, this conversation is over.” She moved to close the door, the heavy oak catching on Lindell’s boot. “What, Shirin?”

“I thought you’d want to see the scene at the river.”

“And I thought you had banned me from all active crime scenes.”

“The sheriff didn’t agree with my call.” Lindell coughed, looking to the side. “And, much to my fucking dismay, I am forced to admit that you do have a keen eye. This case is only getting bigger, and we need to get this shit under wraps as soon as possible. The sooner, the better, or we’re all going to wind up being hounded by the press.” She narrowed her eyes at Virginia for a split second before her face returned to a neutral expression. “And I’d think you’d want to stay as far away from that limelight as possible.”

“Fine,” Virginia said, opening the door again. “Jolie, take the spare coat from the closet, that blanket isn’t enough to keep you warm. And a hat. We’ll need to hide your hair.”

Chapter Twenty-Eight

Virginia had almost expected the body to be a fake. A dupe, or unrecognizable, or something that would prove that it wasn't actually Ursa, but it was. There they were, still drenched from the river, algae-ridden rivulets cascading, careening down the slope towards a city drain. Something about the recognizably sickly pallor pulled at her, and she had to turn away before it pulled her under the riptide of another failure.

"What the fuck," Jolie whispered at her shoulder. "We just saw them."

"Shh."

"Ginnie, you're here," Arthur said. He pulled off his black leather leather gloves, revealing the lambswool inside. "I have to admit, I was hoping that you weren't right about this one." He tilted his head in concern. "What happened to your eyes? You look like you spent all night having a bender." He examined her, searching for a reaction she refused to give.

"Just coffee, Arthur."

"Maybe you should switch brands. You look like hell."

Virginia stared, challenging him in a way she knew he wouldn't meet. "I'm glad everyone feels so comfortable telling me what I look like, but let's get back to the situation at hand, shall we?"

"Who's this?" he asked, jabbing a thumb towards Jolie.

"Intern."

"You have an intern?"

Virginia nodded. "Yep. Work experience. I get a grant for letting her tag along. Don't worry, she knows not to get in the way."

"I didn't agree to this," he complained.

"I don't remember asking. As a consultant, I am not under the purview of the VCPD."

"Fine," Arthur relented. "Just make sure you keep an eye on her."

Virginia nodded, her hands shoved in her pockets. The day was so bitterly cold, the damp so threateningly pervasive, that she was regretting not putting on an extra layer before she'd left. "So walk me through this, Arthur. When did the call come in?"

"Just before noon. Bunch of Nether-heads down at the embankment saw something that looked strange, fabric they said, or something. One of them called it in when the current turned them over."

"Noon," Virginia repeated. It would have happened so soon after she'd left Anya's shop. She glanced at Jolie, throwing her a knowing look. Virginia cleared her throat. "You're sure?" she asked.

"Damn sure. Someone upriver confirmed that they saw someone matching Ursa's description skulking around the bridge, you know the one."

She nodded. "The railway bridge."

"The very same. Hard to know if it was the cold, drowning, or the impact," Arthur answered. "The coroner is on it, of course, but it's likely to be a combination of all three. It's a forty foot drop from the bridge, so they probably went into shock the moment they hit the water. Painless, maybe."

"I doubt that," Virginia said. "Death is rarely painless."

"Oh, and you're some expert?"

"More than you, if memory serves." She shivered, resenting the automatic reflex. "No one tried to pull them out before the paramedics showed up?"

"The current is strong near the bridge. They couldn't, not without getting pulled in."

She followed the trail of the draining water, watching as it slipped beneath the river's lazy winter foam. "They're a shifter too, you know."

Arthur sighed, rubbing his temple. "I figured as much."

"There's no way they had anything to do with Nether. They were dead set against it, working two jobs to keep the lights on and their brother away from all that." She turned back to the corpse, her stomach churning, but she forced herself to look anyway. "It didn't work, in the end. Now they're both dead."

"Might still be Fiske. Collecting for debts unpaid, that sort of thing. It's not unheard of, Ginnie."

"Of course it's not unheard of, but I... Ursa is another case entirely." She looked up at him. "I want off this case."

"What? Why?" He asked, almost laughing. "When have you ever wanted to be off a case?"

"I don't think it's relevant."

"Have you lost your mind? Of course it's relevant. The brother disappears for weeks, resurfaces as a powered up shifter, almost tears you limb from limb, winds up dead in a swanky uptown apartment, and now the sibling, too?" He shook his head in disbelief. "This is clearly connected to Fiske."

Virginia shook her head. "Not Ursa."

"How?" he demanded. "*How* can you disagree, Ginnie? It's clear as day that this is Fiske."

"It does seem like that," Jolie offered, taking a step back when she caught Virginia's glare. "I just mean, you know, in terms of what's been going on, lately."

"See? Even the kid can see it," Arthur said. "I can't force you to work on the case, but I am asking you to as the sheriff of police." He paused, looking out over the river. "As a friend, even."

"Ask Lindell to update you on the apartment, I found a couple of other things that might lead to some new information. A photo frame, a false bottom in the closet." Virginia shook her head. "I won't work this one. It's a clear conflict of interest. Lindell was right about that."

Arthur's face hardened, his dark gaze flat and uncompromising. "If you won't work this case, then you can't work any of them."

"Alright." Virginia turned, walking swiftly back to her car.

"Hang on!" Jolie shouted, running after her. "Wait!" she hissed. "What the hell was that all about?"

"Anya had something to do with this," Virginia replied, still marching towards her escape. "There's no way Ursa went to a healing appointment just to throw themself off the bridge. Something happened, something isn't adding up, and I don't want to get caught in the crossfire when Lindell finally figures that out. When she does, you can bet your ass she's going to be on our doorstep demanding all kinds of answers I don't have."

"I didn't think it would be Ursa."

Virginia wrenched open the car door. "Me neither, kid. I was expecting plenty of things, but I wasn't expecting that."

"Vane, what the hell do you think you're doing?" Lindell was striding across the petulant patches of dead grass, peeking out from under dirty, crushed snow. "You can't just quit, we're in the middle of an investigation!"

"Sheriff said that if I don't work this one, I can't work any." Virginia shrugged. "So I'm not working any. I thought you'd be pleased, since you were the one all bent out of shape about conflicts of interest with this."

"That's—you know what I meant!" Lindell turned, pointing at Jolie. "And you let her out of the car?"

"What did you expect me to do, Shirin? Keep her cuffed and covered in the back seat for days while we try to sift through this fucking mess? I hardly think that's going to endear her to the idea of talking to the shadows-damned cops."

"I expected you to have more sense!"

Virginia tilted her chin upwards towards Shirin, challenging her. "Sorry to disappoint you."

"She's going to end up blowing this whole thing wide open and it's going to be my ass on the firing line, Vane. You're not willing to play the game? You don't want to work on this case anymore because your *feelings* are hurt?"

Virginia stared at her, cold and unmoving. "Get out of my face, Shirin."

"You're selfish."

"Alright."

"Selfish and completely infuriating."

"I think we've covered that," Virginia said coolly. "I have work to do, so if you don't mind, I'm going to get to my office. I haven't been there in days, which hardly implies professionalism."

"Professionalism," Lindell spat, leaning in towards the car. "Professionalism would be not hanging my ass out to dry because you can't handle the heat in the kitchen."

"You have no idea what you're talking about."

"You can't stay away from this case, Vane. It's under your skin. I can see it plain as day, but let me tell you this—if I catch you fucking around with any part of this case, now that you've walked away from it, I will have your license stripped before the sheriff even gets word, and I will happily take that demotion knowing that it kept you out of police business."

"I look forward to it," Virginia said, looking forward as the car roared into life. "You'd better move, before I run over your foot."

Captain Lindell, still glaring, stepped back from the car, her hands balled into fists at her sides. "You're going to live to regret this, Vane."

"Let's hope I die first, then we can both be right."

"You can't keep carting that kid around forever, not with those enforcers looking for her. You're putting her into danger, you know." Lindell pointed at her, boots crunching as she backed away from the car.

"Making a play at my non-existent sentimentality is to be admired, Shirin, but I can personally guarantee you that if Fiske sends anyone after me, they're going to leave the same way the other two did."

Lindell barked out a laugh. "Don't call me when you're bleeding out on the floor."

"Fine."

Lindell still stood, still staring. "Fine." Regret traced its way through the sharp lines on her face before she turned back to the crime scene, waving to a new batch of detectives that had just arrived.

"So..." Jolie started. "Are we going back to Anya's?"

"After this morning? No. I'll call her from the office, but I'll have to be careful. Her phone is probably still tapped. If we show up out of nowhere, she may well hex us both." Virginia pulled into traffic, swallowing back the heavy sigh in her throat. "Or tell Astrid what I've been up to."

"Astrid?"

"Long story."

"Seems like you have a lot of long stories."

"When you get to be my age, you will, too." Virginia swallowed hard and checked the mirrors, always watching to see if she was being tailed. It wouldn't have been the first time, and with Lindell on the hunt for any hint of a mistake, it wouldn't be surprising if she'd asked some rookie to follow Virginia. "Guess I failed this time." The distant lake was choppy and unsettled underneath the persistently grey skies, reflecting back a distorted skyline.

"I've never seen a seer do what you did in Ursa's apartment, though," Jolie said, hand crammed into her pockets for warmth. The coat was too big for her, almost comically so, making her look even smaller than she really was.

"Do what?" Virginia asked. She waited for three squad units to roll past before she pulled out onto the road, gravel crunching with an ugly noise beneath her tires.

"Whatever that was. In the closet."

"It was nothing. A headache or something."

"Are you sure about that?" Jolie asked. "Maybe it was something else."

"Of course I'm sure, don't you think I'd notice?" Virginia asked with a snort. "The Rupture would have proved that easily enough."

"I don't know. I didn't know who I was until six months ago," Jolie said with a resigned shrug of her bony shoulders, barely visible beneath the bulk of the coat.

"I'm not a seer," Virginia insisted.

"Do you think Lindell will turn me in now?" Jolie asked, following the skyline as they passed the city, driving wide around the outside of it. "Now that you don't have a deal?"

"I don't think she would do that."

"She said you'd live to regret not working on the cases."

"She says a lot of things." Virginia sighed. "Listen, kid, it's been a really long few days. Week, really, and I could really just use some quiet."

Jolie turned back to the window, pulling her arms tight around herself.

"Alright."

* * *

Something slithered into Virgina's gut the moment she laid her hand on the doorknob to her office. Bracing, she threw the lock and pushed open the door, revealing a fine powder of shattered glass, the larger fragments sparkling in the fragmented sunlight. Virginia held out an arm to keep Jolie at bay, to keep her out of harm's way, unholstering her gun as she stepped inside.

But there was no one, only a jagged brick laying on the floor behind her desk, a note tied to it with wet twine.

"What is it?" Jolie asked, creeping around the glass.

"Probably nothing," Virginia lied. She untied the paper, the ink half smeared across the stained white page. *Stop looking for trouble,* it read, with the florid signoff of *RT.* Ruby Thorns. A clear enough threat, if she'd ever seen one, but certainly not her first. "It's a prank," she said, crumpling it into the trash. "Bored teenagers, if I had to guess."

Jolie's face contorted with confused suspicion, the the guilt of her expression sparked shame in Virginia's lungs. "Teenagers threw a brick through the window?"

"Wouldn't be the first time." Virginia scowled at the broken window, drawing the blinds across to cover the damage. She took a broom from the maintenance cupboard in the hallway and swept up the rest of the evidence, depositing it into the small wastebasket under her desk. As glass filtered down the collection of trash, the phone began to ring, somehow more insistent than usual.

"Vane," she answered, nodding at Jolie to close the door.

"Vee?"

Virginia sat in the chair. "Astrid?" She waved at Jolie to leave, but she didn't. Damned kid. "Astrid? What's the matter?"

"I've been calling since yesterday, Vee, where have you been?"

"Busy."

"I'm looking at a dead bartender, and you're *busy*."

"Shit. What happened?"

"Your guess is as good as mine, dollface, but he's in my shadows-damned cellar and I need you. I can't call the cops, they're already looking for any excuse to bust in here."

"I can't just... help you. Not with that." Virginia twirled the receiver's cord around her fingers, weaving an intricate knot that matched what her gut felt like. "Not again."

"I promise I'll never ask you for anything again, not for as long as I live," Astrid pleaded, her usual sultry voice laced with the high-pitched tones of panic.

"I doubt that."

"What do you expect me to do? Leave him there?"

"I don't know, Astrid. Call one of your bouncers to deal with him."

"You know I can't do that, they're all brawn and no brains. Blockheads make great bouncers, but shitty cleaners, if you catch my drift."

Virginia sighed, leaning back in her chair. It creaked, drawing more of Jolie's attention as she sat rapt. "Get better bouncers, then. I don't know what to tell you." She turned in the chair, uncomfortable under Jolie's stare. "What happened, anyway?"

"I'll tell you, if you agree to help."

The cases that were still open waited inside her desk drawer, but there weren't many left that hadn't ended in death. Virginia's best shot at closing the rest before they turned up dead was dragging Fiske out from hiding, and she knew his fingerprints were all over whatever was going on at the Sphinx. "No funny business, and no guarantees, Astrid," she warned. "If it's... if the situation is too messy, if it's too closely linked, if I think for even half a second that you are trying to set me up, I am gone."

"When are you coming?"

"I don't know. I have other things to sort out first."

"Vee, he's rotting in my basement," Astrid snapped.

"Fine. I'll be there before the club opens tonight." Virginia hung up the phone with a hesitant sigh, her fingertips brushing the brass handles of the desk drawers. "We're going to take a field trip."

"Where are we going?"

"You are staying in the car," Virginia insisted, her mind still on the brick lodged beneath her desk.

"Come on, haven't I proved that I can behave myself?" Jolie said, pouting. She looked younger than her age when she did that, sticking out her lower lip with huge, pleading eyes. "I won't say anything. Promise."

"It's not about behaving yourself."

Before they could debate further, Virginia's office door hit the wall, taking a chunk of plaster with it. "You said that you'd look into things," Mona said, pointing. "You said that you'd make sure Rickarton was fine." She whirled around, gesturing at Jolie. "Who the hell is this?"

"Intern," Virginia deadpanned. "Mona, what in shadows are you talking about?"

"Arthur just let slip that Benjamin turned up *dead*, Virginia. And his sibling, too. What the hell are you doing, if you're not trying to find out who did this?"

"Your marital discord isn't really my purview, Mona."

"Marital discord?" Mona snapped. "I hired you for a job, and you're fucking around with interns!"

Virginia pressed a hand to her forehead, savoring the distraction of her frosty fingertips. "I am no longer working with VCPD on those cases, not since they became homicides. You'd be better off harassing your other little pet Captain Lindell from now on."

"What do you mean, you're not working with them? That's not what Arthur said, and Lindell said that you had things handled."

"And was that before or after noon today?" Virginia asked. "Listen, Mona, I've done everything that I can on this, and I've come up empty. At this point, my involvement is a conflict of interest, whether Arthur or Lindell want to admit it or not."

"To hell with a conflict of interest, if someone is going around scooping up shifters, I think I have the right to want to protect my family."

"Your husband is the sheriff of police. You are better protected than almost anyone in the city." Virginia waved a hand. "Ask for more patrols around your house."

"That's not enough, and you know it. Penny could be in danger," Mona said, and she was almost shouting in her growing panic.

"If you're half as terrifying with enforcers as you are right now, I think she'll be fine," Virginia said coolly, far too preoccupied with Astrid's call to deal with Arthur's damned wife.

"Stop *mocking* me, Virginia. I came to you in good faith, and because you're... because you're so bitter and pissed off about what happened fifteen years ago, you're laughing at me instead of helping."

Virginia stood, bracing against the desk. "I have done everything I am able to within the law on this, and plenty outside it, too. This runs deeper than Rickarton, Mona, I'm sure he told you that much. I am sorry that I cannot single-handedly become your child's bodyguard, but it has nothing to do with what happened fifteen years ago. You want answers? Ask Lindell."

"One of Penny's classmates went missing. She's ten years old, Virginia."

"Was it reported?"

"You know it wasn't." Mona sighed, releasing the chair. She turned, her brown skin bronzed by the sudden appearance of afternoon sun, sparkling dust particles floating through the air, never settling. "Arthur said there's nothing he can do unless a report is filed."

"He's right," Virginia admitted. "Mona..." She trailed off, already sifting through details about the bartender in Astrid's basement. "There's too much going on right now. I'm sorry."

"You can't keep away from this any more than I can stop asking you to help," Mona said. "This is more than just a case for you, and I'm just trying to keep my children safe."

"Nowhere is really safe. Not for mythics." Virginia opened a drawer, setting files inside, willing Mona to leave her office. "The Rupture changed things. Half the world wanted to turn you into weapons, and the other half wanted you to go back into hiding." She shrugged. "Some did. *You* did."

Mona met her eyes. "I don't want to make things difficult for you, Virginia." She fumbled with her gloves, unsure whether to take them off or put them on. "Please find out what's going on at Rickarton."

Virginia sucked her teeth and inhaled, blowing air from the corner of her mouth. "I think the only thing that's going on there is them covering their asses. Other schools reported even higher numbers of disappearances, but they're all poor kids from poor families too afraid to talk to the VCPD." Virginia slid a page across the desk. "A few kids, here and there. Mostly teenagers, all of them registered mythics. It's Fiske, Mona. Once Arthur gets him behind bars, things will calm down."

"You took this on the moment Arthur set foot back in town, and again when I asked for help, and again when you found that boy. You took this on when you found that kid over there, and you can't fool me, Virginia, I know she's no intern. She's a mythic, and why you're hiding her from Arthur I don't know, but I do know that I won't hesitate to let that drop of information slip from my lips if you continue to refuse to help."

"You really are a piece of work, Mona."

Mona laid her hands flat on the desk, her doeskin gloves running along the surface. "Please, Virginia. The sooner he's put away, the safer my girls will be."

"Fine. But stay out of my way." Virginia faced her, really seeing her for the first time. Determined, strong, fierce. A woman to be feared, maybe. "And don't come here again."

Chapter Twenty-Nine

Virginia parked, trying to rub the growing headache out of her skull. Exhaustion didn't even begin to cover how she was feeling, and there was no end in sight. "Stay in the car."

"Come on, don't make me wait out here. I won't do anything, I swear," Jolie pleaded, going so far as to press her palms together like she was praying to the god that had long abandoned them all.

"I won't be gone long, for one, and for another, you probably don't want to see what I'm about to deal with. This place is like a trap. It sucks you in, and before you know it, you're a year older and somehow everything is worse."

"It's just a club."

"It's a lot more than that." Virginia slammed the door, pointing through the window. "I mean it. Stay hidden. If I'm not back in an hour..." she trailed off, the biting cold night air searing her lungs. "If I'm not back in an hour, leave. Get the hell out of here."

"I can't drive," Jolie said. "Not officially."

"Okay, if I don't show up, *unofficially* drive yourself home. Drive yourself to my apartment, I mean. There's a spare key hidden inside the third light fixture on the left, if you're looking at the door."

"And then what?" Jolie asked, climbing into the back seat so that she could hug her knees to her chest, fitting her legs up inside the oversized coat.

"And then if I'm still missing in the morning... I don't know. Call Lindell.

Or Anya. Hell, call Arthur, even, because if I'm not back, I'm probably dead."

"All this just for a quick job?"

"Nothing is ever quick with Astrid," Virginia grumbled. "Can you handle all that?"

Jolie nodded. "Yes, but I'd rather not, so maybe you could work real hard at not dying?"

"My complete disregard for self-preservation has yet to fail me." Virginia turned towards the club, already regretting showing up at all. Damned Astrid. It felt like she'd never be rid of her, the siren always calling her back. Calling her lapdog to heel.

If Lindell found out about it, Virginia would probably be in a cell by dawn.

"Club entry is around the front, but we're not open for another hour," a bouncer said. "Oh, it's you. Astrid said you'd be here."

"And here I am."

"He's, uh... he's in the basement."

Virginia nodded. "And Astrid?"

"Upstairs. She's getting ready for the show."

"Of course she is." Virginia rolled her eyes. "Far be it from Astrid to delay or cancel a show, despite the corpse in the basement."

He moved aside, opening the back door with a noisy creak, the hinges half frozen from the cold and in dire need of greasing. "You're the one we took to see Anya Quinn," he said, his stare falling to her shoulder. "You look better."

"Why, because I'm upright, and not bleeding all over the parking lot? It's a marked improvement," Virginia said dryly, ignoring the way his eyes wandered from her shoulder to her scars, resting there. Most people did. "So what happened to your bartender?" she asked, stepping over the threshold into the dark club. "He get in a scrap with someone? A distributor, a patron?"

"No, we just... found him there. Yesterday, when the rest of us got here for opening."

"You found him dead and waited this long to take care of it? It might have just been something to call a coroner for, a heart attack, a stroke, or—"

"You should take a look before you say anything else." He gestured to the stairs, old, painted wood flaking at the edges, disappearing into the darkness. "Down there."

"Did you find him in the basement?"

"No. Found him slumped over the bar, like he was asleep or something." The bouncer's eyes flicked from her to the stairs. "He wasn't asleep."

"Obviously." Virginia peered down into the darkness, unnerved. "There's no light down there?"

"Nah, burned out last month. We never go down there, so it didn't get replaced."

"You first."

"Sorry?" he asked, shaking his head.

"I said, you first. I'm in no mood to get ambushed."

He laughed, and it was easy, light. "I've got to watch the door. Astrid will have my head on a silver platter if someone gets in." He shrugged, giving her an easy gesture. "No one here's going to ambush you."

"I've heard that before, and I have the scars to prove it." She tilted her head in challenge. "You first, or I leave and tell Astrid you're why she still has a corpse in her basement."

He groaned, looking between the back door and the basement. "Fine, but you have to make it quick." He eased down the stairs, each step screeching with a chorus of creaks. "I hate it down here," he mumbled. "Even when there aren't any corpses."

"Do you store many corpses in the basement?"

"Only when necessary."

He said it with such ease, such a casual, light tone, that Virginia couldn't tell if he was being serious or not. "Right," she said simply, following him down. The hand railing was smooth but vaguely sticky, and she wiped her hands on her pants. "Doesn't anyone ever clean down here?"

"I told you, we don't use it much. No need."

"The rest of the place is immaculate, Astrid can't spare a few extra bucks to make sure the basement doesn't look like a portal to hell?"

He didn't reply, choosing instead to focus on each step in front of him until he reached the bottom, the thick sole of his boots landing with a thud onto the unfinished concrete floor.

"At least cleanup won't be too bad," Virginia said, noting the absence of both carpet and wallpaper. "Where is he?"

"Corner. Can I go? This basement gives me the creeps."

"Not yet." She squinted into the darkness, her eyes finding a crumpled form, folded over on itself, half braced against an exposed wooden beam. She moved closer, the hairs on the back of her neck standing up.

"Come on, I hate this place," he whined.

"Shut up." As her vision adjusted, her stomach turned at what she saw. It was Bryce, and his eyes were missing. "Shadows fucking shit," she gasped. "What the hell?" She turned on the bouncer, pointing at him. "You didn't say it was a hit job."

"How can you tell?"

"His eyes have been plucked out, you brainless fucking squid, how is that not obvious?" she snapped.

His form shifted in silhouette, the guilty balancing of weight sliding from one foot to the other. "So, are you going to get rid of him?"

"And cart around an obvious target of a hit job in the trunk of my car? No, I will *not* be doing that."

"But Astrid said—"

"Astrid conveniently left out some pretty important information that would have made a pretty big impact on whether I agreed to help her or not. Who have you all been pissing off, then? Fiske?"

"I don't deal with that end of the business," he said, shrugging. "I wouldn't know."

Virginia rolled her eyes, pushing past him to climb the stairs. "Astrid can clean up her own messes."

"She said you might say that."

"Great."

"She also said that if you did say that, I should tell you to talk to her first. Upstairs." He phrased this like two questions, rather than statements.

"No."

"Listen, Vee, or whatever your real name is—she was very clear in her instructions. I'm, uh... I'm not supposed to let you leave until it's dealt with."

Her fingers closed around the knuckles in her pocket, her other hand reaching for the revolver holstered under her shoulder. "You don't want to fight me," she said, staring him down, despite being half his size. "I *will* win."

"There's no need for all that," he said, taking a step back. "Just go talk to her, I'm sure she'll explain everything."

Virginia huffed out a sigh, stomping up the back stairs, an eye over her shoulder to be sure he wasn't following her. Something about the whole situation felt off in the same way it had four years ago. She threw open Astrid's door, hand still on her revolver. "Enough of the bullshit, Astrid."

"Vee, you came!" Astrid cried, turning towards her. She was barely clothed, a silk robe draped around her shoulders. "I knew you'd come to save me."

Virginia averted her eyes, fixing her stare at the wall. "I'm not here to save you. Your meathead bouncer said I wasn't allowed to leave until your little problem was solved."

"Oh, he's just a big softie, really. Takes things a little too much to heart."

"Why didn't you tell me it was a hit job, Astrid?" Virginia questioned her. While Astrid was likely in need of a good questioning, there wasn't much point with a siren. Three notes out of her mouth and they'd be freeing her.

"I was afraid you wouldn't come."

Virginia let out a frustrated growl, advancing on her. "This isn't a game!"

"I know it's not a game, dollface, that's why I called you. Repeatedly, in fact, for two days." Astrid looked up at her from the chair, her eyes wide and pleading. "Where were you when I needed you most?"

"Working!"

"With the VCPD?"

"It's none of your business how I conduct my affairs."

Astrid's face shifted, cold now. "It is when you drag me into it."

"I didn't drag you into anything, even though most people would definitely agree that I have the right to, after what you did."

"It was just a little bit of Nether, Vee," Astrid replied airily, toying with the white tie of her silk robe, twirling it in a lazy circle. "Don't be so dramatic."

"They were going to charge me with distribution."

"But they didn't!" Astrid protested again. She dropped the tie of her robe, perching at the end of her bed, smooth skin against wrinkled sheets. "Can you get him out of my basement or not?"

"Not," Virginia answered. "I'm not your corpse mule. I'm not going to throw a dead body into my car, drive to the lake, and toss him in like it's nothing, hoping all the while that I won't get caught and charged with murder. It's your club, Astrid. You deal with it."

"The cops will be all over me, Vee, and you know exactly why," Astrid whined.

"Yeah, I noticed the vials of Nether in the basement," Virginia replied, doing her best to be unmoved by Astrid's pleading. "Get rid of them. Problem solved."

"I can't just get rid of them, dollface, that's not how this works." Astrid tucked a pin into her hair, securing a curl in place.

Virginia released the revolver, setting the hand on her hip instead. "Hide them, then. Move them, I don't care, but I don't want any shadows-damned part of this."

"You're already a part of it. You're here, and that's exactly what I'll tell that very handsome police captain when she shows up asking questions about the stiff in my basement."

"I thought I was free of getting sucked into your vortex of horseshit, but apparently not," Virginia spat. "How do you know Lindell?"

"She came in here the morning you left, asking questions," Astrid answered. "I covered for you. Said we were old flames, sometimes you drop in. That's all."

"You are fantastically efficient at making everything worse." Virginia sighed, trying not to notice the way that Astrid was sitting, her robe falling open just so. "Keep my name out of your mouth, Astrid."

"Oh? I thought you liked your name in my mouth." Astrid stood, sauntering over, tracing a fingertip over the collar of Virginia's jacket. "Why are you so upset?"

"Because you have a corpse in your basement."

"Come on, Vee, just indulge me a little. You're always so stony, so walled off." Astrid smirked, leaning into her, breath ghosting against Virginia's throat. "The temptation is in the game. In getting you to finally bend."

"Tell me how he died, and I'll consider indulging you."

"After."

"Now," Virginia insisted. The heady cloud of perfume raked at her senses and threatened to pull her under, feeling Astrid's breasts pressed against her, the feel of lips on skin and losing herself to it all over again. She shook her head. "Now, or I leave."

"You're so stubborn." Astrid traced a finger along Virginia's jaw, following up towards the scars that crested her cheekbone, falling down from her hairline. "He got mixed up with the wrong crowd. He was trying to organize a deal to undercut Fiske."

"With who?" Virginia asked, pulling away from her, seeking something like fresh air to clear her head, but there was none available in the perfumed cloud of Astrid's presence.

"I don't know their name," Astrid answered, pressing closer. "Only that they're new in town and already attracting a lot of negative attention. Whoever it is boosted a huge shipment of Nether from some place uptown."

"Oh?" Virginia asked, despite already knowing how that scenario had played out. "Where did it end up?"

"That's the thing, no one knows. Franky reckons this new gun in town is angling to overthrow him, so he's a little keyed up."

"I don't know if I'd call a murder every other day *a little keyed up*," Virginia replied, her arms tight at her sides, determined not to give in to Astrid's advances. "So what did this newbie have to do with your bartender?"

Astrid lit a cigarette, leaning close. "I wish I knew, dollface. Bryce never brought it up with me. My guess is that he wanted to have details on the table before he came to me with a proposition."

"But he never did?"

"No."

"Don't lie to me, Astrid."

"I'm not lying. In fact, this is the most truthful I've been in years."

Virginia exhaled a laugh through her nose. "I'm not so sure that's saying much."

"It is what it is. We live, we fuck up, and we die." Astrid offered her the cigarette. "Not much unavoidable other than those three things."

"Taxes." Virginia took it, drawing a long drag. It wasn't her brand, but the tobacco hit just the same, swirling in her mind.

"Oh, you can avoid those just fine, if you know who to talk to." Astrid smiled easily, completely unbothered by the prospect of jail time, but then women like her never actually wound up in a cell.

Virginia took another drag of the cigarette, irritated how grateful she was for the smoky taste in her mouth. "Why am I not surprised that you're committing tax fraud, too?"

"Not fraud, Vee," Astrid corrected. "It's avoidance, not evasion. All perfectly legal with the right accountant."

"Do you ever worry that maybe you're not a good person?"

"No," Astrid replied simply. "I think the ideas of good and evil are unnecessarily stark and functionally useless, when we all exist in the in-between." She took the cigarette back, setting it to her lips again. "You're hardly so innocent yourself, dollface."

"Ancient history."

"You and me, are we ancient history?" Astrid asked, turning her head to exhale.

Virginia tilted her head, watching. "Maybe not as ancient as I might like."

"I gave you your information, are you going to get the stiff out of my basement?"

"No."

"Come on, Vee," Astrid whispered, pressing closer, her lips brushing against Virginia's. "I know you can do better than that."

Virginia swallowed hard, unable to bring herself to pull away. "I can't."

"Sure you can, you're one of the best investigators in the city."

"One of?"

"Are you fishing for compliments?"

"No, I'm questioning your judgment."

Astrid leaned closer, her tongue tracing along Virginia's bottom lip, pleading for entrance. "I've never had good judgment when it comes to you, dollface."

"The feeling is unfortunately mutual." Virginia let her in, groaning softly when their tongues met, hasty, careless strokes that pulled at her center, tempting and treacherous. Astrid's hands were on her waist, the cigarette stubbed out and the smell of sweetly acrid smoke clouding the air.

Astrid pulled her to the bed, her silk robe falling open to expose juicy flesh, soft and inviting, deliriously appetizing like a feast after a famine. "I knew you'd come to me," she whispered, delivering a soft bite to an earlobe. "I just wish we hadn't lost those four years."

"We didn't lose—" Virginia started, but was silenced with a kiss. Her fingertips pushed past silk, resting against skin, and the heat of it was a wildfire, uncontrolled, calamitous, and needlessly beautiful in its destruction. It was knowing she couldn't look away, like staring straight into the sun until her retinas burned and left her blinking, hands grasping for something that felt like earth.

There was nothing she hadn't felt before, but it was needy and insistent, a demand, an order she couldn't ignore, or walk away from, or pretend she hadn't heard. It was Astrid's body pressed against hers, and too many layers of fabric between them, and the sick twist in her stomach as she fell back into the void, like diving off a cliff when there was no water at the bottom to catch her fall.

A sigh crept into a moan that sat against her lips, breathing into her mouth, forbidden but absolutely at its own behest. She hated herself for giving in, and she hated herself for denying herself the saccharine pleasure for years, when she could have been in Astrid's bed all along, content to dismantle herself, piece by piece, giving herself away one pound of flesh at a time. A palliative destruction, expected and without nuance.

She was lost in it. Lost in Astrid, again, and slipping down the embankment into the river she'd always known she'd die in with her around. Astrid was poison, and Virginia was eagerly lapping her up, forever a moth to the flame. She inhaled the essence of her, toxic and alluring, the end of days compressed and delivered in the form of soft breasts and curved hips that fit neatly beneath her palms.

Something, somewhere in the distance, shattered. A glass from the bar, or a vial of Nether, or maybe even Virginia's ability to maintain her own composure. Tongues, heat, the yearning desperation to be torn apart just to prove that she could survive it again, even if she couldn't. Wouldn't.

Another thud, dull this time, like the sound of a door slamming against the frame. "Virginia!" Jolie's panicked voice shot through the fog and the panes of glass in the window, coming from the parking lot below.

Virginia shoved Astrid away, turning for the door. "Jolie!" she shouted, panic rising in her throat. "What did you do, Astrid?" she demanded, pulling out of her grip. "What do you think you're doing?"

"What are *you* doing?" Astrid shot back. "What are you doing with an inferno witch?"

"I should have known better." Virginia threw open the door, running down the stairs two, even three at a time, using the hand railings to vault down the final third. "Jolie!" she shouted again, her revolver already unholstered and ready.

She grabbed the bouncer by the neck, shoving him against the wall. "Where are they taking her?"

"I don't know," he replied, holding his hands up in surrender.

Virginia slammed him into the wall, stalking out into the night. "Jolie!" she yelled. "Where are you?"

A black car peeled out from the lot, the windows tinted. A revolver appeared through the rear end, firing wildly, more a deterrent than a real threat. She dodged the shots, running for her own car. "Shit!" she hissed, seeing the flattened tires. She climbed in anyway, only to find the car dead in the water. The slimy shits had drained the battery.

Slamming her fist against the steering wheel, she cursed herself for being so stupid to trust Astrid again. Virginia steeled herself before heading back into the club, rage boiling in her gut.

"Tell me what they've done with her," Virginia demanded, pressing the revolver to the bouncer's throat. "Tell me, or I swear to shadows I'll decorate the wall with your brains."

"I—I don't know, honest!" he said, sobbing. "Probably to Fiske!"

She pushed the barrel of the gun in further. "Where is Fiske?"

"They don't tell us. I'm just a bouncer, I don't know!"

"Did you know this was a fucking setup?"

He only stared, his eyes wide.

"I said, did you know?"

"Y—yes!"

"Tell me why!"

"Fiske wants her. Threatened to call the cops about the stiff in the basement if we didn't comply."

Astrid descended the final seven steps airily, as though she hadn't just betrayed Virginia all over again. "I'm asking you as a friend, dollface, please don't murder my bouncer. We have enough problems in the club tonight as it is."

"A friend?" Virginia hissed, turning on her. "You think that after all that's happened, after what you chose to do tonight, that we're *friends?*"

"What is some random girl to you, anyway? Fiske would have gotten her one way or another, and you know that's true."

"I know that it's your fault she's in the back of some car right now, you useless fucking monster," Virginia seethed.

Astrid's eyes narrowed. "You know, Vee, I would have thought you would understand our dynamic by now. In the moment, you never see what it is I am trying to do for you. Fiske is ruthless, and he'd slice you in half in a second if it meant getting what he wanted. I'm only trying to protect you."

"Protect me," Virginia scoffed. "*Protect* me? Are you serious? You tried to have me framed for Nether distribution."

"Would you have preferred a murder charge? Because that's what the state's attorney was aiming for after that guy turned up dead, dredged up out of the lake. I saved you, Vee, and you're too stubborn to admit it."

"My lawyer saved me, not you. Sadie Sinclair saved my ass, Astrid, not you." She struggled to regulate her breathing, the anger overtaking her. "I'm only going to ask you this once," Virginia said evenly. "Where is Fiske?"

"If I tell you that, you'll drive off half-cocked and get yourself killed." Astrid's gaze flicked to the car outside. "Although given the state of your car, I imagine you'd have to procure a mechanic, first."

"Where."

"He has a warehouse down by the docks, but it's so heavily guarded, you'll never even get close. Just drop it, Vee, or sooner or later I'll be saying my goodbyes to you in a cemetery."

"I'd rather be dead than get back into bed with you, literally or figuratively." Virginia's voice was pure venom, and it burned her tongue with every syllable. "Don't ever call me again. Don't breathe my name, don't even dare try to remember what my face looks like. If you were anyone else, I'd kill you with my bare hands."

Astrid dismissed the bouncer with a wave of her hand, and he disappeared behind a heavy door into the club. "If she's as strong as he thinks she is, you won't have anything to worry about. I'm sure she'll be fine. Sleeping in a work dorm down at the docks will be an improvement from sleeping on the streets for her anyway."

Virginia leaned in close, so close that her lips almost brushed Astrid's. "Fuck you," she breathed, pushing her against the wall. "I meant what I said. We're done."

"We'll see about that," Astrid replied, leaning in for one last kiss.

Virginia flinched away, releasing her. The wildfire of passion that had so recently bloomed had turned to ash inside her, smoldering into bloody embers of hate that would to engulf her if she wasn't careful. She turned, throwing open the door and stepping out into the frosty night.

Fiske had better run.

She'd tear Verdance to the ground before she'd let herself be fooled again.

Chapter Thirty

Captain Lindell looked up at Virginia from her desk, golden amber eyes staring over the lip of her mug. "What do you want, Vane? I thought you had asserted you were done consulting for the VCPD, which is why your presence here is so deeply confounding to me." She turned the page of the newspaper in front of her, setting the coffee to the side.

"I know where Fiske is."

"I doubt that."

Virginia pressed a hand to her hip. "Excuse me? You *doubt* that?"

"We have the full might of the force on high alert, and they haven't uncovered a single thing. What makes you think that you're special?" Lindell glanced around Virginia, eyes narrowing. "Where is the kid?"

She couldn't bring herself to answer. She only met Lindell's eyes for a moment before averting her gaze, staring at the worn floor, the wood in dire need of treatment.

"You lost her, didn't you?"

"It's more complicated than that."

"Is it? This is the second one, Virginia, how is that complicated?"

"Because she was thrown into the back of a car and taken," she shot back. "She didn't escape my grasp, she was kidnapped." She couldn't bring herself to admit the brick through her office window. Lindell would only judge her more harshly if she knew.

"Sounds the same to me." Lindell sighed, folding up the newspaper. "I can only imagine what the hell you were doing when all this went on."

"I would say that you don't want to know, but given your closeness with the owner of the Sphinx, I'm guessing you already know. In fact, I'd bet my right eye that you've been sitting there at your desk, posing with coffee and the evening paper for at least an hour waiting for me to show up."

"I don't think closeness is quite the right descriptor in this scenario."

"Isn't it? Astrid sure had a lot to say about you. A handsome police captain who questioned her the morning I left? Please, Shirin, you can't think I'm that dim."

"Handsome?"

"Keep it in your pants, Captain. I guarantee you don't want to be traveling down that road."

"By experience, I imagine."

Virginia closed the door, sitting in the chair. "She's got a stiff in the basement of the club. Funny that you missed that one, isn't it? I guess you also missed the enormous stash of Nether she's got down there too, did you? Excellent investigative work, *detective.* Keep it up and you might make sheriff one day."

"I didn't have a warrant for the basement, Virginia."

"Since when has that ever stopped you? Didn't have a warrant to be going through my sealed personnel record, either, but you had no problems with that."

Lindell tilted her head slightly, holding their eye contact. "Okay. What would you have me do, now?"

"Arrest her, obviously."

"For what?"

"Homicide. Manslaughter. Distribution. I don't give a shit, Lindell, arrest her for obstruction if you want to. Just get her the hell off the streets."

"She set you up."

"Obviously," Virginia spat, and the shame of it burned bright in her belly. Once more, she'd been sucked into Astrid's gravitational pull, only to be offered up as a sacrifice, as collateral damage to her fucking empire. It didn't even matter that her empire was no more than hordes of desperate, lonely people looking for comfort, Virginia was expendable.

"I can't say I didn't see this coming."

"Yes, I'm sure you're absolutely fucking thrilled that you get to parade around with that smug look on your face."

"I'm not smug, Virginia."

"The hell you aren't," Virginia accused.

Captain Lindell interlaced her fingers, strong, callused, and then flattened her palms against the desk. "I find you difficult to be around for a number of reasons, so whatever you are reading on my face, it isn't born of egotism nor self-satisfaction."

"What?" Virginia asked. "I don't even know where to begin with that, you—" Interrupted by a sharp rap at the door, she turned, and rolled her eyes. "Great."

"A surprise to see you here, Ginnie," Arthur said, and his tone was guarded, almost harsh, in a way she'd only ever heard him speak to members of the city council, or suspects being questioned, or a member of the press who had gotten too cocky for their own good. "I thought you were through with us."

"She might have a lead on Fiske," Lindell offered, "and she was wise enough to bring the information to me first, instead of trying to crash in on her own."

Virginia shot her a look, but remained seated, waiting.

"Alright, and where is he? Allegedly?" Arthur asked.

Lindell ran her fingers over the worn wood, almost hesitant, like she was about to plunge into a pool with an unknown depth, her eyes without their characteristic steadfast confidence. "We hadn't gotten that far before you came in just now."

"The docks," Virginia offered, after clearing her throat. "There's a warehouse at the docks, but heavily guarded."

"We've swept the docks four times," Arthur countered. "There's no way we missed something of that size."

"I think it's hidden beneath one of the storage houses out there. Maybe the one owned by Fiske Enterprises."

"Since when does Fiske own a building at the docks?" Arthur asked.

Virginia pulled a leaf of paper from her shoulder bag, holding it out to the captain. "Since he bought it under a shell corporation six years ago."

"How did you get this information? This isn't from the public records office," Lindell said carefully.

"Don't you worry about where it came from, the source is legit."

"We can't use that for a warrant."

"Then use something else for a warrant. Scoop up a witness, anything." Virginia snatched the page back, handing it over to Arthur. Ursa would have been the perfect person to act as a witness against Fiske, at least enough to get a warrant, until... well. Until.

"If you're consulting for the VCPD, you can't just be breaking and entering, Ginnie. You have to think these things through, or we're going to blow this case before we even have the chance to consider the repercussions," Arthur said, folding his arms across his chest, the gentle tan fabric of his coat wrinkling in response.

"No one broke or entered," Virginia shot back. "All I did was to call in a favor to someone who owed me one."

"Was it Zin?" Lindell asked. "The librarian, was it her?"

"Yes," Virginia answered through gritted teeth. "It's not technically illegal to find this information out, it's just more of a challenge, and one that most people couldn't be bothered with."

"I'm surprised she didn't read you to rights, given what that fire dem—" The captain stalled, covering the slip with a loud, overdramatic cough. "What that inferno witch did to the building."

"I more or less owe her my soul now, but at least we have somewhere to start," Virginia explained. "Zin really came through."

Arthur leaned against the closed door, one of his legs stretched out in front of him. "There's no guarantee they're keeping her at the docks," he mused.

"Who?" Lindell asked.

"The inferno witch. Ginnie's intern." He scratched his beard, gracing both of the women with a smirk. "Oh, you two thought you were being clever? No. I knew what you were doing from the moment that kid showed up at a crime scene, which reminds me, Ginnie, do *not* do that again. We have enough problems trying to keep things under wraps without adding more people to the mix."'

Virginia searched his face, and found what she knew would be there. "Mona told you."

"Of course Mona didn't—" he started, and then sighed. "Mona told me."

"Figures," Virginia said with a huff. "She only knows because once again she barged into my office demanding to know answers about Rickarton."

"I'll speak to her."

"No, don't. I can..." Virginia trailed off, searching for her footing. "I can understand her concerns." She picked at the lint deep in her pocket, ripping it away from the threads it had become entangled with. "We need to raid this warehouse," she declared.

"Absolutely not," Lindell said. "Even if there was Nether hidden in there somewhere, we have no warrant issued, we have no idea what we'd be walking into, and everyone in this room knows that Fiske has an army of attorneys ready to slap us with injunctions at every damned turn."

"Lindell is right," Arthur agreed. "We can't rush this."

"What about Jolie?" Virginia demanded.

He shrugged, holding his palms out in resignation. "We have to hope that she will be able to fend for herself until the time is right."

Virginia stood, pointing at him. "Just like all the others did? Are you serious, Arthur?"

"You know as well as I do that there are rules and regulations for the VCPD to adhere to." He lowered his voice, pointing back now, "And you should damn well know what happens when we skirt them."

"That never would have happened if you'd listened to me," she spat. "Those people died because you were too much of a chickenshit to pull your pants up and do something," Virginia hissed. "I told you there wasn't enough time to get them out *and* take down that crew, but you refused. You turned your back on them, just like you were already turning it on me."

Arthur's glare flicked to Captain Lindell, settling back on Virginia. "I'm not sure right now is the right time for this conversation, Ginnie."

"Isn't it? You had no problems flaunting it when I took the fall for what happened, even though you were just as much at fault as me." Virginia squared her shoulders, glaring. "You may be bound to bullshit protocols and paperwork, but I'm not."

"You are not busting into a warehouse full of Nether all on your own," he ordered. "Have you lost whatever sense you once had? You'll get yourself killed."

"It's better than another dead civilian on my conscience," she hissed. "It may not keep you up at night, Sheriff Dixon, but I haven't had a good night's rest in fifteen shadows-damned years."

He stared, unblinking, for longer than he should have. She'd known him well enough and long enough to realize that he was trying to decide whether to throw her out of the building, have her license stripped, or toss her in a cell to make sure she didn't do exactly what she was planning to do. "So much for our ceasefire," he said, finally.

"I'm not even firing yet," Virginia retorted.

Captain Lindell stood, bracing herself against the desk. She waited for a beat, looking between them before inhaling softly. "Virginia, as much as I am on your side with this, we can't go riding in there like it's a shootout. If we do, people will die, and not just civilians, but officers, too. And you, maybe, although you do have a strange knack for getting yourself into and then out of perilous situations."

"On my side?" Virginia asked, laughing. "You haven't been on my side since the moment we met at the quarry."

"All I'm trying to say is that we can do the most good here if we are calm and measured," Lindell said.

"Don't talk to me like I'm some rookie cop fresh on the force. I've been around just as long as you have, Shirin."

"Not on the force, you haven't. You're missing fifteen years in comparison."

Virginia's fists clenched, unavoidable, unconscious, and pulsing. "You're just as bad as the rest of them, and you don't even realize it," she whispered. She had to whisper, because otherwise, she would scream or cry, and neither was conducive to getting Jolie the hell out of there. "You're just one more crooked cop."

"Get out," Captain Lindell said evenly. There was no trace of anger on her face, only a strange, unreadable neutral expression, one that held no hint of what she was thinking. Like an erased chalkboard, or a page of notes that had been scratched out beyond comprehension, or a book with all the pages torn out.

"Gladly," Virginia retorted, picking up her bag and slinging it over her shoulder.

Arthur blocked her way, holding up a hand. "Ginnie. Wait."

"For what? You to get the lead out? For you to fuck me over one more time?"

"I'm only suggesting that this case bears a striking similarity—"

"Of course it fucking does, Arthur, why do you think I'm in here trying to make sure we don't make the same shadows-damned mistakes again?" Virginia asked, scoffing loudly. "Shadows on high, you've got your head buried so deep within the confines of paperwork and protocol that you can't even remember that's what led us to what happened last time."

"What happened last time?" Captain Lindell asked, face still neutral.

"The case file is sealed," Arthur said simply. "We signed contracts to keep things under wraps."

Virginia pulled at the cuffs of her sleeves, vaguely aware that she hadn't slept in a day and a half. It was wearing on her, and the weight of it dragged. "A bust went bad," she said.

"Ginnie," Arthur warned.

She ignored him, turning back to Lindell. "A bust went bad because we had to choose between saving eight people, or rounding up the lice who'd done it. Things were different in those days, it was before the Rupture. No one knew about mythics, there were none on the force, and it was more a numbers game, us versus them."

Arthur advanced on her. "*Ginnie,*" he repeated.

"I wanted to save the eight. Higher ups disagreed, they wanted to wait, to see what happened, to try for better evidence, for better witnesses." Virginia leaned forward, rubbing the newsprint under her fingers. She had always loved the soft feel of it, pliant and fragile. "I went anyway. Someone ratted me out, the entire force descended, eight people died, the scum-sucking crew got away, and I was kicked off the force." She shrugged. "Is that what you wanted to know, Shirin? How I fell from grace?"

Lindell held her stare, but said nothing.

"Don't worry, Arthur," Virginia said, putting on a light tone that did not match the subject, "I won't implicate you, or tell your subordinates how you were involved." She turned back to face him, his wide eyes blinking back at her. "After all, *officially*, you weren't."

"Ginnie," he said for a third time. "I thought we had agreed—"

"We did, and as you might notice, I've kept my mouth shut for fifteen years." She leaned in, whispering. "But for what?"

"You can't do this alone, Ginnie, no matter how angry you are. You're going to wind up dead." He was forceful now, challenging her. "You'll wind up dead, and it will be me in the morgue to identify you."

"Good," Virginia shot back. "Give your wife my regards."

"If you walk out that door, you're not coming back."

Virginia fumbled with the brass buckle of her bag, the metal cold under her fingertips. "Is that a promise, Sheriff?"

"This is a fool's errand, Ginnie!" Arthur shouted, and the windows of Lindell's office rattled. "I cannot sit by and watch you do this again."

"There is no again, Arthur. Last time never happened, remember? It was nothing more than a blip on the radar for the press, thanks to you. There aren't eight now, there's one, at least as far as we know, because Fiske keeps killing his damned distributors."

"One person isn't—"

She pressed her fingertips into his shoulder, pushing him a step backwards. "One person *is* enough, Arthur. That girl is enough of a reason to do something, and not sit around waiting for her corpse to wash up on the shore."

"Who is she to you?" he asked. "Why all this for some kid?"

"Because it could have been me, had I not run into you all those years ago," Virginia answered. "Because I have too many sins on my conscience this late in the game."

He nodded, his eyes softening. "Do I need to throw you into a cell for your own good tonight? Or can I trust that you will at least wait until morning? That you will, I hope, go home, sleep, and meet us at nine?"

"No. She's out there, but if we don't move now, she might not be by tomorrow."

"Ginnie…" he sighed, rubbing his head. "You look like you're about to collapse. You're not any good to that kid right now."

"He's right," Lindell offered.

Virginia turned and shot her a look. "You stay out of this. If you hadn't been sniffing around the Sphinx, Astrid never would have tried to pull me into this mess."

"First I'm not a good enough cop because I didn't check the basement without a warrant, now you want me to stay out of it?" The captain shook her head, scoffing. "You're a real piece of work, Vane."

"Captain," Arthur said evenly, "perhaps we can hold off on the ad hominem at least for tonight."

"She started it."

"The both of you can go and fuck yourselves," Virginia said, reaching for the door. "The VCPD might be more than happy to throw civilians to the crews, but I'm not."

"You're no good to her dead," he said quietly, in a soft tone she hadn't heard since they were married, and it gave her enough pause to let her hands fall back to her sides. He moved to lay a hand on her shoulder, but thought better of it, pulling back. "It hasn't even been a full week since you were attacked, and despite your protestations to the contrary, I know you're not back to full strength."

"Seamus really needs to learn how to keep his mouth shut."

"He worries."

Virginia sighed, the exhaustion pulling at her again. "He should worry about himself. Only a matter of time before these crews go after the weres, too."

"We'll cross that bridge when we come to it."

"I can fend for myself, you know, I'm not helpless. I've been just fine on my own for fifteen years." Something like pity flashed in Arthur's eyes, and she hated him for it. No, hated herself. The deep and inextricable loathing settled into her again, a thin poison that always dripped down her spine, one desperate molecule at a time. She lifted her chin. "I nearly took out a bouncer without even thinking earlier tonight."

"Just wait twelve hours, Ginnie."

"Fine." Virginia grabbed the knob, wresting it from the door frame with a noisy grinding sound. "But if anything happens to that girl, I will personally see that everything classified leaks to the press."

Chapter Thirty-One

Fiske wouldn't be so stupid as to send Jolie straight back out on the same night, but it didn't keep Virginia from returning to the Sphinx. She waited around the corner in the shadows, hoping. Willing Jolie to show up in some car with a shipment of Nether, unharmed, unscathed, and ready to turn the whole operation on its head.

No one came. Astrid was smart enough to know that someone would be watching the club that night, whether it was Virginia, the VCPD, or both. She'd know not to risk her livelihood on a top up shipment, not when the stakes were so high.

The car would have to be towed. It sat there, as useless as it had been hours before. Checking her pocket watch, she sighed again, heavier, the weight of it filling her chest with the guilt and regrets she'd always sworn not to have. Dawn was almost cresting the horizon, the pink glow looming, ominous, the frustration of a new day and the heaviness of what it meant for Jolie.

People who were missing longer than a few days were rarely found. Benjamin had been unusual in that regard, but he'd wound up dead anyway, just like his sibling. Just like so many others that were foolish enough to trust Virginia Vane. She shook her head, eyes squeezed shut. She'd made so many mistakes, such callous disregard for anyone other than herself, and it showed.

It showed in her personnel file. In the sealed case file, too. It showed in how the only person who had spent the night at her apartment in years had been that kid. Other dalliances were brief, calculated, triaged, and dispatched long before the sun rose. Most dispatched themselves. Virginia directed the rest to the door, craving silence again. Craving the comfort of her own broken mind, maybe, or just afraid to get caught in another web.

It hadn't mattered. She'd done that anyway, though not out of affection for Astrid—no, there had been affection, once. Guarded, but it was there nonetheless.

"Can I safely assume you spent all night out here?"

Virginia turned, arms folded over her chest, defensive at the sound of Lindell's raspy voice. "Tailing me again, Shirin?"

"No, I just correctly assumed this was where you'd be." Her hair was still damp, almost frosted in the icy air. "Don't make me tell the sheriff you still haven't slept."

"I'm fine," she replied, betrayed by the yawn that demanded to be released.

"At least let me take you home."

"I'll walk."

"Where's your car?" Lindell asked, leaning against the cold bricks of the building.

Virginia nodded to the parking lot across the street. "Sphinx. Bastards slashed the tires and drained the battery."

"Sounds like your reputation preceded you."

"Astrid will have warned them."

"Better to be feared than pitied," Lindell said, tucking a stray wavy lock behind her ear. "I didn't know about what happened before. It doesn't seem right."

"It wasn't." Virginia breathed a sigh, the cloud dissipating into the air, lit by thin streaks of dawn. "Isn't."

"He has some brass balls, coming back to Verdance after what he did to you," Shirin said, and there was an earnestness that hadn't been there before.

Crispy snow on the tree branches started to sparkle in the early light, almost like thousands of tiny sequins gently laid atop the empty wood, waiting patiently for spring. "It was a long time ago," Virginia said, and meant it. "I should be over it by now."

"I don't know if that's something I'd ever get over." Lindell looked out at the horizon, a tiny patch of road between endless buildings, stretched out to the lake in the distance. "It does explain a lot about... how you are."

"How I *am?*" Virginia asked with a sardonic laugh.

Lindell toyed with the sleeve of her cuff, but maintained eye contact, staring at her with those piercing amber eyes. "You're abrasive."

"I'm sure plenty have said the same about you."

"They have."

While there was never silence in Verdance, sometimes there was a moment of respite, most often near dawn, when the night owls had long since left the clubs, staggering home, and the early birds were rising with the sun, preparing for one more hopelessly short day. "They're going to destroy that girl, Shirin," Virginia said. "They're going to realize what she is, and they're going to rip her apart by the time they're done."

"I know."

"Why the hell does Fiske need a fire demon, anyway? What the hell is he protecting down there? It can't be just Nether, can it?"

"Hard to say."

Clouds were beginning to gather over the lake, heavy and ominous as they began to block out the weak rays of sun. "I miss the days before all this. Before the shadows-damned Rupture," Virginia said after a long, uninterrupted moment.

Lindell shifted her weight, the metal of her belt grinding against the holster at her hip. "I think many of us do. Mythics and mortals alike."

"A stupid saying. We're all mortal. All capable of dying, of being dispatched, of being hurt."

"We'll find her," Shirin promised.

"And if we don't?"

"If we don't..." The captain sighed. "I don't know. We try again." Shirin watched as a man delivered crates of milk to the apartment buildings across the street, the delicate sound of the glass almost like wind chimes. "Let me drive you home, Virginia. I'll get your car picked up by the civilian contractor."

"I can wait a little longer," Virginia replied.

"She's not coming. They're not sending her here, probably not ever, knowing that you'll be watching, and they definitely wouldn't have tonight. You need to sleep."

"Getting some sleep will be worse than not getting any at all," Virginia retorted. "I'm fine."

The first true beams of sunlight crested over the road, illuminating everything ugly that collected in the gutters. Slimy, discarded newspapers clogged the grates, along with half-frozen piles of days-old snow, a few broken bottles, and inexplicably, one boot. Verdance did always look better at night, or from a distance. Despite her love for the city, it was ugly, and undeniably so.

"I don't know if I would have survived it, getting thrown off the force," Shirin offered, her eyes always traveling, always looking, always analyzing. "I think I might have just died instead."

"Mm." Virginia didn't offer the truth of it, that she almost had, that she'd spent months alone in that apartment, drifting from empty room to empty room and feeling the loneliness and disuse creep up behind her like some vengeful, forlorn shadow, inescapable and foreboding. Even the memory of it still twisted like a knife in her side, even all those years later. "Alright," she relented. "I'll let you drive me home. I should get a shower in, at least."

* * *

A part of her had almost been foolish enough to hope that when she reached the top of the stairs on the fourth floor, that Jolie would be there, standing at the door with a big smile and a wild story about how she'd escaped.

What Virginia hadn't anticipated was Anya, standing at the door, wringing her hands. *Fuck.*

"Vee, you're here!" Anya said, relief flooding into her. "I need to talk to you." She hardened, her mouth set with a deep frown. "Captain Lindell.

You're here, too."

"Shirin, I'll meet you at headquarters later. Thank you for the ride," Virginia said, willing her to leave.

Captain Lindell smirked, tucking her cap under her arm. "I think I'll stay, actually. Make sure that you're alright."

"I'll come back later," Anya said, moving to push past Shirin, her skirts whispering curses against the floor, but Virginia caught her by the arm.

"I probably won't be here later, for one thing," she said, unlocking the door. "For another, I'd love to hear how you got my home address."

"From Ursa."

The name gave her pause, and she laid her palm flat against the door before she pushed it open. "Oh."

"I don't know what happened, they were—" Anya glanced at Lindell again, clamping her jaw shut. "They seemed fine, the last time I saw them."

"And when was that?" the captain asked coolly.

"Shirin," Virginia said, flashing her a glare. "Not now. If I'm supposed to be sleeping, I can't have the two of you bickering in my kitchen." She dropped her bag on the counter, leaning against it with a beleaguered sigh. "One or both of you needs to leave, or I'm going to snap."

"Fine," Anya said, still standing in the hallway. "Will you call when you get a moment? Or stop by the shop?"

"I will, when I get a moment," Virginia promised. "Probably won't be until tomorrow."

"Why?"

Lindell stepped between them, offering Anya a condescending smile. "Police business. You understand."

"You planning to toss a few more shops today, Officer?" Anya shot back, her aqua eyes almost steely in their defiance.

"Maybe, if they are hiding information from the police, or stocking illegal reagents."

"Those were for personal use."

"I'm sure," Lindell said, and it was more than a challenge, it was derisive.

Virginia blinked for one second too long and already the weight of sleep pulled at her, begging her to rest. The room almost spun around her, taunting and cruel. "Anya," she said again. "I'll meet you the moment I can."

Lindell closed the door, turning to the kitchen with her brow furrowed in accusation. She opened her mouth to speak, but Virginia held up a hand to silence her. "Not now, Shirin. I know you're about to tear into me about that, but I need a shower and I need sleep. I am not able to have yet another argument with you on the subject."

"Alright."

It was all she said, but the momentary lapse in aggression was welcome. Virginia nodded towards the cabinets. "Coffee's in there. I'm sure you can figure the rest out." Virginia pushed off the counter, stripping off her coat to hang on the rack. She unbuckled the holster, laying it on the table along with the knuckles from her coat pocket. She glanced between the weapons and Lindell. "You're staying, then?"

"Why, is that an invitation?"

"If you're staying, I can leave the gun out here."

"Do you usually shower with your firearms, Vane?" Lindell asked, tapping her boots against the worn mat inside the door to slough off the clumps of wet, muddy snow.

"Within reach, yes."

Lindell stared at her for a moment before shaking her head with a blink. "Seems a little paranoid."

"Don't call me when you're bleeding out on the floor." Virginia arched an eyebrow. "Isn't that what you said to me?"

Lindell didn't reply, but raised an eyebrow and sucked her teeth instead.

"There's not much food around, but help yourself I guess."

The captain pressed a hand against the green wallpaper, leaning easily, almost nonchalant, almost performative in the gesture. "I already ate."

"Okay then. Well, I'm going to shower." Virginia hesitated, her stomach knotted. It had been a long time since she had showered with someone else in the apartment watching the door. Even with Astrid, even with the others that had come and gone over the years, she was never bare. Never vulnerable. The realization sat heavy on her mind, despite the door that would separate her from Lindell.

"Are you going, or what?"

"Yeah. Yeah, I'm going."

* * *

A soft knock roused Virginia from her sleep, and before she even opened her eyes, the headache began to pound.

"Fuck," she muttered.

"Are you alive, or do I need to call the coroner?" Lindell called through the door.

"I'm alive," Virginia groaned. "Unfortunately."

"The sheriff called."

"Okay."

There was a brief pause, and the sound of Lindell's boots against the hallway floor. "Are you coming out?"

"Shadows, yes, give me a moment to regain consciousness." Virginia threw off the blanket, pressing a palm to her forehead. The throbbing in her skull was insistent, drawing focus away from all else. She'd done it to herself by not sleeping, but knowing that didn't lessen the pain.

She pulled on a pair of fresh trousers, a dark green wool, paired with a crisp white shirt from her closet and a pair of suspenders. There was no sense bothering with a tie. Pushing her hair out of her face, she fixed it back with pins, securing it out of her face. Virginia stared blearily at the silver-framed mirror hung on the wall and sighed. If it was even possible, she looked worse than she had before.

"Alright, Lindell, what is it?" she asked, opening the door.

"Right. Well." Lindell stepped aside, allowing her to exit the room. "The sheriff called, and they went back to the docks this morning to—"

"He sent squad units there? Without us?" Virginia demanded. Fucking Arthur. She should have known he'd go behind her back.

Lindell sucked her teeth, as though she was bracing for an outburst or an argument. "For reconnaissance."

"And?"

"And they didn't find anything."

Virginia huffed out an angry sigh, petulant and unguarded. "No shit they didn't find anything, I'll bet he sent the fucking rookies, didn't he?"

"I'm not aware of who he sent."

"What about the Fiske warehouse?"

Lindell shook her head. "Nothing."

"That can't be true," Virginia said, already regretting that she'd succumbed to sleep. "They must have missed something."

"There was a full sweep done, every stone overturned, every crate inspected, and there wasn't so much as half a vial of Nether."

"No!" Virginia shouted. "No. Maybe there's an underground area we haven't yet uncovered."

"That close to the river?" Lindell said, shaking her head. "It's impossible, it would be nonstop flooding."

"Something else, then. A loft, a false wall, a—"

"Virginia, there was nothing." Lindell clasped her hands behind her back, looking oddly formal. "He's asked us to go in for a strategy session tomorrow."

"Tomorrow?" Virginia exited the hallway, greeted with the deep fuchsia glow of a Verdance sunset painted across the walls. She reached for her pocket watch, laying next to her holster, and groaned. "Why did you let me sleep for so long? Twelve hours, he said. Twelve."

Lindell looked to the side, fixing her stare on a bit of blank wall. "I called and told him that it could wait, that you weren't..."

"That I wasn't *what*, Shirin?"

"Fit for duty. Fit to consult."

"How is it that every time you try to make amends, you turn around and make things worse?" Virginia demanded. "Leave."

"Excuse me?"

"You heard me," Virginia ordered. "Leave. I'll find the kid myself. Shadows know that the VCPD is apparently good for nothing. You're both content to let Fiske keep running his little racket, waiting for a picture-perfect opportunity instead of doing your damned jobs."

"You aren't hearing me, Virginia. It's not about being afraid, it's about trying to control the seemingly unparalleled amount of Nether being trucked throughout Verdance every day, it's about trying to keep people safe, it's about making the hard choices." Lindell shrugged, and it was aggressive. A challenge.

"You think I haven't had to make hard choices?"

"Of course you have, but that's why you're not on the force. Don't you think that—"

Virginia glared at her, regretting ever letting her through the door in the first place. "*Leave*, Lindell."

"If I leave you're just going to throw yourself back onto the streets, dragging yourself across the city looking for the kid, looking for Fiske—"

"You're damned right I will!" Virginia spat. "What other options are there, when the shadows-damned VCPD refuses to lift a single finger?"

"There's nothing at the docks, Virginia! Already the sheriff is in hot water with the city council, asking where that tip even came from. Do you know how much money the Fiske family gives to mayoral campaigns in this city? To the governor, for her reelection? Use your brain, instead of just your gut for once! Do you really think Fiske would be stupid enough to hide his criminal enterprise in a building he owns?"

"I think you and Arthur agreed that you'd babysit me to keep me out of the way," Virginia snarled. "I think you decided how today would go, and didn't let me in on it. At what point does it become more important to serve the city, and less to cover your asses?" she asked. "I can't wrap my head around the idea of letting Fiske do whatever the hell he wants just because he's connected."

"Because not everyone is you, Virginia," Lindell replied, running her hands through her wavy hair, tousling it out of frustration. "Not all of us are trying to die in the line of action."

"You think I'm *trying* to die?"

Lindell sighed, tucking her shirt back in and straightening her badge.

"It sure as hell seems like it." She approached the kitchen softly, with apprehension. "I'm just saying that you take more risks in the field than most would, and it's usually to your detriment. It's not even been a full week since you were attacked, and you're barely sleeping, you're messing around with Astrid again—"

Virginia turned towards the sink, flexing her hands in and out of fists, her head throbbing. "I didn't offer to deal with the stiff in the basement, in fact, I told her she was on her own because I wasn't about to get involved in a hit job."

"The corpse was gone by the time a squad unit got there," Lindell replied. "And the terrified bouncer, I assume that was your doing?"

Virginia sighed. "Maybe."

"You probably shouldn't be sticking guns into people's faces."

"And you probably shouldn't be holding me prisoner inside my own home, but here we are, Shirin."

"I'm not—I'm not holding you prisoner, Virginia, I'm asking you to be sensible and wait for more intel for once. Don't fly off the handle and get yourself captured or killed. Fiske will be on high alert, and if you go flying in there, guns and knuckles blazing, that's it." Lindell moved out of the way, allowing Virginia to pass. "This is all too messy to be half-assing it. Too many connected murders, too many incidents, your best girl Astrid will almost certainly wind up in prison—"

"Good," Virginia said, rage bubbling up in her throat. "She belongs in prison."

Lindell arched an eyebrow, but didn't move. "You all but threatened me to keep me out of that club and away from her business."

"Because I knew she had more information on Fiske, not because of any... lingering affection. Astrid clams up around cops."

"Is that how your relationship started?"

"No, I was long gone from the force by the time I had the extreme misfortune to fall into her little trap." Virginia turned the tap on, allowing the cold water to shock her senses, to give some semblance of distraction, to let her forget for just one precious millisecond that most of this was entirely her own damned fault. "This isn't how I like to conduct my life, it's just that this is all rather uncomfortably strung together. Arthur, Astrid."

"I don't judge you for what happened with the sheriff."

Virginia splashed her face with the frigid water, welcoming the bracing jolt. "And Astrid?"

"I judge you a little for that," Lindell said, but she laughed. "Who hasn't fallen into bed with the wrong woman once or twice?"

"Oh yeah? Did yours ever try to frame you for Nether distribution?"

"No. She did empty my apartment while I was on shift, though."

"That sounds like an interesting story." Virginia turned back, cringing at the unexpected wistful look on Lindell's face. "Oh," she said softly.

"It was seven years ago," Shirin said. "I never found out where she went. The one that got away, I guess."

Afternoon was quickly turning to dusk, the morning's sparkling pink snow fading into Verdance's dark recesses, cold, lonely, and stark, giving way to the growing clouds over the lake. Virginia braced herself against the counter, waiting, hoping the right words would come, and when they didn't, she cleared her throat. "So are you going to help me get Jolie back, or not?"

"Virginia..." Lindell started, a quiet sigh passing her lips. "We have to wait. I know it's hard but it's how things have to be, at least for this moment."

"Then I will be at the station bright and early."

"Will you promise me that you won't do anything that might get you killed?"

"I can't promise that," Virginia said, and nodded towards the door. "I'll see you in the morning, Shirin."

Chapter Thirty-Two

The night was cold, even more frigid than it had been in recent days. Whatever snow was left roving over what would someday be thick grass had crusted over with ice, crunching delicately under Virginia's boots. Tugging her coat tight around her, she flinched against the involuntary shiver that crested neatly over her spine.

She knocked, quietly at first, and then with more force when there was no answer. "Come on, Anya," she grumbled under her breath.

The shop door swung open despite the desolate darkness within, the only light pooling under the door that led to the tiny clinic, and the ghastly yellow pallor of the street lights reaching with bony fingers through bare branches to rest uncomfortably across the floor. "You came," Anya said. "I was afraid you wouldn't."

"After that display at my apartment? How could I resist the intrigue?" Virginia stepped inside, stomping the remains of slush from her boots.

Anya reached around her to throw the lock, being careful not to disturb the closed sign that hung on the door. "If there was anyone else I could go to—"

"I get it, you're not my biggest fan." Virginia bristled, thrusting her hands into her pockets. "Do you want my help with whatever this is, or not?"

"How is your shoulder?"

"Fine."

"Let me take a look." Anya waved her towards the clinic door, the silver bangles at her wrist clinking softly with every gesture.

"I said, I'm fine," Virginia insisted.

"I want to see how well that poultice worked. It's a fresh blend, and it's never been used on a puncture before."

"So I was a test subject?"

"Are you complaining?"

Virginia followed her through the shop, petulant. She wouldn't have come, if she'd known it was only for that. "No."

"Strip," Anya said, with all the warmth of a block of ice. Clinical. Professional, but in a distant way.

"Usually I ask women to take me out for a drink, first." Virginia closed the door behind them, squinting into the vague candlelight that spread across the pristine tiles laid into the floor. Flames flickered, dancing with shadows on the whitewashed walls in a strange, unchoreographed dance.

"Do your dates usually come with free medical care?" Anya asked.

"I thought Astrid was paying you."

"She was. This, however, is complementary."

Virginia shrugged off her coat, laying it across the cot. She unbuckled her holster, keeping it in her lap as she unbuttoned her shirt and slid the suspenders down over her shoulders. "So what happened with Ursa?" she asked. "That's why you really wanted me to come here, right?"

"Dual purpose," Anya said, inspecting the wound. It had almost healed completely, despite the ugly scar that spread across Virginia's shoulder. "It's looking good. How is your range of motion?"

"Fine. Ursa, what happened?"

Anya traced a finger around the edges of the wound, and it was so gentle that it was almost imperceptible, yet the feel of it made Virginia's breath catch in her throat, unexpected and perilous. Anya frowned at the scarring and pressed gently, testing the skin for infection. "I don't know what happened, Vee. They were here, and they were gone."

"How did you find out? I wasn't aware their death had hit the papers."

"Whisper network."

"Cops?"

"No," Anya said, turning to a cabinet to rifle through a set of jars. "I am old friends with the coroner."

"She could get fired for leaking information." Virginia flinched now that Anya wasn't examining her, poking at the wound herself. It was still tender, not that taking punches from Seamus had helped it much.

"It's only to me, and only when relevant," Anya replied. "Only when it's a mythic, or someone connected to... well, you know."

"Connected to Fiske."

Anya nodded, unscrewing a lid from a small, palm-sized jar. "I've been trying to keep tabs on him, but it's almost impossible."

"Yeah, you're telling me."

"This will be cold, sorry." She approached slowly, with too much caution, hesitating too long before she smeared a sweet smelling ointment over the wound. "Where is your intern?"

"Fiske."

Anya glanced up at her. "Shit."

"Yeah."

"She run, or...?"

Virginia gripped the edges of the cot, bracing against the cold slime of the ointment. "No. Astrid set me up." She sighed, and it hissed past her vocal cords. "*Again.* I don't know where the kid is, but I need to find her. If they figure out what she really is..." she trailed off, unwilling to finish the thought.

"What is she?" Anya asked.

"A fire demon," Virginia answered, already regretting saying it aloud.

Anya jerked back, her ointment-covered fingers hanging in the air. "What?"

"We—Captain Lindell and I, that is—thought she was an inferno witch at first."

"She'd be in enough danger if that was the case," Anya said. "This is much worse. Fire demons are very rare." She returned to the wound, massaging the sticky mixture into raw skin. "Extremely powerful."

Virginia nodded. "They've been after the kid for weeks. One of them chucked a brick through my office window, I didn't think they knew I had her." She hissed out a grunt between gritted teeth. "They don't know what she is, they just think she could hold her own in a fight."

"And could she?"

"Maybe. She's young, inexperienced. She's only had her abilities for six months or so."

Anya smoothed the surface of the remaining mixture, melding it at the edges. "Did you see the body? Ursa's body?"

"Yes."

"And it was definitely them?"

"Whatever it is you're dancing around, Anya, get to the damned point."

"I think something happened to Ursa."

Virginia squinted at her. "Obviously."

"No, I mean…" Anya pulled back again, scraping more ointment out of the jar. "They were trying to get out of the city."

"And you think Fiske's enforcers got to them first?"

"Not exactly."

"You're going to have to give me a little more than that to go on, I'm not a mind reader." Virginia did her best to not think about the warmth spreading through her shoulder, but it was such a welcome, desperately craved feeling that she couldn't help but lean into Anya's touch, savoring the feel of the medicine. "What happened when Ursa left here?"

"Nothing out of the ordinary, I—they wanted a clean escape."

Virginia sighed. "They tossed their own apartment, didn't they?"

"Yes."

"Any ideas what they were keeping in the closet? Something… shiny?"

Anya tilted her head, smoothing over the last of the ointment. "Shiny? No. Why do you ask?"

"No reason. I just thought if it was important, they might have taken it with them, but nothing was found on the body."

Anya stood back, examining her work with a curt nod before handing over a clean bandage, this one light and thin. She bit her lip, hands shoved deep into the pockets of her skirts. "I need to tell you something, but I need you to listen until I am done, and not start shouting."

"Ominous, but alright."

"The body pulled from the river wasn't Ursa." Anya turned to the sink, washing her hands. "It was an illusion. Magic."

Virginia shook her head, pulling her shirt back on. "No, that's not possible. No illusion could look... quite like that."

Water splashed into the basin, creating a fine spray of mist that hung in the air for only a moment before crashing back down into the porcelain. "Mine can," Anya said simply.

"Since when is a witch with a healing specialty capable of advanced illusion magic, too?" Virginia asked.

Anya dried her hands and put the jar away, her fingers lingering on the brass knob. "Since it's me, and I can."

"Impressive, but then what the hell was the corpse?"

"Sometimes, sacrifices have to be made to achieve higher levels of magic," Anya explained. "Significant ones."

Virginia drew in a breath, somehow simultaneously relieved that Ursa may yet be alive, and terrified of what Anya was about to say next. "I sincerely hope this isn't a homicide confession."

"Not unless you can be tried for buying a pig from the farm just outside the city limits."

Exhale. "No."

"My bet is that you'll get about thirty-six more hours before the coroner sounds the alarm. They'll probably think someone stole the corpse, replacing it with a pig. Most illusionists..." Anya sighed before continuing, "most illusionists wouldn't deal in matters such as these. Not anymore, anyway."

"Is this a service you frequently offer?"

"No. First time for everything, right? And I don't think I'll be doing it again," Anya admitted. "Too messy for my taste."

"Messy," Virginia repeated, buttoning her shirt, her fingers sliding up the seams as she covered herself. "Okay, so Ursa is alive, I guess, but what I'm still missing is why you showed up at my apartment looking like someone had left the corpse in your bed."

"I don't know if they're alive."

"But you said—"

"They were going to wait a few days, let me get clear of suspicion," Anya said, wringing her hands again, now that they were finished with their work. "Ursa was supposed to call me when they crossed state lines, to let me know—I don't want to get pulled into a homicide investigation, Vee."

Virginia sighed, and then nodded, showing that she understood. "We might be past the point where that's avoidable."

"I'd have been the last person to see them alive," Anya agreed. "And I knew you would tell Lindell." She tugged at a long silver necklace around her neck, pulling the sapphire pendant back and forth over the chain. Virginia had spent enough time in interrogation to recognize anxiety when she saw it, and maybe even guilt.

"I didn't tell Lindell," Virginia said, tugging the suspender straps back over her shoulders with a snap. "But I had a feeling that there was something you weren't telling me, and I knew that filling in the VCPD would only complicate matters at this point."

"Thank you."

"It's not a favor."

Anya leaned against the door, fidgeting with the apron she wore over her dress. "I realize that, but my thanks are genuine, all the same." She tightened the looped tie at the back of her head, pushing a few stray hairs back into the loose bun. "In any case, Ursa didn't call."

"Do you think Fiske got them?"

"I'm hoping that's not the case, but with the heightened awareness around their brother's disappearance and death, that may well be what happened," Anya said.

Virginia restrained a heavy sigh, releasing it from her lungs slowly. "So, what, you want me to find Ursa? Again?"

"I don't know, I just thought you should know. Just in case," Anya offered. "In case he comes for you."

"Fiske?" Virginia asked, biting back a laugh. "No. It's Fiske who should be worried about *me*."

"He's dangerous, Vee."

"I'm aware, but that kind of intimidation only works on people with something to lose."

Anya held her stare for a moment, her brow furrowed, before looking away, busying herself with tidying the tiny vials of reagents. "I would think you have plenty to lose."

"You'd be surprised, then." Virginia left it at that, not thrilled at the idea of sharing more than she should with Anya again. "I'll go down to the docks and have a look for myself. Rumor has it Fiske has a warehouse down there. Lindell made sure to keep me out of it today, because I think that sending a bunch of rookies that are still wet behind the ears to flush out Fiske is an empty-brained idea. There must be something else," she said. "Something underground, maybe."

Anya's hands brushed over each vial, twisting until the label was facing forward. In the orange glow of the candlelight, they looked almost sinister. "Underground? But the river—"

"I know, I know, Lindell said the same thing. But there has to be something down there."

"Unless it's another setup. Who told you that Fiske was at the docks?"

Virginia's hands fell to her sides, resting against the soft white sheet. "Astrid's bouncer."

"Right. *Astrid*."

"That's a fair point." Virginia rubbed at her eyes. "Shit." She chewed on her lip, rebuckling her holster over her shoulder, wincing at the fresh tenderness. "Something isn't adding up about it, though. Why hide the warehouse within a shell corporation if there's nothing illegal going on down there? Why go through the trouble of all of it, of it looking suspicious as a shadows-driven hell, if it's just a warehouse?" Virginia paused, running through every possible scenario in her mind. "It could be that it's something illegal, just not Nether."

Anya nodded thoughtfully, chewing on her plump bottom lip. "Gambling?"

"Maybe," Virginia admitted. "Or illegal imports skating around outside the embargos."

"Is it wise to go after Fiske for something other than the Nether?" Anya asked, fingers trailing over the collection of vials, all alphabetized now, straightened, prim in their places. "Wouldn't he just get out of it again?"

"It's hard to say. I can't just leave her with them, Anya. I know every reason why I shouldn't go down there, why I shouldn't risk tipping them off, why Lindell and Arthur are probably right—I'd listen to them if all of this wasn't my fault—but—"

"How is any of this your fault?"

"I was the one foolish enough to cozy up to Astrid in the first place." Virginia sighed, pushing her hair out of her face. "I was the one who let Benjamin leave, who didn't keep tabs on Ursa, who was foolish enough to fall for a setup."

"Don't pull all that misery to yourself, Vee, it will bury you alive."

Virginia rolled her eyes. "Probably too late for that," she muttered. Running a finger over the stamped brass buttons of her coat, picking at a frayed thread. "It's complicated."

"You know, there'd be no harm in taking a walk down by the docks," Anya suggested. "I hear Verdance looks beautiful from the Inner Avenue bridge over the river."

"Are you asking me on a date, Anya?"

"You did say that you prefer that before being asked to strip, maybe I just got the order wrong." Anya matched her expression, pausing, almost daring Virginia to break the silence first. "You're not so bad when you're not being a pain in the ass." She turned, selecting a jar from the cabinet. "Or outright hostile."

"Harsh," Virginia retorted. "I don't think judging me when I have a panther fang puncture wound is very fair. I have to say, your bedside manner leaves a lot to be desired."

Anya set two vials into tiny straps inside her bag, folding the top closed and latching the buckle. "I can say with complete certainty though, that you have one hell of a right hook. That guy who showed up here the other night had a jaw fractured in three places."

"Glad to have your seal of approval," Virginia said, wrestling with the temptation of laying into her about hiding the fact she'd treated both of those enforcers from the alley. It wasn't the time for that, and much to her dismay, Virginia needed Anya's help at the docks if she was going to get close without being scooped up. "What are the vials for?" she asked, gesturing.

"Insurance." Anya slung the bag across her body, adjusting it so that the pack laid against her hip. "I'm still waiting for you to replace my reagents."

"They're in lockup, and I don't have access."

"Some ex-cop you are, you can't even kick in a door for me?"

"You know, I keep trying to burn that bridge, but the shadows-damned thing won't stay lit." Virginia blew out a line of candles along the wall at Anya's gesture, shooting tiny plumes of smoke into the air. "Maybe breaking into lockup will do it for me."

Anya unlocked the back door, gesturing to the alley behind the shop, a gentle snow drifting through the air, content to float on the breeze from the lake. "I hate to say it, but you're not very much use to me in a cell, and I don't think I'd visit you in prison."

"Wow," Virginia said, stepping out into the cold.

"Years later, when you were finally eligible for parole, you'd come back here, hoping for a reunion, or maybe revenge, but the windows would be all boarded up and I'd be long gone."

"This is some web of fantasies you're spinning," Virginia replied, buttoning her coat before too much of a freezing draft could snake its way around her hips.

"Or maybe the shop would have been replaced with a book store," Anya continued. "Or a place to get rare tea blends, or imbued soaps, and you'd find yourself wondering if it had all been a dream."

"Except for the court record."

Anya laughed, turning to lock the door. "Yeah, except for the court record."

Chapter Thirty-Three

The snow, which had started so gently, so polite and unassuming, had quickly begun to settle on the roads. The flakes that fell from the sky grew thick, heavy with damp and the looming threat of a blizzard. Verdance was no stranger to it, and so the cars kept driving through the streets, and pedestrians trudged home in the early darkness, and Virginia swiped another laden piece of snow from her cheek.

"Lovely night for a walk," Anya said lightly, disguising the sarcasm in her tone, but poorly. "Some would almost say it was romantic."

"Calm down, Quinn, there's no need to put on that much of a show," Virginia retorted.

"We both know that Captain Lindell could very well be around any corner, waiting for you to do exactly what she asked you not to."

Virginia shifted her weight against the railing of the bridge, leaning out over the half-frozen river below. "We can only hope that I've convinced her to trust me this once."

"Given what you're doing, I doubt it."

"You're one to talk, you tried to help someone fake their own death. That's hardly legal, is it?"

"No," Anya admitted, dragging the word out as she squinted up into the harsh orange glow of the street lamp, "but neither is anything you've done recently. I'm surprised they haven't already pulled you in for obstruction."

"That might still be how this ends, you know."

"If Captain Lindell shows up, I'm running for it."

Virginia laughed. "Some alibi you are."

A car drove past, the tires making wet tracks in the burdened snow, crushing it into water that would become ice as the moon rose in the sky, crescent but clouded over. Virginia waited until the sound of the engine died down, fading as the car rounded a corner. "We need to get closer, I can't see shit from here." She looked out over the water, watching the eddies as they swirled lazily around ice, kicking up sticks and debris from the river's bed. "I can barely even see that warehouse from here."

"Which one is it?"

"The one with the orange lights outside the loading door."

"Looks quiet."

"Too quiet, maybe. These docks usually keep busy through the night. See, look," Virginia said, pointing, "the others are midway through shipments."

"Seems like if you were smuggling embargoed goods, you'd do it at night."

"Not if the VCPD knows that and sends more patrols at night, then you're going to be aiming for shift change, near dawn."

Anya groaned, wrapping her arms around herself. "I'm not standing out in the cold all *night*, Vee."

"You're free to leave if you can't handle it," Virginia offered. "No one made you come here, you know."

"I have a feeling you're much more interesting outside the law," Anya said with a distinctly mischievous tone. "Outside the precinct."

"I wouldn't go back now, even if they let me. Too much water under that bridge. As soon as this case is done, I don't know. I need a change of pace for a while."

"What you need is a vacation, Vee."

"Fat chance of that happening," Virginia replied with a scoff.

"Come work at my shop," Anya suggested. "You can scare away all the paying customers."

"We'd kill each other," Virginia said simply. "We're like piss and petrol."

"Which one is piss, and which one is petrol?"

"Depends on the day."

Anya gripped the railing with her mittened hands, leaning out over the water, her silvery hair like pristine moonlight as it swayed in the breeze. "I don't think you could walk away from this work, Vee. It's in you, somehow."

A horn sounded from somewhere a few streets over, the harsh brashness of it pulling Virginia back to whatever reality it was that she was being forced to live in. "I'm going to get closer."

"You'll get caught, is what you'll do."

"I can handle myself." Virginia gave a vague gesture to the holster under her coat. "Besides, even you admitted that I have a hell of a right hook."

"You know Captain Lindell is going to be watching that place like a hawk. It's a foolish move."

"The whole of the VCPD is convinced that my tip was garbage." Virginia watched the movements at the warehouses adjacent as crates were unloaded from the barge three at a time. "Arthur has the mayor and the governor breathing down his neck, I doubt if they'll even be running the usual patrols past this place. The other warehouses, sure, but not this one." The cold of the steel railing bit into her hands, and she let it, feeling the sting clear her head of the fog within. "I think Fiske is up to something. A turf war doesn't seem important enough to be taking these risks, but you never know. Maybe he's losing his grip." she shook her head. "It's impossible to know without more context."

"What about Astrid? What does she know?"

"Shadows only know what Astrid knows. You said it yourself, she's not just unreliable, she's outright damaging." Virginia sighed. Too much talk of Astrid was burning a hole in her chest, a fire built of shame, and guilt, and something else entirely that Virginia didn't care to investigate. "I'm going down there," she said finally, pushing away from the frosted steel. "You can either come with me, or you can stay here pretending to be a lost tourist, or you can go home and pretend this never happened."

"There's something you should know about me, Vee," Anya said, a heavy weight to her voice.

"Oh? And what's that?"

"I have an insatiable sense of curiosity that may well kill me one day.

Let's go."

Virginia laughed softly. "I hope your stealth training is better than your bedside manner."

"My bedside manner gets rave reviews," Anya argued, her tone light despite what they were doing. "How close are we going to get?"

"As close as we can, and hope we don't get nabbed," Virginia said, the soles of her boots echoing strangely against the metal grate, stilted by the ice, the frozen air, and the low hum of cars driving across the girders.

"I'm less worried about Captain Lindell, and more worried about Fiske's enforcers."

"You should be worried about both equally. Lindell might separate my head from my shoulders if she finds me down here." Virginia checked her pocket watch, frowning at the time. "Hopefully, she's off-duty by now. She spent all day babysitting me."

Anya followed behind her, moving quietly. "I didn't think that's something you would allow."

"I was asleep."

"And you let her stay in your apartment?"

"With Lindell, you rarely get a choice on the matter. I'm quickly learning that," Virginia said, exiting the bridge onto the ice-slicked sidewalk. "Careful."

"I've lived in Verdance a long time, I know what ice is."Anya stepped carefully onto the grass, her coat pulled taut over her shoulders. "I hate winter in this city."

"Everyone does. Shadows only know why the hell we stay."

"Because there's nowhere else in the world like it?" Anya offered, but it was clear that she hadn't even convinced herself.

Virginia pressed her fingers against the faded metal sign that directed towards the docks, and the rivets felt like waves under her palms. "I don't think that's it. I think it's because starting over now would feel like signing my own death warrant."

Anya was silent, joining Virginia behind a brick outbuilding. She tilted her head, looking up at the growing clouds, and exhaled, her breath a fog, and then it was gone. "I know what you mean."

Growing uncomfortable with their conversation, Virginia ignored the comment, rubbing her hands together and wishing she'd brought gloves. "The warehouse is three buildings to the north. Are you still up for this?"

"Too late to back out now."

"Nah, you could try to climb the slope back to the bridge, just to prove to me that you know what ice is."

"Tempting, but I think I'll stick with you," Anya replied, tucking her hair back into the wide, fur-lined hood of her coat.

"There are three night guards at the next building. Follow my lead, and we might manage to get out of this unscathed." Virginia eased around the brick corner, her steps light, trying not to step through the crusted snow. One of the guards leaned against a wood post at the end of the dock, his cap pulled down over his eyes. Sleeping, hopefully, if they had any luck. The other two, standing at the loading door, were embroiled in an argument she couldn't quite discern over the sound of the river.

"There's a truck over there," Anya said, pointing. "They left the lights on."

"A quick drop, maybe, or they're draining the battery of some poor fool they've already picked up." Virginia stiffened, glad that she'd left her car back at her building, just in case Lindell drove past to check. "Looks empty, at least."

The uncovered bed of the truck was quietly, slowly filling with snow, the miniature drifts cresting and cascading against the metal, hiding whatever lay beneath, if there was anything at all. The headlights glowed sadly beneath the caps of snow, obscured by the growing cover.

"Who do these warehouses belong to?" Anya asked.

Virginia shrugged. "Various companies, all of them vetted. One carries spices, one deals in textiles, and this one we're passing has a vested interest in automotive manufacturing. Parts come here to be sorted, and then get packed up north. There are usually large trucks coming through here in the day, which is why they prefer to take in shipments at night. More time to sort."

"What else does Fiske have his fingers in? Any other businesses that might be protecting him?"

"It would be easier for me to tell you what he *doesn't* have his fingers in."

They approached the first warehouse, easily skirting the half-asleep dock worker, pausing behind a cord of wood, nestled beneath a slapdash tarp. Several logs were already covered in snow, and now would be useless for months yet.

"Shh," Virginia urged, placing a finger to her lips. It was more a gesture than a sound, but Anya nodded all the same.

"When does the next boat come?" one guard asked, his red scarf a beacon against the encroaching gloom. He sighed. "I'm bored off my ass out here."

"Thirty minutes, maybe an hour depending on the lock operators."

"It's too damned cold to be waiting outside."

"You know the rules, O'Doyle, if we get caught waiting inside again, they're going to give us the boot."

"I'm so cold I don't even care right now."

"You will when your house is just as cold because you have no cash to pay for wood or oil." Further down the river, a loud horn sounded, reverberating along the embankment, signaling a ship's arrival. "See? That's probably it. Not much longer to wait."

Virginia watched them, tracking their movements. Satisfied they wouldn't turn around, she darted to the next building across the gravel track, set deep with fissures drawn by the many trucks that loaded up at the docks. Anya followed, almost dancing over the rocks. "Impressive," Virginia said. "You were almost as silent as me."

"Please, you sounded like an elephant on the gravel. I'm surprised every alarm in the tri-county area isn't sounding right now."

"Alright, Anya."

"Did I wound your pride?"

"You're getting on my nerves." Virginia grappled with the side of a window, standing on the sill to grab the gutter, pulling herself onto the slanted roof. Hiding behind the chimney stack, she peered across the dockyard, eyes following the rutted truck tire tracks from one loading area to the next, scanning for movement. There were none at the Fiske warehouse, and something about it didn't seem right.

"I hope you don't think I'm climbing up there," Anya whispered.

"Shh," Virginia hushed. "No one is asking you to. I'm just getting the lay of the land. There's no movement at the Fiske place."

"Maybe that's good?"

Virginia sighed, dropping back to the ground with a soft thud, her boots crunching against the snow. "It means they're laying low. Might be that he's already moved everyone, or everything. Spooked by the VCPD raid." She shook her head, a low grumble emitting from her throat. "This is why I told Lindell it was a bad idea to rush in there like that, rookie detectives, no way to track where people were being moved to because the force is spread too thin."

"Sounds like you should have been sheriff."

"In another life, I probably would have been." Virginia glanced at the seemingly empty warehouse again, brow furrowed. "But the VCPD is too far gone now. You can't reform what's rotten from the foundation."

Anya shoved her hands into her pockets, standing back from the building, brow creased as she took in the growing clouds overhead. "So what now?"

"I still want to get closer. It might give us some ideas as to where they might have gone. I should be able to get a general idea of how many trucks went in and out today. At least the damned snow is good for something."

"Seems to me a man like Fiske would have salted over the snow, obfuscate the tracks," Anya suggested.

"Not if he was in a hurry."

"Lead the way, Vee. But I'm not climbing on any roofs. I'm accident-prone enough as it is." Anya flashed her a bright smile, out of place within the context of the situation, and for some reason, it made Virginia want to set herself on fire just to escape it.

"I'm not used to working with other people," Virginia grumbled. "It makes me twice as likely to get caught."

Anya raised an eyebrow. "Okay, well I'm here now, so how about we just focus on getting closer, and we can argue about it later? Maybe you can even tip off the cops again, I had so much fun being raided last time that I definitely want to repeat that experience."

"That's not exactly fair."

"Neither was getting pulled into your bullshit with Astrid. If they hadn't dragged you, unconscious, half-dead, begging me to do something, I wouldn't be standing here in the snow freezing my ass off, waiting for you to make a move." Anya shrugged at her, staring. "So move, Vee."

Virginia let out a sigh, more of a quiet hiss, and stalked to the front of the building, watching the second warehouse for guards. "Two there, just inside the door. We should get past just fine."

"I think I can control myself. Can you?"

"I'll manage." Virginia rolled her eyes, despite the fact she wasn't even facing Anya anymore. She crossed the gravel path again, waiting to hear Anya's soft landing before she sidled against the second warehouse. The workers inside were quiet, but as the freighter approached the first, there was plenty of cover for the sounds of their footsteps.

Fiske's warehouse was just ahead, and the windows were dark, unsettling for the relatively early hour. Nine in the evening was rarely a time for the docks to be silent. The loading door was closed, and a set of iron gates were sealed with a large padlock. "Shit," Virginia whispered. She grasped the steel bars over a window, pulling herself up to peer inside through the dirty window. She squinted into the vast darkness, confronted with the eerie sight of an empty warehouse. "There's nothing inside," she said, lowering herself to the ground.

"Nothing?"

"Empty."

Anya took a step backwards. "Was it empty earlier?"

"I don't know, Lindell didn't mention it. Probably not." Virginia crouched, frowning at the tire tracks in the snow. "Three, maybe four trucks maximum. Not enough to clear a full warehouse, even if they were large vehicles."

"Nether?"

"Could be. Could be everything they moved was above board, and it's just... I don't know, some sort of power play against the city council or the mayor." Virginia sucked her teeth, examining the tread marks. "It would explain why both of the latter parties are putting so much pressure on Arthur."

"Any thoughts on the padlock?" Anya asked, lifting it, turning it over in her mittened hands. "Do you think you'll be able to get inside?"

"Not sure. It's a new model, I've never picked one before."

"Even if you did, if the warehouse is empty—" Anya started.

"It *looks* empty, that doesn't mean that it *is* empty. There could be a trap door inside, leading to some sort of basement, or a false wall, somewhere they could be hiding what would be evidence. Illegal imports, Nether." Virginia took the lock from her, the weight pressing firm against her palms. "People."

She pulled a pick from her inside pocket, thrusting it into the lock. It was an unfamiliar layout, and she closed her eyes to visualize the internal schematic. Five tumblers, each of them with a guard to prevent picking. It would be even more of a challenge with her hands half-frozen from the still falling snow, dense with lake water. "So much for your theories about the blizzard."

"Shadows, Vee, just pick the damned lock already. My toes are starting to go numb."

"It's not my fault you didn't dress for the weather."

"Please, as if you're not cold right now."

Virginia opened her eyes, locking Anya in a challenging stare. "I'm perfectly warm." Her body betrayed her with a visible shiver, and she scowled. "I just don't like the snow."

"Sure, sure." A smile played at the corners of Anya's lips, but she had the decorum to keep whatever mocking comment she had lined up to herself. A rare burst of peace, when it seemed like she never shut up.

"Hmm," Virginia grumbled. "I get the feeling that someone tipped them off before the VCPD showed up."

"Who?"

"Beats me, could be anyone who knew they were going to do the raid today. Any of the detectives, any of their partners. It could be anyone in the whole department if they sent a memo around headquarters." She ran her thumb over the lock, the brushed metal smooth against her frozen fingertips. "Which I'm sure Arthur did."

"How's the lock coming?" Anya asked, rocking back onto the heels of her boots, holding her arms tightly around herself for warmth.

"Slowly, but we may get there in the end."

"A private investigator and a locksmith, what a combination."

Virginia stood, a hand on her hip, firing off a withering stare. "How else do you think I get proprietary information?"

Captain Lindell stepped out from behind an empty crate, arms crossed. "One would hope through means other than breaking and entering."

Shit.

Chapter Thirty-Four

Virginia had hoped she would be able to go the rest of her life without being cuffed again, but clearly, that had been far too ambitious. She shivered again in the frosty malevolence of the squad unit, shoved in the back like a common criminal.

Although, in fairness, maybe she was one.

Maybe she always had been.

"I can't fathom why you always have to make things so difficult for yourself, Virginia," Captain Lindell said, sliding into the driver's seat. She met her eyes in the rear view mirror, shaking her head. "And what's with bringing the apothecary owner with you? That seems very out of character."

"She wanted to come."

"Why?"

Virginia shrugged, unsure of whatever Anya was telling the officer in the other car. "Work experience."

"That excuse isn't going to hold water for much longer, you know. I'm the one who was there when you gave that excuse to the sheriff about Jolie Laar."

"Jolie, who's still missing because your dimwitted department was too hot on the ignition to gather more intel first."

Lindell laughed. "That's rich coming from you, Vane, you were ready to storm the gates, guns blazing."

"No, I was ready to storm the gates with a small, prepared team of those of us with enough experience to know that once the shoe drops, the roaches scatter. And scatter they have, so excellent job, Captain, well done."

"I should think you'd be a little more respectful, given you're in cuffs."

"What, are you going to charge me with resisting arrest, too?"

"No, but your attitude might make me conveniently forget your phone call until tomorrow afternoon." Lindell turned back for just a moment, glancing at Virginia. "Don't test me, Vane."

"You're not even supposed to be on duty," Virginia pointed out.

"And neither are you," Lindell argued. "I seem to remember you assuring me you wouldn't do anything impulsive, and yet here we are."

Virginia scoffed loudly, and she jingled the chain that held the iron cuffs together. "You just wanted to keep me out of the way."

"Because you're jeopardizing investigations."

"No, because I'm jeopardizing your job. Admit it, Shirin, you feel threatened by me, and that's where all your shadows-damned hostility comes from. You lure me in by pretending to be normal, and then bam, you're behind me with a bat, taking me out of the game entirely."

"I didn't hit you," Lindell said, turning back to the front. "And I didn't have a bat."

"You didn't need to."

"You said you'd stay put for tonight!" Lindell said, her raspy voice booming. "You said that you would wait until we had more information."

"I couldn't, because the VCPD fucked up the mission!" Virginia shouted. "That warehouse is empty now, Shirin, and—"

"Captain," Lindell corrected. "I don't think it's appropriate for someone in cuffs to be addressing me so informally."

"Oh, fuck off, *Captain*."

"Very professional," Lindell shot back.

"My professionalism died fifteen years ago when I realized it was nothing more than ass-kissing," Virginia retorted. "I suppose it doesn't matter now that you're going to toss me into a cell for the rest of my days."

Captain Lindell made a noise somewhere between a laugh and a grunt, her hand pressed to the gear shift as she twisted the wheel. "Don't be dramatic, Virginia, it's a trespassing charge, not homicide."

"Why were you waiting for me?"

"Because I knew you wouldn't listen."

"This is entrapment," Virginia accused. "A clear-cut case, Shirin, and the second my lawyer hears about this, she'll have me out on bail and this trespassing charge dismissed."

"It's not entrapment, and you know that," Lindell growled. "You can't go around doing whatever you want! Compromising missions, adding more fuel to a fire that's already starting to burn out of control. We have rules and regulations for a reason, and you choose to skate around them like they don't apply to you."

"You've hated me from the moment I showed up at the quarry," Virginia spat. "You decided then and there that you would do everything in your power to make my life a living hell. Well, great job, Lindell, I think we can safely say it's mission accomplished."

The car was quiet for a moment as they crossed beneath the street lamps, bars of light like fool's gold cresting and falling through the windshield, blurred into a hazy glow by the thickening snow. Drifts were collecting in the verges, and they'd be iced over by morning, waiting on the sun to melt them. Waiting on warmth that was still months and miles away.

Captain Lindell breathed softly, barely audible over the sound of the engine. "I don't hate you, Virginia."

"You have a strange way of showing it."

"I find you deeply frustrating, yes, that much is true, but hate?" Lindell shook her head, stopping at a light. "I don't think I could ever hate someone like you."

Virginia stared out into the snowy landscape, pointedly avoiding meeting Lindell's eyes in the mirror. "Oh, give me a few more opportunities, I'm sure you'll grow to see the inevitability."

"Did you ever think that I waited out here, freezing my ass off in the cold, because I wanted to make sure you didn't do anything that would get yourself killed?" the captain asked. She was trying to sound calm, but the waver in her voice was unmistakable. "That perhaps I might have more information than you? That I wanted to be positive I wouldn't wake up to a police report on my desk, with your name in the morgue?"

"Now who's being dramatic?"

"You're reckless, Virginia. You're reckless, and you don't even realize it."

"Of course I realize it," Virginia said with a laugh. "You think I don't understand what this all entails? We've had a fresh body almost every day for a week, and you think I'm unable to put two and two together? Fiske is running scared from something, and I for one am not exactly thrilled to find out what that is."

Lindell loosened her grip on the steering wheel, sighing. "It doesn't make it better if you know it's dangerous and go anyway."

"Doesn't it?" Virginia asked. She let the question hang in the air, a challenge, like a deflating balloon on a slow descent into one more bad decision, influenced by instinct and reflex. "Isn't it better if I understand the risk?" she asked again.

"I don't know."

"Whatever happens next, Anya didn't have anything to do with it," Virginia asserted. "Not a shadows-damned thing."

Lindell scoffed, the whisper of breath from her lips forming a messy cloud before immediately beginning to dissipate. "Oh, you forced her to come along, did you?"

"Yes."

"She didn't look like her arm was being twisted, Virginia."

"You don't always have to physically force someone into complying, you know," Virginia said, tugging gently at the cuffs. There was no way she could get out, not when Lindell had taken her lock picks, but the metal was beginning to rub her wrist raw. "Maybe I blackmailed her."

"Are you admitting to extortion now, too?"

"Just let her go home, Shirin."

"I can't. She's already been booked." Lindell glanced from one side of the road to the other, squinting through the snow before she pulled across the intersection. "Besides, rumor has it she was the last one to see Ursa alive. Do you know anything about that?"

"I want my attorney," Virginia said simply. "Sadie Sinclair."

"Oh, now you decide to clam up? What wonderfully inconvenient timing for you to grow a sense of self-preservation."

"Dying is one thing, Shirin, rotting away in a cell is another thing entirely." Virginia leaned her head back against the seat, the thinly-covered headrest biting into her neck. "It's no surprise to me that the VCPD has some kind of obsession with me. Once tried, always guilty. That's how things work there."

"That's not—no, Virginia, that's not what's going on."

"Isn't it?"

Lindell huffed out a sigh, throwing the car into park. "Of course not. It's like you haven't heard a word I've said this entire time."

"I'm sitting in your squad unit, cuffed. What more is there to understand, other than that?" Virginia asked. "Spare me the lesson on ethics and self-preservation or whatever it is you're trying to teach me. Charge me or don't, Shirin, but I don't have time for games."

"You're palling around with someone who's about to get charged with homicide, Virginia. How do you think that would look to the press? To the sheriff?" She faced forward, her hands on the door's handle. "I expected to find you trying to break into that warehouse tonight, that I will readily admit. But to find you there with someone who likely had a hand in Ursa's disappearance and subsequent death? Are you *serious*?"

"Anya didn't have anything to do with Ursa's death," Virginia insisted. She couldn't let slip what Anya had done, but seeing her in a cell would only drive home how much of it had been Virginia's fault. "At least, not like that."

"And how do you know that?"

Virginia exhaled through her nose, chewing on her cold-chapped lips. "I think you'll want to talk to the coroner tomorrow."

"What does that mean?" Lindell asked, and when Virginia shrugged, she stepped out of the car and wrenched open the back door. "What does that *mean*, Vane?"

"I'm not sharing anything other than that. It's Anya's story to tell, not mine."

"I will slap you with an obstruction charge so fast—"

Virginia leaned forward, meeting her glare. "Do it then. I dare you, Lindell, charge me with obstruction, we'll see how far it goes, because you and I both know everything I've said in this car is inadmissible."

"What?"

"You fucking rookie," Virginia scoffed. "You didn't read me my rights."

Lindell stepped backwards, stumbling like she'd been punched. "Of course I did."

"No, you didn't. Looks like you've slipped up, Captain," Virginia said, allowing a devilish smirk to ease across her face like a crocodile stalking its prey. "Good luck with the obstruction charge, though. I'm sure Arthur would love to hear about how you forgot to read me my rights when you arrested me after camping out in a damned snowdrift for what, hours? Losing feeling in your extremities, letting snow pile on your cap, waiting for me to show up like some desperate girl at a party."

"Enough!" Lindell shouted, her voice, rich with gravel, echoed across the near-empty lot.

Virginia flinched away from the sound, but held her stare. "How long were you out there, Shirin?"

"It doesn't matter how long I was out there, because I was right. You did decide to deliberately disobey my orders."

"I'm not one of your detectives, if you haven't noticed."

"Of course you aren't, mine would never act so impulsively, so outside the scope of the law." Lindell looked away, blinking, hands clenching and releasing at her sides. "And my detectives—" she shook her head, interrupting herself with a sharp intake of breath, like she'd been forgetting to breathe all along.

"Your detectives what?" Virginia prompted.

Lindell squeezed her eyes shut for a moment, her brow creased with frustration. "I don't hate you, Virginia, but you *infuriate* me."

Wind blew the snow sideways, and in an instant the flakes were twice as large, obscuring the view of Verdance. Virginia could barely see to the end of the lot, much less to the street, and already the precipitation was sticking to the ground, gathering, collecting, growing into something that would undoubtedly mean a busy night not just for the VCPD, but the local hospitals, too.

"You have the right to remain silent," Lindell began.

"What are you doing, Shirin?"

"Reading you your rights. You have the right to an attorney. If you cannot obtain your own counsel, you will be assigned one by law."

"Don't you think it's a little late for that now?"

"You have the right to refuse self-incrimination, and if you are a mythic, you have the right to conceal said information until it becomes relevant by law," Lindell continued.

Virginia sighed heavily, rolling her eyes. "Are you done?"

"You have the right to refuse questioning until your attorney is present. Yes, I am done." Lindell stepped away from the car door, gesturing for Virginia to climb out. "You'll be booked in, though I'm sure at this point you're familiar with the process. If you're lucky, they'll update your mugshot. Did you have those scars the last time you got dragged in here?"

"You've seen my file, so you know the answer to that question."

"Contrary to your belief, I don't spend all my time mining through your files for information."

"Don't you?" Virginia asked, raising an eyebrow. "You sure know a lot about me, Shirin."

"It's hard not to," Lindell grumbled.

"Let's get this over with. I want my phone call as soon as I'm booked."

Captain Lindell held the chain between the cuffs with one hand, slamming the back seat door with another. "I didn't want to have to do this, you know, but you made it impossible to ignore."

"You're not the magnanimous cop you think you are, Shirin. It's not like you have some power over the seedy underbelly of this city, holding the balance in your hands alone."

"Magnanimous," Lindell repeated. "No, I wouldn't say that, either." She pulled Virginia to the back door of the station and pushed her inside, steering her by the shoulder. "You may have lived in Verdance longer than me, seen more than me, but there's a lot about this place that even you don't know." She whispered this in Virginia's ear like a threat, as though she'd known all along how the whole thing would play out.

"What the hell are you talking about?" Virginia demanded, but before she could turn to face the captain, she was pushed into a small room, uncomfortably familiar with its desperate claustrophobia.

"We've got one Virginia Vivian Vane for booking," Lindell announced, shoving her further inside. "Watch her like a hawk, she has a bit of a reputation."

Virginia jerked at the sound of her middle name, one she hadn't heard aloud in years. It wasn't even on her personnel file, at least, not that she could remember. "Don't worry, Captain, I won't tell them that you forgot to read me my rights." She offered a wide smile, like a predator coming to dinner.

The officer looked to Lindell, eyes questioning. "Captain?"

"She has been appropriately dealt with, and read her rights. Get a move on, there will be another one here shortly. The roads are getting rough out there."

"Blizzard tonight, ma'am, they said."

"So it would seem." Lindell hovered in the doorway, amber eyes flashing. "Something you should learn about me, Vane, is that I'm not as quick to abandon my principles as you are. Maybe someday you'll learn that lesson."

"You might think you hold all the cards here, Lindell, but you're about to find that's not the case."

"Is that a threat?"

"No, rocks-for-brains, it's a warning," Virginia said, allowing the snide laugh in her throat to bubble up past her lips. "Whatever Fiske is doing, it's heading underground, and fast. He's getting bolder and more dangerous and you're so tied up with your own shadows-damned ego that you're more concerned with putting me behind bars than you are protecting this city."

"I live for this city," Lindell said.

Virginia tilted her chin. "Oh, that I know. What's unclear is whether you'd die for it, too."

Chapter Thirty-Five

Four years, eighty-two days, and if she had to guess, roughly ten hours since the last time she'd been sitting with her wrists cuffed to a table, thanks to Astrid's legacy.

The incandescent light burned yellow, burned hot, the bulb with its cheap and flimsy shade swinging lazily above her, dragging the shadows along with it. It was just as hard to be on that side of the table as it had been last time, and the shame of it flashed under the surface of her like lightning, unexpected and deadly. If shame could kill, she'd be long-buried. It was too bad that she wasn't, given the circumstances.

"I know you can hear me," Virginia said, staring at the glass she knew was a mirror. "These kinds of mind games aren't going to work on me, Lindell."

She leaned back in the rickety, uncomfortable chair, her spine straining with the effort of being hunched over. Mind games wouldn't work on her, but she wasn't so sure about Anya. She was the one who'd get dragged in front of a judge before the night was out, likely charged with homicide and tossed into a cell. There was no doubt that all of that was Virginia's fault, too.

"Some water would be nice," she grumbled. "What the hell happened to good cop, bad cop? All I've seen so far is one mediocre cop and the inside of this room. No wonder none of you want to be in here, it smells like a bat nest."

The door swung open on its hinges, and Lindell tossed a clipboard onto the table before letting the latch catch in the frame. "Have you frequented many bat nests?" she asked, leaning against the glass.

"Shut up, Lindell. I already told you I'm not talking until I see my attorney."

"If you're referring to the pissed off looking werewolf in the lobby, he's already here."

Seamus. Thank the shadows. "He's not my attorney, he's here to pay my bail," Virginia explained. "I still need my lawyer before I will agree to answer any questions."

"We haven't had a bail hearing for you yet, Ms. Vane."

"Oh, so now that you've got me in cuffs, we're back to formalities? You've seen the inside of my apartment, Shirin, I think we're past that."

"Nevertheless, professional standards will be adhered to. Who is he?" Lindell asked, pen poised over the clipboard.

"I told you, he's here to pay my bail."

"Who is he to *you?*"

"Always with the invasive, irrelevant questions with you," Virginia said, laying her palms flat against the metal table, dented from years of use. Years of intimidation, more like. "What difference does it make who he is? Maybe he's a bail bondsman. It doesn't matter."

"No bondsman would come out in the middle of the night during a blizzard for a bail that's yet to be set," Lindell said evenly. "Highly irregular."

"Eleven at night is hardly the middle."

Lindell tucked a lock of charcoal black hair behind her ear. "If you don't want to tell me who he is, I can always run on the assumption that he's a known associate of Astrid's, seeing as he came running for you the same way that Anya Quinn did. It would be enough to hold him in lockup overnight."

"He's my sparring partner," Virginia grunted through gritted teeth. "He is nothing to you."

"And Anya?"

"Is a healer. She patched me up after Benjamin—after the shifter attack."

Captain Lindell's stare fell to Virginia's shoulder with a curious tilt. "How are you healing, after all that?"

"You'll forgive me for not divulging more information when you have me chained to a desk." Virginia rattled the chains noisily, punctuating her point. "I'm obviously not dead, so I guess she did a good job."

"Mm." Lindell sat across from her, hands folded against the desk. "The judges have all gone home for the night, so your bail hearing will have to wait until morning."

"How *convenient*," Virginia spat.

"Maybe next time, you should plan your heists for a more palatable time of day, and then you wouldn't have to spend the night in this room."

Virginia scoffed. "Great, thanks, I'll keep that in mind."

"While I understand why you are angry, I would ask that you try to see things from my perspective," Lindell said, taking notes in the margin of the page. "You knowingly interfered with a VCPD investigation, and—"

"Interfered?" Virginia interrupted. "Was it not only the other day that you and Arthur were practically begging me to solve your Fiske problem for you?" She glanced at the glass again, unsure if there were others behind it. "Where is Arthur, anyway?"

Lindell's jaw flexed. "He is not on shift."

"Okay, I understand that, but usually when there are issues, like a consultant being arrested for the same crime she's trying to solve, it would be a good time to bring in the sheriff." Virginia caught the flash of uncertainty on the captain's face and leaned forward, her forearms resting on the table. "Unless you haven't told him."

"Of course I told him," Lindell said defensively. "He's just indisposed."

"Indisposed?" Virginia repeated with a deep laugh. "Either he's doing something very embarrassing that he doesn't want his precious wife to find out about, or you don't know where he is."

The captain cleared her throat. "The sheriff's business is his own."

"You know, the last time someone said that to me about him, he was warming Mona's bed." Virginia raised her hands off the table and let them fall back to the metal, the lock and the chain clinking angrily. "Although I guess that wouldn't be such an issue of ethics, now."

"Virginia," Lindell said, sliding into the chair across from her, "I don't want to make this any harder than it already is."

"Horseshit."

"The fact of the matter is that you were caught trespassing—"

"Because you were waiting for me, like a shadows-damned ambush," Virginia interrupted. "I don't know what you're doing, Shirin, but whatever it is, it's not going to help this city. You have Anya in an interrogation room right now, an innocent healer—"

"I don't think a judge will agree with that assertion," Lindell said, cutting her off. "Especially as we just confiscated illegal reagents from her shop days ago."

"Please, as if half the tea shops in this city don't carry the same ingredients. Shadows, I bet half this damn force is using illegal herbal remedies to stay awake on stakeouts, but no one questions that, do they?"

"The law is the law." Lindell gave her a shrug, folding her hands on top of the table. "I can't argue with it any more than you can."

"Maybe not, but the VCPD certainly skirts it whenever it likes." A muffled shout phased through the painted white brick wall, angry and agonized. Anya. Virginia's glance settled back on the mirror, staring daggers at whoever was on the other side. "If she hasn't told you yet, she's not going to."

"I guess we'll see," Lindell said evenly.

"You're using her to get to me, Shirin. I'm not a fool."

"I know you're not a fool, that's why I am forced to go to these lengths in the first place." Lindell sighed, and it was dancing along the edge of resignation. "I didn't want things to happen this way, you know."

Virginia shrugged at her. "Then release me."

"You know I can't do that."

"Release her, then, I know you're just using her as leverage."

Lindell licked her lips, pressing them together. "Anya Quinn is not leverage, Virginia. She was the last one to see Ursa alive, and you know that makes her a suspect. A credible one, at that."

"You're going to look like a fool tomorrow."

"And why is that?"

"Shirin, I know that you have no interest in unlocking these cuffs, but I am begging you to listen to reason. Jolie is still out there, somewhere, being held prisoner by Franky fucking Fiske and his enforcers, and them having a fire demon is the last thing this city needs. You think you have problems now? Wait until they get her juiced on Nether, every damned building in Verdance will burn. There won't even be enough ashes left to scrape into a jar."

"My concern at the moment is Ursa's homicide," Lindell asserted. "That is the department's priority, and specifically, *my* priority."

"Why? Who were they to you?" Virginia shot back, using Lindell's own crappy line of questioning against her.

"Excuse me?"

"What, too personal?"

"You're not in control here, Virginia."

"Don't scold me like a child, you got your way," Virginia snapped. "Here I am, in an interrogation room. So what is it you really want to know, Lindell, hmm? Let's have at it. Ask me whatever you want, and I'll answer it. Drag every bit of my personal life into the light, shall we? We can get down to brass tacks with the real gritty details. Go on, ask me."

"You know I can't, not when you've already asked for an attorney."

"You already slipped up once tonight, what's one more?" Virginia asked, leaning forward in challenge before she shrugged, sitting back into the chair. "You're wasting this opportunity."

"Why won't you tell me how you know Anya Quinn isn't a murderer?" Lindell asked calmly, still taking notes on the clipboard.

"Because I know how this department likes to twist and manipulate information for its own gain," Virginia explained. "I've seen people more innocent than me go down for things they had nothing to do with, just because the VCPD was too lazy to do any real investigative work."

"I wouldn't call you innocent, Virginia."

"None of us are."

Lindell nodded, the lightly swaying light flickering across her olive skin.

"No, I may not be innocent, but I try to do my best by Verdance. You said before, you didn't know if I would die for this city, but I would. I have, in a thousand ways already, and I know the same is true for you."

"Anya shouldn't have been at the warehouse tonight. I made her come with me," Virginia admitted. "Charge me with kidnapping, extortion, whatever you want, but she needs to go free."

"Why are you so hell-bent on this?" Lindell questioned. "She was the last person to see Ursa alive. I am obligated to follow up on a lead."

"You know she didn't kill Ursa, and I know that you know it, and yet we're sat here bickering about it while Fiske is doing shadows know what all over Verdance. Moving his stock, his enforcers, who knows, but you're letting him do it because you're in here preoccupied with me."

Lindell said nothing. Her eyebrows arched towards her thick hairline, and she stared, and she blinked, as though Virginia had reached into her throat and torn out her larynx for good measure.

"Lindell!" Arthur shouted from the corridor. Virginia knew that it was Arthur, because no one sounded quite like him when he was panicked. "Lindell, where—"

Throwing open the door, the captain ushered him in. "Sheriff, what—"

"Shadows, Ginnie, thank goodness you're here."

Virginia sat up in the chair, the air prickling like thorns. "What's the matter, Arthur?" His brow was coated with sweat, his eyes wide with terror. "Arthur," she repeated, locking eyes with him.

"Why are you cuffed?" he asked.

"She was trespassing at the Fiske warehouse," Lindell began, somehow oblivious to the fact that Arthur looked ready to vacate his own skin. "We found her down at the docks with—"

"He took them, Ginnie," he said. "Fiske has Mona and Penny."

Chapter Thirty-Six

Virginia stood in the corridor, a hand on her hip, ready to kick the door in herself. "I don't give one single damn, Shirin, you need to release her."

"Just because the sheriff ordered me to uncuff you, doesn't mean Anya Quinn gets the same treatment. For one thing, she was arrested for an entirely different reason," Lindell replied, arms crossed over her chest. She was standing in front of the interrogation room, glaring, and her rage was apparent. "We need to come up with a plan of action—"

"You're the one who keeps droning on and on about how dangerous Fiske is, don't you *want* a healer along for the ride?"

"She's not an approved contractor. We have plenty of healers who—"

"Oh yeah?" Virginia interrupted, throwing an arm wide towards the window. "How many of them do you think will be able to get here in time, given that blizzard? Or get here at all? You have one of the city's best in that room, and you're being obstinate just because you want to spite me."

"It's not about spite."

"Isn't it?"

Lindell wrenched her arms in tighter, the wool fabric of her uniform pulling taut over her muscular shoulders. "I am more than aware of how grave this situation is, Virginia, I just don't think we should burn down every rule and protocol in our bid to fix it."

"I'm not asking you to burn down all of them, just this *one.*" Virginia stepped closer, challenging Lindell despite the fact that she was at least six inches shorter than the captain. She tilted her chin up, trying to ignore the way Lindell flinched at her proximity. "I'm not going to hit you, Shirin."

"That's not—" Lindell started, shaking her head. "It wouldn't be surprising, that's all."

"Vee!" Seamus yelled, and he was careening down the hall, his heavy brown boots slipping on the melted snow puddled on the dingy tile. "Thank the shadows, you're out. They said you wouldn't get bail until morning, I was ready to start raising hell." He stopped in his tracks, glaring at Captain Lindell. "Oh. Hello."

"The charges were dropped," Virginia said, shoving her hands into her pockets. "I'm trying to get Anya out, we're going to need her for this."

"Anya?" he asked.

"Healer." Virginia gestured to her shoulder. "You know."

Seamus shifted his weight back and forth, a natural consequence to his job as a sparring coach. He was Lindell's height, but leaner, more sinewy. Strong, but lithe. It made him a formidable opponent. "Who is *we*, Vee?"

"Whoever is coming along to knock the crap out of Fiske once and for all." Virginia cocked an eyebrow. "I'm sure Captain Lindell here would love for you to come along, if you don't have any plans in the middle of a blizzard."

"It's not a full moon, Vee."

"No, but you have an uppercut that almost dislocated my jaw." Virginia tilted her head towards him, leaning closer. "It's Arthur's family, Seamus. Franky Fiske scooped them up a couple of hours ago."

He paused from the movements, cracking his knuckles a fist at a time. "Mona? The kids?"

"Mona and Penny." She gestured to her own skin. "Shifters."

Seamus nodded, sinking back into the rocking movements, rolling onto the balls of his feet. "I'll come," he agreed. "Tell Arthur it's non-negotiable. I send those kids cards every year on their birthdays, I'm not turning my back on them or on their parents."

Lindell sighed angrily. "Virginia, we can't let this become some kind of vigilante shootout."

"Who said anything about guns?" Virginia asked. "I don't think Seamus here could hit the broad side of a barn."

"Even more reason for him to go back home," Lindell replied.

He shrugged, but there was the barest hint of aggression hiding there. "I'm here now. Might as well use me."

"Fucked shadows," Lindell hissed, turning to the door, keys rattling in her hands. "I hope to shit that we catch this bastard tonight, because if I have to spend one more day getting pushed around by a fucking private investigator, I'm going to explode."

"We're going to need all the intel your dipshit rookies picked up earlier. If that warehouse is hiding anything, maybe we can tell."

"I've already told you everything they discovered."

"Lindell, for shadows' sakes, Arthur is about to crawl out of his skin with worry, do you think that maybe you could relax for half a second and stop stonewalling me?" Virginia's attention was pulled by movement at the far end of the corridor, a flash of blue and silver. "Detective," she called. "What are you doing?"

A young woman stepped around the corner, sheepish and unsure in her movements. "I was waiting on orders from Captain Lindell."

Virginia gave a dramatic, sweeping gesture. "That's all you, Shirin. Far be it from me to order around your baby underlings."

Lindell glanced at Virginia, a rare flash of respect crossing her face. "Detective Baker, report to the beat desk. We're going to have a hell of a time tonight with that weather."

Baker chewed her lip, approaching with apprehension. "Is that really the best use of my time and skills? After all, maybe I would be better served working on this bust. I did manage to bring in three enforcers last week, and—"

"Beat desk. Now."

"Of course, ma'am." Baker backed away, disappearing down the adjoining hall, the sound of her boots meeting the tile fading alongside the echo.

"I bet you didn't have to deal with this," Lindell muttered, turning back to the door. "Half these rookies think that they know better than anyone else on the force."

Virginia snorted a quiet laugh. "Sounds like someone else I know."

The door swung open, and Anya's head snapped up, her eyes swimming with incandescent rage. "Fuck you, Lindell, I already told you I'm not saying anything."

"I'm not asking you to," Lindell replied, bending to unlock the cuffs. "Your temporary release is conditional on you running a raid with us. You'll be in back, out of harm's way, we just need to make sure we have a healer coming along. The weather doesn't bode well."

"Temporary release," Anya repeated.

"Yes, unfortunately we can't just drop all the charges just because you decided to use your magic for good on one or two occasions."

"Lindell," Virginia said, pushing past her, "we can work out the rest later, alright? You can do paperwork to your heart's content."

"Come up to the conference room in ten minutes, the sheriff is working on an action plan." Lindell turned on her heel, disappearing down the hall.

"No surprise he waits until his own family is in danger to give a shit," Virginia muttered. She leaned against the table, trying to meet Anya's eyes. "Are you alright?"

"You mean other than getting arrested?"

"Yes."

"I'm fine." Anya shot her a look. "No thanks to you."

"I got you out, didn't I?"

"*Temporarily.*"

Virginia sighed, pushing herself upright. "Like you said, by tomorrow the coroner won't even have a body to autopsy. In Verdance, there's no case without a body. And I convinced Lindell to drag you along, so that there will be a veritable sea of cops to act as witness that you were nowhere near the morgue, and couldn't have done anything to destroy or replace a body." She shrugged. "Alright?"

"That is a surprisingly detailed plan," Anya admitted, standing up. She rubbed at her wrists, red raw from the cuffs. "Shadows, they make those tight."

"Standard operating procedure for mythics, especially witches. You all have a tendency to slip out of cuffs, given the opportunity."

Seamus lingered in the doorway, leaning against the frame. "Hey. I'm Seamus." He nodded in greeting. "Vee's sparring partner. Coach, whatever."

"Depends who is kicking whose ass that day," Virginia added.

"Anya Quinn." She extended her arm, shaking his hand. "I have to admit, I didn't expect to be roped into all this tonight. I thought I'd be home in bed by now."

"Never assume that, when it comes to Vee," Seamus said with a laugh. "Seems like she's in trouble every time the sun comes up."

Virginia frowned at him, crossing her arms. "That's a bit unfair, I'm usually in more trouble at night."

He shrugged. "*Plus ça change*, Vee. Some things never change."

"Thanks for coming," she said, and meant it. There weren't many people she could drag out of bed at nearly midnight to bail her out of lockup, and her lawyer hadn't picked up the phone. "I wasn't sure you'd even be home."

"You're lucky my date canceled." Seamus tugged at the sleeves of his coat, a deep teal wool that hung down to his knees. "It's a good thing he did. I wouldn't want to wake up to hearing the news on the radio, and know I could have done something." He shook his head, inhaling deeply. "I can't believe Fiske took Art's wife and kid."

Anya picked up her bag from the table, examining the contents. "That's a big move, even for the head of a crew. It's reckless."

"There has to be a reason he's ramping up," Virginia said. "No one paints a target like that on their backs for fun."

"Ransom?" Seamus asked. "Arthur's family could fetch a pretty penny."

"No, it can't be that. If it was ransom, those kids at Rickarton would have been ransomed, and they weren't." Virginia let out a hiss. "Shit. I'm betting Mona wasn't only talking to me and Lindell about this."

"Another private eye?" Seamus asked. "That's bold."

"Bold or efficient, depending on how you're looking at it."

Anya leaned against the wall, pressing her head back against the brick. In that light, she almost looked like a painting, every drape of her heavy skirts immortalized in oil. "Do you think this other investigator sold her out?"

"Could be," Virginia said. "Fiske has very deep pockets, after all." She nodded towards the door. "Let's get upstairs. Arthur is probably losing his mind with worry, and I'm betting Lindell has no idea how to handle that."

"And you do?" Anya asked, laughing.

Seamus grimaced.

"Unfortunately," Virginia said, turning down the corridor.

The precinct was unusually quiet, despite the crisis at hand, and despite the heavy snow outside. It was eerie, like a department bracing for death. Virginia gave a small wave to the receptionist, who'd grown to recognize her, and pushed through the swinging door into the stairwell. Every time she was there, it was like getting yanked back into a memory, into a time before she'd been disgraced, before she'd been forcibly removed from the force, before Arthur had all but left her for dead in that apartment as he ran off to the coast. Fool. Asshole.

Yet, he was a desperate, foolish asshole, and she was unable to turn away from it, despite all the water that had frozen under that bridge.

They could hear the shouting before they even exited the stairwell. Virginia glanced at Seamus from the corner of her eye, and noticed his shoulders tense, already working to subdue his temper. "Relax," she said quietly. "It's just Arthur."

"Old habits."

"I know."

The door opened onto worn parquet flooring, and Virginia flinched. Arthur's hands were shaking as he held the sides of his head, pacing like an animal that knew it was cornered.

"No, no!" he shouted, pressing his temples. "That's not good enough, Lindell, we need every available unit out there right now."

"Sir, every available unit is either trapped in a snowdrift or already attending to calls. We've got emergencies all across the city, half the paramedics are stuck at the hospital, and the fire brigade can barely get their trucks out of the station, much less get across the city to anything else."

"This is my family, Shirin," he spat.

"And I realize that, sir, but I think you need to take a breath and—"

"Take a *breath*?"

"Lindell," Virginia said, one part quiet warning, and the other part reassurance.

Captain Lindell wheeled around, pointing. "You stay out of this, Vane."

"I can guarantee that you don't want me to stay out of this." Virginia turned into the conference room and sat in the chair nearest to the door. She'd seen Arthur at his worst, and his worst was volatile. Not violent, but chaotic. Impulsive, when he was supposed to be the rational one. It was what got them into trouble the last time, and she didn't want a repeat performance.

Anya joined her in the chair to the right, wordless, probably afraid to say anything lest Lindell revoke the temporary stay of imprisonment. She clutched her bag close to her chest, like she was afraid someone would take it from her again.

"Art," Seamus said, laying a hand gently on his shoulder, "you know me, and you know I love you, and Mona, and the girls, both of them. Where is Orren?"

"With my parents upstate," Arthur replied.

"That's a fate worse than death," Virginia grumbled to herself, but Anya laughed, covering her mouth with the back of her hand.

Seamus shot Virginia a look. "Art, I'm here. Whatever you need."

"Thanks, Seamus," Arthur said, and he was calmer now, if resigned. "I can't believe I let this happen to them. I should have listened to Mona."

"We're going to get them back. This is a desperate move from this Fiske character. He's not thinking clearly, but we are, Art," Seamus soothed. "You've got a solid team right here. I can hold my own, you've got Captain Lindell, you've got a good healer, and we all know that shadows themselves couldn't kill Vee. She's too fucking stubborn."

It was Virginia's turn to shoot Seamus a look, scoffing with indignation and a little bit of misplaced pride. She stood again, rearranging the evidence board, sorting clues by date, grouping them by district.

"What do you think you're doing?" Lindell demanded.

"Shirin," Virginia said quietly, "Arthur is going to blow a shadows-damned gasket, and probably get himself killed if we don't keep it together. You can either help me with the evidence board, or shut up."

Captain Lindell clenched her jaw, released, and eased out an exhale that was somehow both heavy and resigned. "Fine. But you put that first one in the wrong place, that was the day before."

"Alright." Virginia moved the card to the left, raising her eyebrows. "Okay?"

"And I'm not sure grouping by district is that helpful," Shirin said, the contempt slowly melting from her voice. "Not when Fiske has control over the entire city. They're able to move people and product quickly."

Virginia nodded, rearranging the cards to reflect the change. "Fine. So if that's the case, they probably have a fleet of vehicles?"

"Yes, but from what we know already, most of them are privately registered, so nearly impossible to track. No notable plates, or colors, anything like that," Lindell said, adjusting one of the cards herself.

Virginia winced at the window, watching as more snow dumped on top of the squad units in the parking lot below. They wouldn't even start to plow until the blizzard was over.

Captain Lindell surveyed the board, holding her chin in her hand, brow furrowed. She stepped forward, moving a photo from the quarry from one end to the other.

"Oh?" Virginia prompted.

"What if the coroner was wrong, and that body was a few days older than we thought? The bottom of that pit was filled with water, it could have inhibited decay." Lindell glanced at Virginia. "What do you think?"

"Plausible, but how does that impact where Fiske is hiding?"

"We found a burned out black model S down by the river four days before the quarry," Lindell explained. "Serial numbers mostly filed off the engine block, but someone slipped up. There was a partial, we were able to trace it to a dealership over the state lines."

"I don't suppose they had a description of the buyer to hand?" Virginia asked, already knowing the answer. "Something to point us in the right direction?"

"Owner reported it stolen a week before we found it. Due to the partial serial, it took some extra time to join the dots. I pulled Detective Baker's notes, and there was a sighting near an older building on Poe." Shirin shook her head, rolling her eyes. "Shadows-damned new detectives, not logging their notes fast enough, we could have caught this a week ago." She turned, shuffling the cards on the board once again. "If they have a base that close to downtown..." she trailed off.

"It would make sense as to why they were able to jump me at the Sphinx." Virginia massaged her temples. "Astrid waited until I arrived to make the call."

"That is my guess, but what I'm still unclear on is how she knew you had Jolie Laar in the backseat."

Virginia sat back down next to Anya, resting her elbows on the table. "I think you might have a mole in the department, Shirin."

Captain Lindell stared at the board, refusing to turn around. "If that's true, then we have no chance at getting our hands on him."

"Don't involve anyone else," Anya said. "Just us. You, Vee, Seamus, me, and the sheriff of police. None of us are the leak, we know that for sure, right?"

Virginia nodded. "Yes."

"What's your stake in this, Quinn?" Lindell asked, finally turning around. "Why are you so invested?"

"Exoneration," Anya said simply. "I'd rather be back at work tomorrow, and not rotting away in a cell."

"A biased stake."

"Sure, but if I was really working with Fiske, would I be offering to go out with you?" Anya asked. "If there is a mole in the department, which seems likely, he'd know immediately that I'd switched sides, and it would be no skin off his nose to have a witch killed." She fumbled with the pouch at her hip, securing the toggles. "He may think that regardless."

"Virginia, do you think you can see if Fiske owns that building?" Lindell asked. "This one on Poe?"

"I don't think Zin will be at the library in the middle of the night during a blizzard," Virginia said. "Actually, scratch that. Where's a phone?"

"Next room." Lindell smirked. "I thought you would have remembered that."

"Not as many phones then, Shirin, but thank you for your snide remark." Virginia rolled her eyes, slipping into the next room. Seamus still had his hand on Arthur's shoulder, talking to him in low tones. For a werewolf with an attitude problem, he was surprisingly good at defusing potentially explosive situations. It was just a shame he hadn't developed those skills fifteen years earlier.

She dialed, almost expecting the line to disconnect. "Reference desk," came Zin's distracted voice.

"I didn't think you'd answer after hours."

"Virginia," Zin said in a tired voice. "Did you know that there is still a hole in my wall?"

"I know, I'm working on it," Virginia promised. "Listen, remember when I asked you to check out that warehouse at the docks? I need you to look into ownership of a building at..." she took the filed from Lindell, squinting at Detective Baker's chicken scratch writing. "Seventh and Poe."

Zin sighed into the phone. "I'm going to start charging the VCPD a consulting fee." The sound of papers being shuffled crunched over the line. "Hold on. The cord doesn't reach far enough for that filing cabinet."

"Alright." Virginia perched on top of the table, folding her legs beneath her as she waited, picking at her shredded cuticles, wincing at the pain with every tear. Winter was murder on her hands, and the past week had only made things worse.

"I'm back. Looks like there was an application for renovation a couple of years ago, submitted to the city council?" Zin sucked her teeth. "It was denied."

"Denied?" Virginia got down from the table, starting to pace. "Then how was it renovated?"

"Under the radar would be my guess, and if you're asking me, a hefty payout to that district's alderman. Ms. Eugenia Patten is her name, she's already been dragged into inquiries on similar matters three times, but she's never been indicted, and always reelected."

Virginia gripped the side of the table, eager to steady herself. "That sounds like Fiske, alright."

"Ownership is listed as the same shell corporation as the warehouse." The line crackled with static. "This information isn't supposed to be public, Virginia," Zin warned. "It's accessible, but only with a warrant. I could lose my job if this isn't done carefully."

"We'll get you that warrant."

"You'd better. No one else here is going to waive your late fees like I do," Zin teased.

Virginia exhaled a soft laugh. "That book isn't due for two more days."

"Tick tock, Ms. Vane."

"Okay, I hear you."

"Take care, Virginia. I have plans next week, and I don't want to have to reschedule them for your funeral."

"Noted." Virginia placed the phone back in the receiver, her muscles already tensing for the battle ahead.

Chapter Thirty-Seven

Eleven-oh-six Poe Street was suspiciously dark for a night so heavily coated in snow. It had taken them three times as long to get there, taking detour after detour, the streets piled high with drifts. Virginia had finally given up a third of a mile out, opting to walk the rest of the way.

The blizzard was raging. Visibility was at a minimum, and she squinted into the night, the street lamps arguably making things worse with their omnipresent halo glow.

"Fucking hate winter," Seamus said, shivering in his coat.

"Aren't you supposed to have resistance to cold?" Virginia asked over her shoulder.

"Yeah, when I have fur, Vee. I am currently a fleshy sack of skin."

Captain Lindell eased closer to the building, pressing a hand against the brick. "Doesn't seem like anyone is home."

Seamus grimaced. "That doesn't mean there aren't sixty-five enforcers waiting just inside the door, ready to beat us all to death with crowbars."

"You volunteered to be here," Virginia challenged. "Besides, this is for Arthur."

Arthur was following fifteen paces behind, despite demanding he lead the charge into the building. He was a good man in a crisis, unless the crisis was his own.

"Do you think they'll be here?" Anya asked. "I always thought this place was just housing."

Virginia crept closer to the door, still twenty feet away. "Hard to know for sure until we see the inside. If there were renovations done without approval, this place could have a basement, or a loft, or nine-hundred and forty-two traps waiting to snare us."

Anya lingered behind, her hand on her pouch. "Always the optimist."

"Could be that all the usual residents are out moving product," Lindell said, pulling her own coat tighter around her as an icy gust whipped up the street, swirling flakes and disturbing the growing drifts that sat in the verges.

"Yeah, and why might that be?" Virginia shot back. "Maybe because someone kicked over the shadows-damned hornet's nest."

"Enough," Arthur said. He unholstered his gun, checking it over before assuming a stable stance, bracing his wrist with the other hand. "It doesn't matter how this happened. If they're—if I—"

"We'll get them, sir," Lindell said, glaring at Virginia. "We're the VCPD."

"Speak for yourself," Seamus grumbled.

Anya pulled a vial from her pack. "I can create a distraction, if that's what's needed."

"Could be," Virginia said. "What kind of distraction?"

"I'm an illusion witch. I can do things you'd only dream of."

There was something hidden in the way she said the words, a threat, or a promise, it was hard to tell the difference. It usually was with witches, especially powerful ones like Anya. "That's unhelpfully vague."

"Do you believe in ghosts, Virginia?"

"I think it would be foolish not to, given all that's happened since the Rupture."

"That's the opinion of most people, these days. It's why they're all so deliciously easy to haunt." Anya smiled, placing the vial back in her bag. "But it's expensive magic. Best to wait until we know there's people to haunt before breaking it open and spilling it over the floor."

"You're a little bit terrifying, you know that?" Virginia asked, turning back to the building. "I'd pick the werewolf to tangle with any day over you."

Seamus scoffed. "Is that an insult?"

"Take it out on me the next time we spar." She glanced down the road, spotting a tall, chain-link fence leading into an alley. "Lindell, Arthur, you take the back. We need to cover the exits in case they run. Seamus, with me. You know my fighting style best, and I trust you to not shoot me in the back and pretend it's an accident."

Lindell glared at her, but said nothing.

"And me?" Anya asked.

"Out here on the street, in case something happens. You're the lookout."

Anya's brow furrowed, but she nodded, the silvery tufts of her hair that had escaped their hasty bun becoming coated with snow. "What should I do if they come back?"

"Scream."

"Anything in particular?"

"No." Virginia gestured to Seamus, waving him along. "Let's take it floor by floor. Meet at the stairwell, bar the doors once you're inside."

Captain Lindell flexed her jaw, frowning.

"What?" Virginia snapped.

"I'm unclear as to why you are calling the shots," Lindell said.

"Because you're taking too long. Let's go." Virginia turned, not waiting for a response. It was just like Lindell to get all tied up in knots about protocol right when it mattered the least. The entire city was poised on the precipice of whatever Fiske was planning, and Lindell was worried about paperwork. "Seamus, take left," Virginia said.

"Aye," he replied, slipping his fingers through brass knuckles on both fists. "Shadows, I hope they're in here."

"Me, too." Virginia nodded to him once before leaning back and kicking the door in, splintering at the hinges. "No going back now."

"Nice hit."

"Thanks."

Seamus whipped into the building, moving left into a utility room, his long coat swirling around his legs. Virginia spun to the right, peering into an empty foyer lined with mail boxes. "Clear," she said.

"Clear," Seamus replied.

Moving up the corridor, they came to the first residential units. The door Virginia was facing had a gold number one hanging under the peep hole. She slammed her boot into this door too, but this time, it didn't budge. "Deadbolts," she said.

"We don't have time for you to pick every lock in this place," Seamus said. "Here." He crossed the corridor, landing a kick into the door handle, leaving it rattling.

"I could have done that," Virginia grumbled.

"Yeah, but it's more fun to show you up," he replied. "I so rarely get the opportunity."

Rolling her eyes, she repeated his motion, and heard the doorknob detach on the other side of the door, rolling across a hardwood floor. She yanked on the side facing her, reaching through the new hole to unlock the deadbolt. "In," she said, pulling open the door.

"In," Seamus repeated, entering the other room.

The apartment was sparse, but tidy. A cheap sofa, slightly tattered. Whitewashed walls, a small kitchen, a bathroom barely big enough to get inside and close the door. No wonder the city council hadn't wanted to approve the renovation plans, the place was tiny, only suited for single occupancy.

The bedroom was dark, the bed made with standard-issue white sheets and a charcoal grey wool blanket, rough to the touch. Someone had been living there.

"Empty," Seamus called from the other room.

"Yeah," Virginia echoed. "Not the nicest place, is it?"

"Are Nether dens usually nice places?"

"I don't think they're using it as a Nether den, I think it's for new recruits. There's a strange air of desperation in here."

She exited into the corridor, and Seamus was already waiting there, leaning against the wall. "There's another utility closet behind the stairwell, I'll check it out."

She nodded, waiting for him to ease the door open, her muscles tensed despite knowing almost for certain all he'd find in there was a collection of mops and cleaning supplies.

"Nothing," he confirmed. "Next floor?"

"Shirin?" she called. "Arthur, where are you two?"

"Upstairs," Lindell called back.

Virginia rolled her eyes. "So much for sticking to the plan," she grumbled.

"You just make friends everywhere you go, don't you?" Seamus asked under his breath.

"She makes it difficult." Virginia climbed the stairs, revolver still at the ready. Each step creaked under her feet, the wood polished on the surface, but old and worn beneath.

"I trust you didn't find anything downstairs?" Lindell asked, poised to break into another one of the residential units.

"Nothing. It's lived in, but barely. No sign of anyone," Virginia answered. "If there were any enforcers here, we'd know by now. Kicking in doors is hardly the utmost in stealth."

"There could still be some in here," the captain protested.

"And if it's empty, my guess is that something else is going down elsewhere," Virginia said coolly. She leaned forward into the short hallway, glancing out the window. Anya was still standing guard on the street, leaning against a lamp post. She looked up and nodded in affirmation, which Virginia returned. "All good on street level, it looks like."

"We can only hope that stays the case," Arthur said. "We'll take this floor. You two head up the stairs."

Seamus clapped him on the shoulder. "We're gonna find them, Art. I can feel it. Fiske would be stupid to do anything too rash, he'd be bringing the whole damned city down on his head, along with the rest of the county."

"Desperate people do desperate things. I just hope—" Arthur drew in a breath, ragged at the edges. "I just hope Mona and Penny can escape that fate."

"The sooner we clear this place, the sooner we can move on," Virginia said, already heading up to the third floor. She paused, laying her silver knuckled hand against the banister, and bile rushed into her throat. She shook her head violently, swallowing it back.

"Vee?" Seamus asked. "You alright?"

"Fine. Follow me up." Hands back on her gun, she inhaled slowly, urging her heartbeat to slow. Something felt off about the building, something like screaming, or struggle, or the desperate need to be found.

"Are you gonna tell me what the hell that was back there?" Seamus whispered over her shoulder.

"Nothing."

"You looked like you saw a ghost."

"Maybe it's one of Anya's," she answered, moving to the first door on the right. "Wouldn't be the first time that woman has thrown me off-guard with her magical bullshit."

Seamus arched an eyebrow before turning to the other door. "Whatever you say, Vee." He kicked it in, weaving around the corner and out of sight.

"No closets on this floor, just the two apartments," Virginia called out, leaning over the banister. "I'll yell when it's clear." She aimed a kick, opened the door, finding another identical living space to the one down the stairs. This one had a set of keys laying on the counter, which she pocketed, but everything else was the same. "Clear," she announced.

"Same," Seamus said, returning to the corridor. "What now? There isn't a fourth floor."

"No, but there's a roof."

"I don't see an access panel."

Virginia pried a grate off the wall, reaching inside for the lever she knew would be there. A ladder descended from a hatch in the ceiling, and she turned, smug. "I did."

"How in shadows did you know that was there?"

She shrugged. "Lots of these older buildings have them."

"Hidden in a grate?"

"Sure." She'd never actually found one behind a grate before, but that wasn't important. A boot on the first rung, she paused. "I'll go first, in case of an ambush."

"They won't be on the roof, Virginia," Lindell said, cresting the final steps to the third floor. "There's a blizzard outside, if you haven't noticed."

"I thought you wanted to be thorough, Shirin. My mistake." Virginia holstered her gun to allow her to climb, hoisting herself up into a dark loft area. She reached out, searching for a light switch, or a string, and finding none. "Dark up here," she said, "but no sign of anyone yet."

"I'm going to head back to the squad unit and radio the precinct," Arthur said. "It's unlikely they're here, and we need to be combing the city."

"Sheriff, I think we should stick together," Lindell said. "I'm sure Virginia will be done in a moment, and we can all go together. We don't know what's hiding around a corner, or—"

"Don't act like you're the authority here, Lindell," he snapped. "I am the sheriff of the Verdance City Police Department, and you're my captain, and it's my wife and daughter who've been taken, so if you'll excuse me, I'll—"

"It's exactly that reason why I'm trying to keep things on an even keel!"

Virginia groped through the darkness, finding the metal latch for the roof access. She slid the bolt across, pushing the large square panel up and out. The wood was frozen under her fingers, a cutting reminder of the weather, swiftly followed by a blast of snow to the face as she hoisted herself onto the roof.

She could barely see in front of her at that height, with the wind unbroken by the buildings down on the street. It was harsher, more treacherous. Leaning over the side, she couldn't even see Anya, or the squad unit, or anything other than the growing blizzard.

The roof was clearly not in regular use, with several haphazard piles of unused bricks scattered across the surface, covered in snow. They looked like tiny hills, a miniature landscape stretched from one end to the other, with nothing between them but an expanse of freshly fallen snow. Lindell and Arthur were still arguing, but it was muffled and indistinguishable amid the dampened sounds of the blizzard.

She shuffled through the snow, aware that she was leaving obvious tracks across the roof, the soles of her boots dragging. She brushed flakes aside, tilting her head at what looked like a scorch mark.

"Vee? Anything?" Seamus called up to her.

"I don't know," Virginia admitted.

"Well let's go, Arthur and Lindell are about to come to blows, I think."

She glanced across the roof one last time, something pulling her to stay. A feeling mostly, a tightness in her gut that frequently preceded a break in a case. "They won't. Neither of them would throw the first punch. Just give me a minute longer."

"Hurry it up then, would you? This place gives me the creeps, and we haven't found Mona and Penny yet."

"Or Jolie," Virginia added, annoyed that everyone seemed to be forgetting that poor kid. "Just one more minute." Crossing the roof, she kicked over one of the piles of bricks, revealing nothing. "There's an out building up here, but I don't hear anything from the inside of it. Another storage closet."

Arthur and Lindell's voices were beginning to carry up onto the roof, and Virginia flinched. "Tell them to keep it down, they're going to wake up the whole shadows-damned neighborhood."

She wasn't quite sure what she'd expected when she used the keys she'd found to unlock the padlock, frosted over with ice, onto the ground. More building supplies, maybe, or a cache of tools for maintenance. She did not expect Jolie to fall into her arms as soon as the door opened.

"Shit," Virginia hissed. "Seamus! Get up here!"

Tinges of purple lined the young woman's eyes, her pupils dilated to such a degree that you couldn't even see the bright golden glow of her irises. Loaded with Nether and left to die on the roof? It didn't make any sense. Virginia whipped off her own coat, wrapping Jolie in it. She picked her up, heading back towards the access hatch, no longer caring if she left boot prints in the snow.

"Is this her?" Seamus asked, taking Jolie's legs.

Virginia nodded. "Her name is Jolie. We need to get her to Anya. She needs to be somewhere warm." They carried her down the ladder, one rung at a time, until Virginia was able to slam the roof access shut, bolting it again.

"Shadows," Lindell uttered. "Is she alive?"

"Barely."

Arthur looked from Jolie to Virginia. "Ginnie, I—"

"I know, Arthur. We need to get her safe and conscious, she's our best lead to finding your wife and daughter."

"If they're on a roof somewhere in this weather—"

"There'd be no reason to keep shifters in the cold," Anya said, reaching the landing.

"You were supposed to stay outside," Lindell snapped.

"Oh, I'm sorry, I heard Vee start yelling for Seamus, and I made some executive decisions. Lay off, Lindell." Anya pushed past her, already reaching for the pack that was slung over her shoulder. "They kept her in the cold to keep her controlled. She might be a fire demon, but they don't fare very well in freezing temperatures. Less powerful, even laden with Nether."

"Can you save her?" Seamus asked.

"I might be able to, but we need to get her someplace warm, and fast."

Captain Lindell frowned, looking out the window. "I hate to be the bearer of bad news, but we've got company."

"Shadows," Virginia swore. "Of course." She shifted Jolie so that the young woman was draped over her shoulder, reaching for her gun. "How many?"

"Hard to say. Looks like seven."

"We can take seven," Seamus said, already leaping down the stairs. Even as a man, his movements were sometimes unmistakably wolf-like, and his angry grimace would have been a snarl if on a snout. "I can take seven on my own, given the chance."

"Don't do anything stupid, Seamus, Anya is going to be busy enough tonight without any of us getting our asses kicked," Virginia added. With one arm around Jolie and the other on the gun, she descended the stairs, tension mounting with every step.

"We know you're in here!" one of the goons shouted from the ground level. "Come out before we start shooting!"

"Same to you!" Lindell shouted back, moving right behind Seamus. "Surrender now, and we might be lenient."

They fanned out across the second floor before starting the descent anew.

"You don't know what you're doing," the goon shouted again. "We've got an inferno witch here so powerful, she'll make you wish for death."

"Yeah, and you almost fucking killed her," Virginia shot back. "You bunch of thick-skulled garbage rats almost killed your best asset, and what would Fiske think of that? Hell, I think he should be doing me a favor for keeping her alive."

"We were gonna come back for her." The sound of guns cocking snapped up the stairwell, and it sent tendrils of fear to snake around Virginia's heart, not for her own sake, but for the others'.

"This is going to get messy," Arthur muttered, squaring his shoulders. "Seamus?"

"Yeah, Art."

"Whatever happens, you have to get Mona and Penny."

Seamus crouched into a stance. "We're all walking out of here, Art."

"Shit," Lindell said, glancing out the window. "Two more cars just pulled up."

"How are they even getting through this blizzard?" Seamus asked. "We barely even made it here."

"I'm guessing they'd have been here earlier if not for the snow. The blizzard did us a favor. Looks like eight more, and two of them have sub-machines, military grade."

"Yeah, to shadows with this," Anya said, pulling out the sparkling vial. "Shield your eyes!"

Virginia barely had time to blink before the vial shattered on the ground, exploding into a blindingly bright shower of silvery sparks that looked like they should burn, but didn't. They landed on the polished wood floor like beads, first scattering, and then drawing back together as if by magnetism, forming the shape of a ragged, thin woman, her eyes sunken into her skull, her hair wild and wiry.

"Fucked shadows," Seamus whispered.

Anya uttered something ugly under her breath, a curse maybe, something ancient and dangerous, too powerful for mortals to comprehend, and the ghostly figure screamed. Virginia staggered backwards as the windows first fractured, a spiderweb of cracks whispering along glass, before falling out of their frames, some to the outside, smashing against the pavement, and some inside, glittering against the floor.

The ghost, or illusion, whatever she was, descended the steps to the ground floor, one at a time, her hands stretched out, bony fingers grasping at air. She screamed again, the sound so shrill and piercing that Virginia's ears continued to ring after she stopped.

Shots rang out on the ground floor and didn't cease. They were scrambling, and from the broken window Virginia caught sight of the first few stumbling back into the street.

"Now's our chance," Lindell hissed. "Back entrance. Anya, Virginia, take the kid, get far from here."

Virginia shook her head. "Staying to fight is an empty-brained idea, Shirin. The entire point of a distraction is to get away, not to stay and fight."

"If we nab one of them," Arthur said, "maybe they can tell us where my family is."

"We already have a source, Arthur, don't be foolish," Virginia argued. "We will find them, and I don't want the first words out of my mouth to be that you got yourself killed because you didn't stop to think."

Another shriek shook the building, and more shots rang out.

"She's not going to last forever," Anya said, already descending the stairs. "We've got maybe five more minutes, and that's if they don't realize she's not really a banshee."

Virginia followed, nudging Seamus in front of her. "I don't want you to get hurt, either," she whispered.

"Don't worry about me," he replied. "I'll make sure they follow, if I have to physically drag them."

"Pick up the pace, people," Anya shouted over the din of the illusion. "I don't have any more of those."

Jolie shivered anew against Virginia's shoulder as they exited onto the street, pushing through the gate in the chain-link fence. There was no seeing through the snow that pelted down from the sky and whipped around her ankles. Virginia backed down the road, keeping her gun trained where she knew the enforcers were.

Flashes of gunfire glinted through the snow as they shot at the illusion, advancing on them, reaching as she screamed. It was a terrifying sight, even with the knowledge that it was only magic.

Virginia wrenched open the car door, laying Jolie inside, propping her up against the seat. She climbed in next to her, followed by Anya, who was already pulling various things from her satchel as Lindell swung into the driver's seat.

Seamus was all but dragging Arthur down the street, pleading with him, until the illusion blinked out of existence, and the confused shouts turned in their direction. Arthur turned to shoot, steadying his stance in the road, when Seamus picked him up and ran for the car, waving for Lindell to start the engine.

With everyone in, Lindell peeled off down the street in the opposite direction, tires unable to get purchase against the snow, sending the car careening from side to side. Virginia braced against the door with one hand, the other holding Jolie in place. Anya looked up at her, a guarded look in her eyes.

"She's not going to make it."

Chapter Thirty-Eight

The squad unit skidded from side to side, Lindell's knuckles clenching the steering wheel. "I can't see anything!" she shouted. "Not a shadows-damned thing!"

"No one is on the road, just keep driving!" Seamus replied.

Arthur was hanging out the window, firing shots at the two cars in pursuit, reloading his revolver every chance he could.

"You've gotta get them off my tail, Sheriff," Lindell said. "I can't keep driving at this speed or we're all going to end up in the river."

Arthur only grunted in response, and let three more rounds fly. One disappeared into the snow, one lodged itself into the windshield of a pursuit car, and the third hit there again, breaking through the glass and sending the car swerving onto a side street. "One down," he said. His voice was gruff and emotionless, devoid of tone. Virginia hadn't heard that voice in years.

Anya pressed some sort of salve to Jolie's forehead that smelled like charcoal, dust, and something unfamiliar. "She needs to get warm, and fast."

Virginia leaned over Jolie, a protective position, trying to guard her from the cold. "Come on, you damned firefly, don't burn out on us just yet."

"My shop isn't far," Anya said. "Get rid of these assholes and we can go there."

"We don't know how many more are in pursuit," Lindell said. "It's too risky. We need to go back to the precinct where we have backup."

"That's halfway across the city, this kid will never make it. Besides, they won't touch the shop. Trust me."

Lindell looked at Anya in the rear view mirror, an eyebrow raised. "We'll be discussing that later, Ms. Quinn."

"It isn't what you think it is, so relax. Drive, Lindell."

Arthur ducked inside the car, fumbling to reload his revolver. Virginia batted the rounds out of his hands, replacing them with her own gun, already loaded and cocked. He nodded to her, springing his torso out of the window again. Seamus gripped him for stability, arms around his hips. Arthur breathed, and fired again. The shot shattered the windshield of the other car, and it spun out of control, slamming into a telephone pole. "We'll call that in from Ms. Quinn's shop," he said simply, pulling back inside the car and cranking the window closed.

"Nice shot, Art," Seamus said, nodding.

Virginia rubbed her hands over Jolie's arms, trying to generate enough friction to convert into at least some warmth. She would have thought it was too cold for snow, but the wind whipped around and pierced straight through the skin, settling deep within bones and sinew, an inescapable cold. A deadly cold, and Jolie had been out in it for hours, wearing nothing more than the thin sweater Virginia had first found her in. They'd taken her coat. Bastards.

"How is she?" Arthur asked, turning around in the seat. He was searching Anya's face for an answer. Virginia knew that look, packed with panic, hoping against the odds that what he suspected wasn't true. "Is she going to be alright?"

"I don't know," Anya answered. "I've never treated a fire demon before. They aren't common this far north." She returned to smearing the strange ointment across Jolie's forehead. "This is precisely why. Too easily controlled in severe weather. It makes them vulnerable."

"They aren't common at all," Captain Lindell said, pulling onto a side street. She was driving slowly now, the car only gently sliding across snow. "Not for years."

"Not since the Rupture," Anya agreed. "So many mythics chose to meld back into society, rather than risk discovery." She glared at Lindell, who wasn't watching. "Cops and feds certainly haven't helped things."

"We're bound by law, even if we think it's wrong," Arthur said. "I don't think we should be conscripting mythics, but what the hell can I do? I'm a police sheriff, not a politician."

Virginia bit back the reply that was dancing at the tip of her tongue. It wasn't the time for that particular argument. "The Rupture changed things for all of us," she said. "Mythics and mortals both."

Jolie gave a quiet whimper, shivering anew. Virginia tucked the coat close around her, rubbing the arms with more vigor. "How much further, Lindell? She's frozen back here."

"Not far. Almost there."

"If we were even fifteen minutes later," Seamus said quietly, trailing off. "It's a frightening thought."

"Remind me to buy Zin a drink," Virginia said. "Better yet, Arthur, get some damned funds allocated to fix the hole in the library. Don't make her wait for the city council."

Arthur nodded. "First thing in the morning."

"We're here," Lindell said, guiding the car to the side of the road, or at least, what looked like the side of the road, given the thick snow. The streets were nearly silent, the only sound that of flakes landing on the metal fence posts around the side of Moonshadow Botanicals before they dropped off in fat clumps, exploding against the ground and melding into the other snow.

Virginia carried Jolie inside, depositing her on the table. She looked so small in Virginia's coat, like a child despite her eighteen years, so fragile and frail, so vulnerable.

"Everyone out," Anya said. "I need space to treat her, and you're all going to annoy me." When Virginia hesitated, she glared. "You too, Vee, you're not exempt. Out."

"I could help," Virginia protested.

"No, you can't. Out."

Anya all but shoved them through the door into the shop, locking it behind them. "I'll update you in a bit. Keep it down, the shop next door has a residence above."

"Maybe we should have taken her to a hospital," Captain Lindell said, wringing her hands. "They have a bigger team, with more staff, and—"

"What makes you think an average medical staff would know what in the hell to do with a fire demon?" Seamus asked.

"They could just treat the hypothermia, surely that would be better than nothing."

"Hospitals are rife with staff that quietly report mythics to the feds, Captain Lindell. Why do you think most of us choose to visit healers instead?" Seamus asked. "Shadows, doctors are half clueless about most of us, anyway. They weren't trained to deal with anything other than mortals. Before the Rupture, three quarters of the planet didn't know that the monsters under the bed were real, and suddenly we're showing up in emergency rooms with strange magical problems? It's a nightmare."

"Maybe I think that hospitals should be for everyone," Lindell said, picking up a small glass orb, black and shining in the darkness.

Virginia took it from her, placing it back on the dusty shelf. "You're naive. And don't touch anything. I'm surprised Anya even let you in here, given what you did the last time."

"I can't help that she was in possession of illegal reagents," Lindell argued.

"Why do you think they're illegal?" Seamus shot back. "It's so we're more easily controlled. We can't get what we need to be healed from illness or injury, we're forced into hospitals where they pump us full of stuff that doesn't work, we get reported to the feds, spend the next thirty years being thrown at whoever the nation is fighting that day." He turned towards a bookshelf, tapping the spines of the old leather tomes. "You have no idea."

"I'm sorry," Lindell said. She blinked, clenching her jaw like there was something she wanted to say, but couldn't, or wouldn't.

"What time is it?" Virginia asked, before pulling out her own pocket watch to answer her own question. She grimaced at the position of the hands, the face barely visible in the darkness. "Nearly two in the morning. The streets are going to be bad until at least six, depending on snowfall."

"I need to call the precinct," Arthur announced, reaching for the phone behind the cash register. "We need an all-points bulletin on Mona and Penny. And Fiske."

"Sir, we can't bring in Fiske until we have some evidence, or he's going to slip the net," Lindell cautioned. "You know how he is, and—"

"Don't fucking lecture me, Captain," he snarled. "I don't care if I have to destroy this city alongside my own career, I *will* get my family back."

"I'm only trying to keep a lid on this. *Sir.*"

No one spoke for a long moment, and the only sound was that of gentle glass rattling from the clinic on the other side of the door, and hushed tones from Anya that were unintelligible, but unmistakably encouraging, trying to rouse Jolie from her stupor.

"I understand," Arthur said finally. "There are days I wish the Rupture had never happened."

"Some of us like that we can live freely, Art, even if it's harder," Seamus said gently. "I know that now may not be the right time to say that, but, well, I think it's important to note." He shrugged, leaning against the door frame, his coat brushing against the closed sign. "We don't really know what Fiske is up to, right? Maybe this is a final desperate act."

"It could be ransom, even now," Lindell offered. "Maybe he's waiting for you to panic, so when the demand comes through, you'd pay it without regard to the law."

Arthur's face twisted into a hateful frown. "I don't give a damn what the law says. If I get a ransom note, I'll drain half the city's funds to pay it, and happily sit in prison until my dying breath."

"Let's not get ahead of ourselves," Virginia said, laying a hand on the cash desk. "Fiske has more money than the city's budget anyway, it's not going to be ransom. At least, not that sort of ransom."

Lindell let out a hiss. "He's going to bargain for prisoner release."

"Probably," Virginia agreed.

"We picked up a couple of high level enforcers last week. They haven't said a word, they've got an army of attorneys, and..." Lindell pressed three fingers to her forehead, grimacing. "I should have expected this."

"It's bold, even for Fiske," Arthur said. He leaned his head against the window. "I should have listened to Mona," he said again.

Virginia hated herself for the bitterness that rose up in her throat. "Call the precinct, Arthur."

He nodded, picking up the receiver. She pressed her ear to the clinic door, hearing only muffled sounds, all of them Anya's, and her stomach twisted with regret. Jolie might not make it, and it was Virginia's fault. She should have known better than to go to the Sphinx that night. Without thinking, she punched the door frame at the thought, rage bubbling up inside of her. *Astrid.* Always at the center of her problems.

Anya yanked the door open. "I said I'd update you, Vee."

"Sorry. That wasn't for you. Just—guilty. I feel guilty, I mean. About the kid."

"Fine," Anya said with a sigh. "Come in. But everyone else has to stay in the shop." She glared at Lindell, her eyes narrowed. "She better not touch anything."

"She won't," Seamus said. "I'll make sure." He flashed a wolfish smile, an eyebrow cocked.

Virginia stepped into the clinic, her breath catching in her throat at the sight of Jolie, shivering, her lips blue, frost still melting from her eyelashes. "Shadows," she whispered.

"I won't lie to you, Vee, it's not good. I'm doing everything I can, but my resources are somewhat limited, especially after getting cleared out by the shadows-damned VCPD." She yelled the last part of the sentence through the door, wiping her hands angrily on her apron.

"What can I do?"

"Talk to her."

"Talk?" Virginia asked, taking a step backwards towards the door.

Anya gestured towards the stool near the cot. "You're the one who wanted to be in here, Vee. The serum will take a while to get into her system yet, and even then, I'm not sure if it will be enough to bring her around." Anya thrust a small glass bowl into Virginia's hands. "Hold this," she said. It was filled halfway with ash, a large, triple-wicked candle nestled in the center.

She uttered something soft as she held a match to each wick, setting them alight. One burned blue, one red, and one orange. "Let me know if it gets too hot."

"I'm fine." Virginia shifted, watching the flames as they danced. "If we lose her, we lose any chance of finding Fiske before things get worse." She sighed, and her breath made the candle flicker. "Sorry," she preempted.

"Be careful. Do you have any idea how long it takes to make those candles? I don't have another one of these to start over with if you blow it out." Anya reached over, gently pushing the bowl into Virginia's lap. "Admittedly, I am unprepared for this."

"No one expects a fire demon."

"I suppose not." Anya tucked the heavy blanket tighter around Jolie, leaving no gaps around the edges. "I don't know how long this will take." She leaned back against the sink, brushing her hands against her apron, closing her eyes for just a moment. "Why did you keep her around, instead of tossing her to the VCPD?"

"I don't know." Virginia looked down at the candle, the glass bowl warming rapidly in her lap. It was an intense, direct heat, and already she could feel it leaching through her trousers into her knees. "Come on, kid. I know you're stronger than this. You can't let a blizzard take you out, that's just embarrassing."

"Embarrassing?" Anya asked with a soft laugh.

"Yeah. Embarrassing. Imagine I died, and the papers said it was a little bit of snow, and not one of the dozen other things that should have taken me out by now? People respect someone who kicks the bucket from a panther bite, or poisoning, or—"

"Who poisoned you?"

"Guess."

Anya sighed. "Astrid."

"When I say that we have a long, sordid history, know that I mean it." Virginia met Anya's eyes for just a moment before tearing her gaze away, embarrassed at what she'd admitted. "It feels like it was a hundred years ago, now."

"How'd she try to poison you?"

"It was a weak poison. She only did it to prove a point."

"You have terrible taste in women," Anya said, pulling more vials from the shelves, rubbing her hands together between each one.

Virginia flattened her palms against the glass, enjoying the vivid heat radiating through it, feeling it melt the iciness that had settled in her bones throughout the long winter that still had months yet before it finished. "Not all of them. Just her." She grimaced again at herself. "What does the candle do?"

"You're the one holding it, I imagine you can tell already."

"It's like spring, or early summer, maybe."

Anya nodded. "Enchanted to melt the frost within. Particularly useful for hypothermia, although I'm not sure it's potent enough for a fire demon."

"She's looking better." Virginia tilted her head, scanning Jolie's face for injury. "Nether is fading, and her lips aren't blue anymore, either." She moved the candle closer to Jolie, holding the bowl in her hands once more. "What's the worst-case scenario?"

"A relapse," Anya replied, "usually caused by shock. I'd be surprised if she didn't, after what she's been through."

"The Nether can't have helped."

"No, it won't have. Makes people more vulnerable to cold, even mythics. I doubt there's any records on what it would do to a fire demon, but then, they thought she was an inferno witch."

"What does it do to inferno witches?" Virginia asked.

Anya turned back to the sink, arranging some bottles above on a shelf. "An inferno witch wouldn't have made it this long," she admitted.

Virginia shifted, holding the bowl closer to Jolie, trying to direct the radiant heat towards her. "And illusion witches? What does Nether do to them?"

"I'd prefer not to answer that," Anya said. "I think you would judge me for what it makes me become."

"So you've tried it, then?"

Anya sighed, keeping her attention fixed on the bottles, arranging and rearranging them. "Once or twice, just after the Rupture." She turned back to the table, looking over Jolie. "The color is returning to her cheeks, that's a positive sign."

Virginia didn't blame her for changing the subject. Plenty of people were cagey about their Nether use, and for good reason—not to mention, there were two cops just on the other side of the door. "Come on, Firefly, we need you to tell us where to find these assholes. We're fresh out of leads."

"Here, hold the bowl with me." Anya pulled another stool to the other side of the cot, holding out her hands. "Over her middle. If we can warm her torso, maybe that will be enough. The candle, the serum, and the poultice."

Virginia carefully lifted the bowl, moving it slowly, watching the wicks as they moved. Anya took one side, their fingertips almost touching on the underside of the glass. "This is at least more than a hospital could have done."

"Hospitals weren't built for people like us," Anya agreed, and Virginia didn't want to ask which *we* she was referring to. Anya breathed quietly for a moment before she said anything else. "I was on a date when the Rupture happened."

"Oh?" Virginia prompted, after a sizable silence. "That must have been something."

"Being visibly marked in the middle of small talk certainly puts a damper on things. She just started staring at me, and this look of horror came over her face. By the time I pulled a mirror from my bag and saw that ugly black mark across my face, she was gone."

"The one that got away."

Anya shrugged lightly, careful not to jostle the bowl. "It's for the best. Even without the Rupture, she probably would have found out eventually."

"How long did your mark stay?" Virginia asked.

"A month. Most weren't surprised, but then, I've run this place since I was twenty-eight. It doesn't take a genius to connect an apothecary with a witch." Anya searched her face, but Virginia couldn't figure out what she was looking for.

"What?" she asked.

Anya shook her head. "Nothing. You're an enigma, Vee."

"You're not the first person to tell me that." Virginia stared into the flames, willing them to revive the girl in front of them. "It's a good thing you were along tonight. I'm not sure we'd have survived it otherwise," she said, looking down at Jolie. She'd stopped shivering, finally, her unconscious breaths slow and even. "That was a hell of an illusion you pulled off."

"One of my best, if I do say so myself."

"How did you do it?"

"Oh, you know," Anya said, shifting her palms around the glass. "A little bit of magic. A lot of luck." Anya leaned over the table, a devious smirk playing at her lips. "Truth be told, I'd been hoping for an excuse to try her out."

"Oh, so we might have all died as part of your experiment?"

"It's not like anyone else had a better idea, Lindell was about three seconds from piling down the stairs and becoming a martyr for the sheriff of police." Anya nodded down towards Jolie. "Look who's coming around."

Jolie's eyes fluttered open, their warm golden hue returned. "I know where he's keeping them."

Chapter Thirty-Nine

It wasn't yet dawn, but the snow had finally slowed to a light flurry, and the trucks were already beginning to plow the streets. Virginia leaned against the facade of Moonshadow Botanicals, flicking ash onto the ground below. If she couldn't get sleep, she'd at least need a cigarette. Maybe three. "Arthur, stop pacing, you're going to wear a hole in the earth."

"We should be moving now," he said. "We have a lead, we need to follow it.

"Let Lindell get intel first. You know procedure."

Arthur shot her a look, his hands shoved into his pockets. "Since when are you one for protocol?"

"Since we all nearly died last night rushing into something, and if you'll excuse me, I don't want any more blood on my hands." She took another drag, blowing the smoke out. "The fact that Jolie has that information at all is a good sign. It means Fiske is getting sloppy. He's spread too thin."

"You can't even imagine how I'm feeling right now, Ginnie."

She clenched her jaw. Released. Took another drag. "No," she said. "I can't." Her old, scabbed-over sins throbbed from deep within her, from wherever it was she'd shoved them when he'd left.

Arthur stared out over the dark road, the hem of his coat flapping in the breeze. "I'm surprised you're still here. You got what you came for, your fire demon is safe and sound."

"She's not *my* fire demon, Arthur. She's just a kid who got taken under my watch." Virginia sighed. "For whatever it's worth, I feel like at this point in my life, I need to start—" she cut herself off, inhaling the last of the cigarette before tossing it to the ground. "Start, you know, balancing the scales. Atoning."

"What happened wasn't your fault, Ginnie. I told you that, even then."

She pulled out a fresh cigarette, striking a match against the brick of the building, the flame faint in the growing grey dawn, the second she'd seen that week. "And of course I'm here, you fucking bonehead. You were my best friend, once."

He turned to face her, his expression unreadable, and said nothing.

"When you left, I lost more than a husband and a captain. I lost the last thing anchoring me back to reality. I was adrift, Arthur. It took me years to find shore again." Inhale, and the winter birds started their incessant song, another morning beginning against her will. Exhale, and it was one more loss in a sea of shipwrecked dreams. "But I understand why you left, and it doesn't matter now, anyway."

Wind blew between the buildings across the empty street, whistling softly, rustling with a new chill as it settled beneath her coat. "You shouldn't smoke so much," he said finally.

She caught his gaze with a smirk, responding with another drag. "I'll keep that in mind, Arthur."

The door swung open with the quiet jingle of bells, just as their larger counterparts four blocks down sounded in a forlorn church steeple. Six in the morning. "She's asleep, but Ms. Quinn assures me that's normal after what she's been through," Captain Lindell said, breathing into her cupped hands for warmth. "Shadows-damned cold out here."

"It's winter, Shirin. Of course it's cold," Virginia said, watching as smoke curled up into nothingness.

Lindell looked at her, jaw flexing, before turning away. "I called the precinct again, Sheriff. Once the roads are cleared, we're pulling in however many reserves we have on roster."

"Thank you, Captain Lindell."

"And I've also confirmed that no demands have been left at your residence. I am still awaiting a call back from the state penitentiary, however."

"I think we can all assume what that will look like," Arthur said, hands in his pockets. "Ginnie is right on that account. We should have figured it out sooner."

"I would have, had I known you were making moves on top-level enforcers," Virginia said, inhaling again. "If you had kept me in the loop, Shirin, I might have been of more use."

"I'm too tired to argue with you, Vane," Lindell said, and her voice was heavier than usual. "It's been a long night, and we've still got a hell of a lot more to cover before we're done."

The snow had ceased, finally, leaving a glittering coat across the abandoned landscape. It wouldn't be long before the city awoke to begin fighting back mother nature, shoveling snow out of paths and lighting wood fires to keep out the cold that so desperately belonged in their bones. It was the eye of a storm, and snow would certainly return. Virginia took the final drag, stubbing the rest out against the wall. She leaned her head back against the brick, letting the rough ridges tangle in her hair.

"Spare one?" Lindell asked, leaning on the wall adjacent.

"I didn't know you smoked," Virginia replied, offering her one from the silver case, monogrammed with her initials in a florid, looping script. A gift from Arthur for her birthday twenty years before, and the tarnish showed its age.

"We all have our secrets, Virginia." Lindell took it, accepting the light from the freshly struck match. "A habit I prefer to keep hidden."

"You're too tired for arguing, I'm too tired to hide my bad habits."

"I'm going to call the penitentiary again," Arthur announced, easing back inside, as though the creak of the door was something to apologize for.

Captain Lindell exhaled, smoke coupled with a sigh. "They're going to have that place stacked out with enforcers." She inhaled, looking at Virginia out of the corner of her eye. "Fuck."

"We won't all make it out of there alive, and Arthur knows it."

"The mayor already said he's not allowed to use the VCPD to raid it," Shirin said, blowing smoke out the side of her mouth.

"When did that happen?" Virginia asked.

"When you were in with Anya and Jolie."

"Fucking corrupt city."

"Yup." Lindell blew a pillar of smoke skyward. "You know, I feel for him. Barely a week back in Verdance, and already his family is getting abducted. I'd be surprised if he stays after this."

Virginia buried the toe of her boot in the snow, flicking a clump into the air. "He'll stay. I'm not lucky enough for him to disappear back to the coast." She sighed, fingers rubbing against the matchbook in her pocket. "I don't think he was ever going to stay away from this cesspit forever. It was always going to pull him back."

"I don't know if you're easier to talk to when you've had a smoke, or if I am," Lindell said, exhaling. "Either way, it's preferable to being at each other's throats."

"Lindell, if letting you bum cigarettes off me will keep you off my ass, I'll start buying them in bulk."

"I didn't promise that," Captain Lindell replied, a laugh escaping, despite everything. "I wonder if this would have gone another way, if we had played our cards differently."

"The problem wasn't the play, Shirin. It was the cards we were dealt." Virginia crossed her arms over her chest, shivering. The glow from being inside, from holding the glass bowl, had long since faded. "The city wasn't built for justice. That's not how it works."

The first cars started down the roads, trudging where the plows hadn't yet been. Milk trucks still made their rounds, stopping outside the apartment buildings down the street. Wordlessly, Virginia lit a third cigarette, offering Lindell a second. She took it, and they shared a light.

"A chain smoker, too?" Virginia asked, almost chiding.

"I have to make up for all the smokes I'll never have if I die later today." Lindell smirked before turning away, looking down the street towards the encroaching sunrise. "You know, Virginia, you're a complicated woman."

"Not so complicated, actually."

"I disagree. It's almost impossible to talk to you." Lindell turned back to face her, but something was different this time, there was some hidden note to her face that made Virginia's stomach knot. "Half the time, I don't even know how we ended up arguing in the first place, and it's infuriating."

"Because you piss me off," Virginia answered plainly.

"Clearly, but I—" Lindell stepped closer, hesitant, her boots crunching softly on the crusted snow. "I don't want to upset you, I just think we have different methods."

"Methods."

"Sure."

She was closer now, but Virginia stayed, a strange, sick sense of curiosity settling in her chest. "Okay."

Lindell pressed a gloved hand to either side of Virginia's face, bracing against the wall. She leaned in, and Virginia was still surprised when their lips met, like she'd been expecting to wake up from a confusing dream, covered in sweat and in dire need of coffee and a smoke. But she wasn't asleep, and knew it for sure when Lindell leaped away at the sound of the door.

"Oh, shit—shadows—sorry," Anya spluttered, turning in the opposite direction. "I didn't know anyone was out here, I needed some air."

"I was heading inside anyway," Virginia said, her head still swimming. She tossed what was left of the cigarette into the snow, pushing open the door. Warmth washed over her as she went inside the shop, aiming for the clinic door.

Seamus caught her by the arm. "Hey. You alright?"

"Yeah." Virginia shook her head, offering her the opportunity to rearrange her face. "You know. Tired."

"You know what we never do anymore?" Seamus asked, musing. "Brunch."

Virginia snorted. "When have we ever done brunch?"

Arthur slammed down the phone, and the force of it jostled the bell within the receiver, echoing across the small shop. "Ginnie was right. Fiske wants those enforcers released."

"What's the plan?" Lindell asked, coming through the door, summoned by the sound of the phone.

"Plan?" Arthur spluttered, almost laughing with incredulity. "There's no plan. I'd never get clearance to have them released. Fiske will know we're coming if we do anything stupid."

"Tell him you agree to terms," Virginia said, shoving her hands into her pockets. "Get word to him you'll release his enforcers. Buy us some time, Arthur. Make him think we're playing his game, it's what he expects anyway. Everyone else in this shadows-damned city does whatever he wants, so it's what he'll want to think about this, too. Buy us time to take a breath."

"If he tells the mayor—"

Virginia shook her head. "He won't tell her. Let him think you're going around the law, he'll believe it, and he'll keep his trap shut."

"And then what?" Arthur asked. "What then? I can't follow through with that promise, Ginnie."

"We make a plan that doesn't get us all killed. Get some rest. Meet back here at dusk, because we don't want to be putting a target on this place." Virginia leaned back into the bookshelf. "We get Mona, and Penny, and whoever else Fiske has got. We all move on with our lives."

"You make it sound easy," Lindell said.

Virginia met her glance, and it had an intensity that both terrified her and ignited some kind of lightly uncomfortable curiosity. She looked away, fixing her eyes on the floor. "Oh, it's not going to be easy. It's going to be the hardest thing any of us have ever done."

"Anya Quinn should remain here," Arthur said. "In case we are in need of..." he trailed off, but they all knew what he meant.

"Take that up with her," Virginia replied. "I'll take the kid with me so she can get some sleep on something other than a table. Anya should rest, too."

"Sheriff, this is probably the best play we've got," Lindell said. "We've got reserves coming in to patrol, to note any abnormalities, we have bulletins out on every known vehicle Fiske is associated with, every known enforcer, and we can keep it quiet until tomorrow if any of them get pulled in. We don't want him to see us coming."

"Alright, then," Arthur said with a weary sigh. "Dusk."

* * *

Morning was streaming through the windows of her living room, an uncomfortable reminder that it had been another sleepless night. Virginia poured herself a glass of gin, hoping against hope that it would calm enough of her nerves to let her get at least a few hours of sleep. "You okay on the couch?" she asked with a nod.

"I'm so tired, you could have left me in the park and I'd have curled up under some leaves," Jolie answered, unfolding the blankets.

"After last night, I didn't think that would be a good idea."

Jolie laughed quietly. "Were you considering it?"

"I wasn't not considering it." Virginia almost offered her a glass, but stopped herself, remembering the untouched glass from the night she arrived. "Tea? I have some of that stuff Anya sent with you."

"Sure."

Virginia turned, filling the kettle from the tap. She opened the tiny brown paper pouch of herbs, and it smelled like summer, like freshly cut grass, ripe raspberries, and the way the sun glistened against water at noon. She packed the tea leaves densely into the strainer, turning to Jolie with a raised eyebrow. "You want to use your little party trick, or should I do things the old fashioned way?"

"Might as well see if I've got it back," Jolie said, crossing the room to stand at the counter. She furrowed her brow in concentration, aiming at the kettle. A tiny, weak flame sprang from her fingertip, dying against the cold kettle with a hiss. "I guess not."

"Anya said it can take time."

"I went most of my life without these... abilities, I guess, but now that they're gone, I feel strangely vulnerable. Weak, I guess."

"Be grateful. Fiske doesn't want weak mythics, maybe this will get you some peace. For now, at least."

Jolie sat on the couch, pulling the blankets over her lap. "You came back for me."

Virginia didn't reply, didn't know how to, so she concentrated on the tea leaves, instead, and lit the burner of the stove with a long match. It was her fault the kid had been taken in the first place. She should have been smarter, sharper, seen that it was coming from a mile off.

"I wasn't sure that you would, but you did." Jolie shifted, the sound of fabric rubbing against fabric. "Anya said I would have died if you hadn't found me when you did."

"I'm sorry I didn't get there sooner."

"No one else would have come for me at all." Jolie folded her legs to her chest, turning to look out the window. "That estate will be hard to breach. They have ten foot fences all around the perimeter."

"I know. I've seen it before, and so has Arthur. It used to be owned by someone else, a wealthy widow. Eccentric. She had a huge greenhouse filled with rare plants."

"It's still there."

Virginia nodded in acknowledgment. "There was a break-in at the property a long time ago, when Arthur and I were still working together. She owned a lot of antiquities from around the world, rare books, crystals, artifacts, you know the type. Fiske bought the place about seven years ago."

"Did you ever solve the break-in?"

Virginia nodded. "We did. It was some kids from this side of town, trying to make a quick buck. They didn't realize how hard it would be to shift some of that stuff. Too recognizable." The kettle hissed quietly as it heated, and she found herself extending her hands towards it, trying to ward off the chill of the apartment. She shook her head at herself, moving to the radiator against the wall to open the valve. "Should get warmer in here soon."

"I saw Fiske, for a few moments, before they took me to that other building. The one where you found me. I think he's on Nether." Jolie shifted on the couch, stretching her legs out over the cushions. "A lot of Nether," she corrected. "Maybe it's why he's slipping."

"Could be." Virginia searched Jolie's face for lingering signs of illness. "How are you feeling after that detox?"

"Like I got hit by a train."

"Sorry about that. It should wear off in a few days."

"I just wish I could help tonight." Jolie sighed, pulling the blankets tighter around herself. "It's this feeling of not being able to get warm, it's unnerving. Like ice in my veins."

The kettle whistled its readiness, and Virginia poured the water over the leaves, letting them steep in silence. The water turned a rich amber first, slowly leaching into a deep ruby red, the color of summer flowers. She handed the mug to Jolie, returning to her own glass at the counter.

"Thanks," Jolie said, inhaling the steam. She closed her eyes, taking a sip with a quiet groan. "That already makes me feel better."

"I'll start another cup for you, then."

"So, you're a seer," Jolie said casually, her hands wrapped tightly around the mug.

Virginia laughed, swirling the gin in her glass. "What gave you that idea?"

"How did you find me on the roof?"

"I was being thorough."

"But the roof access was hidden, wasn't it?"

"I know my way around old buildings," Virginia replied with a shrug. "It's nothing another decent private investigator worth their salt couldn't do."

"And the picture frame at Ursa's."

"Thorough."

"And the closet," Jolie argued.

Virginia set the glass down. "I'm not a seer."

"Are you sure?"

"Do you really think I wouldn't know if I was or wasn't? Of course I'm sure, I'm old enough to remember the Rupture, even if you aren't. I was never marked."

"I was only five years old," Jolie said. "I wasn't marked, either, at least, not that the orphanage told me."

"They wouldn't tell you, they'd be trying to protect you from people like Fiske, if they knew what you were. It was a time of chaos. No one knew what was happening, mortals least of all. Violence in the streets, people turning in their neighbors. Family rifts. Companies collapsed. It upended everything most of us knew about the world. There were plenty of mythics that had no idea there were other kinds in the world."

Jolie pulled a small, onyx orb from the bag she'd shown up with. "I'm glad I didn't take this when we went to the Sphinx. I don't know what I'd do if I lost it."

"What is it?"

"Here," Jolie said, tossing it across the room.

Virginia caught it one-handed, more out of instinct than thought. It singed her fingers, and dragged bile up through her throat. She nearly dropped it in response, but set it on the counter, stepping away from it. "What the hell is that thing?"

"To most people, it's just a sphere of onyx. That's all it is, really. It was left with me when I was abandoned." Jolie waited a moment before continuing. "What did you see?"

"Nothing," Virginia lied. She could feel her world starting to crack at the seams, sending a spiderweb of unease across every impossible case she'd ever solved, every strange memory, every time she'd gotten sick after running evidence when she worked on the force. "I didn't see anything."

"I won't tell anyone what you are."

"I'm not anything." Virginia could hear the panic rising in her own voice, and struggled to tamp it down, turning to the kettle once again. "There's nothing to tell."

"You didn't know," Jolie said quietly. "All this time."

"Anya said you should have two cups of this in the morning, and two at night, until you start feeling better."

"Vee—Virginia—I'm sorry, I didn't mean to upset you."

"I'm not upset. There's nothing to be upset *about.*"

Jolie drained her mug, holding the emptiness in her lap. "I know that seers are in high demand with the feds."

"Good thing I'm not one, then."

"How do you explain what just happened, then? What *keeps* happening?"

Virginia let out an aggravated sigh. "You're welcome to stay here until you're recovered, and then Anya and I will help you find a place. There are some decent group homes on the east end of the city." She poured another mug of the tea, taking it to Jolie, swapping it with the empty one. "I'm going to get some sleep. You should, too."

Chapter Forty

The glass of gin sat untouched on her bedside table, glinting in the morning light. Virginia had her head between her knees, trying to gulp at breaths that wouldn't fill her lungs. The panic was strangling her, crushing the air from her chest, her ribcage contracting in on itself. She hadn't felt like that since she was a teenager, not since—no. She dug her short nails into her thigh, through the fabric of her pants. Had her mother known? Had she, all along?

It wouldn't have been the first mistake she'd made, where Virginia was concerned.

Or the tenth.

Or the hundredth.

She reached out with a tentative hand, brushing gently against the glass. Nothing happened, so she took it into her hands. This, at least, was safe.

Maybe it was a coincidence, a series of unusual happenstance that led the kid to that conclusion. She was only eighteen years old, what could she possibly know that Virginia didn't? That all the others who had spent time around her hadn't? That Arthur hadn't? They'd spent their childhood summers together, whipping through the cornfields, screeching like banshees. Joined the force together. Worked cases together, and he hadn't known?

Virginia gritted her teeth against it, as though sheer force of will could push it from her body, a gelatinous lump of black slime that could be coughed up out of her. Perhaps it had come from her absent father. She took a sip but the taste was wrong, marred by whatever it was that was inside her, growing exponentially now that someone had said it out loud.

She'd always known, maybe, in a way. Shoved down and ignored like so much else about herself, unworthy, unusable, one more black mark against her.

The Rupture happened just after Arthur had left.

She hadn't looked in a mirror for months after it happened, unable to face the ugly scars that were red-raw and weeping, taking far longer to heal thanks to the poison in the wounds. If she'd been marked, she wouldn't have known it. She didn't leave the house for months. Arthur took off to the coast with Mona, and that was that.

When news of the Rupture broke, it was days before people connected the marks to what they were, identifiers of mythics. Even that hadn't spurred her with enough bravery to look at herself in the mirror, and besides, it may well have faded by the time she had.

She rubbed her fingertips against her forehead, the ridges of the scars long since smooth. Had there been a mark there, when the Rupture happened? Had the scars prevented a mark from showing up at all?

If she was a seer, she wasn't a very good one, only getting flashes here and there, and never anything concrete. She'd spent years attributing her caseload to gut feelings, strong pulls alongside skilled detective work. The church bells four streets over chimed ten, the faint peals ringing over snowy roofs. She wasn't going to sleep, clearly. Not after this.

The forest green curtains were drawn, but light streamed through them anyway, disregarding the thick weave of the fabric and the fact that Verdance functioned much better under the cover of clouds. Half the city would wind up snowblind if the sun didn't go in.

Virginia opened her door quietly, moving to the far living room window for a smoke. She opened the case, running her fingers over the monogram, the delicate engraving persistent against her skin. Striking a match with shaky hands, she lit a cigarette, holding it out the window. She watched Jolie for any sign of waking, but the fire demon was dead to the world, snoring softly on the couch. It was better than a cot in the healing clinic, at least.

The black cat landed silently on the windowsill, having leaped down from above.

"Hey," Virginia hissed, shooing at it with her free hand. "Get out of here, you'll wake her up. I don't have anything for you right now."

The cat ignored her, sauntering across the side table towards the couch. Virginia was afraid to wake her, afraid the cat would, but was frozen in place by indecision. It decided for her, curling up on top of Jolie, emitting a quiet, stable purr. In her sleep, Jolie gave a contented sigh, smiling gently.

She'd never be free of Fiske, not so long as they both walked the earth. He wanted Jolie to be his prize, a powerful mythic that would make him more money than he could spend in an entire lifetime. He'd continue to hunt her, and wreak havoc in Verdance, and Virginia was just so shadows-damned *tired.* She just wanted the whole thing to be over. She wanted to sleep deeply, be it in her own bed or in a grave, at least it would be done once and for all.

The smoke in her lungs was at least proof that she was still breathing, still capable of inhaling and exhaling, and that point had been at odds in the bedroom. The others would already be asleep after one of the longest nights she'd endured in years. Shadows, but that fatigue nestled deep down within her, knowing it was far from done. She was just so desperate to be free of it all.

Lingering questions pierced through the fog of fatigue, even as she tried to bat them away. She focused her gaze out the window, against the bright glare of sun on snow, garish and tawdry. Time refused to stand still, and the minutes ticked by, sliding them all closer to dusk, to a fight, to certain death.

If she was smart for once, maybe she could stop it all in its tracks. Atone. Balance the scales that had been uneven for so long, the weight of her sins dragging her closer to whatever the emptiness of damnation held for her.

Eight had died fifteen years ago because she made a bad call. Benjamin had died because she fell asleep. Ursa was still missing or dead.

She could save five that night, and by extension, two more. They'd all be free to live their lives unencumbered by it all, and all she had to do was throw herself into the lion's den and hope that it was enough. Maybe it would balance. Make her life mean something other than the solitary, frozen landscape that it was, choosing the wrong thing time and time again, always facing the same decisions and always defaulting back to where she never wanted to be again.

Cyclical.

It was no different than what her mother had done, revisiting the sins of her own parentage onto Virginia. How do you break the kind of curse that runs through your veins, blood-red and ruinous in its intent? How do you filter out the imaginary pathogens that live there, infesting every cell, a complex fabric of generations upon generations of always getting it wrong?

Virginia stubbed out the butt of the cigarette, leaving it on the windowsill. She closed the window and bent to open the valve on the radiator below to match the other across the room. Jolie shouldn't get cold, not if she wanted to make a full recovery.

It was strange how automatically she buckled her belt, tucking in a fresh shirt pulled from her closet. Her mind was barely present as she shrugged on a waistcoat and tie, buttoning it. If she was going to die, she might as well look halfway decent. If she was going to die, it was best to treat it like a Sunday service, reverential in her own demise. The freedom was in the dying, after all, and that's the story that had always been told.

Gun, holster, knuckles. The three things she never left home without, even as she readily left any semblance of self-preservation cowering under her bed. If she was a seer, then she had power that the others didn't. If that's really what she was, then there was no better time to use it to absolve herself of fifteen years of crushing, inevitable guilt.

She paused before putting on her coat, stopping for just one wasted moment to be sure Jolie was well and truly asleep. If she woke too soon, she'd alert the rest of them, and none of it would have mattered at all, just one more mess to Virginia's name. More blood on her hands, more souls weighing heavy on her conscience because it *had* been her fault, no matter what Arthur said. It had been her, and her alone. The cat purred, and Jolie slept.

The doorknob was strangely warm under Virginia's fingers.

She didn't even mind that it would probably be the last time she closed that door.

Virginia descended the stairs like royalty cascading to the guillotines.

Chapter Forty-One

Frederick Fiske's compound was almost exactly as she had remembered it, at least from the front gate. High, iron fences, although now they were topped with razor wire instead of ivy. The greenhouse was just where it had been left, but the disused path leading to it suggested that whatever had been left inside had been left to rot or thrive, whichever the elements allowed.

Enforcers made their rounds, most of them huge and hulking, and if Virginia had to guess, most of them shifters. The pang in her shoulder was an unpleasant but timely reminder of the last time she'd tangled too closely with one.

She was parked on the street, leaning over the passenger seat with a pair of binoculars she always kept in the glove box for stakeouts. Usually she'd be hunting for a wayward spouse, gambling the family's money away on horses or crashing into bed with a lover, not scoping out the base of one of the most renowned criminal enterprises in Verdance.

There were twelve enforcers on the outside of the house, and no telling how many were inside. She was good with a gun, but once shots rang out, it would alert anyone and everyone within a half mile radius. Fiske owned most of that half mile, at least down to the river on the south side of the property.

It was already noon, and the sun was unacceptably bright after such a tumultuous blizzard, but then, Verdance weather was known for its juxtaposed behavior. Despite the bright glare, and the cloudless sky, the air was still cold enough to sear the lungs, so she breathed through the fabric of her thick wool scarf. It at least took the bite from the chill.

She'd have to get inside first. If she didn't free Penny and Mona before she was discovered, the whole thing would be up in flames. Probably literally, if Fiske had anything to say about it.

It was already too late for rethinking. Too late for cowardly posturing, for pushing the ignition and driving home, slinking back into the apartment like she hadn't failed all over again.

The entire estate was bathed in the cold light of winter, the trees bare and incapable of blocking the sun, the bare, grasping branches content to ignore all of them until spring. Stasis. Hibernation. Death, in a way, and Virginia was envious of it. Of the cold peace, of the quiet, of being released from expectations.

She was almost surprised that no one had found her yet. That Jolie hadn't woken up in a panic, alerting Lindell and Arthur, sending them on their way to stop Virginia in her tracks, but the street remained as quiet and unperturbed as ever. Shirin would be angry when she found out what she'd done. Shirin was usually angry at her though, which made the kiss all the more confusing. There was something there, Virginia couldn't deny it, but it was too hungry, and she was still too afraid of being torn apart.

And yet, throwing herself into a heavily guarded compound had taken almost no consideration at all.

She climbed out and closed the car door quietly, leaning against it until the lock latched.

Iron gates closed off the property, secured with a wide padlock. Two enforcers were just inside leaning against a small shelter, shading their eyes against the glare of the snow. They wore thick coats with emerald vines embroidered across the sleeves, adorned with scarlet thorns. Fiske's taste in uniforms was unparalleled. She noted their position, and how many guns they were carrying—two each—and skulked towards the fence. Virginia strapped clay impressions of hooves to her boots, buckling the leather straps and securing them under the laces. Leaving footprints was a fast way to get caught.

It had been a long while since the last time she infiltrated a compound. Ten years, maybe more. Fiske's house had a basement, and that's likely where he was hiding Arthur's wife and daughter. Virginia had seen it working that case so long ago, and while much could change in the ensuing time, she hoped the access points were still the same. A staircase, nestled back behind the large kitchens.

She crept through the snow, staying low to the ground, cursing herself for not owning a white coat. The glint of a small window half hidden by the earth caught her eye. The basement. Another access point, if she wasn't able to get to the stairs.

The gaps between the fence posts were wide enough for a cat, perhaps, but not a person. Virginia sucked her teeth. Rope would be too obvious. A tall oak towered near the iron, one branch extending over the danger of the razor wire. It had been decades since she'd climbed a tree. Grasping the bottom branch, she pulled herself up into the tree's crook and untied the hooves from her boots.

Her stomach twisted at the shining threat of the razor wire. She inched forward along the tree's limb, pulling herself towards the compound. Some faraway part of her begged to get back into the car and leave, to wait until dusk as they'd all agreed, but she swallowed it down without much thought.

On the other side of the fence now, she dropped to the ground with the quiet thud of boots against snow. There were plenty of boot prints this side from the enforcers, so she kept the clay hooves in her pocket. They'd only make her unsteady. Virginia moved quietly, always looking over her shoulder for any sign of movement or detection, but mercifully, there were none.

It was far too early to breathe a sigh of relief. She was barely breathing at all.

The greenhouse was lit like a beacon, taking in the glare of the sun on snow, reflecting some of it back onto the grounds to such an extent that the old, dead grass of autumn was poking through the melting drifts surrounding it. The handle was rusted, and from what she could see, the inside was overrun with untended plants. She touched the brass lock and seethed with a hiss at the vibrant, vivid memory that came rushing back. She and Arthur had sneaked into the very same greenhouse all those years before, looking for evidence. She'd cracked some snide remark about pruning shears as a murder weapon, and he'd rolled his eyes and laughed.

It was like being back in the moment, dragged backwards in time, so heavy and pristine that Virginia had to plunge her hands into nearby snow to focus her mind. She'd always had problems escaping the past. Memories too sharp, too present to forget.

Three enforcers stood at the kitchen door, leaning against it. She couldn't take three out silently, not all at once. If she survived it, she'd take up knife throwing. If she survived it, she would smoke an entire pack of menthols and chase them with a bottle of good gin.

It would have to be the window. She edged closer to it, keeping her eyes on the three enforcers. They looked bored, and probably were. Working security was hardly the most mentally stimulating thing she'd ever done, either, and that was back when she was working for Astrid at the Sphinx. Virginia flattened herself against the wall, reaching down to touch the window, tentative, almost flinching away from it. No flashes, no twists of her gut came, and it was a relief given all that had probably happened in that house since Fiske bought it.

She pressed against the glass, testing its resolve. The hinge squeaked gently, and Virginia froze, glancing from side to side. When no one turned around the corner to shoot at her, she pulled at it again, releasing the rusted pin to drop silently into the snow. She pressed at the second hinge, this one more resolute in its job. Virginia tapped at it quietly, trying to knock off some of the powdery rust that kept it firmly in place. It was staunch, and stiff, and she glared at it as though that would change its mind.

With the silver knuckles slipped over her fingers, she tapped at the hinge quietly, pausing after each time metal connected with metal. She was lucky that the nearby enforcers were engrossed in some conversation about Nether drops, she couldn't hear much of the details from her position. It didn't matter. They'd deal with the Nether later, when Fiske had lost his most potent bargaining chips. No doubt he was already incensed at losing

Jolie, if those enforcers had even been brave enough to deliver the news yet.

The second pin scraped free of the hinge, and she removed the pane of glass, bending down to the ground to peer inside. She could barely see, her eyes still instinctively flinching from the bright sun outside. The basement was dark, the only light coming from the window she'd just opened. She was sure he'd be holding them in the basement.

She slipped through the window, taking the pane and the hinges with her. Most wouldn't notice that the glass was gone, but they would if she left the evidence in plain view. Setting the pane down on the floor, she unholstered her gun, holding it at the ready.

The basement was different than it had been twenty years ago, although she'd anticipated that. Before, it had been mostly a storage area, stacked high with boxes and unused furniture. Now, it was fitted with lush carpeting, the wallpaper crisp and clean, and a billiards table situated in the middle of the room. It was a recreation room, not a place to store hostages.

"Shadows," she uttered under her breath. Had their intel been wrong all along? Maybe Mona and Penny weren't even in the building at all. For all she knew, they could have been moved back to the warehouse at the docks, left to shiver and freeze in the winter cold like Jolie.

Virginia slunk through the basement, her muscles tense and aching from the effort. Footsteps sounded upstairs, dull echoes, but she hesitated just the same until they faded. There was a light switch on the wall, the plate smudged from years of use, but she left the basement bathed in darkness. A closet beckoned her to the corner of the room, and she tried the handle, surprised when it was unlocked.

Empty, except for a few boxes of files. She rifled through them quickly, folding and pocketing a few pieces that looked relevant. A property deed for some place upstate, pages of what looked like payroll notes, and in the margins of those notes, comments about payments to Eugenia Patten, the alderman, and Detective Baker, the young woman on the force. Virginia sucked in a breath. Corruption was spreading through the VCPD, and Arthur had no idea.

The wooden stairs hosted only a narrow strip of fabric that ran up the length of them. Virginia kept to one side, wary of creaks, wary of enforcers that may or may not careen around the corner at any given second and plow right into her.

Still, she continued, anticipating capture, or worse. Crews like the Ruby Thorns were very well known for what *worse* could entail, and your body being dredged from the lake was on the lighter end of the scale. The three enforcers outside the kitchen were still there, still gossiping, but now, their voices were clearer.

"He's going to get us all killed, you know," the one with the long blond braid said. She tossed it over her shoulder with a quiet swish. "I'm surprised we haven't been inundated with cops already."

One enforcer with a small tattoo on his hand, a rudimentary dagger, leaned against the door. "Come on, Jen. Fiske has never done us wrong before, has he? Hell, he managed to get everything moved before that raid on the warehouse. Imagine where we'd be sitting if he hadn't."

"There wouldn't have even been a damned raid if he'd just slow down on this whole thing for ten seconds. It's not just about Nether anymore. Now it's politicians in his pocket and money laundering and expansion, expansion, expansion. It's all he ever talks about."

"You're free to leave, you know," the final enforcer said, tugging his black wool hat down over his ears. He cleared his throat harshly, spitting something wet and horrible onto the ground with a disgusting splat. "No one is forcing you to stay here."

"Hey, fuck you, Paul. I don't have to take this shit from you. I've been picking up your slack for weeks because you can't be bothered to do your job." Jen huffed angrily, cracking her knuckles. "I'm going to check the perimeter."

"Why? There are plenty of us out there already," Paul said.

"Because I'm tired of looking at your ugly mug, that's why. Fuck." She stomped off towards the greenhouse, and Virginia's stomach clenched, waiting for her to notice the window, until the enforcer had passed it with no alarm sounded.

"She's such a bitch," Paul said.

"You could go easier on her. She *has* been picking up your slack."

"You too, now? Shadows, and here I thought I'd get a moment's rest working around here, but I guess not."

"You can take it easy when we're not spread thinner than last week's butter over this week's bagel, alright? All I'm saying is that it's been a tough few weeks, and we're all tired, Jen included. I bet if you lay off, she'll cool down."

Paul huffed out a laugh, striking a match on a Sphinx club matchbook. The sight of it burned Virginia's lungs anew with resentment for Astrid. "You're all a bunch of babies," Paul said, lighting a cigarette. "Jen most of all. You can't say anything to her without her flying off the handle."

"I don't know what to tell you, pal. She's not like this with me."

"Yeah, because she's sweet on you."

"Fuck off."

"Just make sure her old man doesn't see you coming or going, eh Anthony?" Paul chided, elbowing him in the ribs.

Virginia's knees were beginning to ache from squatting in the same position, unmoving. She shifted one foot to the side, stifling the sigh of relief when she removed the pressure. She had to get the hell off the stairs and find Mona and Penny.

"Nothing is going on with me and Jen. You just see things where there isn't anything. It's annoying." Anthony turned away, coughing. "Come on, man, can't you do that somewhere else? I can't stand when it blows in my face."

"What's the matter, can't handle a little smoke?" he asked, and Virginia felt her own craving for the tobacco spark at the back of her skull.

"Asshole."

Paul took a long drag from the cigarette before discarding it onto the ground. "What did you just call me?"

"I called you an asshole, you incompetent sewer rat. Listen, go check the hostages. Take them some water or something, Fiske said we're not supposed to be harassing them."

"Why don't you go play maid service for them?" Paul shot back. "I'm no one's errand boy."

"I can't wait to see Fiske knock the crap out of you. Fine, Jen can go when she's back. It's not like they can get out of that bedroom on their own."

Bedroom. Excellent. All the sleeping quarters in that house were on the third floor. Virginia eased into the kitchen, staying low to the ground. It was the same tile flooring as it was twenty years ago, intricate and impressive, although if she had to guess, the grout had recently been redone.

There was another enforcer in the living room, but she could easily skirt him by taking the back stairs, once only used for the servants of the house, now used by everyone and anyone, judging by the streaks of mud on the carpet. Virginia climbed to the second floor, grateful for the carpet that muted her movements. The large room at the end of the narrow corridor, lined with damask wallpaper, was likely Fiske's office. Her jaw ground together, and in another life she would have kicked the door in and fired on him then and there.

That wouldn't get Mona and Penny released, though it *would* sign Virginia's death warrant. She turned, ready to climb another flight of stairs, still cautious, still expecting and preparing for the worst. The navy blue carpet was strewn with huge flowers woven right into the texture.

The third floor was mercifully empty, devoid of enforcers and more importantly, devoid of Fiske. She knew better than to breathe a sigh of relief, so she inhaled again, cramming her lungs with unspent oxygen. She'd need it if she got caught.

She tried the first door, and it opened into a dark closet piled high with boxes. Flipping open the corner of one, Virginia expected to see the telltale glow of Nether, but instead found political canvassing pamphlets. Fiske was going to run for mayor. Shit. One more notch in his belt, and another foot in the grave for Verdance.

The second door was a small bedroom with rumpled linens and the stench of stale sweat. It was Fiske's room, and surprisingly bare. A bed, a wardrobe, and a shallow closet, and that was all. She backed out, grateful for the cool, fresh air of the corridor.

The third and final door was locked. "Mona," Virginia whispered through the door. "It's Virginia."

There was no answer, and the silent absence filled her with a sick dread. She tried the doorknob again, but it didn't budge. Kicking it in would alert the whole damned house, and picking it would leave her vulnerable, out in the open. It was risky, but the only option.

She thrust a lockpick inside, feeling her way around the tumblers. Only two, and no secondary lock. She tapped one into place, feeling the quiet click more than hearing it, and starting work on the second. In two minutes, the door was open, and she rushed inside, bolting it behind her.

Mona and Penny sat on a wide bed with navy sheets, bound, gagged, and blindfolded.

"It's Virginia," she hissed, reaching for the blindfolds first. "Don't scream."

The little girl was terrified, shaking like a leaf in her gingham pinafore. "I'm a friend of Arth—of your father's," she whispered. "I'm here to help." She removed the gags next, pulling a small pen knife from her inside coat pocket to cut the ties at their wrists and ankles.

"Virginia, thank shadows," Mona said, helping her to pull off the remaining ties. "Where is Arthur?"

"It's just me."

"Just you? But there are dozens of them—"

"Keep your voice down, Mona."

Mona stood, rubbing at her wrists before enveloping her daughter in an embrace. "It's alright, we're going to get out of here Penny, alright?"

The girl nodded, stealing a glance back at Virginia. "Why does she look angry?"

"She always looks like that."

Virginia rolled her eyes, checking the lock on the door. "Did they give you inhibitors?"

"Yes, but not for a while. They've been putting them in our tea."

"Then we don't have long, because I already heard a trio of them arguing about who was going to do it. Can you shift?" she asked the little girl.

Penny bit her lip. "I can usually, but I haven't been able to here."

"Mona?" Virginia prompted. "What about you? Because I sure as hell can't."

"Let me try." Mona eased the window open, crouching at the edge first to check for enforcers at the perimeter. She stretched her arms over her head, shifting into pigeon, her clothes falling away. She began to shift back, and Virginia turned to face the wall, her face reddening.

"I guess so," Virginia said.

"I don't want to be a pigeon, Mama. I'd rather be a hummingbird."

"Not this time, Petal, it would draw too much attention. It won't be for long. We'll fly straight home to see Daddy, yes?"

Soft footsteps outside the door drew Virginia's glare, and she leaped across the room to lean against it just as a key was thrust into the lock. "Go!" she shouted.

"What about you?" Mona asked. "I can't just—"

"I said go!"

Mona and Penny flew out the window to freedom just as another enforcer joined in the fight to break into the room, throwing Virginia backwards against the floor.

"Well, well, well," Paul said. "What the fuck do we have here?"

Chapter Forty-Two

Paul was almost twice her size, a huge, hulking man, and if she had to guess, a werewolf, and a nasty one at that. He had that same wolfish grin that Seamus did, but without any of the warmth. He tossed her into Fiske's office, leaving her sprawled across the floor.

"Found this upstairs, Boss," he said. "She let those two shifters go, they flew out the window when she cut them loose. I already took her gun and her knuckles."

"Knuckles?" Fiske asked, leaning across the desk, his lean frame dwarfed by his enforcer and the strange angle of his cheekbones casting a gaunt shadow over the rest of his clean-shaven face. The hard parting of his hair on the left presented a stark contrast between the paleness of his skin and the dark, overly oiled bluish-black of his cropped mane. "Odd choice for a woman."

"Challenge me to a fight, let's see how odd it is," Virginia shot back.

Fiske drummed his fingers against the leather-topped desk, the pin stripes of his neatly tailored suit following his movements. He raised one dark, bushy eyebrow and nodded to Paul, who punched her square in the mouth. Pain exploded across her face, blood already dripping from her nose.

"Cheap shot," she said, wiping her face with the back of her hand. Blood smeared across her skin, and dripped onto the carpet.

"Winners rarely abide by the rules of engagement, Ms. Vane." Fiske stood, his hands clasped behind his back. "Oh, yes, I know exactly who you are. You've been a nuisance for years, although never worth dealing with before now." He tugged at the cuffs of his crisply starched shirt, the same Ruby Thorns symbol embroidered on a handkerchief that peeked out of his breast pocket. "Paul, you're dismissed. Tell Jen to wait outside the door, just in case Ms. Vane has any other tricks up her sleeve." Paul turned to leave, and Fiske pulled a revolver from his holster, shooting him dead.

Virginia flinched at the thud when Paul's body hit the ground, the vibrations traveling through the floor and directly into her lungs, which again ceased to function. "Seems like overkill," she wheezed, trying not to choke on the blood running down the back of her throat, thick and viscous.

"It's a challenge to find good help these days. Although apparently not for Sheriff Dixon. He wrangled you back onto the force less than twenty-four hours after he landed in Verdance." He stood from the desk silently, moving across the soaked rug like an eel.

"I'm not on the force," Virginia protested, her voice thick.

"Yet you're here, freeing his family and ruining my plans." Fiske sighed, nudging Paul with the toe of his polished shoe. "I did tell him this would happen. Poor, foolish Paul. He never was very bright."

"So, what now?" Virginia asked, sitting back on her haunches. "I have plans later that I'd rather not be late for."

Fiske turned the gun on her, tutting softly. "Plans with our Astrid Frost, I imagine?" He gestured with the revolver lazily, waving it to the side. "No sudden movements now, Ms. Vane, I would hate for you to spook my trigger finger."

"Astrid can rot in hell, as far as I'm concerned," Virginia growled. "I don't give a shit who she's doing business with."

"Yes, I did gather that you were less than thrilled with our little arrangement after you stole my inferno witch from me. Very clever, that illusion." He leaned against his desk, keeping the revolver trained on her. "I'm well aware of where that came from, and I can't say I'm thrilled that Anya Quinn chose her side quite so... irrevocably."

Virginia wanted to stand, but wasn't yet confident of the strength in her legs after that punch. "Leave Anya out of this." She spat a glob of clotting blood onto the carpet, staring at him in challenge, waiting for him to shoot her.

"Where are the rest of them, Ms. Vane? I've already alerted the rest of my enforcers on the property, it won't be long before they are found."

"It's just me."

"I don't believe that for a moment. You've been inseparable from Sheriff Dixon and Captain Lindell for a week now. I know they must be here."

Virginia lifted her face, ignoring the blood dripping down her chin. "They aren't. I didn't tell any of them that I was going. Our plan was to strike at night. I jumped the gun." She needed him to believe it had just been her, to leave the rest of them out of it. If she died, it was expected. If they did, it was another failure on her conscience, and just before death, too.

"Why?"

"To catch you off-guard." She smirked. "Looks like I did. Your leverage has flown the coop."

He shrugged, giving her a dangerous smile. "Not all of my leverage. I still have you."

Virginia laughed, and it caught in her throat, gurgling with blood. "I'm worth far less."

"Perhaps so," he said easily, waving his hand in a mocking, deferential way. "After all, you aren't the sheriff's wife."

"No, I quit that job," she retorted.

"From what I heard, you were unceremoniously fired. From both positions, in fact, as I seem to recall." He sighed, looking out the window over the grounds. "I didn't want things to end up like this, you know. One simple exchange was all it would have taken, and no one would have needed to get hurt. A gentlemen's agreement, a trade, and we all could have gone about our days." He looked down at her, tilting his head. "And you would have been able to make your dinner plans, whatever they may be."

"A pack of menthols and a bottle of gin."

"Keep on like that, Ms. Vane, and you'll land yourself in the morgue with no help from me." He twirled the gun around his finger three times, catching the trigger lightly each time it was pointed in her direction. "If you last that long."

"Where is Ursa?" Virginia demanded, spite in her tone fueled by the blood in her mouth.

"Who?"

"Ursa, their brother was a distributor of yours. He punctured a hole in my shoulder a week ago."

"Oh." Fiske popped the chamber from the revolver, spinning it before snapping it back into place. "I imagine they ran off after they killed their brother."

"What?" Virginia asked, stifling the gasp blooming in her throat. "Ursa didn't kill Benjamin."

"Oh, you didn't know? Yes, well, it's a common situation these days, isn't it?" Fiske asked, nonchalant, still twirling his revolver on his bony fingers. "Benjamin ran off back to me, back to his job, and Ursa tried to stop him. Things got... messy."

Virginia shook her head, the room spinning around her from the hit. "That can't be true."

"I am more than happy to take credit for my own untidiness, Ms. Vane, and I can tell you with full authority that Benjamin's death had nothing to do with me." He shrugged at her with a smirk, refastening his sparkling cufflinks. "He was unwilling to leave his post, they fought. He didn't survive, and his sibling fled the scene. Truth be told, Ms. Vane, I'd love another shifter with that kind of grit, so if you see this Ursa again, make sure you send them my way."

"Please, it had everything to do with you," Virginia hissed. "He never would have been there if not for—"

"For what? For rampant inequality in Verdance? For a lack of opportunities for young mythics?" Fiske asked, pacing circles around her that grew tighter and tighter with every pass. "You may hate me, but I'm doing more for the prosperity of this city than anyone else is. If his sibling had stayed away, they would both still be alive and living in that ramshackle little apartment across from yours." He glanced up, nodding to an enforcer in the doorway. "Jen. Take Ms. Vane here to the greenhouse to cool off.

Tell the others to dispose of this." He nodded at the corpse. "Consider yourselves lucky that I didn't also blame you for this little fiasco."

"Yes, sir," she said, grabbing Virginia roughly by the arm.

"Bind her, Jen. She's feisty." He holstered his gun below his shoulder, sliding it neatly into the leather. "And send cars to sweep Moonshadow Botanicals, Sheriff Dixon's home, that dingy gym on the southwest side, and Ms. Vane's apartment."

"Of course, sir." The enforcer pulled a length of hemp rope from her shoulder, tying Virginia's wrists together. "The two shifters?"

"Gone, unfortunately, but we're already working on retrieving them."

Virginia groaned as she was pulled roughly to her feet, focusing intently on even minor movements. "You'll never get them," she mumbled. "They'll know you're coming."

"Ms. Vane, if there's one thing you've yet to learn about Verdance, it's that men like me always get what we want." Fiske pulled a cigar from his pocket, lighting it easily with a gold lighter. "Get her out of here. I'm tired of looking at her face."

Jen dragged Virginia backwards out of the room, pulling her down the stairs. "Don't start any bullshit, and I won't have to cave in your skull," she threatened. To prove her point, she took Virginia by the shoulders, slamming her head backwards into the painted brick wall along the staircase.

Her vision swum, and her knees buckled beneath her. "Fuck," she grunted, falling forward. She would have careened down the rest of the stairs, if not for Jen yanking at her wrists, pulling painfully at her shoulders.

"Don't fuck with me," Jen said. "I've taken out worse than you without a second breath."

"Fucking... bastard," Virginia slurred, alarmed at the sound of her own voice. Blood dripped down the back of her neck, oozing into the collar of her shirt. She blinked furiously, trying to clear her vision and failing, barely even able to see each step in front of her.

Jen tossed her into the greenhouse and slammed the door, securing a padlock to the outside. There were four enforcers outside, one on each side of the outbuilding, their forms obscured by the thick foliage that wound its way up over the arch of metal holding it up. "Don't let her move a muscle," Jen instructed. "Fiske said to go grab the rest of them. You know the drill."

Cold leached through Virginia's pants and she pulled her coat close around her, lamenting her empty holster and lack of knuckles, burning with impotent rage that Fiske had stolen the latter. Wrists still bound, she reached up, feeling the back of her head, her fingers coming away bloody, just as she had expected. At least it was thick, oxidized, beginning to clot already.

Virginia sank down slowly to the ground, not making any sudden movements that would earn her a bullet in the chest. Dying was one thing. Failing was another.

Chapter Forty-Three

She wasn't sure how long it had been when a car pulled up, and three figures were dragged from the back. Seamus. Anya. Jolie. Virginia stood, peering out the frosted windows, squinting through the cold and her bleary eyes.

"Throw them in with her," Jen barked. "Bind them first, and give them all inhibitors. They're all mythics."

Another enforcer injected syringes into all three of them before dragging them to the greenhouse and tossing them in. "If the VCPD cooperates, you'll all walk out of here," Jen called to them from across the stone courtyard. "Try my patience, and I won't hesitate to bury every single one of you."

"Bitch," Anya muttered.

"Vee!" Jolie said, her eyes wide. "What happened to you? Why are you here, did they take you? How?"

"I came alone," Virginia answered, feeling the shame boil inside of her like lava, singeing at her veins and filling her with guilty smoke. "I wanted to keep you all safe."

"What about Mona and Penny?" Seamus asked.

"Gone. Shifted, flew away. I hope they weren't taken, too."

Seamus shook his head. "No, the enforcers driving the car said as much. Fiske killed one of his own?"

"Yes." Virginia breathed a sigh of fragile relief. "I'm glad they weren't recaptured. Arthur?"

"At headquarters," Seamus answered, tugging at the worn cuffs of his gym-branded sweatshirt, olive green with embroidery across the chest.

"They'll be trying for the ransom again, trade, whatever."

"Lindell?" Virginia prompted. "Did they get her?"

Anya sat down, folding her legs beneath her. "We don't know. She wasn't in either of the cars. There were six or seven enforcers, too many to fight off."

Virginia hung her head, the shame pulsing through her more steadily than the pain. "I'm sorry. I should have warned you."

"You look beat to shit," Anya said, reaching out with bound hands. "Are you okay?"

"More or less."

"Your nose looks broken."

"Probably," Virginia admitted. "Took a few hits to the head."

Jolie leaned against one of the cluttered potting benches, looking up through the glass roof of the greenhouse. "Did you leave because of what I said?" she asked, quieter, her voice barely above a whisper. "Are you angry?"

"I'm not angry." Virginia sighed. "Not with you. With myself, maybe."

Seamus tilted his head. "What did she say? What in shadows is—"

"Later," Virginia growled, cutting him off. "If we make it out alive. But not here."

"Have you been keeping secrets again, Vee?" He crouched closer, staring, willing her to admit what she was aloud.

She shot him a look, regretting it when her head began to pound again. "Enough, Seamus. Later."

The padlock unlatched again, the door swinging wide to reveal the bright glare of the snow. "You, inferno witch," Jen said. "With me. We have a job for you."

"You just gave her an inhibitor," Virginia protested. "You're going to send her on a job *now*?"

"She'll be fine, it's a routine drop." Jen smirked. "Probably. You can never tell what will happen these days, not with cops swarming the city, and that's all thanks to you."

Virginia coughed, spitting out a fat glob of thick blood onto the tiled floor.

"Wait," she said. "Take me instead." She held up her hands, climbing unsteadily to her feet. "I'll be of more use in the long run than a baby inferno witch, anyway. Let these three go, and I'll stay. I'll join the ranks with no fight."

"Vee, no," Jolie hissed. "It's fine, I'll just—"

"What makes you think I have any use for a busted up, has-been of a disgraced cop?" Jen asked. "Over an inferno witch?" She laughed, throwing her head back with enough force to swing the braid hanging from the nape of her neck. "Maybe I rattled your brains too much back on the stairs."

Virginia took a deep breath, squaring her shoulders. "I'm a seer." The admission felt foreign, like she was sharing someone else's secret. She wasn't even sure she really believed it herself, but it was the last chance to save the others now that Fiske had captured them, too. The sharp sting of failure cut through the throbbing ache in her skull, too present to ignore.

"Bullshit," Jen said.

"I'll prove it," Virginia said. She slowly reached out for the enforcer, keeping her gaze, and brushed a finger against the button at the cuff of her coat. Closing her eyes she strained, focusing, trying to pull something to her that would prove what she was. The vision came in pieces, fragments that could just be her imagination, one last desperate effort to atone. "You grew up on a farm out of state, up north. A dairy farm." She inhaled, holding the air in her lungs, bracing for a hit that didn't come. "You cried the first time a cow was taken to slaughter."

Jen yanked her sleeve away. "Don't touch me."

"The buttons on your cuffs were your grandmother's. She raised you, but died when you were young? Fifteen?"

"Fucking hell," Seamus breathed.

Virginia stumbled backwards, reeling, pressing her hands to her head as best she could with her wrists bound. It was the most she'd ever seen, and the only thing that distinguished it from a daydream was the shocked expression sinking into the enforcer's face. Virginia shrugged lightly, as though the admission was a casual one. "Like I said. I'm a seer."

Jen stared for a moment, fumbling with the buttons on her cuffs. "Go get

Fiske," she shouted over her shoulder. "Tell him she's a seer." When none of the enforcers moved, she barked, "Now!"

"If you want me, they go free," Virginia said.

"You're in no position to negotiate," Jen declared, almost crowing with her victory. "We have plenty of ways of making you work," she said, twisting a ring on her finger. "You can take my word on that."

Virginia straightened again, trying desperately to ignore the pounding in her head. Whether it was from the smack against brick or the Seeing, she wasn't sure. "I have a very high pain tolerance."

"We'll see about that," Jen snarled, still keeping her distance from the greenhouse.

"Vee," Anya said in a warning tone, "don't do this. There's still time."

"We're fresh out of time," Virginia replied. "Time, time. We're all so fucking beholden to it."

"Are you alright?" Jolie asked.

"Sure."

Seamus shifted his weight, the same way he did in the sparring ring, a nervous habit now that he relied on it so much to keep himself calm near a full moon. "I wish you'd told me, Vee."

"I didn't know until today. How about that?" Virginia asked. "One more thing I never asked for. Didn't ask for any of this, you know. It makes sense, really, when you think about it, but damn, I have spent forty-eight years not knowing a shadows-damned thing."

Fiske strode across the courtyard, his tailored wool coat flapping angrily with every step he took, the soles of his shoes tapping indiscriminately against the stone. "What a fascinating development," he said, calling across to the greenhouse. "You failed to mention this earlier, Ms. Vane."

"Wasn't relevant then," Virginia replied.

"She says she only found out this morning," Jen said. "But that can't be, because—"

"We're all well aware of the Rupture," Fiske interrupted. "Move." He pushed past the line of enforcers, taking black leather gloves off his hands. "What's this bargain you want, Ms. Vane?"

"I'll work for you," Virginia offered, her speech still slow and lightly slurred. "Do whatever you want, whatever nefarious bullshit you require. Infiltrating politics, since that's clearly your next step, given those pamphlets I found. Or undercutting your competitors? I hear there's a new source in town, and you're none too pleased."

"The source has been taken care of."

"So you think."

"Okay," Fiske said, stepping closer. "Enlighten me. How does this play out if I let these little birds fly free, just like the ones you released from their cages earlier? How would that then impact the deal I have going with the VCPD?"

"You won't need those top-level enforcers if you have a seer." Virginia bit back a retch that stalled in her throat, coated in blood and saliva. "Not even the feds know what I am. I'm free and clear, I won't be conscripted. You and I both know that you could accomplish incredible things with access to a seer."

"Perhaps," he said, rubbing a thumb over his knuckles. "But then, if I kept all of you, I could accomplish even more."

Virginia shook her head. "Can't keep all of us, Fiske, it's a liability and you know it."

"A liability, or an ace in the hole?"

"It depends. How long do you think you could keep all of us under control?" Virginia asked. "Inhibitors, sure, but then we're useless. We're no better than half of the mortal enforcers you've got here. Cannon fodder. Scraps for the meat grinder."

Fiske stepped closer, pressing his lips together and releasing them with a quiet pop. "I had anticipated that you would be trouble, but I can't say that I saw this coming." He still stank of cigar smoke, the overly sweet scent drawing another gag into Virginia's throat. He rubbed at his goatee thoughtfully. "It's certainly an interesting proposition. If I free your friends, I don't get my top-level enforcers back. If I don't get them back, I lose loyalty here in these ranks, Ms. Vane. Do you understand?"

"You're not getting them back," Virginia replied. "The mayor already decided."

Fiske leaned forward on the balls of his feet and jabbed Virginia in the jaw. She grunted, stepping backwards, but bit back any other sound. She'd trained how to take a hit, and smiled at him again with blood-stained teeth. He smirked, pulling his arms back to his sides. "I think the mayor will change her mind soon enough."

"Why, because she's in your pocket?" Virginia snarled.

"No, because we have an arrangement," Fiske replied evenly. "That's how real life works, Ms. Vane, I would have thought you would understand by now."

She tilted her chin up, daring him to hit her again. "I've always been a slow learner."

"Hm." He punched her again, this time in the ribs. She flinched, but said nothing. "I do wonder about this supposed ability. How does it work?"

"I don't know," she said, pain radiating through her body. "I'm not a fucking expert."

"What do you see when you use your abilities?"

Virginia squared her shoulders, preparing for another hit. "It depends. Sometimes nothing. I'm new to this."

"From what I was told a few moments ago, you had a very clear reading on Jen, here. Why is that?"

"Beats me," she answered. "Now, do we have a deal, or not?"

Fiske brought a finger to his lips. "Shh, Ms. Vane. I am still making my decision." He waved to Anthony, cocking his head. "Tony. Let her do a reading on you."

"I'd rather not, Boss," Tony answered, but held out his arm anyway when Fiske rubbed his hand against the revolver under his coat. "Alright, here."

Virginia stretched out her bound hands, first smoothing over a shell button and getting no reading, and then the wool of the coat, and his watch. "Nothing," she said.

"See? She's bullshitting."

"Either I'm bullshitting and Jen is working with me, or not." Virginia shrugged. "It's your call, Franky."

"I'm not working with you," Jen shouted from the side of the greenhouse. "She's lying, Fiske, she's trying to stall for time so we miss this drop, and you know what happened last time we—"

"Shut your mouth," Fiske said icily. "We don't need to give away all of our trade secrets, now do we?" He searched Virginia's face, his brow furrowed, looking for answers he clearly wasn't finding. He leaned forward again, and this time, Virginia was ready for it, taking the hit in stride. The chunky gold ring he wore on his finger connected with her cheek, and she felt the skin tear.

Again, she said nothing, only standing upright again. "Your father gave you that ring."

Fiske's eyebrows raised in surprise. "Go on."

"I didn't get much more than that."

"Allow me to give you another chance at redemption, then." He threw another punch, landing in her stomach. It doubled her over, and she struggled to regain the breath that had been knocked from her lungs.

"Stop," Anya pleaded quietly. "Stop this."

"I'll deal with you later, Quinn," Fiske said. "We have business of our own to attend to, but I'm sure you're already keenly aware of that." He turned back to Virginia. "Well?"

"I don't think you want me to say the next part out loud, unless you have a much closer relationship with your enforcers than I had originally anticipated." Her lungs burned, stunned from the hit. She leaned forward to whisper in his ear, "You killed your father yourself."

"Very good, Ms. Vane. I have to admit, I am impressed," he said, wiping the blood from his ring with the handkerchief from his pocket.

"Then hire me," Virginia offered again. "Let the rest go, leave them alone. You want your enforcers back? Fine, let me help you do it in a way that's quiet."

He stalked around her, appraising her like she was a prize haunch of meat. With every step he took, snow crunched under the soles of his shoes, showing off the silence of the courtyard. "It is tempting, but I prefer games where winner takes all. I will hire you, that much is certain. The idea of you falling into the hands of the feds is deeply repulsive—but I also don't have any interest in losing grip on the inferno witch," he said, turning his attention to Jolie like a snake would coil around its prey. "She's young, but oh, powerful. More than any others I've found, and she will grow to be my right hand, if she plays her cards right."

Virginia turned, giving Jolie a stare that she hoped would keep her quiet. Jolie opened her mouth, but closed it again, eyes narrowed. "Fiske," Virginia said, pain radiating from her skull all the way down into the frozen earth beneath her boots, "it's time to make a decision."

"You're right, it is." He smiled. "Thank you for sharing this personal tidbit with me, Ms. Vane. Your honesty will be remembered in the future, I guarantee it. My decision is that I'll have all of you, regardless of your pathetic little warning, because you don't get to come into my home, let loose my hostages, and try to upend everything before throwing yourself on my mercy."

"I was never under any illusions that you possess even one iota of mercy," she hissed.

Fiske folded his hands in front of him, lacing and releasing his fingers. "Mercy is for cowards and the weak-minded. Yet, I do find myself compelled to attempt to harbor something that looks like goodwill to my newest recruits." He turned to Jen, nodding. "Take the rest of them, get them outfitted. Burn everything they have, especially that shop and the gym. The girl doesn't have anything to burn, but be sure to get Vane's apartment. Douse the one across the hall while you're at it, and don't leave any loose ends."

"Arson?" Virginia asked, laughing. "That's how you're going to press us into service?"

"It's rather effective, I think you will find in the coming days." He pulled her silver knuckles from his pocket, slipping them over his fingers. "I've always wanted to try some of these." Hauling back, he slammed his full weight into her, the metal ripping at her jaw. She stumbled backwards, unable to swallow back the quiet whimper as her head detonated with pain and the fight with Benjamin replayed, clear as day in her mind.

Fiske smirked, examining the knuckles, flecked with her blood. "I think I'll keep these. We'll call it payback for being such a pain in the ass."

"Enough," a voice said, followed by the sound of a car door slamming.

He turned, face reddening with rage. "What the hell are you doing here, Morrison?" he demanded. "Tell her I don't need a shadows-damned babysitter."

Someone wearing all black, head to toe, face covered in a silk mask, folded arms over her chest. "She says it's enough."

"She can take it up with me personally, if she has a problem with how I am conducting my affairs," he retorted.

"You've gone too far, Fiske," Morrison said. "You're drawing too much undue attention, and she's tired of cleaning up your messes."

He snorted a derisive laugh, shooing her away with a dismissive flick of his wrist. "Tell her that I'll give a shit what she thinks when she's woman enough to fight her own battles. Until then, I'm the one running this city, not her." Fiske slid the knuckles from his fingers, pocketing them. He reached for his revolver, holstered under his shoulder, when the masked woman shook her head.

"I wouldn't do that, if I were you," she said.

"If you don't get off my property in the next fifteen seconds, I'm going to have you weighed down and tossed into the lake," Fiske said, waving Jen forward.

"Do you really think she would send me here if she hadn't already paid off every one of your enforcers?" Morrison asked with a curious tilt of her head. "She's the one who divvies out their pay, not you, and they know that." She turned to Jen. "Correct?"

"Yes," Jen mumbled.

Fiske twitched towards his revolver, his wrist already reaching for the holster. Somehow, beyond the blood in her eyes and the haze in her head, Virginia saw him do it. She surged forward, her forehead colliding with his temple, sending him sprawling to the ground. The force of the impact sent Virginia to the snow-soaked dirt as well, the world spinning dangerously around her.

The masked woman turned, unholstering her own gun and firing two rounds into Fiske's chest. "I told you not to do that," she said. "You forced my hand." She turned to the rest of the enforcers, holstering her weapon again. "Stay out of trouble until a new head is chosen. It will be one of you. If I catch wind of any backstabbing, literal or figurative, you're done." She looked around, her mask impenetrable. "Clean this place up."

She was still talking but the world was fading around Virginia, dimming at the edges. Maybe she'd finally managed to take enough hits to kill her. Two strong arms lifted her from the ground, carrying her across the courtyard. Virginia squinted up at the mask, reaching out to touch it. The black silk was soft under her fingers, but still managed to conceal every feature of the woman's face. "Who are you?" Virginia asked weakly.

The woman leaned away from her touch. "You don't want to know." There was something strange about her voice, something strained, but Virginia blacked out before she could put the pieces together.

Chapter Forty-Four

The first thing that Virginia noticed when she woke up in her own bed was that someone had washed the blood from her face. Sitting up with a palm pressed against her pounding forehead, she turned towards the mirror and recoiled at the battered, bloody reflection. Bruises painted along her left eye socket and jaw, streaks of pink still lingering under her chin. Her face was swollen almost everywhere, and the stitches along her cheekbone were perfect and precise. She might not even scar.

Lifting her shirt she pressed her ribs gingerly, giving a soft gasp at the pain that shot through her. "Fuck," she said. If this was what she looked like after Anya had healed her, she must have looked like roadkill before. She stood, unsteady and wavering, blinking at the strange, sweet smell wafting under the door.

Maybe she was dying, after all. Maybe the blood had pooled in her brain, and she was starting to hallucinate. Maybe she'd taken one hit too many.

She pulled a worn wool sweater on over her head, wincing at the pain in her shoulders and tugging up a pair of soft sleep pants so she could investigate her apartment. How the hell had she even made it back here? There was nothing but grey, swirling fog in her memory after that woman had carried her out of the greenhouse. Morrison, they'd called her.

Virginia opened the door, staggering out into the narrow corridor. Before she could even open her mouth to ask who the hell was in her apartment, Jolie swung around the corner.

"Vee!" she shouted, her arms flung wide for a moment before she reeled them back in, thinking better of the hug. "You're alright."

"I don't know about alright, but apparently, I'm still alive," Virginia grumbled. "Unfortunately."

"I made pancakes."

Virginia laughed, but it still hurt, the sound of it reverberating against bruised ribs. "You what?"

Jolie bit her lip, backing up into the kitchen. "Pancakes? I thought maybe you might want something to eat. Anya dropped some things off last night. She said she'd be back this morning, but she hasn't stopped by yet."

"How did I get here?" Virginia asked, squinting at the light streaming through the blinds. Her head continued to pound.

"You don't remember?"

"No."

"That woman, whoever she was, deposited you into your car. Seamus drove us all here, wanted to avoid Anya's shop, just in case. She healed you as best she could with what she had at the time."

Virginia nodded. "Arthur?"

"Sheriff Dixon called four times last night, until Anya told him you needed sleep."

"Mona and Penny?"

"Are fine," Jolie answered, "but I don't know any more than that."

"Fine," Virginia said, breathing in a sigh of relief. "Good." She sat at the counter, leaning against it. She barely even had the energy to sit up straight. "So. Pancakes."

Jolie grinned, flipping a stack of fresh ones onto the plate, dripping with butter and maple syrup. "There are more, but I wasn't sure how hungry you'd be."

"It's been a very long time since someone has made breakfast for me," Virginia said quietly, trying hard not to remember. It had been after the attack fifteen years ago, and it had been Arthur, his face pained and terrified as he handed over a plate of burnt scrambled eggs. "Thank you."

Jolie turned back to the cast iron pan, pouring in the last of the batter. "You saved my life, you know."

"I wouldn't say that," Virginia argued. "We'd all be pushing up daisies by now if Morrison or whoever she was hadn't showed up." She cut a triangle of pancakes, syrup dripping from her fork. It was like heaven in her mouth, sweet, buttery, and hot, straight from the pan. "These are good."

"Why did you go without us?" Jolie asked.

"Why do you keep asking me that?" Virginia replied, preferring to focus on breakfast instead. "I told you. Seemed to make more sense to have one of us go down than all of us." She shrugged, cutting another forkful. "Sometimes, you run out of other options."

Jolie nodded thoughtfully, giving the last pancake one deft flip in the cast-iron pan. "Thank you," she said softly. "For everything."

"Thank you for breakfast," Virginia replied, cutting the remaining portion into three bites. She chewed and swallowed, one by one, feeling it fuel her. "Coffee?"

Jolie nodded, firing a blue snap of flame at the kettle, boiling it instantly. She poured it over the press, letting it steep before pouring it into a mug, adding sugar and milk. "Coffee," she said, sliding it across the counter.

"Your party trick is looking good," Virginia said. "Feeling better, I take it?"

"Good as new."

The mug sat in front of Virginia, a tempting cup of normality after chaos so thick it had nearly drowned her in its current. "How did you know how I take my coffee?" She asked, taking a sip and savoring the beautiful lifeblood of the hot beverage. "It's perfect."

"I pay attention," Jolie answered. "At least, I try to."

"You'd make a good detective."

"Or a good private investigator."

Virginia raised an eyebrow over her mug, but said nothing. It was too early, whatever time it actually was, to be thinking about anything other than remaining upright. A knock at the door pulled her attention, and Jolie opened it, Anya rushing through.

"Vee, you're awake!" Anya said excitedly, already kicking off her snow-laden boots and flinging her coat at the rack with such force, it nearly toppled over.

"It would appear so," Virginia mused.

Anya began unpacking glass jars and things wrapped in brown paper from her satchel. "I brought things to do more healing. I didn't continue last night because I didn't want to wake you as I worked."

"Thank you." Virginia pushed away her empty plate. "Jolie made pancakes."

"I see that. It's good that you're eating, and it's even better that it was something with a little sugar and fat to keep you going. You took a beating yesterday, Vane."

"You don't have to tell me that, I'm well aware." She turned to face Anya but stopped, the pain twisting in her side and in her face, and she flinched from it.

"Couch," Anya directed, pointing. "I'll start with the ribs."

"Bastard had a hell of a punch."

"Dead bastard now," Anya said, choosing two vials and a paper packet of herbs. "Jo, I'll need some hot water for—" Jolie interrupted her with an already-boiled kettle, setting it on the counter with a bowl. Anya smirked. "Thank you."

Virginia moved to the sofa, internally chastising herself for how slowly she was moving. She probably looked like her mother, and the thought of that made her want to hand herself back over to the Ruby Thorns. She sank into the cushions, leaning back against the neatly folded blankets and pulling up her sweater and undershirt just high enough to expose the ugly, mottled bruise there. "I'm ready to not feel like I got the shit kicked out of me," she said.

"Good thing I came prepared for that, then." Anya sat next to her, applying some sort of sweet smelling ointment that landed somewhere between the strange scent of marigolds in autumn and earth after the rain. Petrichor. It was oily as Anya delicately pushed it into her skin, her fingertips so light that Virginia barely felt it.

"Feeling better already," Virginia whispered, unsettled at the gentleness of the touch.

Someone pounded on the door, and all three of them froze, staring at the lock. "It's Arthur," the voice said.

Virginia groaned. "Let him in."

Jolie barely had time to flip the deadbolt before the door burst open, the gust rattling pages of the book on the table. Arthur was rubbing his head, panic-stricken. "Ginnie, shadows, I tried calling all last night but—" He strode through the door, stopping short at seeing Anya. "But Ms. Quinn insisted I wait until you had rested." His eyes fell on the bruise, and his face fell. "Ginnie, I—"

"Stop," Virginia interrupted. "Whatever it is you were about to say, I don't want to hear it."

"I have you to thank for my family being alive and safe," he answered, shoving his hands into the pockets of his coat. "I don't really even know what else to say."

"Lindell?" Virginia asked, and Anya cocked an eyebrow, her expression awash with something Virginia couldn't identify, before returning to work on the bruise. "What?" Virginia asked.

"Nothing," Anya answered.

Arthur sat on the stool at the counter. "Captain Lindell led the raid on Fiske's compound as soon as we had the numbers to do so. Unfortunately, his enforcers had already cleared out, leaving no evidence to speak of behind."

"My coat," Virginia said, nodding towards the unbalanced rack. "I nabbed some property deeds. Might be helpful."

"Good, I'll take those back with me." Arthur took the mug of coffee that Jolie handed him, looking surprised. "Er, thanks, Jo." He took a sip, still watching Anya cycle through ointments and poultices. "This is only going to get messier."

"I don't know who *she is*, this mystery woman that Morrison or whoever mentioned, but it sounds to me like this whole thing goes right up the food chain," Virginia said, reaching for her own mug as Anya worked.

"I can think of a few places to start looking."

Virginia glanced up at him. "You'd better be careful, Arthur. Whichever way this thing goes, it's not going to be good. What did Lindell say?"

"The same."

"I'm surprised to hear we agree."

"I should have known you two would fight every step of the way, you're both stubborn and resistant to criticism."

Virginia shot him a look. "I'm not resistant to criticism, I've been taking nothing but criticism my entire life."

"Be that as it may, Ginnie, I hope you will continue to consult with us. From what I understand, we're going to need you." He searched her face. "Ginnie, you never told me about being a seer. Why?"

She shrugged, ignoring the pain. "I didn't know." She hissed through a patch of pain as Anya pressed further into the bruise, seeing the guilt shoot through his face like lightning. Virginia looked away, not willing to relieve his fifteen-year-old guilt. "Can I trust that you're not going to turn me over to the feds?"

"Of course not."

"Because I don't want to work for the shadows-damned feds, Arthur."

"Cross my heart and hope to die," he said, repeating an oath they used to make as children. The memory of it shook something loose in Virginia, like an avalanche, or a rock slide, screaming down the side of a mountain but she couldn't face it. She never had been able to. He sighed, his eyes falling on her broken skin and her swollen face for just a few seconds before he had to look away. "You're going to have to talk to your mother about this, you know."

"I know."

"Sooner, rather than later."

"I *know*," Virginia said, closing her eyes. The last thing she wanted to do was drive the three or four hours downstate to ask questions she'd never really wanted the answers to, and to deal with someone she hadn't spoken to in twenty years.

"When are you going to go?" he pressed.

"Can I please get a little further out from this shit storm, first?" she snapped. "I took a few hits yesterday, if you hadn't heard."

"Of course, and I know, and I'm—"

"Arthur," Virginia said, interrupting him. "Enough." She closed her eyes again, the pain starting to recede from her ribs. "Seamus?" she asked.

"He's fine," Anya answered. "He slept on my couch. Is still sleeping on my couch, actually."

"Why didn't he go home?"

"He's the one who carried you up the stairs, Vee," Anya explained. "He stayed until I made him leave. I let him sleep, because he needed it. Full moon in two days, I'm surprised he was even upright yesterday."

"He's spent most of his life training himself to do so," Virginia said.

"I have some things that may help him, if he still finds it a struggle."

Virginia tugged her shirt down when Anya moved away, finished with her task. "Do you think I'll be all set to spar tomorrow?" she asked.

"No."

"I was joking."

Anya gave her a skeptical look. "No, you weren't. Besides, Seamus already told me that you're banned from the gym for at least two weeks while you recover."

"I didn't even take that for the panther fang."

"Even more reason, then."

Virginia sat up straight. "Ursa. Fiske said they took off, after—" She stopped herself short, not wanting to reveal the truth of what had happened between the two siblings. "You know, after Benjamin."

"They cropped up on the west coast. Lindell found them, using a fake name."

"What now?" Virginia asked.

Arthur swallowed another mouthful of coffee. "Let it lie, for now. Close their homicide investigation." He glanced at Anya. "And hope that certain illusionists don't offer that service again in the future, especially if they want a cushy job as a VCPD healer."

"I don't know what you're talking about," Anya said lightly, standing to pour hot water over a poultice, mixing it up with a spoon. "But I appreciate the offer. Maybe it will keep things a little quieter at Moonshadow

Botanicals."

"I should hope so," Arthur said. "Not to put too fine a point on it, Ms. Quinn, but I would expect that your little clinic would keep to treating the general public, and not be fixing up crew enforcers in the middle of the night."

"That is what I meant by quieter." Anya checked the consistency of the poultice, letting it fall from the spoon back into the bowl with a wet plop. "After everything that's happened in the past week—"

"Ten days," Virginia corrected.

"After everything that's happened in the past ten days," Anya continued, punishing Virginia for her interruption by slathering the warm poultice across her jaw, "I'm not keen to work with Astrid or her people. I'd hope that other people would give her a wide berth as well."

Virginia flinched away from the poultice and from the barbed comment. "I'm sitting right here, Anya."

"I never would have put you with Astrid Frost," Arthur said, stroking his close-cropped beard. "That's not the Virginia I knew."

"The Virginia you knew is dead," she shot back.

"No, she's right here. Just... different." He gave her a strange smile, the kind he used to give her when they were kids back in the corn fields. "It's good to be back, despite everything."

"No hope of you running back to the coast, then?" Virginia asked.

"None. Even after everything, Penny wants to stay, and Mona wants to let her. She thinks we can do good here." He finished his coffee, setting down the empty mug with a hollow clank. "It's going to get worse before it gets better, but we will make Verdance City safer."

"Same old Arthur," Virginia said, rolling her eyes. "Ever the idealist. Too bad it won't help me get rid of you any faster."

"You're not getting rid of me that easy, Ginnie."

Virginia let a growl escape from her throat, knowing he wouldn't take it seriously. It's just how things had always been with them, even when they were young. "Give Mona my best," she said, leaning back against the sofa cushions once again. "And make sure Penny does her homework." She opened an eye. "Any news on Rickarton, after all this?"

"I had a word with the principal. They were concerned donations would dry up if they didn't cover up the disappearances."

"Typical," Anya said. "But then, Vee knew that already."

"We're going to do a thorough investigation of all the schools in the city," Arthur said. "There's already a task force to collate anyone who's still missing, but there was an additional outbuilding at the compound, we found most of them we hadn't already."

Virginia waved him away. "Alright, get out of here, Arthur. I need peace and quiet, and you're not going to shut up. I'll come into headquarters tomorrow."

"Monday," he corrected. "I don't want to see you, either of you, until at least Monday."

"But the task force—"

"Can wait." Arthur stood, dusting off his coat. "Ms. Quinn, welcome to the VCPD. Jo, you make coffee better than Ginnie, but don't tell her I said that."

Virginia rolled her eyes. "Out!"

* * *

Virginia stood at the living room window, blowing a plume of smoke out into the night air. It was quiet, soft snow falling from a cloud-dense sky, settling prettily atop the drifts that still sat in the verges, collected from the blizzard. They'd be there until spring, slowly hardening into ice until the sun grew warm enough to melt them.

One more drag of the cigarette and she savored it, the cool menthol crisping in her lungs, welcome despite the rush of icy air from the window. It was methodical, and it was routine, but it was necessary, especially as she started to plan when she would travel down to see her mother. Her jaw clenched as she stubbed out the cigarette, already reaching for another to dull the realization of what had to be done. Sooner or later, it would have to be done, and there was no escaping it, not if she wanted to grasp whatever this was within her, this latent, passive thing that had waited under her skin for nearly half a century.

Or maybe it had never been latent at all, and she had just been foolish. Young anger and stubbornness, growing stagnant as she aged, unchanging, petrifying herself into stone.

Her fingers brushed against the silver cigarette case when there was a hesitant knock at the door, almost apologetic. "Did you forget something, Jolie?" she asked, opening the door. "Oh," she said. "Shirin."

Captain Lindell stood in her doorway, probably fresh from work in her uniform, holding her cap in her hands. "Hello."

"Is everything okay?"

"I wanted to see if you were alright." Her eyes trailed across Virginia's body, finally coming to rest on her face. "You look better than I thought you would, given what I'd heard."

"Anya is good at what she does." Virginia moved aside. "Did you want to come in for a drink?"

"Only if you're up for it, I know you must be tired." Virginia nodded, and Lindell crossed the threshold, unbuttoning her coat. "Where is Jo?"

"With Anya for a few days. They thought I should get some rest."

"And are you?"

Virginia reached for the bottle of gin, setting it on the counter. "More or less."

"So," Shirin said, taking a long pause between locking the door and leaning against the counter. "You're a seer. You kept that one awfully quiet."

"Even from myself, it seems." Virginia poured into two glasses, nudging one across to Shirin. "It was a surprise to me, too."

"But the Rupture?"

She gestured at the long-healed scars on her face. "It was a busy time for me, and it's possible I may have missed the whole thing."

Shirin nodded. "Of course." She took a sip of the gin, but her eyes never left Virginia's.

"I was wondering where you've been," Virginia said. "I haven't seen you since—" she let it hang in the air, unfinished, because it had felt unfinished, whatever it was.

"I've been busy. I'm sure the sheriff told you it was me who led the raid on Fiske's compound."

"He did."

"Dealing with the fallout from that has been excessive." Shirin took another sip. "Lots of paperwork."

Virginia smirked, her lips itching for another smoke, even if Anya had told her to stop while she was healing. "Paperwork. My favorite."

"And yesterday, when the sheriff was here, I was at headquarters." Shirin leaned into the counter, her forearms bracing against the wood. "I'm deputy sheriff, now."

"Congratulations."

"I can never tell if you're being sarcastic or genuine, Virginia."

"Genuine," Virginia answered, running a finger around the rim of her glass before bringing it to her lips. She inhaled softly, letting the smell of juniper flood her senses. "It's good to know that someone sensible is at the helm when Arthur isn't there."

"High praise, coming from you."

"Don't get used to it."

Shirin set the glass down, searching Virginia's face. "I don't think I can get used to anything where you're concerned. I feel perpetually off-balance whenever I'm around you. It's—" she tilted her head, and her face flashed with vulnerability for just a second before it disappeared. "It's unsettling."

"Now who's handing out the high praise?" Virginia asked, cocking an eyebrow. She knew what she was doing, and she didn't care. Maybe life was too short to give a shit about making another terrible mistake.

"You find being unsettling high praise?"

Virginia nodded, fingers reaching for the bottle again, but falling short. "The highest."

"And why is that?" Shirin asked.

"It is an acute and arcane power for a woman to be unsettling. It is to be unknowable, unpredictable in her wants." Virginia held her gaze. "Her desires, the way she moves through the world. Wouldn't you say that's compelling?"

"I would."

"As would I."

Captain Lindell nudged her glass across the counter, watching as Virginia poured more gin into the bottom, the clear liquid quietly swirling in the dim light of the apartment. "As compelling as unsettling is, I do find it a challenge to be around you, to figure out what it is that you want."

"What do you think I want?"

Shirin exhaled a quiet laugh through her nose. "You're playing games with me."

"Maybe," Virginia answered, pouring gin into her own glass. "But you're the one who started this, Shirin."

"It couldn't be helped." Captain Lindell stood, shrugging off her coat, draping it over the counter. "Not around you, apparently." She moved closer and this time there was no hesitation. Virginia barely had the chance to set her glass down before Shirin pressed her into the wall, so close that Virginia could smell the soap she'd used, cedar and something spicier, black pepper maybe, the notes of it filling her senses.

Shirin kissed her, and Virginia couldn't stifle the audible sigh that whispered past her lips, like she'd been waiting years to be kissed that way, and maybe she had. It hadn't been like this with Astrid, she had never been someone who had been so *hungry* for her. Lindell pulled back, her amber eyes intense and ravenous before she kissed her again, pressing a uniformed thigh between Virginia's legs as she melted back into the wall.

The apartment was silent, except for the incessant ticking of the clock on the wall and the quiet, eager sound of lips on lips and tongue against tongue, and it was still a terrible idea but what difference did that even make? Whatever problems it wrought, and it would, they were for the morning to uncover when the sunlight burned through the creeping shadows and cast it all into sharp relief. But in the moment, it was night, and the soft cover of darkness made the consequences so easy to ignore.

Shirin touched her with a fierce, greedy ferocity, like a starving wolf fresh from a failed hunt. Virginia let her, because it had been so long since she had been devoured. Parts of her were falling away along with her shirt and Lindell's jacket and she didn't even care, because she'd spent years pretending to be dead, and feeling so alive was the kind of dangerous exhilaration most people lived for.

Her fingers brushed against smooth buttons, pushing each one through, her eyes closed because if even she couldn't see what she was doing, then it couldn't be wrong. The draft from the window, or maybe the almost rough pull of Shirin's hands against her hips, pulled goosebumps across her skin. She reached for Shirin's belt, the quiet rattle of the brass reaching across the stillness as she pulled it free.

"Wait," Shirin said, pulling back, gasping for air. "Are you sure you're alright? I mean, the hits you took, I don't want to hurt you, and I—"

Virginia reached up, tangling her fingers in Shirin's short, wavy hair, pulling her in for another kiss, pressing against her, already feeling the need start to build between her thighs. "I'm fine," she growled, falling prey to it, letting it envelop her and pull her from the kitchen to the bedroom, falling back on the bed with a soft grunt.

The bedroom was dark, Shirin only visible in silhouette, the profile of her face glancing to the window first before looking back to Virginia for just a second. She leaned over her, a knee on the bed, the frame creaking softly as she bent, lips pressed against Virginia's neck as her hands roved over hips, pulling at the waistband she found there. She flipped open the buttons with one practiced hand, trailing her callused fingertips across Virginia's skin, a sweet temptation of what was to come, like a square of bittersweet chocolate as it melted across the tongue.

It was a game, and she was the mark. She didn't even care because she'd almost died twice that month and may the shadows corrupt her from the inside out, but the feel of Shirin's lips as she roamed, silent and pensive across her body was like coming up for air. It was like breathing again after diving too far into the deep ocean, after the riptide nearly pulled her under, after she'd almost let it happen for no other reason than the fact that there wasn't another option, not when she was faced with the swirling chasm of sea and sky and the inevitable long press of reality back into her skin.

Shirin's hair dragged over Virginia's hips as her pants slid to the floor, and she was rapt in it. There was an urgency in her touches as she pulled at fabric, teasing, waiting for only a few painfully lingering moments before she bent her head, kissing deeply where Virginia's thighs met, pressing into her with tongue first, and then fingers when Virginia pulled her closer.

Moonlight crested across the window, and the room was drawn into a cool glow through the clouds, through the clearing even as the snow continued to fall, dampening all else. Virginia opened her eyes to it, looking up through the window and then down at Shirin, surprised to see her looking back with such intensity that it pulled her to the edge, and she fell over it with a gasp and a shudder.

She lay there, letting the tremors in her legs pass. It might have been five minutes or an hour, it was impossible to know. Virginia sat up, pulling Shirin onto the bed with a questioning look.

Shirin shook her head gently, tracing a finger along Virginia's jaw. "Enough for me," was all she said, still staring.

"Alright." Virginia pulled a pack of cigarettes from her drawer, along with a silver lighter, engraved with florid swirls. She lit one, the orange glow emblazoned against the dark as clouds sat over the moon, diffusing the pale light into a barely discernible glimmer. Inhaling, she let it sink into her, bringing her to life once more. She hadn't died, and this was proof, the fading pulse between her legs, and the smoke in her lungs, and the knowing. The deep, inexorable knowing of what she was hung heavy in the air, and it was promise, and it was threat, but either way, she had lived.

She passed the cigarette to Shirin, who took it, a smirk playing at her lips. "We'd better not tell the sheriff."

"No," Virginia said, trailing a finger over Shirin's bare shoulder. "We'd better not."

Before Virginia could protest, Shirin was already off the bed and getting dressed, fastening her belt buckle and reaching for her shirt. "Could be the precinct," she said.

"So? Arthur doesn't know you're here."

"So I thought we just agreed to keep it that way," Shirin said with a wink, tightening her tie. "And I have a meeting with a couple of feds first thing in the morning."

"Feds," Virginia repeated, propping herself up on an elbow. "Why?"

"Routine." Shirin bent, kissing her on the cheek before buckling her holster under her arm. "I'll see you soon, alright?"

Virginia followed her out, a blanket pulled tight around herself. She threw the deadbolt and threaded the chain. She pulled the cigarette case and a Sphinx matchbook from her coat pocket, hanging limply on its hook. She opened the window and lit one, reveling in the soft plumes of smoke that escaped from her lips, twisting and dancing in the night breeze.

The black cat appeared from the broken fire escape, mewing softly. It hadn't done that before, spoken to her in the way that only cats could. It invited itself inside and jumped up onto the kitchen counter, waiting patiently.

"Oh, alright," Virginia relented, putting out her cigarette to open a can of tuna for the ungrateful creature. After it ate, it looked at the sofa, head tilted. "She's not here," Virginia explained. "She'll be back in a few days. You'd better be careful, she might try to name you next."

The cat stayed in the apartment, despite the open window, and despite Virginia finishing her cigarette in the cold air. It twisted around her legs, purring softly until she closed the window. It sauntered over to the overstuffed, raggedy chair, where it curled up on the arm, next to the book that had brought Jolie to Virginia.

"You can stay one night," Virginia allowed, settling into the chair. For the first time in a long time, she was looking forward to sharing her apartment again. She'd call in the morning and invite Jolie to stay for a little while longer.

The radio scanner hissed with static as a new transmission crunched over the airwaves. "Calling all units, we have a ten-sixteen in progress. Fire department already en route, but fellas, I hate to say it, but it's looking like another arson."

Virginia glanced at the radio with suspicion, waiting for another call that didn't come. Good. Verdance could be someone else's problem for one night.

End of Rhapsody in Flames

Keep reading for sneak peeks of the next books in The Ruptured Realms Universe: Exiled Advocate, the first Sadie Sinclair Esquire book, and Clocktower Elegy, exhibit B in The Vane Dossier.

Want to get sneak peeks, exclusive sales, and free books? Join the newsletter at Linktr.ee/RyannFletcherWrites

Enter The Ruptured Realms Universe

The Ruptured Realms encompasses three different series, with three different main characters. Read them in linear order:

1. Rhapsody in Flames (The Vane Dossier, exhibit A)
2. Exiled Advocate (Sadie Sinclair, Esquire: book one)
3. Clocktower Elegy (The Vane Dossier, exhibit B)
4. Séamus Carlucci: new series coming soon

The Ruptured Realms will contain twelve novels across these three series! Sign up for the newsletter at Linktr.ee/RyannFletcherWrites for access to beta reader signups, advanced reader copy giveaways, and sneak peeks.

Preview for Exiled Advocate (Sadie Sinclair, Esquire: book one)

She raced down the crystal-paved path towards the lake, face held to the sun as she shrieked with excitement. Stark birch trees rose up out of the earth, their foliage thick and verdant in the warm summer sun. She had everything she could ever wish for, and in that moment, she was the happiest she would ever be.

"Shailagh!" her mother called, smiling broadly with her arms held wide, beckoning her down to the water. "Would you believe that it's the perfect temperature?"

"Coming!" she squealed, tearing past an errant bramble bush. The delicate silk of her silvery dress caught on a thorn, rending apart each shining thread with the quiet yet insistent snap of permanence. Panic began to rise in her chest as she grasped at it, trying to hide the tear in her clutched fist.

"Shailagh!" her father shouted, grabbing her by the hand. "What have I told you about running like that? It's not befitting of a princess. It's not befitting of royal lineage."

"Faarys, she's just a child," her mother chided, standing up. She straightened her own dress, moving to smooth out the wrinkles. "Royal or not, she deserves to have some fun." She approached, resting a hand on his arm. "It's only fabric, dearest."

"The finest fabric in either realm," he replied sternly. "Child or no, she needs to learn how to hold her place in Fae court. She's old enough to start understanding the consequences of her actions."

She stared up at her parents, flinching away from the growing tension between them. It wasn't the first argument they'd had about her, and it was difficult not to feel responsible. Pulling from his grasp, she broke free and ran to the water, kneeling on the edge to stare into the glassy, mirrored surface.

At first, it was just her face that stared back at her, young and childlike and innocent. Her parents, rushing to catch up with her, one concerned, one furious. The crisp teal water rippled, disturbing the picture before her. The earth shook, and the lake boiled, disappearing into the deep chasm that had appeared at the center. In its place, a viscous purple sludge oozed up from beneath, pushing aside the land as if it were made of spun sugar.

The forest disintegrated one giant tree at a time, their limbs floating and carried away by the current. She tried to run, but she was rooted to the ground. She reached for her mother first, but she was no longer there. She reached for her father, who stared down from his safety on the bank.

Screams echoed through the ruined woods at the exact moment that the crystalline sparkling path erupted, shooting streams of purple magma into the air with unrepentant fervor. Pain, suffering, exposure.

She held her dress in her hands, and when she looked down at the ruined fabric, it, too, began to melt through her fingers, the purple fluid burning her skin and drawing ripe blisters to the surface. When she reached out, there was nothing there.

Birch trees swayed in the chaos, their roots twisting up out of the ground like tentacles, the wood far too brittle to bend. Bark splintered, the echo of annihilation like barbed thunder in her ears as one trunk after another cracked into fragments, the snap, crack,

thwack of files against a worn wood table. "Your Honor." Sadie took a breath, and exhaled it quietly. "As much as it pains me to miss the opportunity to spar with the prosecution, we all have to admit that there just isn't enough evidence for them to bring a case against my client."

The prosecution pointed across the table in accusation. His oversized, ill-fitting suit hung off him, nothing more than a mess of navy pinstripes and white pocket squares. "What Ms. Sinclair seems to be forgetting is that the prosecution had plenty of evidence, the cornerstone of which was our eyewitness to her client's crime of insurance fraud!" He sighed angrily, letting his arms flop back to his sides. "Your Honor, I humbly request an audience in chambers to discuss the possibility that Ms. Sinclair engaged in witness tampering."

"Your Honor!" she protested, gasping audibly, the hard intake of breath echoing around the courtroom and settling in the empty gallery seats. "I am appalled that Mr. Link of the prosecution would accuse me of something quite so unethical, not to mention illegal, in open court." She tugged at the hem of her aubergine suit jacket and flipped a dark curl over her shoulder.

The judge picked up his gavel, turning it around in his hands as he considered. "Mr. Link, are you prepared to offer evidence that the defense engaged in witness tampering?" he asked.

"No, Your Honor, we've yet to uncover hard evidence, but given her track record—"

Sadie spat out a laugh. "My track record?" she repeated. "Please, Mr. Link, point me to even one shred of evidence that I've done anything beyond the scope of the law, and I will immediately turn over this case to another attorney." She glanced at the door, the huge wood panels still closed, even as the minutes ticked by on the clock that hung above them. She cleared her throat and turned back to the judge. "Your Honor, I am simply asking for this case to be dismissed, as the prosecution no longer knows the whereabouts of their eyewitness. That's all."

Edward Link offered her an oily smile over the gap between their tables. "Your Honor, the prosecution asks for a continuance, in order to regroup and issue a subpoena to our errant witness. We are still prepared to question her, even if she has decided to be a hostile witness."

"Ms. Sinclair, I am inclined to side with the prosecution," Judge Haber said, clearing his throat with a wet sound. "They have indicated that there may be more evidence to support their claims, even if their witness declined to show up to court."

Hinges creaked open and Sadie had to resist the urge to spin around, triumphant, instead of waiting until Ella tapped her on the shoulder.

"Ms. Sinclair," Ella said in a loud whisper that could still be heard across the court, "I think you should see this." She looked perfect in a sapphire blue dress that skimmed over her shapely hips, her dark brunette hair shiny even in the dark courtroom, braided into an intricate crown around her head.

"Thank you, Ms. Beaufort," Sadie said, taking the envelope. She opened the flap and looked inside, feeling every eye in the court on her. The page read exactly as she knew it would, having prepared it that morning. Evidence, hidden by the prosecution that implicated another perpetrator that had long since fled the country. She raised an eyebrow, looking across to the prosecution. "How very interesting," she said evenly.

Edward flinched, shuffling through his paperwork noisily. He dropped a page, and it fluttered silently to the floor, coming to a rest under his polished patent leather shoe. "Your Honor, I would like to respectfully request a recess," he announced. "Just a brief one, if you will. The prosecution doesn't wish to waste the court's time."

Judge Haber considered the request before nodding. "Fifteen minutes," he said, smacking the gavel against its platform.

"What do you have?" Edward Link demanded, reaching for the envelope. Sadie snatched it out of his grasp, sitting back down in her chair.

"What do you think I have?" she asked. "Come on, Ed, you can't be serious with this case. You've got nothing, and this envelope proves that your office has been—"

He bent down, his face inches from hers. "Keep your voice down, alright?" he hissed. "Now, what do you want?"

Sadie glanced over at her client, a thin, weedy-looking man hunched over the table, still looking as terrified as a wounded gazelle on the plains, waiting for a hyena to finish him off. "Probation," she said. "Six months."

"A year and he has to pay a fine," Ed challenged. "Come on, Sadie, you know I can't go lower than that or I'll be on the chopping block next week." He pulled at his red silk tie, standing up straight again. "Or, we meet the judge in chambers, and I tell him everything I learned about how you employed the enforcer who scared off our witness."

"Do you have proof of that?" Sadie asked. "Because if not, it's nothing more than conjecture. You're grasping at straws, counselor. You and I both know I did not engage in witness tampering." She smiled up at him, clutching the envelope to her chest. "If you want the fine, then no probation."

"Six months probation and a fine, and that's the best I can do," he said. "And don't think I won't be watching you all the more closely next time we face off in court, Ms. Sinclair." Edward huffed out an angry sigh, irritated that he'd let a sure-thing case slip through his fingers. "Take the deal, you're not going to get a better one. Your client is in dire straits. Neither of us wants this to continue in court."

"Deal," she agreed, extending her hand to shake his. "We're ready to sign." She shuffled through her folders, locating the one with the green tab poking out of the side where Ella had placed it. "Fortunately, I already have it drawn up."

Ed narrowed his eyes. "Oh yes, fortunate," he deadpanned. "What a completely unforeseen scenario." He took a pen from his inside pocket, signing each page and dating it after he skimmed through the wording. "Tell your client to keep his nose clean or we'll be back in this courtroom in six months, and next time I'll make sure that he does time."

"Pleasure doing business with you," Sadie said, leaning back in her chair. "Anything good coming up next on your docket?"

"Why, so you can undermine that case, too?" he retorted. "All you shadows-damned ambulance chasers—"

Sadie interrupted him with a theatrical gasp. "Mr. Link!" she protested, folding her hands atop the table. "I've never once chased an ambulance, nor do I make it my business to scrape cases off the public defender's floor. Working on contingency certainly won't pay the rent, now will it?" She crossed one leg over the other, sliding the contract to her client along with the pen, already bleeding black ink into the margins of the first page. "We are supposed to be professional peers, not adversaries. After all, we all have to attend the same dry galas, don't we?"

"I happen to enjoy the galas," he said politely, taking the signed contract from her client and closing it into a folder. "As does my wife. It's an opportunity for the women to get out of the house and get gussied up." He shifted, staring a little too hard. "Perhaps I will see you there, if you aren't busy undermining more of my witness prep."

"I'll try to make time for it," Sadie said easily, ignoring the latter half of his statement. "Judge Haber, I think the defense and the prosecution have reached an agreement," she said, standing again. "I believe Mr. Link has the completed contract."

"Excellent," the judge said, taking the folder from Ed. He settled a pair of wire-frame glasses on his nose, reading over the contracts and nodding. "This all looks appropriate," he said, signing his name on the final page. "Ms. Sinclair, your client is free to go, but will need to stop at the probation office on the way out of the building."

"Thank you, Your Honor," Sadie said politely. The jury began to shuffle out, grumbling to one another no doubt about their wasted time and Sadie couldn't blame them. She hated her time to be wasted, too. "Mr. Pender, you will need to be assigned a parole officer, do you understand?"

Her client nodded, wringing his hands in his lap.

"My payment terms are thirty days," she reminded him. "And you will need to pay the court's fine, there's no getting around that." She nodded towards the door, and he silently followed her instruction, disappearing through the doors along with the rest of the jury.

Sadie turned in her chair, leaning over the divider that separated the attorney desks from the court gallery. "Nice timing," she whispered to Ella. "I wondered for a moment if you'd forgotten."

"Who, me?" Ella asked, batting her eyelashes. "Never."

"That last-minute evidence tactic is going to run out of steam now, at least with Ed Link. That man is out to get me. He hates me."

Ella shrugged, playing with the pearl stud in her ear, dainty and polite in its size. "He only hates you because you beat him." She crossed her legs, showing off shapely calves and a pair of blue t-strap heels that matched her dress. "And if that's the problem, I imagine most of the state's attorney's office hates you."

"Yes, it makes these galas rather uncomfortable." Sadie cast a sideways glance at Ella, wondering if it was worth roping her into it. If nothing else, she'd look amazing, just as she always did. "You wouldn't want to come with me, would you?" she offered, looking back towards the door to make sure her client didn't pass up the probation office on his way out. She'd almost been surprised he'd shown up to the court date at all. He'd made it clear that he preferred the idea of following his ex-friend out of the country to exile, but she'd convinced him to stay and clear his name.

"Oh, I can't," Ella apologized, biting her lip. "Ray is taking me to The Saffron Rose tonight."

"Of course," Sadie said, waving her away while internally roiling with poisonous envy. "I forgot. Your anniversary, right?"

Ella nodded. "One year this weekend!" She smoothed her skirt, plucking an errant thread from the hem. "You have that meeting tomorrow," she said, leaning in close. "Astrid Frost."

Sadie stifled a noise of irritation, aware that Ed was still watching her. "My favorite client," she said. "Her account pays the bills, I'm afraid, but it makes up for her perfectly repulsive attitude." She cleared her throat, watching Ed cross the courtroom once more. "What was it she wanted, again?"

"She thinks she has a squealer in her club."

"I can't imagine why she might require my services, then. Ella, do me a favor, call her when you're back at the office, and tell her to call Ms. Vane for this."

Ella nodded, standing up from the worn wooden bench. "Of course." She laid a hand on top of Sadie's, smiling. "I'm awfully sorry I can't come tonight. I hope it's not too terrible on your own."

"I will likely survive it," Sadie said, feeling like she should wave her off, but being completely unable to move her hand from where it was under Ella's. "It serves me right for being so perilously single all the time."

"Oh, Sadie," Ella sighed. "You'll meet that special guy soon enough, I just know it."

"Perhaps," Sadie said, staring, and she was distracted just long enough for Ed Link to snatch the empty envelope from her table. "Excuse me, Ed," she said, standing to snatch it back, "that's confidential."

"Oh really?" he said, holding it out of her reach, utilizing his tall, wiry frame to his advantage. "Something from my own investigation is confidential?"

"My case strategy certainly is," she said. "If you wanted to know what additional evidence I had, you should have pressed the issue before we signed a deal." She stood, aiming to match his height but falling short by about six inches. She reached for it, breath constricted in her chest, but he stepped backward, pulling at the lip of the envelope.

He held it upside-down and took the page, reading it with bewilderment. Ed looked back at her, fury collecting in the shallow lines on his face. "How did you get this?" he whispered, and the softness of the realization was far more threatening than any raised voice would have been. "You used pitted evidence?" Ed asked, still staring at the envelope. "How many times have you gotten your hands on something like this?" he demanded. "Who do you know in the state's attorney's office?"

"Ed, you and I both know that this never should have happened," Sadie said carefully. She took the envelope, slid it between her other files, and handed it to Ella over the barrier. "Do you mind taking these back to the office?" she asked.

"Of course," Ella said, keeping things short and sweet because she wasn't just one of the most beautiful women in Verdance, she was whip-smart and had saved cases more times than Sadie could count. Before Ed knew what was happening, Ella was out of the courtroom and rushing to flag down a cab from the front of the building.

"I'm taking this to Judge Haber," Ed declared, crowing it loudly, full-voiced as if he had a leg to stand on. "You manipulated this trial, Sadie. That would never have been allowed into evidence."

"Please, I encourage you to take this to him," Sadie replied easily, leaning back against the barrier because it was easier than staring up at Ed's narrow face, cheeks red and blotchy from the barely contained rage. She smiled at him, being sure to show all of her teeth. She'd had the second set of canines filed down years back, but the slight point was sometimes enough to cow people who weren't observant enough to realize why she was as unsettling as she was. "I'm sure the judge would love to hear about how you didn't do your due diligence before presenting a plea bargain."

"You should be disbarred," he growled. "You're an embarrassment to the law."

Sadie straightened herself to her full height, albeit petite in stature. "Mr. Link, I have done nothing that would merit being disbarred. I received new evidence that may or may not have been admitted into the trial, but before you could ascertain the veracity of the documents, you panicked." She tilted her chin upwards, glancing at the mirror just at the edge of her periphery. "You may want to discern why it is that you felt like that was the best option." Standing with every ounce of her tarnished regal expectations, she adjusted the placement of the briefcase handle in her grip. "I hope to see you at the gala later."

Preview for Clocktower Elegy (The Vane Dossier: Exhibit B)

Bright sunlight, humid and oppressive, beat down from the sky, drawing a bead of sweat from her forehead that she magnanimously allowed to slide over sharp cheekbones, falling to drip down onto her collar. Summer in Verdance had arrived, and while heat was a sensible vacation from the freezing temperatures of winter, in the city, it was out of the icebox, into the frying pan.

"Ginnie?" Arthur prompted, his stare boring into her the same way it had for the past six shadows-damned months. "Did you hear what I just said?"

"Yeah," Virginia lied, popping the joints in her fingers just to feel the light pain of relief. "Homicide."

"I never said it was homicide. We haven't confirmed either way." He leaned in closer, so much so that she had to resist the overwhelming urge to jerk away from him. "Did you know that it's homicide because of your seeing?" he whispered.

She took three steps backwards, nearly colliding with the coroner. "Sorry," she muttered, straightening to adjust the twisted strap of her left suspender. "No, Arthur, that's not why. I have eyes, don't I? It's obvious that he didn't do this himself. There's no way that distributor overdosed. He'd know what human limits were better than anyone, even with this new potent stuff cropping up in the city."

"That was my thought, too." Arthur waved several detectives into the room, watching as they observed the body. Approximately six-foot-one, broad shouldered, built like a brick shithouse, it was Merv Knuckles, a known member of the Kraken crew who'd worked his way up from being an enforcer. He was on his back, purple-tinged eyes wide as he stared up at the ceiling, the bleached bed sheets pulled up to his shoulders and topped with a light grey feather quilt. "If we can't get a lid on this, the feds are going to be all over it." He turned, answering some baseline question that the photographer had about the scene. "They're looking for any reason to get overly involved with our cases. That new anti-terrorism Nether law means they have all kinds of jurisdictional seniority over the VCPD that they didn't before."

"I'm not with the VCPD, so I fail to see how this is my problem," Virginia retorted. She tilted her head, examining the scene. "No signs of forced entry," she said. "No signs of a struggle, either."

"Everything points to an accidental overdose, Ginnie," he replied. "Except for the fact that he would have known."

"Suicide?" she asked. "Although, I can't imagine kicking my own bucket if I was running half the city's Nether rings, and living in a place as nice as this one." She gently tugged the blanket down after the photographer had finished, turning over the victim's hand. "No visible defensive wounds, as far as I can see." She pulled it down further, grimacing. "Naked."

Arthur picked at the badge on his arm, the tiny metallic clasps inaudible against the din of the investigation. "I need your help." He sighed, writing something in the margins of the notepad he had pulled from his pants pocket.

"Just say whatever it is you have to say, Arthur, I don't have all shadows-damned day." Virginia folded the blanket down over the bedsheet, leaving the corpse for the coroner. "Out with it, Dixon."

"You haven't been at headquarters much recently."

"And?"

He watched her, moving aside for the additional detectives to exit. "And as a consultant, I would have thought you would consult more." He straightened after they left, the weight of his position already taking a toll in the lightly greying five'oclock shadow that fanned out across his jawline. "Especially after learning what you did at that compound." He turned, staring, the same way he'd been staring at her for months, as if he expected her to look any different than she always had.

Virginia's jaw clamped, her teeth grinding with the indecision. She hadn't told Arthur that she'd been unable to access those abilities again after the raid, and she didn't want to, either. She didn't want to discuss it at all. "I've been busy with clients."

"More missing mythics? Because you know, they really should be reported to the VCPD for—"

"No," she interrupted. "Minor financial crimes. An inheritance, some fraud, a huckster here or there. You know, the kind of stuff the VCPD can't be bothered with."

"That hardly sounds like a full schedule, Ginnie," he replied. "And if I know you, then those cases aren't scratching that itch."

"It's better than almost dying twice in ten days," she shot back. He was right, but she'd never admit it. Virginia dusted along the metal bed frame, hoping for usable prints, but finding none. "It's perfectly respectable work."

"I just thought you'd be reaching for more challenging cases." Arthur was testing her, and they both knew it, but instead of pushing further, he gestured towards the snag in the carpet amid flattened fibers. "What do you think?" he asked.

"I think that no matter what you find here, the feds are going to stick their paws into it." Virginia pushed past the door and down the steps, hunting for any sign that the victim had fought back. "Whoever dragged him up the stairs, it was someone strong."

He nodded, still watching. "Nothing for sure?"

"He was probably dead already," she replied. "Either that, or unconscious. It's plausible, given how much Nether must have been in his system." Virginia inspected three nearly invisible droplets gathered on the stairs, likely old stains. They definitely weren't blood. "Assuming it's a crew hit, do you have any leads?"

"None," he replied, shaking his head. "None of the usual suspects are talking."

"No connections?"

"None that we can find." Arthur stood just over her shoulder, examining the droplets. "But I thought that you might see something that we hadn't."

Virginia turned, brushing him off. "You don't have to hover, you know."

"It would just be very advantageous if we—"

"There's that word again, we." She ducked under his arm and reached for the arm of the dust-covered cash register, setting the drawer open with a dull chime of the half-hearted bell. "There is no we." She rifled through the drawer before slamming it closed again. "No cash. Pity."

"It would just go into evidence, anyway."

"Obviously, Arthur." She allowed herself a private roll of her eyes before she turned back to face him. "Could there have been any witnesses? Neighbors, maybe? Or a gardener?"

"I asked around, but nothing. The bedroom window is blocked by the scaffolding of the neighbor building an extension next door. Shouldn't have been allowed, but Eugenia Patten on the council signed off on it." Arthur followed her into the back room, leaning against the door frame with one shoulder. "It's a shame we couldn't put her away for those documents."

"She's got enough lawyers to get out of anything," Virginia retorted. She was growing tired of his shadow, preferring to work alone, given the opportunity. She reached out, brushing her fingertips against the desk drawer's handle, but nothing came. "I'm not surprised you didn't nab her."

"Do you sense anything?" he asked.

"I don't know, do you?" she shot back. "You're the sheriff, maybe you could deduce something for once."

"And you're a—" he stopped himself, moving closer in the room and reducing his voice to a whisper. "A seer, Ginnie."

"It doesn't work like that." She avoided him again, crossing the corridor into the kitchen. The marble counter tops were spotless, no doubt scrubbed by an underpaid cleaner. "Sends a message, doesn't it? Killing him at home?"

"I was ruminating on that, too."

"Turf war?" Virginia asked, leaning against the smooth, unmarred surface. "Competitor moving into the area?"

"Not impossible," Arthur agreed. "It would be helpful to get a clearer reading."

"It's difficult when you're following me around." She dodged him again, circling the wood island in the center of the kitchen to prod at several untouched, sharpened kitchen knives. "If I could just call it up like that, I would."

"Can't you?" he asked.

Virginia barely repressed a sigh and a snide remark. "Obviously not. If I could, don't you think I would have known a little sooner?"

He peered out the kitchen door, waving an officer down the corridor towards the back entrance. "Have you used it at all since the raid?"

The question hung in the air thicker than the encroaching scent of death and decay. "I have to get to an appointment," she replied, choosing to ignore it entirely. "I'm already running late and midday traffic downtown is a shadows-damned nightmare."

"Ginnie."

"Arthur."

He hesitated, running a hand over his bald head, shiny with the glisten of sweat. "You haven't, have you?"

"It doesn't matter. Maybe it was one too many hits to the skull. Maybe I imagined the whole thing," she sniped. "I told you, I have to get to the office. My office."

"Jo said it was pretty stark, what happened then. Ursa's apartment, then Fiske's compound." Arthur exhaled unevenly, unsure. "Whatever this is, seeing or... or something else, you should try to figure it out. I'm worried about you, Ginnie."

The words sparked through her chest like lightning, destructive and devastating. She drew in a breath and held it, trying to convince herself that punching him in the jaw wasn't in her best interest, and neither was sprinting away from the scene. "I'm pretty sure you lost that privilege a long time ago."

"Wasn't it you who said we were friends once? Why not try to get back there?" he asked gently, too gently, giving her a look of pity that roiled in her gut.

"Now isn't the time for this," she replied gruffly, pushing past him into the immaculate living room. "I have work to do, and so do you."

He grabbed her gently by the elbow, pulling her closer so that he could whisper. "Ginnie, the feds picked up three ex–Ruby Thorn enforcers last week, and they're singing louder than canaries in a coal mine about an inferno witch causing a lot of damage last winter."

"Shit," Virginia grumbled, allowing him to stop her. "Did they know Jolie's name?"

"They knew enough to have feds asking me why I didn't follow up on tips about an unregistered fire demon last winter." Arthur gave her a sideways glance, half squinted in the overbearing sunlight filtering through the large bay window. "They heard enough to know that's what she is, regardless of what the enforcers thought. They'd give her up in a heartbeat if it meant a reduced sentence for themselves. I have to tell the feds something at some point, and I think it would be better if neither of you were in the city."

"I'll think about it." She picked up an expensive, empty vase, blown glass and shimmering. It probably cost more than her yearly salary. "I have to go."

Arthur didn't reach for her again, knowing better than to make her stay. "I thought we could grab coffee with Captain Lindell, really dig into the meat of these deaths," he offered, adjusting the silver belt buckle that matched the badge on his arm.

"I don't need coffee to pass off my notes." Virginia stepped through the front door, squinting at the assault of the afternoon sun. "I've got too many cases on my docket for that."

"You know, I had hoped that by working together on the Fiske thing, you two would at least grow into a professional respect." He eyed her again, and she was so tired of being so exposed, so seen, especially by him.

"Take it up with her."

"Is something going on with Lindell, Ginnie?" Arthur was at her shoulder now, asking her in a muted, overly calm tone.

Virginia barked out a laugh. "No."

"I just wondered, seeing as you've been avoiding the station."

"I already told you, I've been busy." She waved at the up-and-coming north side neighborhood, one more sign of just how much Verdance was changing. "You should make yourself busy with this overdose, or homicide, whatever it is." She shrugged dismissively. "I'd be making it my top priority, if it was me."

"Sheriff Dixon, the coroner needed to speak to you," one of the detectives said. She flashed a smile at Virginia, who decided to pretend that hadn't happened.

"Sure," he replied with a curt nod. "Ginnie, I'll give you a call at the office if anything jumps."

"Call the apartment if it's past five. Jolie will at least be there, she can take a message." Virginia strode away, regretting having picked up the phone that morning. Another mysterious death, feds, and shadows-damned Arthur to deal with. The only thing that would make it worse was having to deal with Shirin, too.

"Vane!"

Virginia groaned and kept walking. If she was quick, she'd make it to her car with plausible deniability that she'd heard anything in the first place. Her fingers were on the handle, almost an escape, when Lindell caught up with her.

"Hey," Captain Shirin Lindell said, pressing a hand against the car door. "Didn't you hear me?"

"I have a lot on my mind."

"If I'd have known you'd be here, I would have—"

"Would have what?" Virginia interrupted. "Called the feds to let them know they'd have jurisdiction?"

Shirin pressed harder against the door, her bicep flexing beneath the crisp white of her uniform shirt. "No, I would have shortened my shift to make sure I didn't miss you. You've been a hard woman to get hold of."

"You need to relax," Virginia hissed, wrenching the car door open anyways, the hinge creaking with protest. "Arthur already suspects something is going on."

"Why, did he say something?"

"Yes." Virginia climbed into the car, shoving the key into the ignition. "And this isn't a conversation I want to have at a crime scene." She settled into the seat, ready to drive the moment she had the opportunity. "My guess is a homicide, he pissed off the wrong undesirable." She nodded towards the bakery as her car's engine rumbled quietly. "Look for yourself."

"Not just plain old overdose, then?"

"Did you really think we'd get that lucky?"

Shirin studied her, forearms rested against the door despite the heat and the black metal of the car. "No, I suppose not, but it's not as if overdoses are uncommon these days."

"It's homicide, Shirin. A crew hit job, one more for the books. Tell the family to contact his life insurance company, and let's call it a day." Virginia slid the car into gear, easing forward enough to get Shirin to release her grip on the door. "I'll see you around."

She pulled off the driveway and back onto the road, the suspension or something else rattling underneath. She turned left, towards her apartment. It was almost lunch time, and she hadn't left anything for the kid to eat.

About the Author

Ryann Fletcher is a writer who lives in Glasgow with too many books and craft supplies. She writes science fiction and fantasy novels because real life is boring without spaceships and magic. She loves to cook and go for long hikes in the wilderness, searching for the meaning of life and probably the keys she lost three days ago.

You can connect with me on:

- https://ryannfletcher.com
- https://facebook.com/RyannFletcherWrites
- https://instagram.com/RyannFletcherWrites
- https://www.tiktok.com/@ryannfletcherwrites
- https://patreon.com/RyannFletcherWrites

Subscribe to my newsletter:

- https://linktr.ee/ryannfletcherwrites

Also by Ryann Fletcher

Exiled Advocate: Sadie Sinclair, Esquire: book 1
When Astrid, notorious club owner, siren, and Sadie Sinclair's premier client is targeted, this half-Fae lawyer has more questions than answers.

How to navigate a legal system which is increasingly weaponized? When laws designed to protect become tools to entrap, can any mythic obtain justice? What to do when "Human Rights" no longer apply?

Only one fact is clear. Being different has never been more dangerous.